SUDAN

SUDAN

based on a true story

Art Ayris and Ninie Hammon

Sudan

Copyright © 2010
Art A. Ayris and Ninie Hammon

Cover illustration by Mona Roman Advertising
Interior Design by Archer-Ellison

Published by Bay Forest Books
An Imprint of Kingstone Media
4420 Bay Forest Lane
Fruitland Park, FL 34731
www.bayforestbooks.com

Printed in the United States of America by
Bay Forest Books

Library of Congress Cataloguing-in-Publication Data

CIP data applied for

ISBN 978-0-9799035-2-6
CIP

Dedicated to our brothers and sisters whose only cry is for freedom.

-Art Ayris and Ninie Hammon-
November 2009

ABOUT THE AUTHORS

A rt Ayris' journey of awareness into the reality of human trafficking began while working on a documentary in Asia when a man tried to sell him a baby girl. Later, while doing undercover camera work in Brazil, he documented young girls being forced into prostitution. In *Sudan*, he directs a modern story of slave-trading, an ancient evil whose prevalence has only increased, with more people in bondage right now than at the height of the North Atlantic African slave trade. Though *Sudan* is a novel and most of the characters are fictional, it is based on a true story. The atrocities described in this novel did not originate in the authors' imaginations. Rather, they were taken from actual news accounts detailing the butchering and enslaving of southern Sudan's Christian and animist people groups during the 1980's and 1990's - and now extended to the genocide of the inhabitants of Darfur.

Art and his wife, Kelly, live in central Florida, where they continue their media work along with raising two great sons.

* * * * *

Ninie Hammon spent a quarter of a century as a journalist, beginning as a reporter and working up to publisher. In 1995, the newspaper she started in Louisville, Ky., had five employees and a press run of 8,000. When she left in 2005, a staff of 23 produced *The Southeast Outlook* for more than 65,000 readers. Her first book, *God Said Yes,* was published in 2007. When she was asked to co-write *Sudan,* she read the true story on which the book is based. She was sickened by the reality of everyday life in Africa's largest country, and by the world's unwillingness to challenge the evil that has been unleashed there. Her own passion on the slavery issue is described by Dan Wolfson, one of the main characters in *Sudan:* "It *is* happening. Right now. This minute. As we sit here safe in this comfortable room, on the other side of the planet Arab raiders are kidnapping women and little kids, tying them with ropes and hauling them off to an auction where they'll be sold, branded, beaten, raped, mutilated and forced to work against their will. I don't need some other deep psychological explanation for why I'm so passionate. That's reason enough. It's wrong. It's just *wrong.* "

Ninie lives near London with her husband, Tom, who supervises an international youth organization in the United Kingdom and Ireland. The couple have six children and seven grandchildren.

SUDAN

Chapter 1

SOUTHERN SUDAN, March 2000

The sound of running feet dashing past her tukul was the first sign that something was not right in Dada Manut's world. She'd been tickling baby Reisha's tummy, sending the little girl into gales of giggles, but now she stopped and listened. She heard shouts in her sharply punctuated Lokuta dialect and then another sound, a sound she had never heard before, a high-pitched whine that couldn't possibly have come from any animal or human she'd ever seen.

She snatched the naked baby into her arms and hurried outside. Her neighbors pointed at something in the eastern sky above the mountains. She squinted into the rising sun, but couldn't make out the source of the strange noise that grew louder by the second.

She shifted Reisha to her hip, shielded her eyes with her left hand and peered into the glare. There! Now she could see it, see *them*. Two silver objects streaked across the sky toward her village, dropping lower and lower as they approached. The sound of them grew louder, rumbled like the thunder of a summer storm. Her heart began to hammer in her chest; her eyes widened in wonder—and growing dread.

Dada had never seen an airplane of any kind, much less a Soviet Antonov fighter. But she didn't have to understand the incredible firepower bearing down on Nokot to sense the danger. Was this the death from the skies some of the other villagers talked about in hushed tones around their campfires at night, the tales of devastation too monstrous to comprehend? Information about the world outside their remote little valley was sketchy at best, but descriptions had filtered into Nokot of massive destruction and bloodshed, vague, shadowy stories as terrifying as bad dreams. Dada had dismissed the stories when she heard them, but now she began to back slowly toward the safety of her tukul, with its solid thatched roof and strong wooden support posts.

She didn't make it inside before the first bomb fell.

The earth-shattering blast detonated less than 100 yards away, knocked her backward off her feet and slammed her to the ground so violently she almost lost her grip on Reisha. She lay there stunned, trying to catch her breath, her eardrums throbbing. In a daze, she turned in the direction of the blast, blinked her eyes, and struggled to focus. But the world was not right. The stately balanite tree she and her friends had climbed when they were children was gone, replaced by a smoking crater of blackened earth with half a bloody zebu carcass draped over the edge. The rest of the animal was scattered in pieces around two other zebu that lay motionless nearby. Another blast hammered the earth on the other side of the village. Its roar mingled with the bleat of panicked goats as they stormed out of their pens, the screaming caw-caws of terrified guinea hens, and the shrieks of women and children in a frantic stampede away from the carnage. Then she heard, as if from a great distance, the terrified screams of her infant daughter in her arms.

Dada staggered to her feet and lurched toward the doorway of her hut. Inside, both her sons sat on their sleeping mats, too frightened and bewildered to move. Dada knelt and pulled them close, held their trembling bodies tight, felt the staccato pounding of their little hearts against her chest.

Above the screams of the villagers and the cries of terrified livestock, she could hear the high-pitched whine of the fighter jets grow louder and louder. They were coming back. The strange other-worldly sound again became the rumble of thunder and Dada had time to wonder if she should run for cover in the woods or stay here where her husband and older son could find her. Then the bombs began to fall.

Four deafening explosions rocked the earth at two- to three-second intervals, cutting a swath of devastation 50 feet wide from one end of Nokot to the other. Huts that took direct hits vanished; others burst into flames. People and animals were indiscriminately blown apart, scattering body parts in a bloody hail in every direction.

Dada placed her shrieking baby on a sleeping mat, but couldn't get Isak and Kuak to sit down beside their sister; the boys were too terrified to let go of their mother. When she finally peeled them off and forced them to stay with Reisha, she stuck her head out past the elephant grass partition in the doorway. Her tukul was one of the few left standing. Four or five of her friends lay motionless on the ground nearby, and she could see the blood-soaked form of her 7-year-old nephew, Kagak, struggling to claw his way out of the remains of his family's shattered, burning hut. But he could not crawl; both his legs had been blown off above the knee. His wailing mingled with the cries of the other injured villagers and animals in a symphony of terror and pain.

Dada's eyes darted frantically from one horror to the next, took it all in. Her heart boomed and she could barely breathe through the rising knot of panic that gathered in her chest and flooded her mouth with a taste like blood. A purple light bloomed inside her head, and Dada felt hysteria crawling up the back of her throat, felt herself slipping, spiraling down toward the oblivion of total collapse. It was close, so achingly, temptingly close.

Everything in the world around her was wrong, *all wrong!* How could this be when the morning had started out like every other morning she had ever known? Dada's mind suddenly reached out and grabbed hold of the morning, fiercely clutched the memory of normal and hunkered down into it. She left the acrid stench of burning bodies behind and snuggled up in a reality that was safe, a reality not defiled by exploding death, flames, and blood.

＊ ＊ ＊ ＊ ＊

She had awakened to the sound of the small herd of zebu lowing outside her tukul, and had slowly raised herself on her elbow, careful not to disturb Reisha, curled up beside her breast. Two of her other children had been asleep on straw mats on the dirt floor of the one-room dwelling, but a third straw mat lay empty. Her oldest son, Koto, was gone. He'd risen early to deliver the first of the zebu, large gray and white cattle with droopy ears, humps, and huge horns, to the pasture lands below their village.

Dada got up from the mat as quietly as she could and carefully nudged a tattered blanket closer to the baby to give her something to bump up against if she awoke. Then she edged past the sleeping forms of her two other children, and marveled again at how alike they were. There were times when even she would have struggled to tell them apart were it not for their lone distinguishing characteristic. Isak, the older of the 8-year-old twins by several minutes, had been born with a mark on the back of his right hand. To Dada, the mark was a shapeless blotch; to Isak, it was a butterfly! She paused briefly above each of the boys and gazed at them tenderly.

The face of the sun had just peeked over the Imatong Mountains on the border of Sudan and Kenya, and smiled down on the village where a half-dozen clans of migrating Lokuta tribals had settled 60 years earlier. Nokot now numbered 45 to 50 tukuls—round, mud or straw huts with conical, thatched roofs.

Several women already squatted by their cast iron pots, stirring their family's morning meal of porridge and cassavas. One of them was her sister, Bette, and she smiled a greeting. Koto was nowhere to be seen, so Dada walked over to their smoldering fire, picked up a stick and began to poke the embers, adding leaves and twigs, and blowing gently until flickering flames leapt from the red coals. Yesterday, she and Koto had gathered a large pile of acacia limbs, enough to fuel the family oven for several days. Like the rest of the families in their isolated village, they kept their fire stoked through the night and added dried zebu dung to produce a pungent smoke to hold at bay the seroot flies that carried the dreaded sleeping sickness. Everything in the village, every hut, mat, dried animal skin, thatched roof—and all the villagers, too—smelled like the smoke, the stink was woven into the fabric of their everyday lives.

Gauging from the position of the sun, she estimated that her husband John, her father, brothers and the other Nokot men had been in the millet fields for at least half an hour, planting the seeds that would produce a crop of sorghum. John's face formed in her mind, and she smiled. She was married to a good man, and not all the women in the village could say that. Some of the men were lazy, but John worked extra hard because his withered right hand made simple tasks more difficult. No one knew exactly what had happened to him. He'd been only 2 years old, too little to tell his mother what had bitten him. A spider, maybe. A millipede. A snake. The list of suspects was huge. His mother had washed the wound with river water and put a poultice of leaves and boiled acacia bark on it. The toddler had been very sick for days; his hand had swollen to three times its normal size. When he recovered, he could no longer move his wrist, fingers or thumb, and over time, the hand withered and hung useless.

When John's father had come to her father to negotiate a marriage, her father had been reluctant to agree, even when John's father offered nine zebu. He'd feared John couldn't properly care for Dada and a family, but Dada had pleaded with her father to approve. For years she had hoped John would be selected as her husband. He had kind eyes, and she'd watched him with his younger brothers and sisters. She knew he would be a good father. And she'd been right. When Isak had been born with the butterfly mark in the same spot on his hand where John had been bitten, Dada was certain that the spirit of John's dead mother had put it there to protect her grandson from the fate of his father.

With the fire going strong, Dada sat back on her heels and relished the early morning. The cool air that caressed her skin was a welcome balm, a short, gentle reprieve from a life sentence of soaring temperatures in the glaring Sudanese sun. The stillness was just as soothing. She cherished the quiet. It nourished her soul, strengthened her for the demands of her family and her life. It was a good life—a gentle, hard-working husband, healthy children, enough to eat. She asked for nothing more. But she loved the stolen minutes of the morning because they were hers alone. In that delicious time before the village awoke, she was not fetching water in a clay pot balanced on her head from the river that flowed southwest into the White Nile, grinding sorghum for the next family meal, washing clothes, gathering wood, tending to a child or nursing an infant. For a brief moment in time each morning, Dada was alone with her thoughts, at peace with her world.

But the solitude of the moment as she knelt by the fire was soon shattered by the piercing cry of her youngest child. Dada poked a few more sticks into the growing flames and then stepped back inside the tukul. As she did, she pulled her left breast out from under her wrap, one long piece of red and purple cloth draped under her right arm, with the ends tied together in a knot over her left shoulder. She snuggled her daughter close and took care of motherly business.

Reisha sucked frantically for 15 minutes until she'd finally had enough. A single drop of milk hung suspended from Dada's breast like a raindrop above the baby's pink lips, but Reisha turned her head away. She was finished. Dada smiled as she reflected on how different her oldest and youngest children were—had been since the moment they were born. Koto had been easily satisfied, hardly demanded any attention at all, and ate solid food before he could walk. Now 15, Koto was tall for his age but thin, not yet filled out with the muscles of a man. He had a high forehead, wide, round eyes, and like the other members of the Lokuta tribe, he was as black as the night sky. Koto had always seemed vastly more mature than his years. His gaze was steady, his movements compact and economical, his temperament calm and confident—almost like a grown man in a child's body. Ah, but this Reisha!

She placed the baby back on the sleeping mat, smiled and tickled her bare tummy. The baby's giggles mingled with another sound. Running feet. Her neighbors shouting. A strange keening noise rumbling in the sky before...

* * * * *

No more than a few seconds after her mind had rejected it, Dada was sucked back into the reality of agonized screams and the stench of burning death, back into the deep, airless ditch of terror. And when she felt Isak wrap his small arms tight around her leg, his body trembling, she knew she had to stay there. She couldn't abandon her children, couldn't leave them alone in this nightmare while she escaped into hysteria. With every ounce of will she possessed, she forced herself to stand perfectly still, to calm down—to *think*.

John! She had to find her husband! He would know what to do. He would save them. She scooped Reisha into her arms, grabbed Kuak's hand and told him to hold onto his brother. Together, they left the tukul and headed toward the sorghum fields where the men had been working. They cut behind two burning huts and came out into the open where Dada could see the fields, and her heart leapt with hope when she saw all the Lokuta men—40 or more of them—sprinting toward the village.

Then she saw why they were running.

Behind them, soldiers in jeeps bounced across the dark earth of the freshly planted fields, the weapons in their hands shiny in the early morning sun. The sharp crack of a rifle shot reached her ears a heartbeat before one of the Lokuta men crumbled and fell. Then another shot rang out. And another. Two more men fell. The gunfire grew more intense; the bodies kept falling, one after another, until there were no more targets left.

Dada did not see John, her father or brothers fall. She couldn't make out anyone in the crowd of running farmers. But she knew John was there somewhere, knew that a bullet from one of the gunshots she'd heard had ripped into his back, and he lay dead in the field beside the bodies of all the other men in her family.

Kuak and Isak stood speechless beside their mother, too dumbstruck even to cry. But there was no time now for grief. The men in jeeps raced toward them, and Dada spun around and began to run with the boys back into Nokot.

In less than 10 minutes, the idyllic village in the green mountain valley had become a fiery deathtrap. Mothers grabbed their children and raced toward the river where they hoped to find safety in the marsh and reeds. Bellowing zebu and bleating goats ran helter-skelter in wild-eyed panic. Dada and the boys dodged burning huts, zigzagged past blast craters and stumbled over the body parts of dismembered villagers, as they made their way to the northern edge of Nokot to the field where Koto had taken their small herd of zebu that morning to graze.

Dada's eyes frantically searched the field for her son, but there was no Koto. Her mind flatly refused to countenance the possibility that he had been hurt or killed. Koto was fine, she assured herself desperately, he had escaped the convoy of trucks carrying well-armed soldiers in combat fatigues that barreled across the field toward the village.

For just a moment, Dada stopped and stared at the approaching trucks bumping down the rutted path, scattering the terrified zebu and kicking up an ominous cloud of dust as they drew near. They reminded her of a pack of jackals she'd seen once, as they circled a wounded doe and fawn. Then she turned to join the rush of other families that scrambled toward the river. But there was no escape there either. Soldiers ran up from that direction, too, cut off any flight, grabbed the screaming women and children and herded them into groups.

Dada stood very still on the dirt path she'd walked every day of her life. She realized she was utterly alone and totally helpless. With all her options gone, she turned toward the village and led her sons back to the only refuge she had left—their own tukul.

Once inside, Dada clasped the still screaming Reisha to her chest and sat the boys against the far wall of the hut. They obeyed her direction without protest. With identical faces that wore identical looks of abject terror, they scooted as far as possible back into the shadows and huddled close with their arms around each other. Then Dada placed herself between the boys and the doorway, and waited.

The sounds outside were hard to follow. She could make out some of the voices, but others shouted in a language she'd never heard before. She tried to soothe her frightened baby—*Shhhhh! Shhhhhh! Hush now, shhhhhh*—as she edged to the lone window her husband had cut in the side of the tukul and peered out. The entire village swarmed with soldiers. She saw one of the trucks parked only three tukuls away. Already, groups of women and girls had been bound with lengths of rope, strung together like beads on a necklace.

She jumped back startled as a soldier ran by. He stopped in the doorway of the tukul where the newly wed Sama Pomwe and her husband, Karal lived. Karal had gone out with John that morning to work in the sorghum fields.

The soldier stood for a moment and stared into the tukul, then shouted something in his strange tongue and two other soldiers ran to him. The first soldier began to unfasten the pants of his uniform and stormed into the tukul with the other two close on his heels. Then Dada heard Sama scream, a high, piercing wail that went on and on and on.

Dada's knees almost buckled out from under her, and she had to grab hold of the pole that supported the wall to stand up. She leaned there for a time, trembling violently; the sound of Sama's cries sliced into her soul.

Then she slowly lifted her head and straightened up. Her hands steadied. The trembling stopped. Desperation had wedged steel down her spine.

She kneeled and whispered instructions to her sons, then picked up the back pack she'd used to carry each of her babies when she gathered sticks or food. She placed Reisha inside and tied it snugly across her shoulders. Reisha loved to ride in the back pack and her cries quickly changed to soft sniffles. Dada had counted on that; Reisha *had* to be quiet now. Then Dada peered carefully out the window. To her far left, soldiers herded a group of women and children into a circle next to a large truck as Dada readied herself for one final flight.

A detachment of soldiers went from hut to hut and dragged out the few remaining inhabitants. They had reached the tukul two down from hers where an older couple lived. If Dada meant to make a break for it, time was running out. With her baby daughter on her back, she gripped each son's small hand, stepped to the door of the hut and prepared for the most important two minutes of her life.

The path leading into the village, the one the trucks had used, looked to be her only escape route. She had been the fastest runner in Nokot when she was a young girl. If she could make it just 200 yards down the road, there were large fields of elephant grass where she and the children could hide.

As soon as there were no soldiers in sight, she eased out her door, hurried toward the road, and caught a quick glimpse through her neighbor's doorway as she passed Sama's tukul. The young girl sobbed quietly as two soldiers pinned her down while a third raped her.

Dada led the children stealthily from the back of one tukul to the next. She saw no one. Most of the soldiers were on the other side of the village where they herded women and children into transport trucks. When she reached the last abandoned tukul on the edge of the village by the road, she paused. She edged slowly around the circular hut and searched for soldiers. She saw none, took a deep breath and made her move.

*   *   *   *   *

Ron Wolfson looked down at the little girl who sat in the dirt at his feet and wanted to cry. Or rip somebody's throat out.

But if he cried every time his heart broke for a brutalized child, or a dead baby, or a slaughtered villager, he wouldn't be able to do what he'd come here to do.

And if he went looking for somebody's throat to rip out, where would he start? The Murahaleen raider who burned down her village, killed her parents and carried her away? The slave-trader who sold her to the highest bidder? The master who bought her? The government that condoned it? Where would he stop?

He knelt beside the vacant-eyed child, flipped the catch on his camera case, reached inside and took out his battered old Nikon. He slid the camera strap over his head and around his neck and wiped the sweat out of his eyes on the dirty sleeve of his shirt. Was it hotter today than usual? Better question: Could a—Masapha would say "pampered"—American from a little Indiana town on the bank of the Ohio River ever get used to the frying-pan heat of Africa?

The blonde man moved so the glare of the sun was at his back, set his knees in the dirt and made his body a human tripod. Then he put his game face on. *I have to tell this little girl's story without any words.* He lifted the camera to his eye and began to fire.

The girl rocked back and forth as she tenderly cradled the cold, stiff body of her little sister in her arms. She was oblivious to the other refugees huddled together in groups around her, speaking in dialects she couldn't have understood even if she'd been listening. She was oblivious to the American, too, who knelt in the dirt in front of her, his aged Nikon click, click, clicking as he captured her pain on film. The child was oblivious to the blistering heat, to the stench of unwashed bodies and human excrement, to everything except her little sister's face—at peace, finally at peace. As she hummed the ancient melody her grandmother had sung to her mother, and her mother had sung to her, she shooed the flies away from the blood clotted in her sister's ears and smeared in caked, dry streams down her neck.

"Some tribals brought her in this morning," Jack Hadley said, as he came to stand beside where Ron knelt. With his red hair and freckles, the Canadian looked even more out of place in a Sudanese refugee camp than Ron did.

"From what I understand, they found her staggering across a field in a daze, carrying the body," Jack continued, his words colored by the Irish-sounding lilt of his native Prince Edward Island.

Jack had told Ron about the child when the 36-year-old photographer showed up that morning to process film in the makeshift darkroom Jack had allowed him to hide in a closet behind the kitchen at CARA, the Canadian Aid and Relief Association's refugee center near Nimule in southern Sudan.

"The other little girl was already dead, had been for some time apparently, but she wouldn't let them touch her. The villagers didn't know what else to do with her so they brought her here."

Ron removed the 28-mm wide-angle lens from his camera and replaced it with an 80-mm portrait lens. He framed the child's expressionless face in a couple of shots, then focused on the still-raw burns on both the little girls' left shoulders. Click-click.

"Those brands are fresh," he said as he stood up and dusted the dirt off his pants. "Slave-traders don't waste time branding captives, so these two must already have been sold. Doesn't look like it's been more than a few days since their new owner put his mark on them to identify his property."

Ron spit the word "property" out of his mouth as if the taste of it on his tongue made him nauseous. "I wonder how they got away."

"Don't know, but perhaps I can find out. Let me see if I can locate somebody who speaks her dialect."

Jack cocked his head to one side and studied the child. "She has a certain look, don't you think? High cheekbones, a thin nose. I've seen that look before."

Ron watched Jack disappear into the teeming city of tents, lean-tos and makeshift huts that housed more than 25,000 people who had nowhere else to go, the hemorrhage of humanity from a society that was rapidly bleeding out. The camp was home to just about every one of the country's 597 tribes—men, women and children speaking 400 languages who had fled the plains, valleys and mountains of southern Sudan to escape the indiscriminate, brutal slaughter of genocide.

Ron turned back to the child and decided that Jack was right. She did, indeed, have a certain look, and he'd seen that look before, too. It was the look of vacant, hollow-eyed shock occasioned by horror way beyond a child's capacity to process. He'd seen it on children's faces in Rwanda, in Kosovo and in Uganda.

"You know what killed her." It was a statement, not a question. Ron's assistant, Masapha, had stepped up un-noticed beside him, and the smaller man's words came out in a voice gruff with restrained emotion.

Ron turned to face the Arab; their eyes met and locked. "Yeah," Ron struggled to keep his own voice under control, "I know what killed her, all right. The insect treatment."

❊   ❊   ❊   ❊   ❊

Idris Apot was tired, bone-weary tired. The day had begun at first light in his small field on the village communal land, where he'd hacked all morning at the ground with a grubbing hoe to break the crust on soil baked rock hard by the unrelenting, dry season sun. It had ended as evening crept into the sky from behind the forest, after he'd scattered handfuls of tiny anyanjang seeds onto the ground for hours and then gently covered them with a thin layer of dirt. When he harvested the sorghum he was planting, his wife, Aleuth, would grind the kernels into flour to make the staples of his family's diet, including injera, the yellow flatbread Idris liked to eat hot, dipped in melting moo-yahoo butter made from shea nuts.

The 33-year-old Dinka farmer grimaced when he arched his back and stretched his cramped muscles. He was stiff from bending his lanky, six-foot, four-inch frame almost double all afternoon as he checked to make sure the anyanjang seeds lay no deeper in the freshly raked soil than the distance from the tip of his finger to his first knuckle. He looked toward the western horizon, squinted and shaded his eyes, to gauge how much daylight he had left. When he turned from the glaring sun, he spotted wispy gray and white streaks slowly rising from the first evening fires in Mondala. The broad smile that lit his face revealed the gap where four of his lower front teeth had been pulled at age 12 as the first part of his rite of passage into manhood. He took in a great gulp of air that held the faint scent of rain and let it out slowly. It was good to be home, he thought.

His village of Moinjaang, "the people of the people" as the Dinka called themselves, had just gotten settled in after their annual migration across the western floodplains to graze their herds of zebu on the banks of the great river. At the beginning of the dry season in mid-December, everyone in Mondala, except the old, the sick and nursing mothers, had gathered up the village cattle and herded them to temporary camps along the Bahr el Jebel, the White Nile, where the annual floods laid down a rich layer of silt that produced lush, plentiful grass. They had remained there for three months, then returned home, a little earlier than usual this year, before the rains came and the river overflowed its banks, making the shoreline camps uninhabitable and turning the verdant grasslands into swamps.

It would never have occurred to Idris to question whether he liked his semi-nomadic life. He had never known any other. He had only twice ventured more than 100 miles from his home, had only been in a city once. But Idris knew that a profound peace always settled over him when he left the vast, featureless, grassy plains behind and returned to Mondala, to the hills and the forest. And he knew that the fulfillment he felt when he harvested the millet he'd planted with his own hands was rivaled only by the satisfaction of bringing home an antelope, gazelle or eland he'd tracked down and killed with a spear or his bow and arrow. Both experiences made him feel strong and capable and in charge of his life.

Some of the other farmers gathered up their tools, and two of the older men headed up the hard clay path toward the village. They shouldered their hoes, spades and rakes as they walked along together, chatting. Like Idris, they wore nothing but loincloths and beaded necklaces. They were tall men, too—several were taller than

Idris—with very dark skin, almond-shaped eyes and narrow, square shoulders. Their height identified them as Dinka, the tribe that had given American basketball fans one of the two tallest players in NBA history—Manute Bol, the seven-foot, seven-inch Washington Bullets' center known as the Dinka Dunker. The intricate pattern of scars on their foreheads identified them as Dinka, too.

Idris stood for a moment undecided. He wanted to plant one more row. He surveyed the partially seeded field and estimated he would have to work three more full days to get the crop in the ground. Given the early planting, he hoped the harvest would yield a bumper crop, like the one he'd produced 11 years ago, the year his first child, Akin, had been born. He hadn't said anything to his wife at the time, but he'd yearned for a boy. As a Christian, Idris no longer believed the ancient traditions that required a man to produce a son or face oblivion after death. He didn't want a son to carry on the family name, to maintain the lineage link from the past, through the present to future generations. He just wanted a boy who would one day help him farm the land, care for the cattle and hunt for game, a boy he could teach to hold a bow steady, shoot an arrow straight and throw a spear accurately. He'd struggled mightily to hide his disappointment when he learned his firstborn was a girl.

Idris almost laughed out loud at the memory. It was hard to imagine that he'd ever been dissatisfied with Akin! She'd been the absolute delight of his life since the moment the midwife placed the squirming infant into his arms. The child had instantly stopped wiggling and looked at him solemnly, her round eyes wide and unblinking. And then she had smiled at him—a wide, happy smile that planted twin dimples in her chubby cheeks and bathed her tiny face in joy. Oh, everyone said he'd imagined it, that newborn babies didn't smile. It must have been some trick of the flickering campfire light, they said—or gas!—and they chuckled good-naturedly at the fancy of a proud, new father. But Idris knew different.

As she grew older, that same dimpled smile lit Akin's face whenever she saw him. She'd toddle toward him on wobbly legs, her chubby arms outstretched, her face beaming, and he'd scoop her up and cuddle her close, certain that she was the most beautiful little girl and he was the most fortunate father in the world.

The image of Akin's smiling face, and the eager faces of his other two children, 9-year-old Abuong and 5-year-old Shema, waiting at home to greet him sealed his decision. He'd stop now; the rest of the work would just have to wait until tomorrow. He picked up his hoe and rake and headed up the clay path toward home.

A village of about 100 tukuls, Mondala was built on a knoll overlooking the river that flowed down out of the range of hills to the north and wrapped around the east side of the village. Beyond Mondala, the river continued southeast, one of hundreds of tributaries feeding the White Nile.

On the other side of the river, the landscape changed, gradually became flatter, with small stands of trees scattered here and there in a sea of grass that in some places grew waist high. It was there that the villagers hunted bigger game like reedbuck, gazelle and kudu.

To the west and south of the village lay the woodland that supplied the tribals mangos, papayas, dates, shea nuts and guavas, and kindling the women carried back to their tukuls in baskets balanced on their heads. The forest of stately mahogany and ebony trees, palms and date palms, was home to flocks of colorful tropical birds, chittering monkeys and hooting Hamadryad baboons. The villagers hunted dik dik and bushbuck there, tracking them through the woods as soundlessly as the leopards that also stalked the small antelope.

North of the village lay the sorghum fields and the grassland where the villagers' cattle, sheep and goats grazed. Beyond the fields, tall, rocky hills rose high above the village, with a trail winding up the side of the nearest one. Steep, narrow and cluttered with rocks, it was the only path north from Mondala.

His stomach began to rumble with hunger and Idris quickened his pace along the path. Aleuth would be preparing boiled potatoes and fava beans by now, and perhaps fresh injera, too. His mouth watered. As he started up the last rise in the path that led to Mondala, he could just make out the form of a young girl running toward him. The light was failing, but Idris didn't need the sun to see the smile on the child's face. He could see her dimples with his heart.

* * * * *

When he stepped out of the blistering sun, the rush of cool air inside the Bata Hotel hit Ron like a blast off an Arctic glacier. With his last reserves of energy, he gripped his weathered travel bag, re-shouldered his equipment bag and battered camera case and marched resolutely into the crowded lobby.

If the clash of incompatible cultures, the cacophony of 400 languages, the utter chaos in the city's streets and the abject poverty didn't do it, the searing heat in Khartoum usually reduced westerners to a state of semi-catatonic submission in less than a week. After three months in southern Sudan, Ron had grown as accustomed to the brutally hot weather as he ever was likely to be, though he shuddered to think that the scorching sun had not yet taken its best shot. Temperatures in Khartoum at the end of the dry season in May and June would reach a balmy 110 to 120 degrees, made even more enjoyable by the appearance of ferocious haboob sandstorms.

Ron's present state of semi-collapse had not, however, been occasioned by life in a microwave set for popcorn. The issue was sleep, or rather the lack of it. After he'd snatched only a couple of hours a night of it for more than a week, he suspected he might literally be slack-jawed and drooling. His weary face, gray with fatigue, looked as worn and tired as the Nile steamer that had been the instrument of his unintended sleep fast.

As he fought the numbing exhaustion, he wandered through the lobby and searched the passing faces for his contact from the BBC. A poof of dust coughed out of his pocket along with the crumpled scrap of paper as he checked the time and date once more. *"Noon, 15 March,*

Bata Hotel, R. R. Olford, BBC." Ron smiled weakly. The R. R. stood for Rupert Reginald. Not many mothers naming their babies *that* anymore, he thought. The two of them had met briefly, had a few beers together a couple of times when both were in South Africa. Ron was confident they would recognize each other. He knew he could pick Olford out of a police lineup: tall, skinny, glasses, and bald—with a really bad comb-over.

An Arab woman wearing a powder blue, knee-length salwar kameez and a black shayla wrap that revealed nothing but her face, brushed by him without acknowledging his unkempt appearance. If she saw him, or smelled him, she pretended not to notice. Dark-skinned businessmen dressed in western-style suits with smaghs on their heads were caught up in a heated argument about something, their voices loud, their Arabic as rapid-fire as machine guns. To Ron's American eye, all men in smaghs looked like Yasser Arafat. A half dozen Zande porters dutifully stood by the hotel's front entrance, and scanned the crowd for potential business. Ron couldn't help noting that none of them had offered to carry his bags.

The first time Ron had stayed at the Bata, he gave the establishment a five-star rating based solely on the gold standard for American real estate—location, location, location. In that department, the Bata Hotel had no equal in all of Khartoum. Half a mile from the Presidential Palace and just over the bridge from the Omdurman markets, the aging edifice offered a sweeping view of the confluence of the Blue and White Nile rivers, a 50-yard-line seat at the birth of the mighty Nile.

Built by a wealthy ex-patriot Spaniard shortly after World War I, the Bata featured an elegant, Mediterranean style red tile roof, spacious balconies and a peach-colored stucco exterior. Though the stucco could have done with a fresh coat of paint, the building still managed a shabby chic that made the peeling paint something of a fashion statement. Inside the lobby, an incongruent mixture of styles testified to the diversity of the hotel's many owners in the past 75 years. Sturdy leather chairs, loveseats and couches rubbed elbows with delicate French ladder-backs, faux Louis XIV tables and porcelain lamps. The most magnificent Moroccan tile floor Ron had ever seen lay beneath the eclectic collection of furniture, and he was convinced the heavy emerald draperies on the huge windows by the door had been stolen off the set of *Gone With The Wind*. Where a fully stocked bar once stood—pre-Islamic revolution—a fairly well-appointed phone bank had been installed that offered remarkably good service. Large double doors on the wall past the phone bank led to what was listed in the Khartoum guidebook as a "five-star restaurant." Ron sincerely doubted the claim, though he'd never eaten there.

He didn't see his contact, so Ron found an over-stuffed chair and gratefully lowered himself into it. The cool and comfort were intoxicating. He'd experienced neither on his trip from Juba to Khartoum. A brief smile skittered across his face as he imagined describing his journey to his college friends who now held cushy stateside media posts. Not one of them had ever seen a conveyance like the one that had transported Ron downriver.

The steamer resembled a Mississippi riverboat on steroids. With motor-less barges attached to both sides, the front and the back, it occupied a portion of river about the size of a football field. The third-class passengers on the barges were accompanied by their livestock. Twenty-four hours after it left Juba, the steamer smelled like a floating dung heap. Ron had spent the trip curled up in a space recently vacated by two rusty, long-empty fire-extinguisher canisters—which he'd chucked overboard. And he only got that choice piece of real estate when he bribed a crew member with his pricy American wristwatch.

Where will I get a replacement for my $19.99 Wal-Mart Timex, Ron wondered as he settled back in a polished leather chair in the cool of the Bata's lobby. And that was his last coherent thought for a while. He only had a couple of tired synapses still firing. They were too exhausted to reach out and touch each other, and the space in between generated random images that appeared, morphed and then disappeared in his head like the shifting mosaic of a kaleidoscope.

Fighting to stay awake and aware, he sat upright in the chair, shook his head violently and dug filthy knuckles into his bloodshot eyes. He forced himself to survey the room, taking in the affluence all around him and pondering a cosmically dark irony. The wealth of the Arabs who glided by him, stirring up the refrigerated air as they passed, kept them pampered and protected, able to sit back and select from the buffet of life only the choicest, tastiest morsels. Wrapped up snug in their oil-driven prosperity and fortified by the rule of *sharia* law, they were safely separated from the barbarity on their doorstep. Most of these men in Armani suits and women in flowing satin-trimmed abayas had never spent five minutes talking to the kind of people Ron had lived among for the past three months. The land where their southern countrymen bled and died, forced to watch in helpless agony as their children were kidnapped and brutalized, lay almost within rock-throwing distance of the hotel lobby where they sat in cool comfort, their own children safe and secure in the penthouse suites upstairs.

Ron's head bobbed only once before he finally lost the battle to keep his eyelids from slamming shut. As his chin fell forward, he slipped his hands through the strap, wrapped his arms around his camera case, and clasped it to his chest like a flight attendant demonstrating how to hold onto a seat cushion life preserver.

Chapter 2

Dada was drenched with sweat. Her heart pounded so hard she could literally hear it thud in her chest. She paused to gather her strength, sucked in a great gulp of air, then leapt from behind the last tukul like an antelope, and sprinted down the road.

Even with a chubby 10-month-old on her back, she ran so fast she had to drag the terrified boys, gripping their little hands tight in her sweaty palms as they struggled to keep up.

She didn't feel the sharp edges of the stones on her feet nor hear the crying/shouting/screaming death throes of the mangled village behind her. Every molecule of her consciousness was riveted on the elephant grass that swayed in the morning breeze 100 yards away, and beckoned her and her children to safety—to life!

The explosion of pain in her right leg took her by surprise. She hadn't heard the crack of the rifle that sent a .308 caliber slug tearing through her body. The force of it spun her completely around, she crashed to the ground, and dragged Kuak and Isak down with her. Reisha flew out of the backpack and landed with a plop on the path a few feet beyond her.

Instinctively, Dada struggled to stand and run. But the shattered femur gave way and spilled her in a heap in the dirt. She looked up helplessly at the boys, shoved them forward and shouted, "Loi! Loi!" Run! Run!

But the twins stood frozen, their eyes wide with shock as they watched the growing pool of blood beneath their mother spread out and begin to soak into the powdery dust on the road.

Dada looked back in the direction of the burning village. She could see women—her lifelong friends—and children, their hands bound behind them, tied one to the next by a long length of rope. The soldiers herded them into the transport like cattle. Then she saw him, the soldier in combat fatigues who had shot her, striding purposefully down the path toward her and her children.

She looked up again at her sons. This time, she didn't command, she pleaded. "Loi! Loi!" But the boys wouldn't move.

Dada's world began to slide in and out of focus from pain and the loss of blood. The soldier was only a few yards away now, and she turned and began to claw her way down the path, smearing blood in a snail-trail behind her.

Dirty and scratched but too stunned to cry, Reisha sat up and crawled toward her mother. Dada reached out and pulled her baby daughter close, to comfort the child as she had done hundreds of times before.

The shadow of the soldier fell over her body. He looked down at her, then barked a command in an unintelligible language. Another soldier ran to him, grabbed the twin boys and dragged them away. The brothers kicked and screamed, dug their feet into the dirt and reached back for their mother. But the soldier effortlessly yanked them along beside him as he headed toward the trucks.

Dada clutched her baby to her breast. She looked up at the re-maining soldier and, in stammering Lokuta, pleaded for mercy. The big man smiled down at her and ejected the spent magazine from his G3 assault rifle. When he slammed in a fresh 20 rounds of shells, the finality of that sound told Dada that she would die.

Reisha rolled out of her mother's suddenly limp arms after the gun blast, her tiny eardrums shattered by the explosion. She righted her blood-splattered body, sat up and began to cry.

Sudan

There was a metallic racking sound followed by a *ka-chunk* as another bullet dropped into the rifle chamber.

The raucous cry of a flock of hornbill set to flight by his second gunshot echoed behind the Sudanese soldier as he walked back toward the remains of the village.

Other than that, it was quiet.

❋　❋　❋　❋　❋

A tall, thin man, with a long neck and a prominent Adam's apple, nudged the sleeping American. Nothing. He spoke his name. Nothing. He spoke it again—louder.

"Ron Wolfson?"

Ron's head snapped upright so violently he almost got whiplash. Even exhausted, he'd only been able to sleep in fitful spurts since his previous assignment in Uganda chasing the ghosts of the Lord's Resistance Army. Machete-slashed corpses and regiments of little-kid soldiers still stalked the dark alleyways of his nightmares. The abrupt intrusion of reality was always startling and usually left him momentarily disoriented.

The BBC correspondent noted the blank, confused look on his face.

"Olford here...," he said tentatively, "from the Cairo bureau..."

The real world downloaded into Ron's brain, and he felt a little sheepish that he had re-entered it like he'd just been jabbed with a cattle prod. Perhaps he should explain his response, but that would require energy and he had none to spare. Instead, he merely grunted, "Yes, I'm Ron Wolfson," as he stumbled to his feet and offered a weak handshake.

"Sorry for the start," Olford said kindly.

And the thing was, he genuinely was sorry. A gentle, compassionate man, Rupert Olford was far too tender-hearted to survive for long as a foreign correspondent. "I was about to give up on you when I couldn't locate you. I was sure I'd recognize you, but... "

"But right now I don't look much like you remember."

"Well, now that you mention it, you do look a bit of a mess." Olford wore a white shirt that looked like he'd just ironed it, and a too-narrow black-and-gray striped tie.

"Back home, we call them red-eyes," Ron said, not referring to the state of his own. "But I don't know what they call all-nighters in the luxurious accommodations of the Nile steamer."

Olford nodded knowingly. His thick, wire-rimmed glasses gave him an owlish look and his head bobbed up and down on his skinny neck. "If that's how you arrived here, I'm not a'tall surprised you look a bit punk."

The Brit's gaze switched from Ron to the other guests in the lobby. His eye swept slowly from one to the next, making certain none of them showed even mild interest in his conversation with the filthy American. When he was convinced they were not being watched, he pointed down a paneled hallway. "I have a room upstairs. We can talk there if you like. I'm eager to see what you have and hear your story."

Ron managed a weak smile and stepped past him. When he did, Olford's face contorted in an involuntary grimace.

Suddenly aware that his clothes reeked, Ron answered the fastidious Brit's unasked question. "It's either goats, zebu dung, dead fish or 2,000 sweating bodies that haven't bathed since the Earth cooled off. Take your pick."

Olford laughed. "You do honk."

"Honk?"

"Believe you Yanks call it *stink*."

Ron's smile broadened as he stooped to pick up his gear. "The assault on your olfactory nerves will be worth the sacrifice when the BBC gets these shots."

"I've looked forward to this ever since the news desk told me 'Mr. C. Dundee' had called." Olford took huge strides on his long, spindly legs as the two set off down the hallway.

Though he wasn't much older than Ron, Olford had gone mostly bald in his twenties. Now, he no longer *combed* his hair, he *placed* it, though his strategically positioned comb-over actually highlighted his lack of hair more than it concealed his shiny, pink scalp.

"After we talk and I see your photos, you can get cleaned up in my room. If you're spending the night in Khartoum, it would probably be best for you to stay with me. I didn't get you a room of your own—I wasn't quite sure you'd show, what with the state of transportation, or lack thereof."

Olford paused, leaned a little closer and lowered his voice, "Actually, I didn't want to bandy your name about, don't you know. If the lads in the government offices down the road knew who your brother was, I suspect they might just string you up from the nearest borassus tree. You'd best hang out with me, no pun intended."

Ron nodded gratefully and slogged on, trying hard to keep up with the Brit, who walked like a stork in the water. When the two got to the end of the hallway, Olford opened the door that lead into the stairwell.

"It's even worse than I thought it would be," Ron began. "And I thought it would be bad. The Nubas, the Neurs and the Dinkas are being decimated... "

Olford put his finger to his lips.

"Hold off until we get into the room," he said. "I suspect you wouldn't be any more popular here than your brother if the wrong people found out what you're doing in Sudan."

They climbed the four flights of stairs in silence. Olford fished the room key out of his deep pants pocket and unlocked the door.

"My home is your home," Olford said, with a bow and a sweeping come-in gesture.

Ron set his travel bag and equipment bag on the stained duvet covering the bed near the window and glanced around the room. Apparently, the hotel owners had sunk the lion's share of their investment into the lobby, the fancy restaurant and the penthouse suites, and consigned ordinary guestrooms to red-headed stepchild status. The walls were unfinished, the paint on the windowsill was cracked and peeling, the spreads on the two beds didn't match, and there were cigarette burns on the nightstand and coffee table.

But on a small table on the far wall sat a perfectly appointed china tea set! Cups, saucers, sugar bowl, milk pitcher, silver spoons and a pot with a cord and a plug that obviously heated water.

"That's *hot* tea, I take it, "Ron said. He set his camera case on the floor by the bed and shook his head in disbelief. "How'd you manage to get a bunch of Arabs to provide all *that?*"

Olford looked stricken.

"I certainly wouldn't expect Arabs to make proper tea," he replied, indignantly. "I brought 'all that' with me. The water's hot. Would you care for some?"

Ron rolled his eyes. "I'll pass, thanks."

"The water's been properly boiled," the Englishman hastened to point out. "It's safe to drink. I got a nasty case of dysentery once in Ethiopia." He wrinkled his nose in disgust. "Horrible place to be sick, absolutely dreadful. Ever since that distasteful experience, I've been extremely careful. I drink bottled water, or boil it, or put those little tablets in it that make it taste like rusty pipes."

"I figured bottled water was likely to be a little hard to come by where I was going so I bit the bullet as soon as I got here." Ron unzipped the travel bag he had set on the bed. "It's a trick an old hippie in Uganda taught me. You add a little tap water to every bottle of bottled water you drink, like one part tap, 10 parts bottled. And you gradually increase the percentage of tap water. I got a little sick a couple of times—actually, I got very sick once—but eventually I could drink whatever the locals drank."

"If I tried something like that, I'm sure I should be dead within the week." Olford shuddered.

Ron reached into his travel bag and took out something wrapped in muslin. He stood for a moment and just looked at the package. "You won't believe what's going on here."

"We never do, do we?" The Brit shook his head. "Until it's too late."

Ron turned and looked at Olford with the hint of a quizzical expression on his face. Even now, it was still hard to believe. "Do you realize there's been more genocide in Sudan than in all of Rwanda, Bosnia, Liberia and Kosovo combined? Two million people are dead. Six hundred thousand have fled the country. Another 400,000 are in refugee camps here."

"I didn't know it was *that* bad," Olford sat down on the bed across from Ron with a thump, as if his legs might have collapsed out from under him.

Ron placed the muslin-covered object on the bed beside the bag and carefully unwrapped it. Clearly, what lay inside was precious. Beneath the final layer of cloth lay a three-inch-thick stack of photographs.

Olford still was amazed that Ron used "film" and produced "photographs," and carried nothing in his camera bag but half a dozen old metal lenses and an equally old, no-bells-and-whistles Nikon that didn't even have auto-focus. Every other photojournalist he knew had long since gone digital.

Of course, Olford had asked why. Everybody always asked why, eventually. One late night when the two worked in South Africa— and Ron had been well on his way to becoming a legend in Olford's mind even then—the Englishman had peered at the American over the foam on his beer and suggested that perhaps Ron might want to consider coming in out of the hot sun someday long enough to participate in the technological revolution.

"I don't do technology," Ron had replied simply.

Olford had pressed the point, made all the arguments for advanced equipment and instantaneous transfer of images.

Ron had only smiled. "Gadgets" were temperamental—get a little sand in them, and they were useless, he said. He'd stick with what he knew. Just a few moving parts. Nothing to break down. He didn't need a camera that was smarter than he was.

It was probably equal parts superstition and stubbornness, Olford thought. Professional baseball players had their special bats, pro golfers their custom-made putters—and Ron Wolfson still used the first camera he ever bought.

But there was certainly no arguing with the quality of his work. Ron was an absolute magician with a camera. His photos were stunning. Some of them packed such emotional wallop they almost took Olford's breath away. Though many of Ron's photos were black and white, the quality of light he captured, the contrasts, the shadows—it looked like each picture had been individually hand-painted. Ron was far and away the best photographer Olford had ever met.

"Where do you want to start?" Ron asked as he straightened up and held out the stack of pictures. "It's a photo tour through hell."

"I want the full Monty. Everything. I'll filter out later what to send on to the newsroom. The problem we have is that every time we get a solid, verified report of atrocities, a government official—sometimes, it's even a U.N. correspondent—releases a report that says just the opposite."

Ron's gaze was unyielding. "The dead are piling up in southern Sudan like Budweiser bottles at a frat party."

The analogy blew right by the Englishman. Guinness had been the beer of choice in the Wheat Sheaf Tavern in the little village south of Coventry in Buckinghamshire where he grew up.

He took the stack of photos, set them beside him on the bed and began to untie his shoelaces.

"It's absolutely unconscionable how Khartoum has managed to bully the rest of the continent—the rest of the world, actually," he said contemptuously, his accent as crisp as fresh lettuce.

Ron smiled just a little. Even as tired as he was, he reveled in the flow and cadence of Olford's speech. An upper-class British accent conferred instant brilliance. Olford could read aloud the ingredients label on a can of Spam and he'd still sound like a nuclear physicist.

"In every way that matters, the Africa Union and the United Nations are impotent." His shoes untied, he took them off, lined them up neatly side by side on the floor and then scooted them carefully under the bed. "Not to mention that the silence coming out of your country is positively deafening."

"Tell me about it," Ron muttered. "Everybody stands by and watches what's going on here without saying a word. Just silence, cold, cruel silence."

"Not everybody. There's certainly no silence coming from your brother, none a'tall. He's shaking things up a bit. I've a little something off the wire about him that I thought you might be interested in reading."

Even the dirt and grime couldn't hide the genuine smile that lit Ron's face.

Olford reached over and opened the night stand drawer to retrieve his pipe and tobacco. "You smoke?"

Ron shook his head.

"I know, I know, your 'Surgeon General's Report' and all that." He wrinkled his nose and muttered softly under his breath, "Rubbish!" He looked up and told Ron with a degree of belligerence, "I am absolutely certain that my food would not properly digest without a smoke after a meal!"

The Brit loaded the small basin, lit the stringy tobacco, took a couple of puffs on the curved mouthpiece and sighed a sweet-smelling poof of white into the air. He propped himself against the headboard with a couple of lumpy pillows, stretched his long legs out on the garish orange-flower bedspread and peered at Ron over his wire-rimmed glasses. "Fire away. I'm listening."

"Just look at those," Ron nodded at the pictures. "They tell the story better than I can."

Olford thumbed through the photos; Ron moved to the window and stared out.

Olford's room was on the front of the hotel and a wide view of Khartoum spread out below the fourth floor window. It was not a pretty sight; the capital of Sudan was not a pretty city. It was hot, dry, dirty, poor, crowded and chaotic. And brown. The dominant color outside the windows of the bus that brought Ron downtown from the dock had been brown. Brown dirt streets, brown thatched roofs, brown bamboo fences separating one brown mud house from the next. No grass, no trees, no shrubs, no flowers, no hills or streams. Khartoum was flat, profoundly drab and almost colorless. Ron looked up and shaded his eyes against the glare—except for the blue, he thought, the relentlessly blue sky that sat like an upturned bowl on top of the city.

The crowds of people and vehicles crammed into the street below also granted a reprieve from the brown. Arab men and women in robes and scarves of white mingled with tribals dressed in bright primary colors—red, orange, purple, green and royal blue. Their wild floral and print dresses stood out against the black skin of women who balanced on their heads everything from water pitchers and trays of fish to baskets of bread and fruit.

It occurred to Ron that the streets of the capital were a word picture of the whole country—diverse, complicated, confused and in disarray. Without traffic lights, drivers of every conceivable kind of conveyance fought their way through the noisy, clogged streets, and stopped wherever and whenever it suited them. Battered blue buses, yellow taxis with loudspeakers mounted on the top blasting words in Arabic that Ron couldn't understand, camouflaged jeeps carrying green-uniformed soldiers, rumbling motorcycles, black stretch-limousines with tinted windows, horse-drawn carts, buzzing mopeds and bicycles all clawed their way forward in the traffic war below.

Ron could see a large, white, sandstone mosque on a busy corner three blocks away, with the spike of a minaret reaching into the cloudless sky. The muezzin proclaimed azan, summoning the faithful to Dhuhr, the mid-day prayer. The crowd of men streaming into the building had traffic snarled for blocks in both directions.

"What is *this?*"

Ron glanced over his shoulder at the photo Olford held up.

"A young man I ran into in the Mangalatore Refugee Camp near Kajo Keji, about 10 miles north of the Ugandan border." He pictured the camp—14,000 people living in mud and straw huts surrounded by plots of limp, leaning corn.

"When the militia raided his village, they tortured him. To finish the job, they tied him down and burned a log on his stomach. Amazingly, he lived through it. His father was the ranking Episcopalian bishop in the region. The militia chopped the man's head off in front of his family."

Ron turned toward Olford and leaned back against the window sill.

"Being an Episcopalian bishop in southern Sudan is like walking around with a 'Shoot me!' sign taped to your forehead. There are a good portion of animists and traditionalists mixed in, but most of the people I've run into in the south are Christians of some flavor."

"I got a quote from Lt. Gen. Omar Bashir's office I plan to use in a piece I'm working on," Olford said.

Bashir was the Sudanese army general who had staged a military coup in 1989 that overthrew democratically elected Prime Minister Sadeq al-Mahdi. Al-Bashir had immediately banned all political parties, dissolved Parliament and allied himself with radical clerics in the National Islamic Front. Two years later, Al-Bashir implemented strict Sharia law throughout Sudan—for Christians and animists who predominated in the south as well as for Muslims in the north. The law was enforced by Muslim judges and a newly created Public Order Police.

In 1993, Al-Bashir was appointed president, and within a decade, he was an annual contender on the Ten Worst Living Dictators List compiled by Freedom House, Amnesty International, Human Rights Watch and Reporters Without Borders.

"Bashir says he intends to accomplish something neither we British nor the Egyptians were able to do, unite northern and southern Sudan. And do you know how he intends to do that?" Olford answered his own question before Ron had a chance. "By Islamizing the whole country."

Olford wasn't saying anything Ron didn't already know, but he enjoyed the accent so he let the Brit talk.

"I'm serious—the bloke's dead set on it. In his radio address last week, he said that within a couple of years he intends to see every man, woman and child in the whole country facing Mecca five times a day to pray—whether they like it or not!"

Olford's lips twisted in a rueful smile. "And if they're Christians or animists and they choose 'or not,' he'll starve them to death or kill them outright."

Olford's words triggered images in Ron's mind so powerful they took his breath away, and he stared at the floor for a few moments before he spoke.

"I was there, just 27 years old, my first job as a free-lancer." His voice was not much louder than a whisper. "I was in Cape Town when apartheid fell, I shot pictures of the prison cells where they tortured Mandela's followers, I talked to the survivors. It was the same year the Hutus butchered 800,000 people in 100 days in Rwanda, and I covered that, too."

He raised his head and looked into Olford's eyes. "I've seen it, Rupert. What's happening right now in southern Sudan is just as bad."

There was silence between them. Olford scrambled to grasp the magnitude of what Ron had said. Oh, he knew there was bloodshed here, certainly people were dying. But he didn't think, never dreamed... He lifted the pipe to his lips, inhaled deeply and created a cauldron of blood-red tobacco in the bowl.

Ron's mind went mercifully blank for a heartbeat, a computer screen after a hard drive crash. It was part exhaustion, part self-preservation. He continued to stare into space for a few more seconds, then his mind re-booted and he engaged the real world again.

"Khartoum has all the cards!" He was as frustrated as his exhaustion would allow him to be.

"Dictators always do."

"Do you know who has veto power over relief efforts—*relief* efforts!—to the southerners?" Ron didn't wait for Olford to respond. "Bingo—Khartoum. Give the man a cupie doll!"

He walked over to the tea set and picked up one of the cups. It had a delicate silver rim around the edge and a crescent on the side, one of those funny-looking eagles with arrows in one talon and a mace in the other. Surely not Olford's family crest; that would be too much!

"I can document that there are more than 500 applications from humanitarian aid organizations gathering dust in some third-string administrator's desk. I know three different agencies ready to air-lift food to the south right this minute, as we speak." Ron turned around and faced Olford. "But Khartoum won't let them, has been telling them no for months now."

Ron spoke to the ceiling, addressed the whole world as it sat in box seats and watched the carnage. "What part of 'the militant Muslim government in the north is trying to starve out Christian tribes in the south don't you understand?"

"Would you mind very much... ?" Olford gestured toward the tea service.

"Huh?"

"Some tea, would you mind?"

'You want me to... ?" Ron was confused. He looked from Olford to the teapot and back to Olford.

"Yes, that would be very kind of you. Mify, please—Milk In First. No sugar. Thanks ever so."

I can't believe I'm doing this, Ron thought, as he poured milk into the cup and steaming tea in on top of it. I didn't travel 10 days up the Nile River on Noah's Ark to fix Icabod Crane here a cup of tea!

When Ron handed Olford the cup and saucer, the Brit's face positively beamed. "Sorry for the interruption," he said. "Do go on."

Ron had lost his train of thought and was rapidly losing his patience, what little of it he had left. The British and their tea! He'd read somewhere that Field Marshal Montgomery had been quietly sipping his tea while his tanks were out kicking Rommel's butt at El Alamein during World War II. Their little piece of civilization in the midst of barbarism.

Focus! The best story in the world won't matter if nobody publishes it. This guy's the key.

"I was telling you about Khartoum's perfect gotcha."

"Gotcha?"

"Gotcha. Catch 22. Heads-I-win-tails-you-lose." Ron could see the Brit wasn't tracking with him, so he just plowed ahead.

"They've done a neat little end run around the United Nations. The Sudanese government forced the U.N. to agree to notify them anytime the U.N. planned to dispense humanitarian aid—basic stuff, food and medical supplies—to the people in the south."

Ron paced back and forth in front of the window as he spoke, venting like steam whistling out of a kettle. "The U.N. has to tell Khartoum when and where the cargo plane will drop supplies. Makes it all neat and tidy. The U.N. gives the government the drop site; the government dispatches a welcoming committee, and... "

He stopped pacing and stood very still. The anger-fired energy drained out of him, and his voice got quiet, like he didn't have quite enough air to speak. "I got to a site near Kapoeta on the Ethiopian border less than an hour after a U.N. cargo plane dropped food out of the sky." His blue eyes turned hard and cold. "I saw what happened to those people." His voice was husky. "I saw."

❋　❋　❋　❋　❋

More than 200 Acholi, Madi, Bari, Lulubo and Lokoya villagers had been waiting for days, hidden in the tall grass and trees encircling the target meadow west of Kapoeta. All of them displayed the ugly visage of malnutrition and starvation. The men's ribs were clearly defined on their bare chests. The women's gaunt limbs poked out of the lengths of ragged fabric that formed shapeless shifts. Their eyes were sunken, their cheeks hollow. The naked children were listless; the babies' cries pathetically weak, like the mewing of tired, sick kittens.

The first sound they heard was a distant drone, more a vibration in the air than a sound. A sudden, instant excitement crackled and sparked in the crowd like static electricity. An airplane was coming!

Sudan

Some of the men ventured into the field and spotted a silver dot in the sky, steadily growing larger as it descended. Once the airplane was clearly visible—a transport!—the rest of the villagers rushed out. Hope granted them energy and they jumped up and down and shouted, waving their arms above their heads to signal the huge cargo plane as it began its low-level approach.

Crouched beneath the protective cover of an acacia tree's spreading branches, an old man and his grandson knelt immobile. Though at 70 his vision had dimmed, the grandfather carefully scanned the trees beyond the field. His black face was leathery under a puffy cloud of white hair and he had no teeth. His skin was taut across his chest; his imbs thin as smoke, his bony frame testimony to his own slow starvation. He wore three strands of beaded necklaces around his neck and displayed the ritual scarring on his chest and face that distinguished him as a Lulubo warrior.

The boy's father and older brother had been killed when a roving band of mercenaries attacked their village. The boy, his mother and two little sisters had been out gathering firewood and hid in the bush until the guerrillas were gone. But the grandfather was too old to fight and too slow to run, so he'd crawled in among the butchered corpses of his son, grandson, friends and neighbors, smeared their blood on his body and face and pretended to be dead.

The grandfather continued to stare out into the field until his nine-year-old grandson could take it no longer.

"Papawa, aren't we going to get some of the food?" The boy was naked except for a small loincloth, his body emaciated. "You're the oldest, and everyone will let you go first, but if we don't hurry, there might not be anything left."

Laying his hand tenderly on the boy's shoulder, the grandfather looked into his upturned face.

"I must look after you and your mother and sisters now and I am old," he said. "That is why I am waiting. I have lived too long to act like a young gazelle that jumps out into the open with no thought of danger. There still could be jackals lurking in the bush."

37

The starving child persisted. "But Papawa, I'm *hungry*."

The old man patted him reassuringly on his small, bowed back and spoke without looking down. His tired eyes continued to examine the field and the surrounding brush and trees. "Filling our stomachs is important, but it is more important to make certain that at the end of the day, we still have stomachs to fill."

The grandfather took his gaze from the field momentarily and glanced into his grandson's eyes.

"No animal is completely defenseless. A gazelle cannot fight, but he does have a weapon—caution. If he is to survive, he must use that weapon. He must be absolutely certain there are no lions lying in wait before he goes into the open field to graze."

The little boy's hunger was far more intense than his sense of caution. "But Papawa, look at all the other men. They've been careful. They've been watching out for danger. They wouldn't be out in the field if they weren't sure it was safe."

"My son, if you wish to grow to be as old as I am, you must learn this lesson. Every gazelle has to take care of himself. He cannot depend on other gazelles to see the danger. It takes just one lion to bring death, one lion hidden so well that all the others missed it. If you are the gazelle the lion attacks and drags away to be devoured alive, it will not comfort you that all the other gazelles thought it was safe to graze in the field."

Flying now beneath the few clouds that littered the sky, the plane slowed its engines. The Swiss pilot spotted the villagers in the field and smiled at his co-pilot.

"Look, there's a reception committee. I'll bank it a little right so the pallets fall clear."

The huge plane leveled off at 200 feet, and the pallets of millet, flour, rice, and powdered milk dropped out of the aircraft, raining life and hope down on the villagers below.

Hitting the ground at intervals of about 100 feet, each tightly wrapped cellophane container kicked up a shower of dirt and sod before tumbling to a stop. Specially packaged and cushioned in high-tech plastic and rubber, the dry goods inside suffered little damage.

The first two packets were still rolling when the villagers swarmed over them, ripping and tearing at the wrapping like a school of piranha. The boy had been wrong. Even if he and his grandfather had been waiting with the others, the old man wouldn't have been afforded the deferential treatment that was his right as an elder. Life in southern Sudan had been reduced to the survival of the fittest.

Without pausing to extricate one parcel at a time, the hungry villagers sliced the bags open, grabbed fistfuls of raw millet and wheat flour and eagerly shoved it into their mouths. They poured the powdered milk into their buckets or folds of cloth held out by the women and children, pushing and elbowing their neighbors who were struggling to do the same thing.

When all the supplies had been dropped, the pilot banked the huge transport and made one last pass over the meadow. None of the relief workers on the plane said anything. They watched in silence as the villagers tore into the food supplies.

To be so hungry you would fight for a handful of raw grain... The pilot shook his head. It was the same every time they dropped supplies, and he never got used to the sight. As the big plane lifted up over the trees and began to climb with a roar out of the valley, the pilot caught one final glimpse of the field. He spotted a very tall villager digging his hands into a torn-open sack of dried milk, his face smeared with white dust like a little kid eating a powdered sugar doughnut. His mind took a snapshot of the man, framed it and hung it up with the caption: *They were starving to death and we fed them.*

There's probably not another thing I will ever do in my life that matters as much as this, the pilot thought as the plane climbed over the ridge. Today, we made a difference. Today, we saved lives!

The young man with white powder on his face could still hear the roar of the departing transport when a bullet tore into his back, ripped through the left ventricle of his heart and blew out his chest.

His spurting blood turned the white powder pink as he pitched forward onto the milk sack.

He was tall, an easy target.

The Fedayeen militia opened fire as soon as the plane disappeared over the ridge. They had been dispatched when the government in Khartoum was notified that the United Nations intended to drop humanitarian aid in this meadow today. Members of the militia had silently edged into position in the tree-line at the far side of the field, undetected by the villagers in a feeding frenzy around the packages.

Within seconds after the first shot rang out, the rat-tat-tat-tat of automatic weapons, the pounding of galloping horses and the shrieking of injured and terrified villagers drowned out the fading drone of the departing transport.

In an instantaneous, mad, screaming, panicked stampede, men, women and children fell over the pallets and knocked each other down as they frantically scrambled to get away from the death bearing down on them. Some raced for the trees, but the distance was too great, the marksmen too accurate. Bullets found their marks with sickening, *thunk, thunk* sounds, and one after another the villagers went down.

…a young mother sprinting for the woods was struck in the back and collapsed, dropping the baby in her arms to be trampled to death by the fleeing villagers behind her…

….a little boy was shot in the leg; his father turned to help him and took a bullet in the face…

…an old man, a teenage girl, a pregnant woman, in rapid succession they collapsed in mangled heaps on the blood-soaked grass.

Rat-tat-tat-tat. Thunk. Thunk-thunk. Thunk. Agonizing, screaming death was everywhere.

Some never made it away from the pallets. Like the young man with the powdered face, they slumped over the feed sacks, their blood soaking into the grain flowing out of the sliced bags.

The Fedayeen continued to fire until the charging horsemen overran the fleeing villagers. Unable to use their guns in such close quarters, they pulled curved, long-handled blades from scabbards at their sides and began to hack the villagers to death. With blow after blow, they severed heads, cut off limbs, sliced children in two.

Though it was a difficult command to follow in the pandemonium of the slaughter, the Arab hunters had been ordered to concentrate on executing the adult males. Later, they would round up the women and children for the slave traders. But there would be no virgins to be sold from this lot of prisoners. The raiders' bloodlust could not be turned off like a spigot after they had reveled in the adrenaline rush of killing. The captives—all of them—would be stripped and raped by one Arab after another all night long.

The old man did not respond in any way to the gunshots that suddenly rang out on the other side of the meadow. His grandson jumped at the sound, his eyes wide with surprise that quickly downshifted into terror. As the massacre rumbled across the field toward them like a blind, rogue elephant, the old man thoughtfully processed his options. It didn't take long because there weren't any. If he and his grandson tried to run, the soldiers would spot them and cut them down. Right now, no one knew they were there. Their only hope was to keep it that way. He put his hand on the boy's shoulder, pushed him down into the high grass and covered him with a large piece of brush and an acacia limb. Moving into a hollow tree several yards away, the old man blended into the shadows and vanished.

As quickly as the massacre had started, it was over. The bodies of slaughtered villagers littered the field. The agonized cries of the wounded were systematically silenced, one gunshot at a time until there was no sound but the frightened weeping of women and children, and the rough voices of raiders, barking orders in a language only they understood.

The horsemen herded their captives to the center of the field. Using raw hemp ropes, a half dozen Fedayeen roughly banded the very young children, all the males and the older women together for what would be a quick, forced march to a rendezvous point where they would be herded into canvas-covered trucks for transport to the slave auctions. All the other females—women, teenagers and young girls—would be left behind; the ones who survived the night would be marched out in the morning.

Other raiders went from pallet to pallet setting fires. Soon, every bundle was blazing, filling the air with smoke and the sickly stench of burning flesh. Then the Fedayeen marched their captives out of the meadow into the woods and were gone.

Crouched in the darkness, the boy had listened in terror to the sounds of the butchery—gunshots, screams, crying, moaning, soldiers shouting. Now it was quiet and somehow the silence was even more frightening. Suddenly, a bony hand reached through the brush and seized his arm. He was so terrified his bladder released and he urinated all over himself.

Lifted into the sunshine, the boy saw that the hand belonged to his grandfather and he was overwhelmed by relief. He threw his arms around the old man and hugged him fiercely. His skinny little body began to shake violently. The boy sobbed, without making a sound, tears streaming down his hollow cheeks and onto his grandfather's bony chest.

The old man held the child and let him cry. When the boy finally stopped shaking, his grandfather slid his arm around the boy's shoulders and wordlessly they turned their backs on the killing field and began the long journey back to the remnant of their family. They had traveled less than a mile when the two heard an approaching vehicle and quickly hid in the undergrowth on the side of the dirt road. But they continued their journey as soon as it had passed. It hadn't been a band of raiders as they'd feared. It was merely a lone jeep with a white man in it, a camera dangling on a strap around his neck, his blond hair blowing in the wind.

Chapter 3

Ron didn't say anything for awhile and Olford was quiet, too, trying to get his arms around the enormity of the horror Ron described. When Ron finally spoke, he was still so stunned by the scene his mind had painted in the air in front of him, his words came out flat and emotionless.

"I counted the bodies. Not a single survivor—219 villagers—pregnant women, little kids, old men were shot or hacked to death when they tried to claim the United Nations' 'humanitarian aid.'"

Ron moved back to the window and looked out with un-seeing eyes. His voice was a tired monotone.

"The government has launched a full bore 'scorched earth' campaign against the south. It's open season on every man, woman and child who lives there, every cow, goat, hut and stalk of grain, too." He stopped and rubbed his tired eyes with his thumb and index finger. "And anybody who survives the carnage is hauled off to the slave traders and sold to the highest bidder."

Olford took a sip of his tea, then set the cup back in its saucer on the bedside table.

"When the truth finally gets out about the bloodbath here in Sudan, they'll have to exorcise demons from the international conscience for the next decade." He shook his head. "And the press hardly says a word. Are all those chaps daft or blind?"

"I really don't know." And he didn't. Here was the biggest story of the century and his colleagues ignored it. "I can't speak to the daft part, but I'm here to tell you that *I'm* not blind. Got both eyes open, even if they are bloodshot. And when I'm finished, this horror show will be coming soon to a theater near you."

Coming soon to a theater near you. Yeah, that's part of the why, Ron thought. Oh, nobody ever did anything for just one reason, but that's where it all started. Only Ron hadn't seen it in a theater. He'd watched it in his own living room years ago, sat glued to the television screen in fascinated revulsion when he was a boy. The images had haunted him for years. Human beings sold to the highest bidder. Plundered villages, raped women, brutalized children, separated families, whips, chains and brands. Watching the "Roots" series in 1977 had been a life-changing experience for 10-year-old Ron Wolfson.

Maybe it had had such a profound impact because he was just a kid, or maybe it was because it was the first time he'd had his nose rubbed in man's inhumanity to man. Whatever the reason, he was never the same. For months afterward, he'd sit in the porch swing at night and gaze into the star-speckled Indiana sky, trying to wrap his mind around the reality that people actually did that to other people; it really happened.

He'd listened to the swing's "eek-eek, eek-eek" tear jagged little holes in the darkness, and wondered if his own ancestors had owned slaves. Surely not! They lived in Indiana and people in Indiana didn't have slaves, did they? But he'd never asked; never brought it up. Both sets of grandparents had still been alive then; he could have questioned them. He didn't. He didn't say anything to anybody, and it was years before he understood that he hadn't asked because he was afraid of what he would have found out if he did.

Now it was happening again, as real as any blood-stained transport ship that crossed the Middle Passage from the coast of Africa to the auction blocks in America in the eighteenth century. Slavery. Here, today, right alongside cell phones, laptops and iPods. An evil buried deep under the years in an ancient and barbaric past had crawled like a bloated, poisonous spider out into the modern world—a world that was trying desperately to pretend it wasn't there.

He turned back from the window toward Olford. "What's going on out there," he gestured over his shoulder, "is an industrial strength nightmare. You name the boogie man, and he's there."

Olford puffed thoughtfully on his pipe and looked carefully at each image in the stack of pictures before he went on to the next.

"Right now, I'm just looking for one particular boogie man, a slave trader." Ron turned back to the window, pulled the curtain aside and leaned his head on the glass. "That boogie man's out there somewhere, and I'm going to find him."

"Which is where I come in, I believe," Olford said.

"Yep, that's where you come in," Ron turned around and pasted his best imitation of an enthusiastic smile on his face. "I give you an exclusive; you blow the lid off the story all over the world—right?"

Typically British, Olford instantly began to hedge his bets. He didn't deal very well in absolutes.

"Well, I shall certainly do the very best I can. This is a huge story, with many, many boogie men, as you say, and I have interested the powers that be in the slavery piece. They're quite excited about this new angle."

The cynic in Ron's head pointed out: Yeah, plain old blood, guts and gore doesn't have a very long shelf life, does it. But he had the good judgment to keep his cynicism to himself.

"So tell me what you've managed to find out."

Ron walked over, sat on the bed opposite Olford and told him about the interviews he'd had with slaves whose freedom had been purchased by Swiss relief agencies, and with a couple of slaves who'd escaped. Then he leaned toward Olford, closer than the Brit would have liked, given the rank odor that rose off the American's body.

"But I still haven't managed to locate—and photograph—a slave auction. That's what I'm looking for. That's the brass ring." He sat back and sighed. "The thing is, they're slick, and they're mobile. It's not like an eighteenth-century Virginia auction, advertised in the local newspaper and open to the buying public. It all happens quickly and privately."

Olford let out a white puff of smoke with his words. "As I understand it, there are so many different sharks attacking at one time it's surprising they don't bite each other. Once they smell blood in the water..."

"Oh, it's become quite a feeding frenzy all right. Government soldiers drop bombs, blow up huts and cattle and people, massacre most of the villagers who survive and capture the rest. Slave traders' hired guns, criminals and mercenaries swoop down out of nowhere and snatch hostages and then vanish without a trace. Murahaleen and Fedayeen guerillas attack with swords and machetes, hack the men to death and kidnap the women and chil... "

"Fedayeen and Murahaleen? Who might they be?"

Ron rested his elbows on his knees and clasped his hands together. "The Fedayeen have been around since the ninth century. I understand they were even chummy with your Richard the Lionhearted during the Crusades."

"You don't say. I knew there was a good reason I never liked that chap."

"Those guys were the original terrorists," Ron said contemptuously. "For the last thousand years or so, they've stolen, kidnapped, raped, traded slaves, assassinated politicians and committed mass murder—all in the name of Allah and Islam. The Fedayeen are the prototype for organizations like Al Qaeda. You do know, don't you, that Osama bin Laden got his start in Sudan?"

Olford picked up his cup and took another sip of the steaming liquid. He didn't say anything, just listened.

"Murahaleen comes from an Arabic colloquialism that means 'a man with a gun on a horse.' To the tribals, the word simply means 'bandit.' These guys are nomadic Arab tribesmen who've fought Africans for generations over water and grazing rights, and now Khartoum has handed them the keys to the kingdom and turned them loose on the south to take whatever they want. Everybody's got a piece of the action—all of them with the encouragement and blessing of the Sudanese government."

Ron reached over and tapped the stack of photos in Olford's lap. "I don't have pictures of a slave auction, but all the rest—all the other boogie men—are right here. Just keep flipping."

He got up off the bed and walked to the window again while the Brit picked up one picture after another. Even exhausted, it was hard for Ron to be still. He lived with an ever-present sense of urgency; time was running out for every tribal in southern Sudan. It was like an itch he couldn't scratch, and it kept him fidgety and restless.

"What on earth happened to these little girls?"

Ron knew which picture was on the top of the stack. He didn't have to turn around and look at the haunting photo of the vacant-eyed child cradling the dead body of her little sister.

"Found them in a refugee camp that's operated by a Christian group out of Canada. The guy who runs it is an old friend from my days in the Peace Corps. He let me set up a darkroom in a closet behind his kitchen—an enlarger, trays, canisters. If Jack didn't have a refrigerator, the only one for 400 miles in any direction, I'd never be able to get the chemicals cold enough to process film."

Olford opened his mouth to point out that if Ron had a *digital* camera, but knew he was beating a long dead horse.

"It took awhile to find a tribal who spoke her dialect and English, too. But once we did, she told us the whole story."

Ron had sat in the dirt and listened to the child's flat, emotionless voice as she answered his questions through the interpreter.

Somebody has to get that dead body out of her arms, he thought. It was gray and stiff—no telling how long she'd been dead—and the flies that buzzed around the dried blood on her neck were so thick the other little girl couldn't keep them shooed away. But the child clutched the body fiercely, tenderly. She never looked at the American as she spoke; her expression never changed. She was so deep in shock that she might as well have been reading the assembly instructions for a mail-order bunk bed.

As he listened, he'd wanted so badly to take the kid into his arms and hold her, tell her everything would be OK. Trouble was, everything wouldn't be OK. He knew it, and so did the little girl.

"Murahaleen guerrillas raided her village. Killed just about everybody, including her father and two older brothers. Gang-raped her mother, slit her throat, and then hauled all the little kids off in the back of a truck. She and her younger sister were sold to 'a man who lived in a big tent and had lots of animals.' Some wealthy Arab trader, I guess. He had them branded right away."

Olford peered at the raw burn marks on the girls' shoulders.

"And everybody would have lived happily ever after—except her sister had the audacity to fight back when they tried to perform an excision."

Olford looked confused.

"A clitorectomy!"

Olford almost choked on his tea. "I didn't think they did *that...*" He couldn't bring himself to use the word for the barbaric procedure that was supposed to keep proper Muslim women pure for their masters. Ron was less squeamish.

"The clitorectomy's just the beginning, "he said. "Sometimes, they also sew the girls' bodies shut with thorns or catgut, leaving just a small opening, until their wedding night—at which point they have to be torn open."

"But these girls are so young," Olford sputtered. "They're probably what, 8 and 10, maybe. Why?"

"I couldn't tell you why, but this guy was thorough. He apparently castrated the boys, too, the day after he bought them at the slave auction. He had a whole lot of slaves to manage, from the girl's description, so I guess he had to run a tight ship. That's probably why he responded the way he did when the little girl dared to challenge his authority. You have to put slaves in their place from the git-go, you see, or they might actually continue to behave like human beings, to have a mind and will of their own. I guess he decided it was worth losing one slave to keep the others in line."

Olford wasn't entirely certain he wanted to know what the slaveowner had done to the child, but he had to ask. Ron answered in three words: the insect treatment. When Olford looked puzzled, he explained.

"They put insects in her ears—it's usually termites, but any boring bug will do—and stopped her ears up with wax. Then they tied her to a tree and watched the insects eat her brains out. From what I understand, most people go completely insane from the bugs running around in their heads before they die."

Ron had held it together pretty well through the explanation, but he began to lose it when the images from the little girl's description started playing on the video screen in his mind. He could hear the tortured child's screams, had heard her shrieking in his dreams for weeks. What kind of human being could do a thing like that to a kid?

"If I had that guy in this room right now," he said through clenched teeth, his voice ragged and his hands balled into fists at his side, "I'd kill him with my bare hands and he wouldn't die fast!"

The two men were silent. The ticking of the wind-up alarm clock on the bedside table was the only sound in the room.

"You can't keep doing this if you let it get to you." Olford spoke softly, compassionately, in his proper British accent. "If you do, you're no good to them or anybody else."

Olford was right, of course. Ron had to disengage somehow, had to reclaim that celebrated "journalistic detachment" he'd left in the ashes of the burned village he photographed two days after he got off the plane in Sudan.

Ron had to... just let it go. He rubbed his face with his dirty hands, took a couple of deep breaths, and exhaled slowly. Then he finished the story.

"The older girl managed to escape. She jumped out of a moving truck on a bridge into a river—can you imagine it—and somehow found her way back to where they'd left her sister tied to a tree. I guess it's the good news that her sister was already dead when she got there."

Ron motioned for Olford to keep moving through the stack.

"I heard of other tortures that I don't have shots of. Tortures just as bad, if that's possible. One of them's called the camel treatment."

"What's that?" The Englishman dreaded the answer.

"Prolonged torture they save for a slave who disobeys his master."

"'Treatment' seems to be a popular word with these people," Olford muttered.

"Beatings, no food for days, tied out in the sun without water. Those are the routine punishments for misdemeanors—spill a drink or drop a piece of firewood or walk too slow. But for felonies, there's the camel treatment. The guilty slave is strapped spread-eagle to the underbelly of a dehydrated camel. The camel is then given water slowly, the belly expands... "

Olford cringed; his face crinkled in a grimace.

"... and the slave's limbs are slowly torn off."

The British correspondent shuddered.

"I can go on," Ron's voice was flat and tired. "Just about anything ghastly you want to see, I can find it for you somewhere in southern Sudan. All the ghastly I could document is sitting right there in that stack."

Olford's hand went up.

"I've heard enough. These photographs are absolutely gripping. I'm sure I can get some of them published, along with your notes. But the slave trade piece is what I'm here to talk about."

He puffed on his pipe only to discover it had gone out. He set it on the night stand beside the bed and looked at Ron.

"I *have* to have documentation—pictures!—of a slave auction, whatever that looks like here. My editor in London says when we provide those, he'll pull out all the stops on the series. But the train doesn't leave the station until we have pictures."

Olford picked up the cup of tea that sat on the night stand beside the pipe, took a sip and wrinkled his nose. It was cold.

"Without pictures, we sound like the *Globe* reporting sightings of Princess Di's face in a lunar eclipse."

"I'm close." Excitement briefly revitalized Ron's voice. "I've found a northerner, an Arab. Lost his job at the university because he was a moderate Muslim instead of a card-carrying, wild-eyed fanatic. He speaks at least a dozen different dialects, probably more. I think he's just what I need. I left him to snoop around and I'll meet him in three days. "

"You be careful!" There was more emotion in Olford's voice than he intended, and he was briefly flustered. He was far too compassionate to conform to the British national character; it was always a struggle for him to maintain a stiff upper lip.

"You sound like my brother. What have you heard about him by the way?"

"I picked up a UPI wire today about U.S. Congressional hearings on the Freedom from Religious Persecution Act." Olford was grateful for the opportunity to pilot the conversation into less personal waters. "That's your brother's bill, is it not? He certainly seems to get quite a lot of press, doesn't he."

"Yeah, that's why my psyche is all messed up. Mama always loved him best," Ron joked. He stuck his lower lip out and tried to look pathetic as he sat down on the bed again. "Spent years on my back counting the ceiling tiles in a shrink's office because of it."

"As I believe you Americans would say, 'Put a sock in it.' "

Ron smiled and kicked off the shoes he'd untied.

"I'm fried. Look, let me hear the latest on Dan after I've had some sleep and I'm not slack-jawed and drooling."

Then he stood up and began to undress. When he slipped out of his pants, a lone Sudanese coin slid out of his pocket and bounced on the carpet at his feet. He picked it up and turned to Olford.

"You did bring along the big bucks so I can keep my Porsche polished and pay off my yacht, right?"

Olford patted the black briefcase tucked against his bed. "Be grateful for the strength of the British pound sterling." There was more than a hint of pride in his voice. Though the Sudanese pound had been replaced by the dinar in 1992, the pound was still in circulation, and that's what Olford had stuffed in the briefcase.

"The international exchange rate of something like 2,000 to one has transformed your pittance of an expense account into a king's ransom."

Olford looked at the American. A fine man, lots of spunk. It would be such a shame if...

"You do know, don't you, what happened to the journalist from the Paris newspaper last year? The word at BBC has it that he was begging to die by the time they got through with him."

"Thanks for the happy thoughts to send me off into Na Na Land."

Dressed only in his boxers Ron collapsed on the bed and lay spread-eagled on the tacky bedspread.

The Brit was horrified. "Aren't you going to take a shower first? You do know there's a shower in there. Soap. Water. Personal hygiene products, things like that."

"In the morning... "

"You smell like a goat!"

"Long as I sleep like one." And then he was out.

* * * * *

Ron had gotten up just after dawn. He felt rested and refreshed. He couldn't remember the last time he'd slept as sound and deep, and he treasured the good night's rest as a gift. A shower, shave and clean clothes had transformed his spirit as well as his appearance. Add to that a good breakfast with Olford in the hotel restaurant, which he wouldn't have given five stars, even though it was certainly better than any cuisine he'd had in a long time. He'd have preferred American ham and eggs, but he'd ordered maschi, tomatoes stuffed with chopped beef, and his all-time favorite dessert, a Sudanese custard called crème carmela.

He and Olford had quietly talked business, and agreed that when Ron had the shots he wanted, he'd contact Olford at the BBC Cairo Bureau, using the Crocodile Dundee password.

Ron had looked at the clock on the restaurant wall—7:30 a.m.—and decided to try to reach his brother. Olford had left to catch the 8 a.m. flight back to Cairo, and Ron needed to get to the dock before the 9 a.m. departure of the passenger barge for the return trip upriver. It would be 1:30 in the morning in Alexandria, Va., but knowing Dan, he would still be up.

Ron left the restaurant and found a comfortable seat in the hotel's phone bank, half a dozen payphones on a wall with carved wooden privacy partitions between them. He punched in the number of his telephone calling card and then followed the instructions of the computer un-person.

Ron heard several clicks and then a female voice, as clear as if she sat right next to him, "Hello, Wolfsons."

"How's my favorite red-headed sister-in-law?"

"Ron?"

"What in the world are you doing up at this hour?"

"Ron! It's so good to hear your voice! How are you?" Sherry didn't wait for him to reply, just laughed tiredly. "And why am I still up? I have two words for you: History. Project."

"What?"

"Don't ask. You don't want to know how I got roped into helping Jonathan build a replica of the Alamo out of sugar cubes."

Jonathan. Ron smiled at the image of the bundle of energy everyone said was the "spittin' image of his uncle Ron."

"Sugar cubes?"

"...or why I'm still up working on it while your favorite nephew snoozes away upstairs."

Ron's smile widened. He could picture Sherry with her long, curly hair pulled back in a ponytail, carefully arranging sugar cubes one on top of the other and—was she gluing them together? Would glue work on sugar?

As Sherry continued her bubbly chatter, Ron thought, as he had hundreds of times before: Bro, you *scored*. Sherry had been his brother's high school sweetheart, and Ron had secretly had a crush on her when he was a lowly sophomore and she and Dan were seniors. He had been the best man at their wedding. Even though a lifetime of serial relationships testified to Ron's determination to remain a free spirit, in his heart he knew that if he ever found a woman who loved him like Sherry loved Dan, he'd get married in a heartbeat.

"So how are the kids, I mean, the *other* kids?" he asked when she paused to take a breath.

"Running me ragged. David made varsity and just started two-a-days, Jennifer has band practice after school and she's determined not to give up cross-country. And Jonathan—don't get me started!"

"And my brother?"

Sherry paused, and her tone grew somber. "Truth?"

"No, lie to me. Come on, Sherry, of course I want the truth."

"I'm worried about him, Ron. He works way too hard, drives himself like...like...oh, I don't know." Sherry's voice trailed off. "I don't want to exaggerate, but if he doesn't slow down—and it's not just the long hours. It's the tension. He's wound up tighter than... well, I can see the stress in his face. That frown crease between his eyebrows, it's so deep right now you could grow ivy in it."

"Don't tell me my big brother is worried he won't get re-elected! I figured all our Hoosier homies made him representative-for-life after last year's landslide."

"Well, it's a different world out there now than it was a year ago. Lots of things have changed. He faces a hunker-down, put-on-your-flak-jackets battle this term. But that's not it. That's not what's eating at him."

"Problems on the Appropriations Committee?"

"No, that takes a lot of his time but... "

"It's the Freedom from Religious Persecution Bill, isn't it." It was a statement, not a question. And in this hotel lobby in Khartoum, Ron said it quietly.

"Ron, that's all he thinks about." There was a mixture of irritation, confusion and concern in her voice. "I've never seen him with this kind of... "

"... fire in his belly?"

"Yes, fire in his belly!"

Ron knew exactly what Dan felt. He felt the same kind of burning urgency to make the world understand what was happening in Sudan. But even if he hadn't, there was a clear picture in his head of that kind of passion.

"It's a shame you didn't get a chance to know Dad very well, Sherry."

"You felt like you knew him, though. Everybody in Southern Indiana did. We saw that face on television—the Rev. Paul Wolfson— in a crusade against drunk driving or child abuse or pornography or... "

"...riverboat gambling or toxic waste or... "

"You know, I never told Dan this, but the first time he asked me for a date—to the Valentine's Day dance when we were freshmen— I almost said no because I was so intimidated that his father was famous. I wish now I could have spent time with your father, but he was never around."

You got that right, Ron thought: he was never around.

"If you'd spent more than five minutes in his presence you'd have seen the fire-in-the-belly syndrome coming a long way out, Sherry. Dan's so much like Dad it's spooky."

"Funny you should say that because he always says the same thing about you."

"Does he *really?*" That genuinely surprised Ron. Dan was the one who looked most like their father—tall, broad shoulders, dark hair and eyes. Dan was the one who stepped into their father's shoes as the crusading social reformer. Dan was the gifted speaker, the charismatic leader. Ron was, well, none of the above. OK, maybe the social reformer part.

"You know, I think deep down in his heart, Dan wants to be you when he grows up." Then she shifted gears. "Look, this call's expensive and you want to talk to Dan. He's downstairs doing research on a bill, guess which one, and you've given me a dandy excuse to disturb him."

"Tell the kids I miss them!"

"I will. Jonathan never shuts up about you. He thinks you're braver than Indiana Jones."

"Tell him I'm better looking, too," Ron said, but Sherry had already put the receiver down on the table beside the sugar-cube Alamo.

Sherry was wrong. Dan wasn't working on the Freedom from Religious Persecution Bill. He had taken a break to recharge his batteries. He sat on the couch in his basement study, his head thrown back, his brown eyes focused on nothing, tenderly cradling his Martin D28 guitar as he finger-picked and sung along. While his deep, booming bass was only a little better than average, his skill on the guitar was nothing short of astonishing. A man with hands as large as his should barely have been able to play at all, but Dan with a guitar was like Ron with a camera—a magician. The big man's musical wizardry had only one limitation...

I fell into a burnin' ring of fire. I went down, down, down, and the flames went higher.

...his musical taste. Dan Wolfson loved country music. Johnny Cash. The Charlie Daniels Band. Allison Krauss. Nitty Gritty Dirt Band. And though he had suffered the raging ridicule of every black basketball player on his team at Purdue—which was just about the whole team—his heart remained true to what Ron had not-so-affectionately dubbed his "twang-twang" music.

And it burned, burned, burned, the ring of fire, the ring of...

56

...the phone. Who on earth would call at this time of night? Then he heard Sherry's shout from the top of the stairs and he couldn't get to the extension fast enough.

"It's about time you called!" Dan said—more like bellowed. Ron could have sworn it was the voice of their father. Both men could address an auditorium full of people without using a mike, and the old ladies in the back row could hear them without turning up their hearing aides. "Where are you?"

"I'm sitting right here in beautiful downtown Khartoum, home of the hottest kebabs and the ugliest women you've ever seen."

"Not exactly a tour bus destination, huh."

"It's best described as the sphincter of the rectum of the universe." Then the playfulness drained out of Ron's voice. "Dan, what's going on in Sudan is worse than anything you've heard."

"Are *you* OK?" There was apprehension in Dan's voice.

"As what's-her-name the housekeeper used to say... "

Then the two responded in unison in a sing-song duet: "I haven't had so much fun since the last time I cleaned the oven."

"Really, I'm fine. Tired, dirty—well, actually, I happen to be rested and clean right now, but it's the first time in weeks, and it won't last. I'm good to go—just massively frustrated. I still haven't found what I came here for."

"And that is?" Dan knew the answer to the question before he asked it. Still, there was always a chance his younger brother had set his sights on a different, *safer* goal. Not a very big chance, but still...

"A slave auction."

Even though Ron spoke barely above a whisper, Dan could hear the steely determination in his voice and recognized it instantly. It sounded just like their father.

"I won't leave here until I get pictures of one. I think I've finally found a guy who can help me. He lost his job as a professor at the university because he committed the heinous crime of being a normal, reasonable, moderate Muslim."

"And the ruling lunatic Muslim fringe only wants wild-eyed, foaming-at-the-mouth crazies to incite the masses to jihad."

"You've done your homework." Ron wasn't surprised by his brother's quick grasp of the situation, but he was glad to hear it all the same. Sometimes, when he was in the middle of a nightmare like Sudan, he'd get to thinking that there wasn't a soul outside that world who grasped, or cared, what was going on. It was reassuring to know that his brother did.

Dan stretched his long legs out in front of him and leaned back. "Yeah, but you're right there in the classroom." He paused. "It's ugly, isn't it?"

"Uglier than you can possibly imagine. I just delivered a stack of documentation to a correspondent." Ron brushed his sun-bleached hair out of his blue eyes in a gesture that had become habitual, and wondered if he could possibly snag a haircut before the barge chugged out of the dock. "I've talked to former slaves in refugee camps. Real horror stories, Dan. You need to be very, very grateful that your kids don't have to grow up on this side of the planet."

There was a heartbeat of silence while Ron switched his focus to his brother's side of the world. "How's the bill going?" He looked around to be sure nobody lingered nearby before he continued. "Unless the U.S., the U.N., or somebody gets some help to southern Sudan soon, there won't be anybody left to save."

Dan's voice sounded flat and tired. "Next Monday I've got a meeting to talk about the bill with a few of my esteemed colleagues, at least one of whom has likened this particular piece of legislation to the warm, sticky substance you find on the south side of a horse going north. I've worked all evening to gather information to include in my presentation."

"You want information, I got information." For the next 10 minutes, Ron told his brother much of what he'd told Olford. Even without the graphic pictures, the descriptions sickened Dan.

"That's really happening?" Dan was incredulous. He'd picked up a pen and had taken notes while Ron talked. He looked down

58

and noticed he'd also doodled spiraling dark circles, like bottomless whirlpools. "Human beings are actually doing that to other human beings?"

"That's the issue—'human beings.' What precisely is the definition of human? It's all about semantics." Ron turned and leaned back against the wall beside the phone bank and surveyed the hotel lobby as he spoke. "Hitler re-defined human to exclude the Jews and eight and a half million 'sub-humans' died. The Arabs here have redefined human and their definition excludes blacks and Christians. Most of the population of southern Sudan has the misfortune of being one or both."

"Well, this bill's moving as slow as a tick on a dog's back." Dan felt frustrated and helpless. "I don't even know who my friends are and who my enemies are on this one."

"Don't the Christians support you? Christian people have been massacred by the thousands because they won't convert to Islam! And African Americans. I mean, we're talking slavery here. Surely..."

"There are lots of people who *should* get behind this bill," Dan interrupted. "But when push comes to shove, I just don't know how many of them actually will."

"I couldn't do your job." Ron raised his voice a little as a group of noisy tourists passed by in the hotel lobby. "I don't know how you have the self-control to sit still while everybody whines and moans and comes up with one lame excuse after another. The real reason your esteemed colleagues won't stand with you, and stand up to this government, is the 'standing' part. Remaining vertical requires a backbone, and those guys are jellyfish in three-piece suits. I think you ought to just deck somebody."

"I couldn't do your job either." And it wasn't just because Dan had never taken a single in-focus photograph in his life. Dan didn't have his brother's wanderlust; he wasn't wired to be a gypsy, a nomad traipsing all over the globe. And he didn't need the adrenaline rush of adventure and danger his brother seemed to crave. He was a fighter, too, but his weapon of choice was persuasion; his battle-field relationships.

Both men fell silent for a moment.

"You do realize, don't you," Dan said, drumming his fingers on the spiraling whirlpools on his legal pad, "that the Wolfson brothers are both tilting at the same windmill this time. That's a first."

"Yeah." Dan could hear the smile in his brother's voice. "I noticed."

Then Ron's voice got soft, distant, and Dan couldn't read it. "I think Dad would be proud of us—both of us."

Before Dan had a chance to respond, Ron changed the subject. "Listen, I need to get down to the docks to catch the boat."

Dan suddenly remembered the pesky man with the nasal voice.

"Oh, I've been meaning to tell you. There's a guy who wants to do a documentary on Sudan, calls my office a couple of times a week trying to track you down. Since *Newsweek* used some of your stuff, he figures you're the go-to guy on the slavery issue. You might want to consider going to work for him."

Having a *boss*? What a horrifying thought! Ron was accustomed to doing things his own way; he couldn't imagine being encumbered by somebody else's expectations. He liked to travel light.

"Thanks for the advice, but I work better on my own."

"I know—that's what keeps me awake nights." Dan wasn't joking. "If you get into trouble out there... " He didn't finish; he didn't need to.

"Indiana Jones always gets away with the treasure, the girl and all his body parts intact. Says so right there in the S'posta Book."

When the brothers were kids, they'd assumed that grownups had a book stashed away somewhere that explained to them precisely how life was s'posta be.

"Give my love to Sherry, and I'll call you again as soon as I can. But don't start to worry when all is silent on the Ron front for a while. There's no phone service where I'm going."

As soon as Dan put the receiver back in the cradle, he went

upstairs to the kids' bedrooms and stared down at his sleeping children. He tried to imagine what it would be like to be unable to protect them, to be powerless when madmen on horseback swooped down out of nowhere to carry them off into slavery. Slavery! David forced to work in the fields; Jennifer turned into a... He leaned over and stroked his 10-year-old daughter's strawberry blonde hair—someday it would be as red as her mother's—then kissed her tenderly on the forehead and went back downstairs to work on his bill.

Ron hung up the phone, checked his equipment, and headed out of the hotel lobby to catch a bus to the riverfront. Three days later, he stepped off the Nile barge onto the gangplank leading to the dock in Conglaii.

Chapter 4

Ron ambled along with the flow of humanity up and down the Conglaii dock for two hours. And still no Masapha.

Half a dozen different tribal dialects babbled around him, mingled with the animal sounds from a menagerie of creatures—cows, pigs, goats, chickens, guinea hens—in a background noise he heard but didn't really listen to.

But it was a lot harder to tune out the stink than the noise. The reek from the fish laid out on the dock when he stepped off the barge that morning had been heightened and magnified by the midday sun to create a stench that was foul beyond description. There was no wind, and the odor hung like a fetid fog in the air.

Ron began to make a mental list of all of his favorite smells: coffee brewing, honeysuckle after a spring rain, steaks on a backyard grill, the upholstery in a new car, a pretty girl's hair.

But the game faded from his mind as his eyes studied the crowd, one person at a time, searching, hoping.

Come on, Masapha. Don't do this to me. I need you, man. Just show up—I don't care if you stink, I don't care if you've been rolling around in zebu dung!

Ron had set up today's appointment the day before he left for Khartoum to meet Olford. He and Masapha had talked for hours and discovered they shared the same theory. Both suspected that the main marketplace for kidnapped southerners had shifted away from Khartoum; what they hadn't figured out was where it had shifted *to*.

Even by conservative estimates, more than 150,000 men, women and children had gone on the auction block in Khartoum since 1990. But with international human rights pressure on President Bashir's government, it was a whole lot easier for him to deny the existence of slavery when human beings weren't being sold to the highest bidder within a few miles of his palace.

While Ron was in Khartoum, Masapha had been out among the people. He'd asked questions, collected information, tried to learn where the slave trade had gone, tried to do what no investigator had ever done—pinpoint the location of a slave auction. That was, as Ron had remarked at the time, a tall order for a short Arab.

The slave traders had perfected a portable collection and distribution system that had operated undetected for decades. It was a ghost, a phantom, a shadow, here and then gone, whispered about in hushed tones in refugee camps and around cooking fires in every village in southern Sudan. Like the hot wind blasting across the Sahel, it was invisible. You only knew it was there because you could feel it and because you could see the damage it left behind in its wake.

But Masapha was confident that if he shook enough trees, some fruit was bound to fall out somewhere.

So where was he? Without a Sudanese guide, Ron might as well flip a coin to determine which way to go from here.

He reached into the pocket of his pants and drew out an American quarter. Let's see, he thought, I'd say north is probably not a good idea. That's where the bad guys live. Southwest is probably out, too. Nothing down there but a swamp the size of Belgium. East? Nope, that's Ethiopia. Sooo, it's heads for west toward the oil fields, or tails for south toward Kenya.

Ron placed the coin on the top of his thumbnail, flipped it into the air...

... and a hand reached out and snatched it quicker than a frog's tongue capturing a fly.

"Yo, Yankee, do not toss the money around," Masapha scolded him. "Soon, we will need every nickel we can lay on our hands."

Ron turned to face the grinning Arab and was so glad to see him he almost threw his arms around him in a bear-hug greeting, even though Masapha's worn chambray shirt and khaki pants did smell a little like he'd rolled around in zebu dung.

But male-hugging was a Western greeting that wasn't a culturally sensitive thing to do in Africa, and Ron always felt silly performing the shoulder shake that was the formal Sudanese equivalent. So he grabbed Masapha's hand and shook it frantically up and down like he was pumping water into a bucket.

"I can't tell you how glad I am to see you!" Ron's jubilant greeting was wrapped around a sigh of relief. "I was beginning to think... "

Ron let the sentence trail off and Masapha finished it for him, extracting his crushed fingers from Ron's death grip as he did so.

"That I had taken your money and spent the whole of it on wild women? I do not have dealings with wild women. Besides, you did not give to me so much money."

Ron looked into Masapha's face and smiled. The man's uncanny resemblance to one of Ron's favorite actors was spooky. Masapha was the living image of Omar Sharif as a young man, the way he looked in "Dr. Zhivago." Their features were strikingly similar—Masapha had the same mustache, the same intense dark eyes, and a lock of hair that always fell down on his forehead. He even had a little space between his shiny white front teeth!

He was drop-dead good looking!

But Masapha was a small man, maybe five-foot-eight, with a slight frame. He wouldn't have weighed 140 pounds with rocks in his pockets and looked even shorter beside Ron, who, at a slender six-foot-four was still two inches shorter and 75 pounds lighter than his brother, Dan.

"I don't know what wild women cost around here, but the money I gave you would have bought a whole herd of them where I come from."

"I did not buy a herd of women, my infidel friend, but I did spend the whole of the money."

Ron looked both surprised and alarmed. "All of it? But... "

Masapha put his hand up to stop Ron's questions.

"I think it will please you, the purchases made by your money." He lowered his voice. There were too many people within earshot. "But it is not to be talked about now. I know a place where so many people are not there. Follow me."

The little Arab didn't wait for Ron's response, just wheeled around and headed back down the dock, past the stinking fish, to a small block building on the far end that hung over the river's edge. The bare block walls, unpainted door and rusty tin roof reminded Ron of the huts that housed the latrines in some of the Boy Scout camps he and Dan attended when they were kids. Dan had been way more into Scouting than Ron, whose only claim to fame was his skill at lighting farts. While Ron was perfecting the art of not setting his underwear on fire, his older brother was racking up badges. Dan made Eagle Scout before he turned 16.

What's wrong with this picture? Ron thought as he followed Masapha into the darkness on the other side of the rough-hewn door. My brother could survive in the wilderness for a month with nothing but a Swiss Army knife. Now he spends his days behind a desk in a posh office, while I'm out here in the boondocks with no matches trying to figure out how to start a fire with flint and the fuzz out of my navel.

Once his eyes adjusted to the dim light, Ron could make out a dozen or so wood-slat chairs around a handful of rickety tables near the back wall and another few scattered in the center of the room. This, he suspected, was probably the finest drinking establishment in the whole town. A group of five or six men huddled in the corner, glasses in hand, and rattled dice in a shot cup. Ron found a couple of seats at a table by a window, away from the other patrons, and set his travel and equipment bags and camera case on the filthy floor at his feet.

Masapha stepped to a counter made from two rough, splintered planks straddling box crates and ordered drinks from the paunchy proprietor, then brought the glasses to the table and sat down opposite Ron. The window let in a breeze that carried with it the smell of decaying vegetation from the river mixed with the fish stench and miscellaneous olfactory delights from the marketplace.

"I haven't spent a lot of time in bars since my fraternity days," Ron said. "But I'd have to say that what this little watering hole lacks in atmosphere and classy clientele it more than makes up for in ugly and stinks."

Masapha didn't catch everything Ron said. Even though he was a language sponge, he never tracked perfectly with the tall, blond American's version of English. Besides his native Arabic, Masapha was fluent in a dozen tribal dialects and could manage basic communication in at least that many others. But English—so many words, strung together in such an odd, illogical fashion. And so many phrases that didn't relate in any way to his world or experience. He just did the best he could, smiled, and tried to act like he understood more than he did.

Ron lifted the glass Masapha had set in front of him to his lips and took a big gulp. A sip would probably have been smarter, then he wouldn't have had quite so much liquid to spew back out of his mouth onto the floor and his shoes.

"What *is* this stuff?" he gasped.

"It is aragi, the local beer."

Ron noticed that Masapha drank only water. "You knew this stuff tasted like paint stripper, didn't you? That's why you didn't order any."

"I did not have the beer because I am Muslim. I do not drink alcohol," Masapha pointed out. "But yes, I have heard it has the flavor of goat urine."

"I don't know about goat pee, but it definitely tastes worse than moonshine!" Ron sputtered, and spit on the floor to get the last remnants of the foul liquid out of his mouth. Then he saw the blank look on Masapha's face. "You don't get moonshine, huh. Never mind. I just hope I don't go blind."

Masapha wouldn't have understood that reference either, even if he had been listening, which he wasn't. He was scanning the room to make sure the novelty of a white man in their midst had worn off and the bar's patrons were occupied with their own business and not inclined to eavesdrop.

He finished his glass of water in one long gulp, then leaned closer to Ron. He paused for effect and then spoke quietly.

"I think I have found it." He enjoyed the impression his words made on the big man who sat across from him. "Oh, I do not have a mark X on the spot of a map, but I believe I have found the big space."

"The area?" Ron's heart began to pound.

"Yes, area where inside there is most of the slave trading."

"What makes you think that's the spot?" Ron tried to hang onto his soaring elation. He wanted so badly to believe that Masapha was right, that he had done the impossible. But he knew he must be prudently skeptical. If Masapha really had found the site of a slave sale, the little Arab with the gap-toothed smile had performed a feat akin to magic. And when something sounds too good to be true...

Masapha glanced cautiously around the room again and lowered his voice. "Many are the wounded people in the south who are being taken to Lokichoggio."

"To the Red Cross hospital?"

The Arab nodded.

"When we left CARA, you went to Khartoum, and I went first to Lokichoggio," Masapha continued. "I thought in my head—the wounded there would have very soon information about the guerrillas, where they attacked and when—and how many captives they took away with them."

He picked up his glass, then remembered it was empty and set it back down again. "The information I got was sketching."

Ron stopped him. "Sketchy?"

"Yes, that too." Masapha tried to sound like he understood the difference. "And all of it was pointed to the same thing. If you study hard where there were raids and when, you can see a ..." he searched for the word, "...a blueprint... "

"Pattern?"

"Yes, a pattern. It would be logical that the Murahaleens, Fedayeens, mercenaries, soldiers—whoever—want to be rid of their captives soon, and the slavers want to bring together so many slaves as they can find at one time—right?"

"Right."

"But they must find a place that is safe, a private place where villagers are no longer there. So I thought, where is such a place? Would it not make sensible for the place to be not far north—so the slavers must not have to travel so big a distance with their captives—and not far south so the SPLA does not stumble on top of them?"

The Sudanese People's Liberation Army was the south's only real resistance force against the Khartoum government. Though poorly trained and totally outgunned by the government soldiers, the SPLA had proven to be formidable adversaries who had racked up a surprising number of military victories—particularly in recent months.

"Makes sensible to me," Ron said.

"Of course, this collecting place would be a target that moves, but if we figure out the area that is best for them to hand off their captives, that is stepping the first time."

"The first step," Ron put in.

"And the second step is that we are to follow the trail of the slavers in that area to the collecting place where the buyers come, and there is the slave auction you want to photograph."

Masapha finished with a flourish. Ron looked at him as if he had completely lost his mind.

"Follow the trail?" he asked. "That makes you Tonto and me

the Lone Ranger, pal, 'cause I couldn't track a herd of elephants through a wine glass factory."

Masapha was a big fan of vintage American television westerns; finally a reference he understood!

"Oh no, Kimo Sabe," he replied with a broad smile. "I do not mean you and I will follow hoof prints in the sand. I mean we will go to the right places and ask the right people the right questions."

"And where are those right places, where we find the right people for all our right questions? Let's go back to step one. This 'area' that we have to search, where is it?"

Masapha spoke the next three words quietly, with an intensity that shouted. "The oil fields."

"The oil fields?" Ron had tracked with the Arab up to that point, but now he was lost.

"You do not see?" Masapha was disappointed; the conclusion seemed absolutely self-evident to him.

"Where is the place that is not so far north and not so far south? The oil fields! The Heglig and Unity fields sit almost on top of the line that divides northern and southern Sudan."

And exactly where that line was located mattered tremendously because it determined how much of the oil revenues Khartoum was supposed to share with the south.

"Where is the place that for certain no villagers are there?" Masapha continued. "The oil fields! The government got rid of all the tribals there long ago, so soon as Khartoum found out it was under the ground oil to be found on their land."

"And where is the place in all of Sudan that the SPLA will for sure not ever be found? The oil fields! The government would not let the resistance army even to get near to them."

Masapha had Ron's concentrated attention as he continued. "And Khartoum would surely turn its eye looking the other direction if southern tribals are sold to northern Arabs in a government place. In fact, it would be making a good guess that Sudanese officials have certain knowledge of slave sales in the oil fields, and the government is—how is it you Americans say?—smiling on the way to the bank."

"The oil fields," Ron said, and this time it wasn't a question. Ron had to admit Masapha made a good case; his logic made sensible. That didn't mean he was right, of course, but his step-by-step theory was a vast improvement over the investigative technique Ron had employed so far. He called it the RGM—Random Guess Method. It had not served him well. But was he convinced enough by Masapha's plan to go for it?

Suddenly, he almost laughed out loud. *I need serious psychiatric care if I'm so delusional that I think I've actually got a choice here*, he thought. Without his Arab guide's help, the possibility of finding a slave auction downshifted from a "slim chance" to "pack your bags, pal, and head back home to Poughkeepsie."

Ron flashed Masapha a broad grin and said the two words the Arab most wanted to hear. "I'm in."

Masapha beamed, and Ron asked, "So where do we go from here?"

"We go toward Bentiu, by a route that is not straight."

Masapha already had it all planned out. They would travel northwest on the road, such as it was, that led out of Malakai through Talodi to Kadugli, then turn south toward Bentiu. The route would take them through the heart of the Heglig and Unity oil fields, the two biggest oil fields in Sudan.

As Masapha described where he intended to conduct his search, he picked up a coin off the rough table top and began "walking it" across his knuckles. "What everywhere I am hearing is that more and more it is government troops who are attacking the villages," he said, "and not just the Murahaleen guerillas and the Fedayeens loyal to Khartoum."

"That's nothing new. They've done that for 15 years."

"True. But the SPLA has been making victories in battle in the past few months, and the north is sending out even more soldiers."

"Goody." Ron pulled back the dirty muslin that served as a curtain and looked at the river.

"My contact in the Ministry of State told me that it has been counted, like a census, and seven from every 10 people in northern Sudan are Sunni Muslim."

"That should be a great comfort to the tribals asleep in their tukuls tonight." Ron let the curtain drop back in place. "Like living next door to the Branch Davidians."

"Branch Davidian?"

Ron waved it off. "Just a fringe group in the western part of the U.S. who dressed hate and paranoia up to look like Christianity."

Ron leaned back in his wood-slat chair, extended his long legs out in front of him and shook his head sadly. "My country has been blessed with the screwiest radical Christian groups and the worst religious, wild-eyed crazies in the world."

Masapha stopped flipping the coin across his knuckles and held it in his palm. He fixed his intense, dark eyes on Ron, and there was no good humor in his voice when he spoke. "When the religious wild-eyed crazies in your country take over it, as they have taken over mine, when they do murder and rape, when they make of any people who are not like them slaves, when they desecrate and defile their own religion—and when the rest of the world looks another way to make believe it is not happening—*then* you can complain about radical groups!"

Ron met his gaze. "Point made," he said quietly.

It was easy to forget sometimes that what were random acts of violence in America were everyday occurrences in a country where the lunatics really did run the asylum.

The two men sat together in silence for a few moments. Then Masapha flipped the coin out of his palm with the end of his thumb and began to walk it across his knuckles again.

"It has been told to me that the SPLA set free more than a dozen villages in just a few months past. And shot to the ground two government planes, too." Masapha's grin displayed the Omar Sharif gap between his teeth. "Our beloved president in Khartoum is not a happy camp!"

"Camp-*er*," Ron corrected.

"He is not that either. And his camp is very not happy that the count of Muslims was also a count of Christians, and in the south, the number of Christians has grown from 5 percent to 20 percent."

Ron thought about explaining camps and campers, but wasn't sure it was worth the trouble. He had figured out that Masapha's almost accent-free English made it appear he understood more "American" than he actually did. Instead of explaining camps and campers, Ron asked a question.

"Where'd you learn to do that walk-a-coin trick?"

"A Mabaan tribesman from the Blue Nile valley taught me," Masapha said, and the memory painted a warm glow on his face. "His name was Sharmad Lemue."

Masapha deftly slid the coin down from the knuckle of his thumb to the nail, flipped it up and snatched it out of the air in one motion. "He was my brother."

Ron waited but Masapha didn't elaborate, just flipped the coin back onto his knuckles and began to move it across again.

"And you're just going to hang that out there like a dead fish on a stick? No explanation? You're a northern Arab, and that makes you a Muslim, right?"

"I am not just a Muslim of culture or geography, as are too many of my countrymen. I am a believing Muslim, in here," Masapha tapped his chest, "in my heart. I am a servant of Allah, may his name be praised."

Ron suddenly wished he was more than an occasional-Sunday-in-church Christian. It once had been in his heart, too, with the same fierce dedication as Masapha's to Islam. But not anymore, though the son of a preacher couldn't have explained what happened to his faith if Masapha had asked. It was just gone, and he had long since stopped picking at the scab that covered the wound of its passing.

"So you're an Arab from the north, and your 'brother' is a southern tribal, and that doesn't strike you as odd in any way? Like perhaps people would be curious about how that came about?"

Masapha held the coin between his thumb and forefinger.

"Sharmad's mother was the housekeeper of my home and cooked food for us, and his father was the driver of my father's car. Sharmad and I were the same age, even our births were on the same day. I have no memory from my childhood that is without Sharmad in it. When we were boys, we witnessed many American westerns. In one of them, a cowboy and an Indian cut their wrists and held them together, mixing their blood up with each other and making them blood brothers."

Ron smiled. He could think of half a dozen movies with that scene.

"There was a lot of that going around in the Old West."

"And it was plain to look in the mirror that the two of us were as different each from the other as American cowboys and Indians. So we cut with a knife our fingers—it would be too much hurt to cut our wrists, and we were afraid—and we made of ourselves blood brothers."'

Masapha sat back in the chair, and even under the weight of his small body, it creaked in protest.

"My mother died when I was 2 years old, and Mama Lemue was like she was my mother. They were a Christian family, but never did it matter that I was a Muslim and an Arab. Almost it was real that I was Sharmad's brother."

Ron thought about telling Masapha about the death of his mother when he was a toddler. But he didn't. He just listened. He had a sense that Masapha was edging further and further out onto a fragile thread, and if he interrupted, the thread would snap and the little Arab would not tell the rest of the story.

"My father worked with the Ministry of State, but he stood against the extremists, and never do bullies like it when you say their bluff."

Ron caught himself before he blurted out *call* their bluff.

"He was not a large person on his outside—my father—but a giant lived on his inside. Nothing scared him. Their threats frightened him like a flea frightens a rhino."

There was more than admiration in Masapha's voice. There was awe. And a strange quizzical quality, as if he still didn't understand the man he most admired in the world. When he continued speaking, his voice was quiet.

"Then, one day he was gone. He woke me up to say me goodbye before he went to work. He hugged me very tight, like he wanted not to let go. Always I have had curious—did he know a thing was to happen? But I do not know. He was vanished—poof!—like never he was there at all. Still, I do not know what happened to him. "

Masapha paused for a beat and then went on.

"And I lost my job teaching electrical engineering at the University of Khartoum two years ago for the reason that is the same. My mouth was running too many times to complain that only radical Muslims were allowed professorships." He laughed mirthlessly. "I should be having grateful that only they fired me." He didn't sound grateful. "Many worse things there are than getting fired. Or getting killed."

Ron said nothing. He wanted to know more, but he wasn't sure Masapha wanted to share it. So he didn't push, just sat quietly, waiting.

When Masapha continued, he wasn't talking to Ron at all anymore. He was narrating a movie that was playing on a screen behind his eyes.

"After my father was gone poof, I was all alone. Just 10 years old, with no family anymore of Arabs. So Sharmad's family took me just like I was their son as was Sharmad. Mama and Papa Lemue no more had jobs, so they moved back to their village on the Blue Nile and I was moved with them."

Sharmad's father had become a Christian pastor with a wide circuit of churches.

"Not even one time in all my days with them did Papa or Mama Lemue or Sharmad try to make of me a Christian. When I knelt to pray five times a day as I was taught to do, they had respectful for my prayers. I served Allah in my way; they served Jesus in theirs."

Often Papa Lemue took both boys with him when he preached, traveling from village to village, tribe to tribe. That's when Masapha discovered his gift for languages; his new family was stunned by how quickly he learned.

Masapha looked up at Ron, who could see him slowly reconnect with the present.

"Those years were the best of my life." He smiled down at the face on the coin in his hand, as if it were an old friend. "Sharmad and I went to a Christian mission school. I was the only Arab, the only Muslim, and Sharmad had so much proud that I was his brother. I learned all to be learned there in a short time, and the teacher said I had very smart and wanted for me to take an examination to be a university student."

Masapha took it, passed and left the lush green of the Blue Nile Valley to attend the university in the capital. He finished in three years, a math prodigy as well as a language sponge, and went right into graduate school, working at two jobs to support himself, and going home to visit his adopted family on the Blue Nile as often as he could. Sharmad became a minister like his father, and Masapha often traveled Sharmad's circuit with him between semesters at the university.

Masapha had leaned his rickety chair back on two legs as he talked, and he set it back down on all four. A lock of dark hair fell over his forehead and a wide smile graced his mustached face.

"Sharmad got married, and his firstborn was a boy. He and Odella named the child Masapha." The Arab conjured up the image of the child's face in the air in front of him and gazed at it lovingly. "So handsome and smart was he! Even he could speak Arabic and Mabaan when he was just 3!"

As Masapha talked about the boy and the two little girls that followed, Ron thought about how much he loved and missed Dan's kids, David, Jennifer and Jonathan. He suddenly was stabbed by a pang of longing—to shoot free-throws with David, to listen to Jennifer's little-girl chatter, to play video games with Jonathan. He was so engrossed in memories, in fact, that he failed to notice at first that Masapha had stopped talking. When he did notice, he saw the look on Masapha's face and a hole suddenly opened up in his belly. He knew what was coming.

"The Murahaleen came in the night," Masapha said. "A neighbor pretended to be dead and saw it all and told me of it."

His voice was flat and emotionless, and he stared with sightless eyes out the window. "Many of the village escaped, and the guerillas thought Sharmad knew of their hiding place. He knew no place to hide, but to make him say, they beat him with their fists and sticks until no more he had a face. They raped Odella—every one of the raiders took a turn—with Sharmad to witness it all." His throat tightened in remembrance. "They had their way with the girls, then killed them both. Still, Sharmad could not say what he did not know, so they tied him to Odella and threw them both into the river and watched the crocodiles eat them."

Ron was so stunned and sickened he could barely breathe. Every time he thought he'd heard the worst story, seen the worst atrocity, witnessed the worst evil, the soul-less fanatics upped the ante.

Sharmad's son, Masapha, was 6. The guerillas picked him up and carried him away.

"That was eight years ago, so Masapha is 14 now." The Arab stopped. He turned back from the window and looked at Ron, and dropped his next words like smooth, hard stones. "He's out there *somewhere!*" The edge of his voice was as sharp and cold as a dagger. "My brother's son is somebody's slave! Somebody owns him, *owns* him! He's been beaten, branded and probably... " The last word came out in a strangled half sob. "*Castrated!* Masapha will never, can never... And every day, *every day*, I... " He couldn't finish, just gritted his teeth, and looked away from Ron and out the window.

Ron's heart went out to his friend as Masapha struggled manfully not to break down. He wanted to comfort him somehow, but he didn't know how.

"Masapha, I'm so sorry."

Masapha took a deep breath and let it out slowly, shook his head and steadied himself. And then the window on his soul that he'd opened wide slammed shut. Vulnerability vanished from his face, to be replaced by his ever-present smile. The smile was plastic, but it announced to the world, to Ron, that that part of the conversation was over.

"We must talk now about Bentiu and how we are to get to there from here," he said, his voice shaky.

Ron stumbled, tried to shift gears. "Uh, yes... you do have a plan, don't you?"

"A plan, yes. First, we buy a jeep."

Buy a jeep? Ron almost choked. "Do you know how much a jeep costs?"

"No jeep, no pictures," Masapha told him matter-of-factly. "Can we chase the slave traders running on our feet?" Masapha paused. "In a city, we could rent. But here... " He thought for a moment and then added, "Of course, if there is not money for a jeep, we could buy camels."

"No camels!" Ron said a little more adamantly than he intended. "I don't do camels. Or yaks either, for that matter. Just a personal policy of mine."

Camels spit; yaks bit. He sighed. Well, it was only money.

"Where, pray tell," Ron gestured out the window at the remote little river village and continued sarcastically, "is the nearest dealership?"

Now, it was Masapha's turn to sigh. He gave Ron a you-still-don't-get-it look.

"There is no dealer *ship* to the oil fields," he said slowly and patiently. "No river launch or steamer either. It is no water there; it is desert. We need a jeep!"

Ron put his elbows on the table, leaned toward the earnest Arab and opened his mouth to explain. But he simply smiled instead.

"You say we need a jeep, then we need a jeep."

"I know a man who will sell to us one, if the money is enough. But you must not display to him your white face or the cost will be bigger times two."

Ron reached down, opened his travel bag and took out a leather pouch stuffed with bills. He opened the pouch just wide enough for Masapha—and no one else—to see what was inside. Masapha looked at the money, then smiled approvingly and nodded. Ron nodded back.

"Hi-ho, Silver," Masapha said.

* * * * *

Idris opened his eyes in the gray, pre-dawn half light, and for the first time in his life, was sorry he was such a good shot. His marksmanship had always been a special source of pride. Even as a boy, he'd had a keen eye and a steady hand. His grandfather had recognized his natural ability and worked with him patiently, hour after hour, until Idris could plant an arrow in a knothole on a tree 75 yards away. At shorter distances, he was just as accurate with a spear.

As he grew older, his family often feasted on kudu, antelope and gazelle, courtesy of his skill. Today, he almost wished he couldn't hit a zebu just 10 paces away.

He got up carefully off the mat where Aleuth still slept, tiptoed past Akin and Shema and out the doorway of the tukul. He sat down beside the glowing embers of the cooking fire, began to poke them with a stick, and added twigs and bark to rekindle the blaze. His 9-year-old son, Abuong, would be baptized today, he thought miserably, and he would not be there to rejoice with the boy because he would be hunting.

When the itinerant Christian pastor came to the village today, new converts from Mondala and two other small villages would be baptized beneath the rock cliff in the bend of the river. That evening, the three villages would gather for a celebration. And it was the task of the best hunters from each of the villages to provide meat to feed the crowd.

The hunters from the other villages would arrive soon; game was more plentiful before the sun became a torch in the sky. So Idris set his bow and larger-than-usual supply of arrows aside and went to find Abuong.

Dawn had just bathed the valley in golden light when Akin rolled over and opened her eyes. She lay there for a time and enjoyed the comfort of her sleeping mat. Then she sat up and noticed her father and Abuong in deep conversation by the cooking fire. Suddenly, the little girl was stabbed by an unfamiliar emotion—jealousy. Akin had always enjoyed a special closeness with her father. She was so snug and secure in her place in his heart that she'd never felt threatened by the affection and attention he also showered on her younger brother and sister.

But she understood that when Abuong was baptized today, he and her father would be joined in a unique bond. All those who had been baptized seemed to draw together in an intimacy that she didn't understand. Now, Abuong would share something with her father that she did not.

She watched her father drape his arm around her brother's shoulder, and the two of them bowed their heads in prayer.

Idris had spent hours telling Abuong the stories of Jesus, and patiently explained how the boy could be in a relationship with the God of the universe. Like every Christian father in the world, he had been delighted when his son understood, believed and asked to be baptized. He sincerely believed that Christianity was the most important gift he could give to his children, and he longed for the day Akin would be willing to sit still long enough for him to have the kind of deep, intimate discussions he had had with her brother. As he and Abuong sat together by the morning campfire, they prayed for Akin. And as she watched them pray, she felt a sudden pang of emptiness. For the first time in her life, Akin had been left out.

She popped up off her sleeping mat and darted out of the tukul.

"Good morning, Papa!" she squealed in delight, and plopped down in his lap.

Idris was so taken off guard that he had to fight to keep his balance on the log where he sat. But his greeting was as warm and loving as it had ever been. He hugged her close and kissed her dimpled cheeks. And the bubbly little girl's jealousy evaporated like dew in the morning sunshine.

The Arab mercenary noted the little girl's dimples as he watched her through the binoculars he had trained on Mondala. Lying with two comrades in the tall grass by the river, the advance scout paused to look at the child briefly before he returned to his surveillance of the village. She was a pretty little thing, he thought—and surely still a virgin. She would bring a handsome price at the auction.

Chapter 5

U. S. Rep. Dan Wolfson stood in front of a small group of fellow legislators in a conference room deep in the bowels of the Cannon Office Building, connected to the Capitol by an underground passageway.

"I just don't know what else I can say to make this any plainer than I already have," Dan said. A hint of exasperation sneaked into his tone uninvited.

He had loosened his red "power tie," and a lock of his dark hair had fallen over his forehead in what Sherry called a "sexy widow's peak." He leaned on the lectern and looked each of the seated men in the eye, one at a time, all the way around the big conference table. "If I'm missing something here, you need to tell me what it is, because for the life of me I can't understand why this bill isn't a slam-dunk."

Dan would know about slam-dunks. Even at "only" six feet, six inches he had jammed many a ball during the four years he started as a forward for the Purdue University Boilermakers. It was his basketball career, as a matter of fact, that had launched him into politics. Or rather, the lack of a basketball career. He'd grown up only 30 miles from the home of Boston Celtics superstar Larry Bird in French Lick, Ind. But Dan was no Larry Bird. He played smart, though, had quick hands and an uncanny ability to see the whole court at once. He always found an open man, and his high, arching, nothing-but-net 3-point shot had sealed the Boilermakers' Big Ten Conference Championship title when he was a junior.

NBA scouts had been checking him out before a torn rotator cuff early in his senior year put him on the bench for the remainder of the season, and as it turned out, for the rest of his life. At graduation, he found himself with a diploma in political science that he would actually have to use to support himself. That led to Stanford University Law School. A brief but impressive law career led to a term and a half in the Indiana state Senate. And that led to Washington.

Now beginning his fourth term representing the southern Indiana district around New Albany, the son of crusading minister Paul Wolfson was considered something of a maverick, and certainly a political anomaly. As anyone who'd been on the Hill more than 10 minutes could tell you, it was virtually impossible to forecast where U.S. Rep. Dan Wolfson would come down on any given issue. He wasn't predictable because he wasn't in anybody's pocket. He'd ridden a landslide victory up to the steps of Congress, and didn't owe the price of the ticket to any big contributors. He was his own man. That made him popular, sought-after and a loose cannon.

Dan had invited to the meeting a handful of colleagues who represented a cross section of the House. With disparate views, constituencies and backgrounds, they were a tough sell. But that's what Dan had been looking for. If he was going to get shot down, this was a better place to take the hit than on the House floor. Better to find out the weaknesses of his argument now than to be blindsided later.

Dan was a convincing speaker—his accent pure "middle America" and his voice pure orator. Even toned down for the small room, its rumble was commanding and impressive. For an hour, he'd presented information and answered questions about his proposed Freedom from Religious Persecution Bill, an unadorned, straightforward piece of legislation that called on the Sudanese government to cease human rights violations against its own people or face a graduated series of stiffer and stiffer sanctions from the U.S. He described what he hoped the bill would accomplish and why it was so desperately needed, and he issued an impassioned plea for support.

Though he had tried to prepare himself, he was still surprised that the presentation provoked such a remarkable lack of enthusiasm from his colleagues. It was as if he had leapt to his feet and shouted: "Hip, hip... " and was waiting for a resounding "hurray!" that never came. There was only silence.

That was not a good sign. He told Sherry later that the meeting had started to go south as soon as he stopped talking.

"Roger Calvin, that little guy from Florida who actually wears a plastic pocket protector, was the first one who bailed," he said, as Sherry poured him a second cup of after-supper coffee. "He said to count him out because 80 percent of Sudan's gum exports come to the U.S., and the gum lobbies and soft drink companies just about own his district."

"Was Raleigh Sutherland there?"

Dan made a *humph* sound in his throat. "Are you kidding? You know he wouldn't miss an opportunity to come down on the other side of whatever I support!"

Then he launched into a perfect imitation of the white-haired legislator's southern drawl. "Ah represent the citizens of the great state of South Car-o-li-na, and far as I know, ah didn't git a single vote from Africa. Much as I'd like to hep ya out, Daniel, ah don't have a dog in that fight."

Sherry began to clear away the dishes as Ron talked. It was Jonathan's turn to help tonight, but he was nowhere to be found.

"Surely, Greg Alexander was on your side. I'd think you could count on a man like him to support a bill to prevent persecution of Christians. "

"Yeah, that's what I thought, too."

Besides bearing a striking resemblance to Brad Pitt, Greg Alexander was an outspoken evangelical who conducted a Bible study in his office every Friday. The young Idaho congressman also was the chair of the Christian Legislators Association, which, oh by the way, had a mailing list of more than 400,000 names.

"I thought I had him when he started out saying he wouldn't be able to sleep at night if he didn't stand up against genocide." Dan sighed. "But he ended by saying the bill's timing was bad and maybe we could try to push it through next spring after we get the budget approved."

Dan suddenly noticed his youngest son's absence.

"Wasn't Jonathan supposed to... ?"

"Help clean up after supper? Uh huh." Sherry looked tired and exasperated. "Sometimes it's easier to just do it myself."

Dan drained his cup, stood and began to gather up dishes.

"Calvin even brought up Ron, implied that because my brother was investigating Sudan, my judgment was somehow impaired, that maybe I didn't see what was going on as clearly as I should."

The big man turned toward the kitchen with a stack of plates.

"My brother is the one who *does* see it all clearly." Dan shook his head. "Ron was right. Maybe I ought to just deck somebody."

❋ ❋ ❋ ❋ ❋

The itinerate preacher, Pastor Maluong, stood on the riverbank, surrounded by a crowd that probably numbered more than 200. Most of them were from Mondala, with a handful from two other villages upstream where he had preached at services last night. The pastor wore western-style khaki shorts with sandals and a bright, African-print shirt loose at the waist.

The crowd was predominantly women and children. The women were not dressed in their "church clothes," but in the shapeless shifts they wore as they went about their chores in the village. Many of the women, particularly the younger ones, were bare-breasted; all the children under age 5 were naked. Most of the men had stayed behind to work in the sorghum fields, planting millet until sundown. But once the workday was over, the men would join the celebration, eating mullaah bamyah, okra stew, and wild water lilies, and the game—gazelle, reedbuck or bushbuck—the hunters brought back, roasted on a spit over an open fire in the center of the village.

He glanced up to see if there were any stragglers before he began the service, and the pastor spotted Akin barreling down the hill, all arms and legs, her perpetual smile snug on her pixie face. The child wormed her way through the people gathered at the river's edge and popped like a cork out of the crowd. She wore her faded smiley-face T-shirt and a stained goat-skin skirt, and she was panting. Obviously, she had run all the way from the village.

"Be careful a crocodile doesn't get you!" Akin called to her younger brother, who stood a short distance away, already up to his knees in the brown river water.

There were, of course, no crocodiles on this particular stretch of water. The river and adjacent sandbar were, in fact, a perfect setting to accommodate the villagers' needs, and Akin was certain the elders who built Mondala on the hilltop had positioned it there for just that reason.

The forest on the village side of the river had been removed so long ago not even the old ones remembered when, to form a bowl that gave the women easy access to the wide, sandbar riverbank to draw water they carried back to their tukuls in clay jars balanced on their heads, and to wash their families' clothes and spread them on the river rocks to dry.

Directly across from the bowl, a huge gray cliff rose out of the water and towered 50 feet into the air. The river bent sharply around the cliff face and cut a deep trough in front of it that created the sandbar on the village side and deposited gravel on the river bottom. Though the cliff face appeared to be perfectly smooth, it offered enough hand holds for generations of boys to climb to the top and leap from the rocks into the deep pool below. But other than climbing the rock wall, there was no access to the top of the cliff from the river. A narrow, winding trail led up a steep slope on the back side of the cliff, but the entrance to that trail was more than a mile upstream. It was the spot where the hunters had crossed the river earlier that morning in search of game for the evening meal.

The road, such as it was, came from the south and split at the crest of the hill. One part continued a quarter of a mile into the village and ended in a labyrinth of interconnecting passageways that wound among the 100 tukuls. Worn by the traffic of bare feet for generations, the trails had been beaten down six inches into the hard clay. The other fork of the road led around a 20-foot stand of bamboo, a wall of sticks that grew so close together even a small child couldn't have squeezed between them. The road ended at the riverbank across from the cliff, where yellow-billed storks, snowy herons and egrets waded on their long legs in the shallow water downstream, feeding among the reeds next to the bank.

The pastor addressed the crowd. "We are here for a very special occasion."

The rock wall and river formed a natural amphitheater that magnified his voice. The sudden sound startled a trio of herons in the nearby reeds. They instantly took flight, protesting loudly before settling back down into the river farther downstream and prancing herky-jerky on their stick legs in the water.

"We're here to stand as witnesses to the faith of our brothers and sisters. Their baptism is an act of obedience that symbolizes the death of their old selves and their birth into a clean, new life."

Even the villagers who opted not to attend the ceremony on the riverbank were welcome to join in the celebration afterward. Only about a third of the 275 residents of Mondala counted themselves Christians. The rest were animists or had no particular religious beliefs of any kind. But the whole village embraced the festivities as a break from the monotony of their everyday lives, and those who weren't at the riverbank looked forward to the evening's feast.

Most who remained behind were men and older boys who

worked in the sorghum fields or looked after the cattle that grazed on the grassy slopes southwest of the tribal compound. The women still in the village cared for small children, finished morning chores or made preparations for the evening celebration.

One villager who'd declined the invitation to join in the Christian baptism service had obligingly agreed to stay behind and help with his neighbors' cattle. Living by himself, Gatluak often traded chores with his neighbors in exchange for meals. It was a useful symbiotic arrangement. For the price of another mouth at the table, his neighbors purchased a hired hand to help them work their crops.

He had taken one of his neighbor's zebu out to the pasture and was on his way back to get the second. As he walked along the path, Gatluak hummed an ancient melody his grandmother had sung to him when he was a boy.

The robed figure who hid behind the hut of Gatluak's neighbor flattened against the wall when he heard Gatluak's voice and the dirt crunching under his approaching feet. The intruder gripped the wooden handles on each end of a strand of thin wire, held his breath and waited. Gatluak came around the corner of the hut, and for an instant that seemed to last forever, the two men faced each other. Then the Arab grabbed Gatluak, threw him to the ground and straddled his back. Before Gatluak had time to cry out, the wire was around his neck, and within seconds, a thin, red line of blood appeared where the wire had dug into his flesh. Gatluak struggled soundlessly, thrashed on the ground as his face turned a deep purple. Then blood gushed from his neck around the wire, and he went limp.

The Arab pulled the gory wire free and joined his companions, who had appeared so quickly they might have popped magically out of the ground. The men, dressed in white ankle-length robes with white shora scarves covering their heads slipped like ghosts into Mondala. They darted from hut to hut and signaled each other with hand motions as they silently infiltrated the village. They killed anyone who got in their way—man, woman or child—using knives, garrotes or machetes so their victims could not sound an alarm that would alert the rest of the villagers before the raiders were ready to pull the noose tight.

Once the advance party was in position, the attackers signaled for the second wave. With a suddenness calculated to stun and surprise, Arabs mounted on horses crashed out of the woods to the south and thundered down the road into Mondala. In seconds, the village went from quiet and peaceful to screaming nightmare madness. Like a pack of wild dogs, the ragtag band of Murahaleen, soldiers and mercenaries dispensed indiscriminate death in a savage, feeding frenzy of blood and destruction. The terrified villagers had no time to react before their attackers were on top of them, swords and machetes drawn, slashing everyone who crossed their path. Shrieking in terror, mothers grabbed their children and tried to escape, but the attacking Arabs yanked babies and small children out of their mothers' arms and sliced them open with shiny silver swords and razor-sharp machetes. Men who tried to protect their families were brutally hacked to death. The pathways of the village soon were flowing streams of blood.

The mounted members of the slave trader Faoud Al Bashara's hired militia carried torches and held the sticks of fire to the thatched roofs of the huts. One after another the buildings burst into flames. The raiders on foot who had hidden in the village went from hut to hut and dragged out any occupants. A handful of women and girls were seized and shoved toward the center of the village. But not a shot had been fired. It was not yet time.

* * * * *

Pastor Maluong talked briefly about the morning's service, that it was the beginning of a journey for those about to be baptized. He described the significance of baptism as an outward symbol of an inward commitment each had made to the God of the universe.

Then he waded into the river until he was waist deep and motioned for Abuong to join him. The boy was already in the water up to his knees, and he made a splashing dash to the pastor that wasn't exactly representative of the solemnity of the occasion. With great effort, Maluong managed not to smile. The others who were about to be baptized, two men, three women and a little girl, waited patiently on shore. When the boy reached the pastor, Maluong showed him how to position his hands in front of his chest so he could hold his nose when he went under the water. Bouncing up and down on his tiptoes in the chest-high water, Abuong did as he was instructed.

Maluong put his hand on the boy's shoulder.

"Abuong, because you have placed your trust in Jesus Christ, I now baptize..."

Suddenly, a piercing scream shattered the reverent silence. Everyone turned toward the sound, which came from the road that led around the stand of bamboo trees that blocked the view of the village from the riverbank. Against a background of rising black smoke, a woman sprinted down the hill, screaming hysterically, and pointed back toward the village. No one paused to listen to her words; the danger was obvious. The village was on fire!

There was a moment or two of stunned shock. Then, as if on cue, the men raced up the hill toward the village that now belched boiling black smoke into the morning sky.

And that was exactly what the Arab mercenaries expected them to do. So far, everything had played out just as they had planned.

The group of women and children left on the riverbank stared at the menacing cloud of thick, black smoke rising from the village. They were stunned, but their surprise quickly downshifted into fear. Mothers called their children's names, searched for their own in the crowd of frightened youngsters—who looked around just as frantically for them.

Akin had moved away from her mother and Shema as soon as Abuong splashed out into the river to stand before Pastor Maluong. The tall grownups blocked her view so she maneuvered her way through the crowd to the river's edge, where she could see Abuong clearly and feel the warm water lapping against her bare feet. When panic broke out, she turned and screamed, "Mama! Mama!" and tried to run back to the spot where her mother and sister had been standing. But the scrambling mass of adults and children got in her way.

Akin looked frantically from side to side, cried out for her mother, her voice gobbled up by the voices of all the other children crying out for theirs. Suddenly, she spotted Aleuth, shoving her way through the crowd to the riverbank with Shema at her side, calling, "Akin! Where are you? Akin!"

"Here! Mama, I'm here, I'm here!"

Aleuth broke free from the tangle of frightened humanity. Akin raced to her, threw her arms around her mother and held on fiercely, her heart pounding, her body trembling.

"Mama, I couldn't find you anywhere and I was so scared. Do you see the smoke, Mama? The village is on fire, it's burning up. What are we...?"

"Shhhhh." Aleuth struggled to keep the sound of her own fear out of her voice as she tried to quiet the frightened child. "Everything is fine. Shhhhhhh. We're in no danger. We're safe here on the riverbank."

That's when the Arabs struck.

As soon as the village men racing toward the burning huts were out of sight around the stand of bamboo, the waiting mercenaries attacked. One band of mounted Arabs thundered out of the reeds downstream and crashed through the tall grass on the riverbank toward the horrified women and children. A second band on foot rushed the crowd from the woods upstream, pinning them against the river. The riders quickly surrounded their prey in an ever-tightening circle as a truck bumped down the road and halted in a cloud of dust.

Chapter 6

With far more bravery than good judgment, the tribal men on the riverbank had bolted up the hill toward the burning village. As soon as the men were in range, the Murahaleen guerrillas snapped their trap shut. The Arabs finally employed their automatic weapons, opened fire, and mowed down the unsuspecting villagers like a scythe slicing through wheat.

One after another they fell. Most were killed instantly by the sickening ka-thunk of bullets ripping into their bodies. Few had time even to cry out. The only men who survived were the ones quick enough to drop to the ground at the first gunshot. One of them was Akec Kwol.

Akec lived in a tukul next to the Apot family, and he would have said that he and Idris were good friends. Idris probably would not have agreed.

Akec was a big man in the village by a couple of standards. He was the tallest, by several inches, in a tribe whose most distinguishing characteristic was height. He stood 6 feet, 9 inches, and was stronger than any other man in Mondala. He also was the richest man in the village. He owned many head of cattle—the standard of wealth among the tribes in Sudan—sheep and goats, and was able to farm a large sorghum field by employing other men to help him work the land. He'd received huge dowries when his daughters married farmers in adjoining villages, and now one of them was about to deliver Akec's first grandchild. His wife, Nhiala, had left at first light that morning to be with their daughter during the birth.

But it was not Akec's wealth that made him so thoroughly disliked in the village. What rankled was his arrogance. He was a boasting show-off, and most of the villagers cut a wide swath around him whenever they could. Except Idris Apot. Idris didn't like the man any more than the other villagers did. But as a Christian, Idris made an effort to treat his neighbor with dignity and respect and had no idea how much his kindness meant to the lonely, friendless man.

Flat on his belly as bullets whizzed over his head, Akec knew his only hope lay in getting his hands on the weapons in his tukul on the edge of the village overlooking the river. With the smell of dirt in his nostrils, he lifted his head slightly and could just make out a group of men running toward the village, farm tools in hand—grubbing hoes, machetes, pitchforks and axes. They were the men who had opted to work in the fields instead of attending the service on the riverbank, and they'd seized whatever makeshift weapon they could find when they saw that the village was under attack.

The Murahaleen saw the farmers, too, turned their weapons on them and mercilessly cut them down, one after the other. With the Arabs' attention focused elsewhere, Akec and the others from the riverbank had a chance to escape.

They crouched low and made a break for the stand of small acacia trees beside the bamboo at the base of the hill between Mondala and the river. From there, they slipped onto the trail that encircled the village and headed north toward the river and Akec's tukul. On the other side of the village, the farmers who'd survived the first deadly hail of bullets made a break for the encircling trail as well and instantly vanished into the labyrinth of paths winding among the huts.

The farmers and the men from the riverbank knew the layout of the village. That was their only advantage. They used the increasing smoke for cover, wove in and out among the burning huts, and quickly intermingled with the Arabs so the attackers couldn't turn their automatic rifles on them without hitting each other. Then, with whatever weapons they could find, they fought back.

One of the farmers launched a pitchfork at a guerilla mounted on a big Arabian stallion. The shot fell short, striking the horse in the side. The animal bellowed in pain, reared up on its hind legs and dislodged its rider before it keeled over on its side. Another farmer leapt out from behind a hut and finished off the dazed Arab with a grubbing hoe.

Akec emerged from his tukul with his bow and arrows. He was not as good a shot as his neighbor, Idris, but at close range he could hold his own with any man. He crouched low behind the only cover he could find, a stack of cooking pots, and fired at an Arab torching the roof of a nearby tukul. The man cried out in pain as the shaft plunged deep into his chest. One of the men from the river launched a spear that just missed its mark, and its intended victim turned his horse and trampled the villager. Akec had to jump out of the way to keep from being trampled, too.

Though the villagers' Stone Age weapons were woefully inadequate, the young leader of the attack had never encountered any resistance at all, and he panicked. He signaled a retreat and his men abandoned the handful of captives they'd corralled in the center of the village. The mounted soldiers galloped off to the rendezvous point a mile from Mondala while the foot soldiers headed down the hill to the riverbank where their companions were rounding up the women and children there for transport.

* * * * *

Aleuth Apot had tripped when the terrified crowd exploded in hysteria, and she lay in the sand for a moment with the wind knocked out of her. But the fall didn't loosen her grip on her daughters' hands, and Akin and Shema stood above her, pulling with all their strength to help her to her feet.

"Mama, get up!" Akin meant to scream the words but terror had taken her breath away and all she could manage was a raspy, choked whisper.

"Mama! *Please!*" she pleaded. "Get up! You have to get up!"

Aleuth staggered to her feet.

Where was her son? What had happened to Abuong?

She'd last seen him with Pastor Maluong in the river before the madness struck. Now she couldn't locate him anywhere. She tried to see past the horses and riders encircling the panicked crowd but the moving wall blocked her view.

Most of the women in the group were too dazed and frightened to do anything except scream. They stood as immobilized as terrified rabbits, with their children gathered around them, as the raiders pulled the noose tighter and tighter.

Aleuth was terrified, too, but she grabbed hold of her fear and hung on fiercely. She looked around, desperate for any avenue of escape, and her eyes locked on the stand of reeds that lined the downstream riverbank and formed a marsh spreading out into the water. It was a place to hide, not a particularly good one but the only one she had.

Grabbing the girls' hands, Aleuth darted behind the horses of two riders struggling with a mother whose two screaming boys were wrapped around her legs, zigzagged through the confused melee and sprinted for the bank of reeds. Somehow in the chaos and hysteria, she managed to make it to the marsh undetected. Once inside the grassy cover, she moved backward slowly and slipped deeper and deeper into the sanctuary of stalks.

Akin clung to her mother's hand. Her heart pounded so hard she feared the raiders could follow the sound of it to their hiding place. In all her 11 years, the little girl had only been truly terrified one time. She had been gathering firewood one day when she was 6 and had stumbled upon a black mamba. No one survived an encounter with a black mamba; a bite from one of the vicious, aggressive snakes was always fatal. Like cobras, mambas rise up off the ground to strike and can sink their venomous fangs into a victim 10 feet away. Akin had been much closer than that. Terror had taken her breath away then, too, and stolen all the strength from her limbs, left her no air to cry for help, no power to run away. She'd simply stood frozen for a five-second eternity and watched in fascinated horror as black death slithered past her bare toes and away into the grass.

Now, she stared with the same fascinated horror at the thin wall of reeds that stood between her and the madness on the riverbank. She knew that at any moment death could rise out of the reeds like a black mamba and strike the three of them down.

High on his Bedouin saddle, one of the mercenaries scanned the river as others lined up the women and children and began to rope them together in a human chain attached to the back bumper of the small truck.

Suddenly, his eye caught something unusual. The tops of the reeds to his left were moving against the downstream flow of the river current. With a quick whistle, he caught the attention of one of the soldiers near him and pointed to the serpentine pathway of reeds moving in the wrong direction. The young soldier smiled knowingly and wheeled his horse into the shallow water.

Aleuth heard the horse's hooves strike the dry reeds less than 30 yards behind her and knew instantly they'd been spotted. She dragged the girls as fast as she could through the boggy water. The spiny heads of the reeds stung her face like tiny sweat bees as she ran.

When the black Arabian horse burst through the reeds, it almost trampled them. Aleuth turned and screamed, and the huge animal reared up on his hind legs—which saved her life. The motion knocked the Arab's aim off center, and the lance thrust meant to impale her struck her a glancing blow on the forehead instead and left a crimson furrow as it raked across the top of her scalp. The force of the blow propelled her backward, and she fell unconscious into the reeds in the shallow water. Shema was so terrified she kept running; Akin stopped to help her mother.

With the speed of a striking snake, the Arab reached down and grabbed Akin. Almost pulling her arm out of its socket, he yanked her out of the water and threw her over his saddle horn. Nudging his horse's flanks, he turned the big horse back toward the riverbank as Akin kicked and shrieked, pounded her little fists against the horse's flank and wrenched her body from side to side in a desperate effort to get free.

The soldier intended to dump Akin into the group of women and children his comrades were tying together with lengths of rope. But when he lifted the squirming child off his saddle, her small foot caught him squarely in the groin. With a roar of pain and rage, he threw her small body like a rag doll over the heads of the half dozen prisoners already tied to the truck bumper. She landed with a bone-jarring crunch in the bed of the small truck, slid forward and slammed her head into a wooden crate. Then she lay very still, blood slowly forming a pool beneath her right ear.

◉   ◉   ◉   ◉   ◉

Idris and the other hunters spotted the smoke from a long way off. Two of the men were carrying on a pole between them the large reedbuck Idris had bagged. Two others were toting gazelles, and the remaining men carried a half dozen bush rats and rabbits.

At first, the men thought the column of black and gray smoke that rose into the late morning sky must be a brush fire. They quickened their pace for another mile, fearful the fire might spread to the village. But as soon as they crested the final hill between them and the river, they could see the roofs of the huts burning.

The hunters dropped their kill in the dirt and started to sprint for the trail that led to the riverbank downstream of Mondala. Idris stopped them.

"Wait! Why do you think the village is burning? It's the Murahaleen!"

The men froze.

"The Murahaleen are attacking the village!" Idris' voice came out in a strangled sob. "They have rifles and machetes. We can't just go running..."

He stopped. His mind was spinning; then his whirling thoughts congealed into a single image.

"This way!" he cried.

He gripped his bow, his spear and his few remaining arrows, turned and raced up the winding, rocky trail that led to the top of the cliff overlooking the river. After a moment, the others followed. They could hear the women and children screaming and the gunfire before they reached the top of the hill, so they dropped low, panting, and crawled the final 50 yards to a collection of boulders that littered the crest of the cliff face.

Idris peeked over the top of the rocks and took in the whole scene in one glance. Women he'd grown up with, children who'd played with his children, were being herded like cattle toward the back of a truck. Dead bodies lay everywhere. *Where was his family?*

There had been a moment as he ran along the trail that Idris wondered if he could do it, if he could actually shoot a man. But there was not a moment's hesitation now. With smooth, practiced skill, he drew back his spear and hurled it with all his strength at the nearest raider. It struck the man in the chest, and he dropped off his horse in a heap.

Idris grabbed his bow, fit the slot of an arrow onto the string and pulled it taut, as the other hunters began firing, too, singling out the mounted soldiers rather than the guerillas mixed in with the crowd for fear of hitting one of the villagers. Aiming carefully, Idris let his missile fly, but as it sailed across the river, someone shouted a warning, his target ducked and the arrow missed its mark.

● ● ● ● ●

The leader of the guerrillas, a bearded man named Hamir, seemed to absorb the light around him into his own darkness. He sat atop his white Arabian stallion like a death angel. His flowing black robe and the black shora scarf on his head blew in the wind as he surveyed the morning's haul. There were perhaps as many as 75 children, and maybe 50 women—it was hard to get an accurate count with them running around screaming. He knew his employer, Faoud Al Bashara would be able to get top dollar for the little girls—the ones Faoud didn't keep for himself. The slave trader they worked for did what was *haram,* forbidden, with children, both girls and boys. There were a lot of young ones here who...

Suddenly, the soldier on the horse next to him let out an odd, gurgling grunt. He turned in time to see the man slide out of his saddle, a spear stuck like an exclamation point in his chest.

A cry of pain squalled out of a rider behind him, and he whirled around to see his second in command shrieking in agony, a feathered shaft buried deep in his thigh.

"Hamir!" a soldier shouted, and the leader instinctively ducked as an arrow flew so close to the side of his head he could feel the air rearrange itself as it passed.

"There, on top of the cliff!" A soldier had spotted the tribals. He and the others raked the rock face with a hail of gunfire from their semiautomatic rifles.

But as soon as the soldiers stopped shooting, arrows and spears rained down on them again. One after another, raiders cried out and dropped to the ground. When an arrow sailed past Hamir's right shoulder and stuck with a resounding *thunk* in the wooden post that supported the canvas cover on the back of the truck, he called it quits.

"Out, *now!*" he yelled at his men, motioning toward the road.

He knew the tribals couldn't hope to compete in a battle of weaponry, but there was no way for his solders to leverage the superiority of their firepower. They couldn't storm the villagers' position on the cliff, and as long as the men shooting at them could hide behind rocks high above their heads, he and his men were effectively outgunned.

"But, the prisoners... " One young soldier started to protest. "How can we... ?"

"Leave them!" the leader bellowed. "I said get out! Now! Get in that truck and drive!"

Hamir turned his horse away from the deadly hail of arrows dropping out of the sky, kicked the animal's flanks and galloped up the road. His men followed suit. They dropped the ropes that bound their prisoners, leapt on their horses and raced up the road behind Hamir. Two riflemen stayed behind to keep the tribals pinned down while the foot soldiers escaped. The small, covered truck brought up the rear. The driver shoved down the accelerator and roared up the hill. The three women and four children who'd been tied to the truck's bumper were yanked off their feet and dragged along behind.

Idris and the other hunters firing from the top of the cliff had crouched so low when the second round of automatic gunfire pinged off the rocks around them that they didn't see the raiders' retreat. When the firing stopped, they peered over the rocks in time to see the rear guard of soldiers disappear over the hilltop.

Idris dropped his weapons, stepped to the edge of the cliff and jumped into the river. He'd done the same thing hundreds of times as a boy, but those memories lasted only until his head cleared the water and he saw the carnage on the riverbank. He splashed out of the water, looked around frantically and called for his family.

"Aleuth! Akin! Abuong! Shema!"

He raced from one bleeding, moaning, injured person to the next, praying that one of them was a loved one—and praying equally hard that they were not.

Suddenly, he heard a cry that stabbed joy into his heart.

"Papa! Papa!" Shema waded out of the reeds and raced toward him. Idris scooped the little girl into his arms and held her tight to his chest.

"Shema, where is your mother?" He knelt and tried to set the child back down on the sand. "Where are Akin and Abuong?"

But the little girl refused to let go of her father. Sobbing hysterically, she wrapped her tiny arms so tight around his neck he could hardly breathe.

Idris finally peeled the child off his chest, stood her on the beach and held her at arm's length to get her attention. "Where is your mother?" He tried not to sound as panicked as he felt. "Where are your brother and sister?"

Shema pointed to the marsh and managed a strangled, "Mama!" between sobs.

Idris splashed through the shallow water into the reeds with Shema one step behind him. He batted the stalks out of his way as he called his wife's name in a high-pitched voice he hardly recognized as his own.

"Aleuth! Where are you? Aleuth!"

When he heard a sound off to his left, he scrambled through the reeds toward it and found Aleuth lying on a pile of stalks bent backward by her fall. For one horrified moment, he thought she must be dead. Then he heard her moan.

"Aleuth! Can you hear me? Aleuth!"

Her face was covered in blood from the wound on her forehead, but her eyelids fluttered open briefly and there was recognition in her eyes before they closed again. Idris knelt, slid his hands under Aleuth's limp body and lifted her out of the water as if she weighed nothing at all. He carried her out of the marsh and onto the riverbank where he laid her down tenderly and knelt beside her.

Her wound was so bloody he could not assess the damage. But she was alive! Alive!

Suddenly, Idris felt a hand on his shoulder and jumped in surprise. The hand belonged to Akec Kwol.

"How can I help, brother?" Akec kneeled in the sand beside his neighbor. "What can I do?"

"Find Abuong and Akin!" Fear locked his throat and Idris found he could only whisper. "I've looked and looked…"

His voice trailed off.

"You take care of Aleuth and I will find your children," Akec said.

Then he was gone.

Oblivious to the pandemonium of frightened and injured people all around him, Idris tore off a piece of Aleuth's skirt and began to wipe the blood off her face. When he went to the river to wet the cloth, Shema was barely a step behind him. The child had stopped crying, but somehow her vacant-eyed silence was worse. She sat in the sand beside him without making a sound, and gently patted her unconscious mother's hand.

Idris could have been kneeling there for five minutes or five hours; he had no sense of the passage of time. Akec suddenly appeared beside him, and when Idris looked up, he knew. He saw it in Akec's eyes and in the blood smeared on his chest.

Idris' anguished face asked the question his lips could not form.

"Abuong," Akec replied quietly. "I found Abuong."

Idris was seized by a nightmare fear so huge he couldn't breathe. His body stood up without him willing it to do so. With Shema as his shadow, he moved along behind Akec, though he made no purposeful effort to follow. He stepped over the dead bodies of friends and neighbors without any spark of recognition.

Suddenly, he stopped, immobilized by horror. The force of what he saw was a physical blow that slammed into him so hard he staggered backward. Abuong was lying face-up on the sand. His right arm was missing below the elbow. The top portion of his body didn't seem to match the bottom somehow. It was contorted, as if the boy wasn't put together right. It was obvious that he was dead.

Idris didn't feel his feet touch the sand as he went to his only son. When he lifted the child up off the sand to cradle his lifeless body in his arms, he saw the gaping wound across his back that had almost cut him in half.

Idris hugged his son to his chest, rocked the boy's body back and forth, and cried. Great gulping, heaving sobs wracked his whole body; his thin frame quaked as he choked on grief so jagged and raw Akec could not fathom it.

Akec had discovered the boy's body caught in the reeds. He had tried to lift the child gently, to lay him out carefully for his father. But Abuong's body almost came apart in his hands.

Suddenly, the big man turned away and began to vomit noisily on the sand. When the involuntary retching finally passed, he straightened up and with the sound of his friend's grief in his ears, he went looking for Akin.

For a long time, Idris was conscious of nothing but the dead child in his arms. The world had stopped revolving on its axis and the moments of his life were without measurement. He was unaware that wounded and dying people lay all around him on the beach, and that others like himself were grieving, cradling dead or injured bodies in their arms. He took no notice at all of the little 5-year-old girl huddled beside him.

Idris could not help imagining what Abuong's last moments of life had been like. What terror and pain his son must have suffered. Just a little boy, not even strong enough yet to pull back the string on his father's bow. Just a child! Idris was filled with a grief and rage so huge it threatened to devour him.

Suddenly, he heard gunfire in the distance. He lifted his head and for the first time noticed the bloody body of a white-robed Arab lying on the ground a few feet away. The man was looking back at him with terror in his dark eyes.

Idris froze. He did not even breathe, just stared into the black eyes of the Fedayeen guerrilla. Then, he carefully placed the body of his son on the sand. As if in a dream, he walked over to where the Arab was sprawled on his back, gasping for air. A huge, gory wound in his belly had turned his white robe crimson. A bloody machete lay nearby. Idris leaned over and picked it up. When the soldier saw what he was doing, he began to plead for his life in a language Idris did no understand, blood bubbling out of his mouth as he spoke.

Idris took the weapon in both hands and began to raise it up over the Arab's body.

"Idris." Akec spoke his friend's name quietly. He took a step closer to where his neighbor stood with a machete in his hands. "Idris."

Idris ignored him. He continued to lift the machete until it was high above his head. Then he stood there lifeless, as unmoving as a clay pot, without a clear thought of any kind in his mind.

"I know what happened to Akin," Akec said.

Idris' arms went limp and he dropped the machete in the sand beside the Arab's head. He knew. Just like with Abuong, he knew.

"They took her," Akec said softly, trying somehow to cushion the harsh reality of the words. "One of the women saw a soldier toss her into the back of the truck before they drove away."

All of the air went out of Idris and he collapsed to his knees beside the body of his son. Shema came and sat next to him, but he did not notice. He knelt silently for a time, his head bowed, his shoulders slumped. Then he began to wail, a high, keening, tormented sound ripped out of his agonized soul. Lifting his tear-stained face to the sky, Idris continued to wail, a sound so desolate and despairing it sent chills down Akec's spine.

The wailing went on and on and on. It was the last sound the Arab soldier heard before his gasping ceased, and he lay with black eyes staring sightlessly at the Dinkan farmer kneeling beside him in the sand.

Chapter 7

The unrelenting afternoon sun beat down on Mondala and on its dead, wounded and traumatized inhabitants. Smoke hung in a funeral pall over the ravaged village, mingled with the acrid stench of burned flesh coming from the ruins of tukuls that had been torched with families still inside. In a symphony of agony, cries of pain and grief rose up with the smoke into the clear, blue sky.

The remainder of the day was a blur for the shell-shocked survivors of the attack. Lifelong friends and family members had been shot or hacked apart, children had been trampled under horses' hooves. The lifeless bodies of the butchered dead sprawled where they had fallen, on the village pathways or in the fields, on the road or by the river.

More than half the tukuls in Mondala had been destroyed. The livestock that hadn't been slaughtered wandered around disoriented, the zebu lowing in the confusion and the goats skittish, calling to their young with baleful maa, maaa sounds. Guinea hens squawked, and fluttered over the puddles of blood spread out around the bodies that littered the village.

The savagery of the assassins who attacked Mondala was nowhere more evident than in the injuries of the survivors, who had been slashed, stabbed or bludgeoned, their bodies riddled with bullets or missing limbs. Many would not live through the night. The survivors did the best they could with what they had to relieve the suffering. They used river water to wash the wounds, and applied herbal poultices and healing roots.

But the need was so overwhelming and their grief so profound, that many who had lived through the butchery went into such deep shock they were almost catatonic.

Idris was not catatonic, though the loss of two children at once was so staggering a blow he couldn't process it. He could only cope if he simply refused to think about Akin. If he did, he'd go mad. She was alive and Abuong was dead. It was time now to mourn the dead.

With his calloused hand, he gently stroked Abuong's cheek, as images of his son flashed through his mind, all in a jumble, too many to see at one time. It was like trying to make out each individual bird when a whole flock suddenly takes flight. A baby crawling on the dirt floor of the tukul. A toddler chasing butterflies in a spring field. A small child sitting on a zebu's back. A young boy's face—so grave and serious, sometimes, asking hard questions about the world and life and God.

Idris bowed his head and tried to pray. No words came, but that didn't matter. Words would just have gotten in the way of communicating his groaning grief to God.

Akec stayed with Idris for a time, stood by his side, saying nothing. It was all he could think to do. But other neighbors also needed help. Finally, he leaned over and told Idris he'd be back, but he wasn't at all certain his friend heard him.

As the afternoon wore on, it became more and more apparent that if the men in the village and on the cliff hadn't fought back, there wouldn't have been a single living being, man or beast, left in Mondala. As it was, the death toll was staggering. More than 100 men, women and children had been killed. Another 50 had been seriously injured. The villagers who followed the mercenaries until their tracks disappeared in the rocks discovered the bodies of the women and children who had been dragged behind a truck and then executed, each with a bullet to the back of the head. With them added to the total, everyone in the village was accounted for. Except one, the one who had been abducted. Akin Apot.

As evening approached, the handful of elders who were left in Mondala gathered to talk. The attack had been so unthinkably catastrophic that the men were still too dazed to get their arms around what the village should do now, how they should respond. They knew they must do something, but they were unable to formulate any plan of action.

Akec stood nearby. He was one of the few people in Mondala who had come through the attack unscathed. His wife and married daughters had not been in the village when the raiders struck. His tukul still stood and most of his livestock had not been harmed. Perhaps he was able to think more clearly because he had not suffered an injury or some traumatic loss, as the others had. But it seemed obvious to him what needed to be done, and though he was not an elder and his counsel was unsolicited, Akec gave it anyway.

"We have to get everyone, the injured and the dead as well, into the village—right now," he said. "It will be dark soon and the wild animals will come."

"The wild animals have already come," one old man said softly.

The others nodded in silent agreement.

"We can go in teams, two men each, so we can carry the bodies," Akec continued.

He pointed to the now empty animal corral in the center of the village, placed there to protect the livestock from predators at night. "We can put the dead there. We will bury them tomorrow."

Wordlessly, the men paired off and went to work as the sun slid down the western sky. The last rays of sunset had begun to cast long, thin shadows from Idris's body over the still form of his son lying in the sand when Akec appeared out of the gloom.

"We've come to help you take Abuong back to the village." Akec laid his hand on his friend's shoulder. "It will be night soon."

Idris nodded. His shadow now covered all of Abuong's body. The darkness had reached out and taken the boy away.

For a moment, Idris stared at the child, aware for the first time how peaceful his face seemed. Abuong had suffered, but he suffered no more. He was in Heaven now; he was home. Idris leaned over, rested his face on the boy's chest and told him softly, "Good night, my son" for the last time. Then he straightened up and got to his feet. He spoke tenderly to the expressionless little girl who had risen with him.

"Come, Shema." He took her small hand into his. "Your mother is waiting for us."

He turned to face Akec and looked deeply into his neighbor's face. "Thank you, friend," he said.

●　●　●　●　●

When the mercenary spotted Akin huddled in a corner behind a stack of boxes next to the cab in the back of the truck, his surprise turned instantly into laughter. With her short hair, black face and big, round eyes peering out of the shadows, he thought she looked just like a baby monkey.

"Come here!" he commanded.

Akin didn't move. She couldn't understand what the man in the white turban was shouting at her.

"You don't want me to come in there after you," he said, menacingly. "I said, come here!"

That time, he motioned with his hand when he spoke, and she figured out what he wanted her to do. Though she was almost paralyzed with terror, Akin understood the threatening tone of his voice if not the words, and she didn't want to find out what the implied "...or else!" might be.

She got up from behind the boxes in the far corner of the truck and timidly made her way to the open tailgate.

Akin had known that sooner or later somebody would find her. Of course, it had taken her a little while to realize she was lost. When she'd first come to, she'd felt an instant rush of relief that she'd finally awakened from a horrifying nightmare. She'd started to call her father to come and pick her up, hold her close and soothe the fear away.

Then she opened her eyes and pain shot down her neck from an inch-long gash on top of a huge bump behind her right ear. It hadn't been a nightmare at all! The raiders really had thundered down on them with guns and machetes and swords. They really had shot her neighbors, stabbed and slashed her friends. The man on the big black horse really had hit her mother, and…

Her mind was confused about what happened after that, before she awoke to find the monsters who'd attacked her village all around her.

As soon as Akin got close to the back of the truck, the mercenary reached in and grabbed her, yanked her down to the ground and dragged her to the spot where 45 or 50 women and children taken captive by the other half of Faoud's raiding party were tied together under an acacia tree.

"Here's another one for you," he said to one of the carbine-toting guards who stood watch over the captives. "Found her hiding in the truck."

The guard put his gun down and picked up the end of the large rawhide rope to which each of the captives was tied with an individual, smaller rope. Half a dozen of the smaller ropes still dangled free at the end, awaiting other captives, and he attached Akin to one of them. He wrapped it mercilessly tight around her skinny wrists. She grimaced in pain, but didn't cry out. Somehow, she knew it wouldn't be a good idea to draw attention to herself.

Akin looked at the other prisoners. Her eyes searched the crowd for somebody, anybody she knew. But there was not a familiar face among them; they all were strangers, frightened strangers. The same look of terror, shock and disbelief was stamped on all their faces. Their clothes were dirty and torn, and several of them were injured. A woman leaned against an acacia tree, barely able to stand. Blood dripped off the fingers of her limp left arm from a gory slash just above her elbow.

Just then, three mounted raiders rode past them toward the front of the line. Hamir ordered his second-in-command to remain with the trucks so the man could get medical attention for the wound in his thigh, and then he shouted to the men who guarded the captives: "Get them up and move!"

The guard in front grabbed the first woman in the human chain, yanked her to her feet and shoved her forward. The other prisoners rose instantly and fell in line behind her. When the captives had been force-marched away from their villages, the soldiers had tossed two young children off the path to die—thirst or the jackals would get them. One of their mothers had been shot when she ran to the aid of her little girl. The other mother had been restrained by the group when her infant son was tossed away. Now, she marched along mechanically, unfeeling, the walking dead; her baby's cries reverberated in her head long after the sound faded away in the distance. Those lessons had taught the group with brutal efficiency that anybody not able to keep up was considered a liability, and would be discarded as offhandedly as a mango peel.

They walked on through the afternoon, followed the setting sun, moving quickly and quietly. The woman whose arm had been bleeding collapsed. A soldier sliced off the rope that bound her in the chain and left her body lying in the trail. All the other captives stepped over her as they trudged along. There was no crying, no conversation, no sound but the padding of their bare feet to mark their passage. During the first couple of miles after the attack on their villages, the group had been shoved and prodded along, to the accompaniment of a symphony of sobbing children, screaming women, shouts in tribal dialects and the sharp, foreign commands of the Arab horse soldiers. But the soldiers quickly silenced the captives. Those who spoke or made any noise at all were slashed with a whip one of the soldiers carried or suffered stinging blows from the other raiders' riding crops. Fear kept the group quiet as they passed through the countryside.

Akin had no idea where she was. Although the other prisoners had been marched away from their villages, Akin had been transported unconscious in the back of the raiders' truck. When she awoke, her surroundings were totally unfamiliar and she had no sense of how far she had traveled from Mondala or in what direction. She couldn't have run away, even if she'd dared, because she didn't know which way to run. The realization that Mondala was completely lost to her, as unreachable as the stars in the night sky, frightened her almost as much as the soldiers.

The purple haze of Sudanese dusk began to settle in, and the long shadows of the trees—ebony, hashab, mango, acacia—dissolved into the approaching darkness.

Akin plodded along at the end of the line. She forced herself to take a step and then another and another, and resolutely refused to allow her mind to process the events of the last 12 hours. She fixed her gaze on the back of the young mother in line ahead of her. Now and then she caught a glimpse of the woman's baby; his doleful, half-open eyes peeked at her over his mother's shoulder.

All of the captives were hungry. They'd had nothing to eat since breakfast—hours ago in another life, in a world that no longer existed. They'd only been allowed a brief water break at a stream in the forest. The soldiers carried food with them. They reached into their knapsacks for hard bread and fruit that came from their supply truck and ate as they rode along. The captives stared at the food; hunger gnawed at their bellies. They were learning the first of many hard lessons about slavery—they were property, and their owners would never invest anything more in them than the bare minimum to keep them alive.

As the sun dipped below the horizon and the color of the sunset drained out of the sky, the raiders steered their exhausted band of hostages toward a particularly thick stand of trees to spend the night.

When they reached the grove of palms and acacias, a few of the riders dismounted and herded the women and children under the boughs of a large palm tree set off by itself. The captives willingly complied and sank down on the cushion of palm fronds atop the soft grass and weeds that grew around the tree's massive trunk.

Since none of the hostages had ever owned a pair of shoes, their feet were tough. But the paths around their village or the pastures where they herded cattle hadn't prepared them for hours of forced march through thickets and over miles of stony trails. Their feet were bruised, sore and bleeding, and they wanted nothing more than to sit down.

Akin collapsed in a heap a rope's length away from the young mother. The little girl had watched the black, velvet sky gobble up the golden sunset, and as the world around her descended into darkness, so did she. She was an 11-year-old child who'd been kidnapped, ripped away from her life by monsters worse than the demons that stalked her most terrifying nightmares. She was alone, famished, tired and scared, so scared the ball of fear rested heavier in her stomach than her hunger. She wanted to cry—no, to *scream*. She wanted to jump up and run away as fast as she could back to her village, her family and her world. But she wasn't even certain that her family and her village existed anymore. She hadn't seen her brother die, but she'd watched the soldiers kill dozens of her friends and neighbors. Had her mother survived the attack by the Arab on the black horse? Akin wondered. What had happened to her brother and sister? And her father, where was *Papa!* The image of his face produced a yearning in her heart so intense it was a physical pain in her chest. Oh, Papa, come and get me! she thought. Please, come and get me and take me home!

For her whole life, her father had stood between her and every bad thing in the world. She had cuddled up warm and secure in her father's care every day that she could remember. When she lay down on her woven straw mat on the dirt floor of the tukul at night, she fell innocently asleep. She was safe. Papa was there;

Papa wouldn't let anything hurt her. But now, in the blackness of this night, Papa was gone. She faced the first night of her life on her own, and she was so scared, so terribly, terribly scared.

Akin started to cry. Not out loud. It hurt too bad to cry out loud. She didn't want to hear the sound of her own grief. She cried silently, her tears streaming down her face and dripping off her chin.

Then she lay down and curled up in a fetal position among the palm fronds. She tried to be small, so small no one would see her or take notice of her at all. Mercifully, her exhaustion overwhelmed her, and she fell asleep.

● ● ● ● ●

Sunrise over Mondala found Idris Apot where he had been at sunset, seated outside the door of his tukul beside the dead body of his only son. Aleuth had been up all night, too. As she sat by her husband's side while the first rays of the sun shot light into the valley, she pulled herself out of the fuzzy cotton of shock and forced herself to focus on the child she had carried, nursed, clothed, bathed, played with, prayed for and loved for almost a decade.

She reached out and took his cold hand, his left hand, the other one was... Silent tears ran down her cheeks.

Though her head wound was not life-threatening, Aleuth had a mild concussion. She suffered waves of dizziness and her vision was sometimes blurry. The neighbors who had carried her unconscious to the village after the attack had refused to allow her to return to the riverbank when she came to. She only learned that her son had been killed when Idris walked up the path to their home with the boy's limp body in his arms. As soon as she learned that Akin had been kidnapped, Aleuth went mercifully into shock. She had sat in the dirt beside her husband and their son's body overnight, staring blankly into the darkness.

But with the morning came reality. She and Idris had to bury their son.

Shema sat beside her mother and held on with both hands to

the hem of her mother's bloodied sack dress. Neither of her parents took much notice of her. She hadn't spoken a word since the attack, except the strangled "Mama!" that told Idris where to find his wife.

Akec had been one of the men assigned to dig graves. When he finished, he went to Idris' tukul and looked down in pity on his grieving neighbors.

"I have made a resting place for Abuong," he said simply.

Idris nodded. He got up on one knee, leaned over and carefully lifted Abuong's cold, stiff body. Akec helped Aleuth to her feet. Then the four of them, three adults and a little girl, set out for the burying ground to lay a 9-year-old boy to rest.

When they reached the freshly dug grave, Aleuth fell to her knees and began to wail. She rocked back and forth and beat her fists into the soft earth as her soul cried out in agony. Shema patted her mother's shoulder, her eyes dry. Something inside the 5-year-old child had clicked off and shut down; she was as emotionless as a stone.

As soon as Idris shoveled the last scoop of dry dirt into Abuong's grave, Aleuth stopped wailing. It was done. Idris helped her to her feet and steadied her as he walked with Akec and Shema back to the village.

Idris said nothing when they reached their tukul, just picked up his traveling sack, the one he carried with him when he went to hunt or trade in other villages, and began to pack it. It didn't take long; he didn't own much and needed little of it where he was going.

Aleuth watched in wonder.

"Are you going somewhere?"

He put the sack over his shoulder, picked up his long ebony spear and stepped out of the tukul. His eyes were steely, set and determined. But when he looked into his wife's face and saw the fear there, he softened. He didn't want to cause her additional pain, but he had to do what he had to do.

"I *must* go," he said simply, then turned and began to untie their lone surviving zebu, slowly unwrapping the knotty, twirled rope from around the wooden peg.

"Go? Go where? And why are you unleashing the cow?"

When he had made his decision, Idris hadn't even considered what he would say to Aleuth. Now, he couldn't seem to find any words at all. There was too much pain in his heart to speak, so he gritted his teeth and continued to untie the family's only cow.

"Idris?" There was so much misery in her voice it broke his heart. He stopped, turned to her and did his best to explain.

"I could not think of Akin before." He stopped. Then started again. "I had to grieve for Abuong, and my heart is broken for him. But he is gone, and now I must not think of Abuong. Now, I must think of the living. I must do what I can for the living."

"The living?" Aleuth stared at Idris, her mind spinning.

Idris replied with one word, dropped it like a pebble into a stream. "Akin."

Aleuth was dumbstruck.

"What can you do for Akin?" she cried out in anguish. "She is gone. The trackers lost the trail in the woods. She is..." Aleuth sobbed out the word, "gone!"

"She is *alive!*" Idris shot back, his voice as hard as a stone.

"And we must pray for the mercy of God to be upon her!"

"I will pray for the mercy of God. But I will also put feet on my prayers."

Other villagers had heard the raised voices and drifted closer to listen to what was going on. In the Dinkan culture, the wife accepted whatever her husband said as the will of the family. Something odd was happening between Idris and Aleuth Apot.

Unmoved by the sudden audience, Idris gathered the rope tied to the cow and looked at his wife. His look was kind but he did not waver.

"I must do this," he said. "I have to go."

"Go where?" Aleuth asked, with shell-shocked incredulity. "I just lost a son and daughter. Am I now to lose my husband as well?"

Though his voice was stern, his eyes pleaded with Aleuth to understand.

"As long as I have breath in my body, my daughter has hope. I am going to find Akin and bring her home!"

There was complete, stunned silence. Aleuth was so shocked she could form no response. A few of the nearby villagers actually gasped audibly. One of the elders stepped forward. It was against custom to interfere in the affairs of another, but these were extraordinary times and the old rules didn't seem to fit anymore.

"There is nothing you or any of us can do for Akin," he said. "If a whole village full of men was helpless against them, what could you hope to do alone? We all loved her, but she is gone."

Idris turned on the old man.

"She is gone until I bring her back! My daughter knows that I will not mourn for her as if she lay cold in a grave like Abuong. She knows her father will not abandon her. She knows I will not rest until I find her."

Aleuth stared at her husband in disbelief. "But why are you taking our cow? It is the only one we have left."

Idris addressed Aleuth, but he was talking to all the other villagers who had gathered there as well.

"I can only fight fire if I have fire of my own. I go to find fire. I will go to Bentiu... "

Bentiu!

The villagers were shocked. The city lay hundreds of miles to the north. Akec was the only one among them who had ever been there. Some of the other villagers had been east to Juba, but Bentiu was four times as big. And dangerous. It was said to be a very dangerous place.

"I will find someone in Bentiu to help me find Akin. And if not there, I will go somewhere else. But I will not stop, I will not rest, I will not give up until I find a man *like* the Murahaleen to *fight* the Murahaleen."

He spit out the word "Murahaleen" as if it tasted foul in his mouth, and without another word, he turned and headed out of the village, his lone gray-and-white zebu plodding along contentedly behind him.

Aleuth stood and watched him go, too surprised and shocked even to cry.

* * * * *

The morning after Akin was captured, one of the soldiers untied her, moved her forward in the line of hostages and placed her among three other young girls.

While the men noisily loaded supplies and gear into the small truck to prepare for the day's journey, the girls whispered urgently among themselves. Like victims of other catastrophic events, they each felt compelled to tell their story, to process the horror in the telling.

The two older girls were from the same village; the third, like Akin was alone. Her name was Omina. At 12, she was a year older than Akin, and had been the only child in her family. But she had no family left now. The attacking Arabs had killed her parents and then dragged her away.

Mbarka was the oldest and had just turned 15. Her mother and her two older sisters had been kidnapped, too, loaded into trucks and hauled off into the night. Bright-eyed and talkative, Mbarka was a sharp contrast to the other girl from her village. Shontal was quiet and reserved. She was barely 14 but looked older. Under the circumstances, that was not a good thing. The terror of the last few days had scarred her worse than the others. She had watched raiders hack her parents apart with machetes. The brown stain that covered most of her skirt was her father's blood. What she had experienced had almost pushed her into insanity.

Akin wanted to comfort Shontal when she heard her story. After all, Akin was better off than the others. Her family was still alive! She knew they were. She couldn't prove it, but it was true. It had to be true.

"I'm so sorry... " she began.

But there was no time for comfort. The guards barked orders in a language none of the captives understood. They stood and marched out in single file across the plains of southern Sudan.

The days blended one into another and she no longer kept count. Every day was the same as the preceding one, little food, little water, walking to the point of exhaustion. Akin's brief acquaintance with the other girls quickly forged into friendship in the crucible of horror. The four had a strength together that none of them could have summoned alone; the presence of Mbarka, Omina and Shontal kept Akin going.

The caravan finally set up camp in a grove of trees beside a railroad siding a few miles south of Wau, a city of about 200,000 on the Jur River almost 200 miles south of Bentiu.

The raiders marched the captives to cattle cars strung along the track and crammed them inside. Akin and the girls tied to her had been loaded first, and about 60 other women and children had been jammed into the transport after that. Akin was mashed against the back wall; the crushing weight of the other captives and the lack of air made her head swim. It got worse when the sun came up; the cattle car heated up like an oven as the train traveled north toward Southern Kordofan. The slits in the side of the rail car provided minimal ventilation, and Akin gasped for air until she passed out. But she remained upright because there was nowhere for her to fall.

Finally, the train stopped and the guards began to unload the captives packed up against her. Suddenly, there was air to breathe. Akin came to and saw the moon through the open door as she stumbled with the others out onto the ground.

The captives were quickly loaded into canvas-covered trucks. Akin caught sight of the other girls' frightened faces, their eyes glowing in the bright headlights of the truck behind them. Then the guard slammed the tailgate shut and the caravan of trucks roared off into the night.

Chapter 8

Idris sold his zebu to a farmer in Vulya, the first village he came to after he left Mondala. The man was a Christian, and when he heard Idris' story, he was so touched that he paid twice what the animal was actually worth.

Unencumbered by the cow, Idris set a grueling pace. From first light in the morning until it was too dark to see, he walked; his long strides ate up the miles day after day. He only took time for essential rest and refused to stop long enough to hunt for food. He ate berries, mushrooms and wild gourds, and scared up enough game to get by—guinea fowl, partridges, pheasants and rabbits. About 10 miles north of Bayom, he almost stepped in a bustard's nest and feasted that night on the land bird's eggs. But there were days when he found no game at all; days he walked 30 to 40 miles on an empty stomach and then fell into an exhausted sleep hungry.

Alone every night in a strange place as the profound African dark gobbled up the world outside the campfire light, Idris was afraid. He was more frightened than he had been as a boy when he and a friend had hidden all night high in an acacia tree as a lioness prowled around beneath them.

But he was certain that wherever Akin was, she was far more frightened than he was. She was just a little girl!

There was a prayer on his every breath. Sometimes his tears and his pain and his prayer mixed together to form something far grander than a simple man could understand. At night on his knees, he petitioned the God of the universe to protect his little girl, to give her the courage to hold out until he found her. And he would find her, or die trying.

He asked nothing for himself, but he was strong after he prayed, his fear left him and he felt a peace that could only have come from God.

Set back from the road in a field on the outskirts of Bentiu, Idris found a particularly tall palm tree on the edge of a small stream. Careful to make sure nobody saw him, he used a stone to dig a hole close to the trunk of the tree, placed his money sack in the hole and covered it with rich, black soil. There were thieves in Bentiu; he needed to be cautious. Idris had never in his life committed an illegal act; today he would search for someone who broke the law for a living.

● ● ● ● ●

Ron lay on the baked sand under the scorching Sudanese sun, shaded his eyes with his hand and squinted at the canvas-topped transport trucks parked below him and at the Sudanese villagers tied up next to them. A small, brown lizard scurried across the top of the rocks he had piled up for additional cover, and Ron edged carefully backward on his hands and chest until he was below the crest of the sand-covered hilltop where he and Masapha had set up shop to capture a slave auction on film.

Masapha had called it, X marks the spot.

Weeks of searching, asking questions and searching some more had come up snake-eyes until the Arab happened upon a woman whose brother worked in a remote oil field. She'd told Masapha about the day her brother had been high up on a rig, and saw in the distance an odd assortment of vehicles, transport trucks, jeeps, a car or two, horses and camels. That was odd enough, she'd said.

What was stranger still was where the caravan was headed. They were going nowhere! There was absolutely nothing in the direction they were traveling but emptiness.

In that emptiness, Ron and Masapha found the final piece of Masapha's puzzle.

About five miles from the lone oil well in Block 8A on the Licensed Oil and Gas Map's grid, a half-mile outcrop of rock jutted up out of the desert floor like a shark fin. Among the barren hills on the undulating plain, it was the only secluded piece of real estate for 50 miles in any direction.

Acacia thickets, brush and groves of stunted trees clung tenaciously to the sand on its boulder-strewn sides; on the desert floor at its base, syringe-needle thorn bushes and brambles grew in tangles so dense even B'rer Rabbit couldn't have made his way through. Its highest point was on the northern end, and below that 150-foot crest, the outcrop curved inward to form a hollow about 300 yards wide that was enclosed on three sides. That was the stage where the drama of the slave sale would be played out; on top of that hill, Ron and Masapha had the best seats in the house.

"You scored, pal," Ron whispered.

"It was not I who made the score," the Arab whispered back. "Mostly, I believe it was stupid luck... "

"Dumb luck."

"... that we found this place."

It wasn't the time or place to argue, but Ron was certain that without Masapha's help, he would have wandered around southern Sudan until he traded his jeep in on an aluminum walker without ever locating a slave auction.

"You're sure everything is OK?" Ron's voice was tense. "You did a trial run with the equipment, right?"

Masapha looked at him patiently and nodded his head deliberately up and down.

"Then we're good to go." Suddenly, Ron's mouth turned to cotton.

Nobody had to tell the two men they were playing in a high stakes game. Get caught, and you lose. Lose, and you die. He looked into Masapha's eyes and saw the same fear he was sure the Arab could see in his. They held each other's gaze for a heartbeat, an unspoken salute. It was Showtime. Below them on the desert floor, the gavel was about to come down on the first-ever filmed and photographed Sudanese slave auction.

When he thought of the nerdy geek he'd befriended at Yale who'd made much of this adventure possible, Ron smiled. His name—no kidding—was Earl Putzler. "The Putz" had built a small company into one of the giants in the aerospace industry. Guys like that either hit it big or became serial killers. When Ron described the state-of-the-art video and sound technology he hoped to lay hands on for this project, Earl had smiled knowingly and said, "You just leave everything to me."

The Putz had come through. The camera and recording equipment Masapha would be using wasn't even on the market yet.

Ron gave Masapha a thumbs-up and they began to inch their way into position at the top of the hill. Masapha placed the infrared/ laser transmitter of the optical audio surveillance system— Ron called it the "corndog thingy"—into a slot in the pile of rocks and pointed it toward the desert floor. Then he checked the radar screen's position where he'd hidden it among the branches of a bush, and put the headphone stoppers into his ears. Flattened out on his belly, he commando-crawled the final few feet to the spot where he and Ron had scooped out side by side mini-foxholes in the sand. He put the camcorder to his eye and focused tight on the scene below. Ron crawled on his belly into his slot beside Masapha, dug his elbows into the sand to steady himself, and made his arms into a tripod. He drew the camera up to his face—the metal was hot on his cheek—and began to frame images in his viewfinder.

On the hard-packed ground below was a consortium of buyers and sellers. Most of the buyers, wealthy Arabs, had arrived in a small fleet of jeeps, trucks and cars that were parked off to one side of the big army transport trucks that were the center of activity. Ron counted five buyers. Two of them were in white robes and shora scarves; the other three were dressed in Western clothing. Each of the buyers was accompanied by an entourage, mostly rough-looking, bearded, bodyguard types who wore sunglasses.

Each of the two sellers had brought a covered transport truck with captives loaded in the back. Both were dressed western-style, but one wore an elaborately wrapped turban, the kind the Bedouins wore to protect them from haboobs. The other, an extremely fat, bearded man with a huge belly that hung over the belt of his pants, wore a floppy Indiana-Jones hat. Each of them had a troop of hired guns as well, a motley collection of mercenaries, soldiers and Murahaleen.

The sellers had unloaded their wares out of two khaki-covered, canvas-topped transports. About a dozen women and children were on display beside one large truck. Another group of three women and several little boys was tied to the back bumper of the other truck.

As soon as they zeroed in for a close look at the collection of trucks and people clustered on the sand, Ron and Masapha were surprised by two things—the large number of Arabs gathered and the small number of slaves for sale. The Arabs outnumbered the tribals two to one.

The conversations 250 yards away filled Masapha's ears as if the men stood beside him. The Arabs had looked over the offerings, made their choices, and now it was time to do business.

Even though Ron couldn't hear or understand the Arabic Masapha monitored, he understood the haggling, bartering body language he could see, and it reminded him of the cattle auctions he'd attended with his father as a boy. These guys were buying livestock.

There was a lull in the haggling and buying while the raiders worked to get purchased slaves safely stowed away.

Suddenly, something flashed across Ron's viewfinder and he looked up over his camera. A boy about 14 or 15 years old sprinted across the sand. His dark, black skin stood out against the yellow-white sand as he flew across it like a high school 800-meter champion.

"What are you doing, son?" Ron moaned under his breath.

He put his eye back to his viewfinder and zoomed in on the men around the trucks. None of them had spotted the boy. They were engaged in conversations, talking and laughing. He panned the camera to the boy, who was still running, partly hidden from the view of the others by the canvas covering on a tall transport truck. He already had covered a hundred yards and only had another fifty or sixty to go. He had a chance.

Then Ron heard a frantic shout. Several more followed.

He quickly panned back to the group of Arabs and refocused. The trader had turned to put the money in his truck and spotted the boy. He shouted something in Arabic and armed men sprinted past the group of slaves toward the boy.

One more shout, then the sharp crack of rifles.

Masapha focused the camcorder on the live action beyond the cluster of trucks. A heartbeat after he captured the boy in focus, he saw the boy spin forward, slammed in the back by a rifle shot. Ron caught the action and froze frame after frame in his Nikon at a thousandth of a second. The force of the bullet hammered the boy so hard he did an automatic double somersault as his body skipped across the hard-packed sand. But to Ron and Masapha's amazement, as the boy completed his second tumble he was back on his feet running. He left a crimson smear where his torn shoulder had hit the ground, but he didn't even appear to slow down as he crossed the remaining sand and disappeared into the tangle of brambles and thorn bushes at the base of the rock outcrop.

The surprised soldiers, who'd assumed they'd bagged their prey, ran to the edge of the brush, but no farther. None of them was willing to dig through thorn-covered vines as close knit as steel wool to find the boy, so they finished him off from where they stood. A sudden *rat-tat-tat* roar, amplified by high-tech sound equipment, stabbed twin ice picks into Masapha's head through his earphones. From point-blank range, the soldiers riddled the brush with bullets, firing round after round from their automatic rifles. With nothing to shield him but a stand of bushes, the boy didn't have a chance. Then the soldiers returned to their leader, who stood screaming at them in a venomous tirade.

Masapha listened through the throbbing in his ears to staccato Arabic voices chattering frantically. It was amazing how quickly the whole lot of them—buyers, sellers and slaves—loaded up and were gone in a cloud of dust.

When the dust settled, the crisscrossed tire tracks and a smear of blood on the sand were all that remained to mark the spot.

Ron slid down the back side of the hill and rolled over next to Masapha. Neither spoke for a time. They'd just seen human beings sold into bondage and watched a boy die rather than submit. Ron felt sick, fouled by the evil. The images in the Arab's head of a little boy named Masapha were private; he would share them with no one.

Ron finally broke the silence. "I thought there would be more."

"More?"

"More slaves. Some of the reports I've gotten said sometimes 200 or 300 slaves are sold at these auctions."

"There may *be* more."

"More slaves? Here?"

"When there was not so much activity, after the ugly man bought the four women, I pointed the mike at the different groups, think-ing to hear, perhaps, some conversations. There was much wind-blowing sound and noise behind, but I believe one of them said they would return to this place in some days for more captives from other raids to be selling here."

Ron tensed.

"I believe we should hang up here..."

"Hang *around* here, or hang *out* here, but not... "

"... for some days and see do they return."

Ron liked the sound of that. He smiled. Yeah, they'd hang here for awhile—up, out and around—and see what else might crawl out from under a rock.

*　*　*　*　*

The big man named Leo, with battle scars on his arms and a twisted, broken nose, was dangerous. He was evil, too. Idris knew that as soon as he got near him. He could sense it the way he could sometimes feel the presence of a black mamba or a puff adder in the grass. And he would back away slowly, carefully. He never turned and ran away. You never turned your back on danger; you faced it head on. That's what he was doing now as he approached the man in the wide-brimmed safari hat.

Idris never found out exactly how Leo had heard he wanted to hire a mercenary. In the two days since he had arrived in Bentiu, Idris had told many people his story, and he clung desperately to the belief that out of one of those conversations would come the answer to his prayers.

Apparently, that's what had happened. As Idris walked down a dusty street the morning of his third day in Bentiu, a voice behind him called out to him in heavily accented Dinkan.

He turned and encountered one of the oddest men he'd ever seen. The fellow's skin was the color of the night sky, the whites of his eyes as yellow as corn meal. Though he didn't appear to be much older than Idris, he had no teeth. He wore bright green pants, a way-too-big-for-him western shirt covered with orange and red flowers, and battered, tied-together-with-string tennis shoes, and he hobbled toward Idris with a pronounced limp.

"I have been sent to find you," he said when he caught up with Idris. His Dinkan was hard to follow. "You are to come with me."

"Come with you where?"

In the few days he had been in Bentiu, he had met more strange people than in all the other days of his life. But this man was by far the strangest of them all.

"You are looking for someone to help you, yes?" the man replied. "Then come with me, and I will take you to such a man."

Idris had turned and followed the toothless man to an alleyway behind a bar, where his guide approached a man who sat in a chair in the shade of an awning that stretched out over the back door of the bar. The man was an Arab. He didn't appear to be tall, but he was big, with muscled arms and a considerable belly. He had his chair leaned back on two legs, balanced against the building, as he sharpened a knife.

Though his black beard was thick and well groomed, the man's nose was the most commanding feature on his face. It didn't seem to fit properly. It bent sharply to the right at the top, then twisted back to the left, and was wide and bulbous on the end. Something had hit that nose, Idris thought, and hit it very, very hard. Probably more than once.

Using a gray whetstone, the man was sharpening a large, double-edged knife, and he seemed to be so engrossed in his work that he hardly noticed Idris and his companion approach.

That was an illusion. From the moment the two men had turned into the alleyway, Leo Danheir had been watching Idris, sizing him up, taking his measure. When Idris' guide bent and said something softly into his ear, the man stopped sharpening the knife and tipped the chair off the wall to place all four legs on the ground. He looked at Idris for a long time without speaking, then reached over and grabbed an empty oilcan next to the wall, slid it out and motioned for Idris to sit on it.

"I'm Leo." The man's voice was cold. "Joak tells me you're looking for somebody to help you; that right?"

Idris said nothing because he could not understand Arabic. Leo gestured toward Idris with the point of his knife and addressed the guide.

"Is this the farmer you were telling me about or not?"

"I guess he only speaks Dinkan," the go-between said, then he turned to Idris and translated the question Leo had asked.

Idris shook his head vigorously up and down, and briefly told the toothless man the story of the attack on his village when his little girl, Akin, had been kidnapped. One of the raiders, a big man on a white horse, was called Hamir, Idris added. He hoped that detail might be helpful.

During his long walk to Bentiu, Idris had played and replayed the events of that day in his mind. His spear had plunged into the chest of the first mounted raider, and he remembered how an arrow aimed at the black-robed figure beside him had missed its mark. A soldier shouted, "Hamir!" and the man on the white horse ducked seconds before the sharp, bone point of Idris' arrow would have torn out his throat.

The odd-looking man turned to the Arab and began to translate what Idris had said. As he spoke, Idris noticed the scars on the bearded man's forearms. They were not the symmetrical, decorative tribal marking of many of the Dinkas in southern Sudan. These were random marks, jagged ridges that criss-crossed each other, some still pink, others shadows of former injuries years ago. Knife wounds.

Leo continued to point the end of the blade toward Idris, but he directed his words to the interpreter.

"How long has she—this little girl of his, Akin—been gone?"

The interpreter relayed the question to Idris.

"She has been gone 12 days, nine before I came to Bentiu and another three since I've been here."

When Leo heard the translation, he swore softly under his breath, picked up the whetstone and went back to work on the blade, which shone viciously.

"Tell him finding one girl gone that long is like trying to locate one ant on a mountain. It's impossible." Then he paused, cocked his head toward Idris and continued. "Tell him for the impossible I will need lots of pay—cash—no cows or sorghum."

Idris and the interpreter spoke back and forth, and often gestured to ensure that the translation was accurate.

"He has almost 100 Sudanese pounds there in his traveling bag from last year's millet crop," the interpreter said. "And he has the price of two cows as well, but he does not have that money with him. He would have to go and get it and bring it back."

Leo held the shiny, sharp knife in front of him, inspected it and said off-handedly to the translator, "Tell him I will try to find his girl. I'm a professional and must be paid like a professional. Tell him to go and get his money and bring it to me here tonight. Tell him if he does that, I will meet him in the morning on the dock next to the shipping company office—the big building that hangs out over the river—and the two of us will head north together. Tell him he must be ready to travel and travel light. I move quickly."

The interpreter began the translation, and Leo interrupted him.

"And tell him there are no guarantees. Make sure he understands that. No promises. I have some contacts. I will ask some questions. I know some places to look. We will see what comes of that."

The interpreter began again, and Leo interrupted him a second time.

"And tell him if I find his girl, it's another 200 pounds before he'll get her back."

As the interpreter relayed all the information to Idris, Leo watched emotions play across the African's face. Somewhere along the way, the African must have decided he believed Leo could pull it off because when the interpreter stopped talking, Idris' face beamed.

In truth, Idris did not at first want to have anything to do with this man. There was a chilling emptiness in his eyes and the gathering darkness of evil all around him. But then it occurred to Idris that the monsters who had kidnapped his daughter were wicked men, too. Who better to look for evil men than a man just like them, a man who understood them, who thought their thoughts and could predict their behavior.

Idris reached into his travel pouch and pulled out the money he had packed there—all the cash his family had, and pressed it into Leo's hand. Then he leaned on his spear and bowed low in the dirt at the tip of the Arab's boots.

Leo didn't appear to notice. He fingered through the wadded-up bills, smoothed them in his palm and counted them.

"I will meet him back here at sunset to get the rest of it," Leo said when he was finished counting. "Tell him he must go and get his money and be back here by then. If he does not show up with the money, I will keep what he has already given me. If he does, we have a deal, and I will purchase the supplies I need—he must purchase his own—and I will meet him at first light on the dock to board the river launch north."

Leo folded the pile of bills and stuffed them into the front pocket of his shirt. He leaned his chair back against the building and continued to sharpen his knife. He ignored Idris as if he were not there and spoke with the interpreter in Arabic.

Idris turned and left the two of them in the alley behind the bar. He had much to do before sunset. As he headed to the edge of town to find the big palm tree, it was obvious his countenance had changed. His mind was filled with plans instead of the pain, grief and fear that had darted around in his head like angry bats. He had something he had not had since he spotted the smoke on the horizon rising from the village. He had hope.

Chapter 9

The noon sun was a flaming torch overhead, but the man feeling his way down the path he had walked hundreds of times neither noticed nor cared. In two weeks, he had aged a year. He had eaten almost nothing, slept very little, stayed constantly on the move. His eyes had sunk deep into his skull, and his trance-like gaze was a guide wire that led him down the meandering trail.

Idris played and replayed in his head all that had happened to him after he left the village to find a mercenary to bring back Akin. And with every replay, despair weighed heavier on his shoulders. With each rehash and recounting, the pain intensified. As long as he'd had hope, as long as he'd had a purpose and a plan, he could keep his anguish at bay. Now that he had nothing, all his sorrow crashed down on him, and he was buckling under the weight of it. His son was dead. His precious little girl was gone. He had gambled everything the family owned on a one-shot chance to get her back, and he had lost.

A villager on his way to the river to water his zebu spotted him on the path. The gait was unmistakably Idris. Word quickly spread through Mondala. Women who had been preparing the noon meal stopped and rose to greet him. Men at work in the millet fields set their hoes aside to welcome him home. The wounded recovering in their huts from the attack heard the commotion and came out to see what was going on.

Aleuth was in the family's tukul caring for a baby whose mother had been slashed across the back with an Arab saber when she heard someone call out, "Idris is back!"

Suddenly, hope shot through her like a bolt of lightning playing on the mountaintop. Akin, their precious daughter. Akin! Riding home on her father's shoulders! And she would grab the child off his shoulders and into her arms; she'd drink in the smell and the feel of her and hold her so very tight.

She leapt up and raced out the door of the tukul. She got as far as the cooking fire out front when she saw him. And she knew. No one could look at him and not know. The joy and hope drained out of her like water from a broken pot.

Her eyes filled with tears. As she watched Idris' slow, deliberate walk, her heart went out to him. But she had no comfort to offer; she felt as dry and barren as the desert. She wiped tears off her cheeks and returned to the tukul. Shema sat in a corner, her face blank. Aleuth looked at her and thought wildly, I have lost all my children! The little girl who had run giggling through the village and chased butterflies in the field had died in the attack on the village as surely as her brother; her spirit had been kidnapped as surely as her sister had been carried away. Now, she was a shadow, a hollow-eyed doll who neither spoke nor responded to the world around her.

Aleuth clamped down on the scream that threatened to rip her heart out, leap from her throat and roar through the village—leaving her behind, dead on the floor of the hut. She gritted her teeth to stop her lip from trembling, and picked up the baby lying on a sleeping mat, held him close and rocked back and forth, humming groans more than a melody.

The other villagers could read Idris' demeanor, too. He had not found his daughter, that much was obvious. What other calamities might have befallen him, they were anxious to hear.

Idris walked slowly into the village, head bowed and shoulders stooped. Men gathered in a group with their farm tools and spears by their sides, silent sentinels showing their support. Akec was among them and he tried to make eye contact with his neighbor, but Idris merely acknowledged the presence of the men with a slight nod of his head and continued toward his hut.

As he passed them, one of the men spoke his name softly. "Idris." And he stopped, didn't look at them, just stopped where he was like a leaf temporarily stuck in the reeds before it floats on down the river.

A small, old man stepped out of the group of men and approached Idris. His hair was the color of clouds, his skin as wrinkled as leather. His name was Durak. A village elder, he was a man respected as much for his kindness as for his wisdom.

"We are your friends, your kinsmen," he said quietly. "We can see that you carry a heavy burden. If you will tell us, we can help you carry it. Many backs will make the load lighter. But if you try to carry it alone, you will be crushed."

Idris turned and lifted his gaze to the men he had known all his life.

"It's gone, all gone, everything I have." His voice sounded hollow and dead. "I went to find Akin and bring her home, but I came back with nothing. No, less than nothing."

There was a despair in Idris' voice that no one had ever heard there before.

Akec stepped out of the group and stood before Idris. "What happened?" he asked, as kindly as he could.

Idris sighed, looked into their sympathetic faces and decided they deserved an explanation. It didn't take him long to give them one. He talked about going to Bentiu, about telling the people he met there what he was seeking. He described his meeting with Leo and his strange, toothless companion.

"He told me to go and get my money and meet him in the alley at sunset to give it to him. I was there an hour before the sun left the sky. He came right on time. He took my money and told me what supplies he would purchase with it for the journey and advised me what I should bring. Then he said he would meet me at first light on the dock and we would go north together."

Idris paused. "He never came."

Even now, the memory still punched him in the belly. He had been early. He couldn't sleep; he was too excited. He stood at the appointed place beside the front posts of the building that hung out over the river and expectantly scanned the dock as the dawn began to break. He remembered the tickle of fear he felt when the sun began to rise and the man named Leo was not there, remembered the growing knot of fear that settled in his belly—and grew bigger and bigger with every passing minute. First light came. Mid-morning. Noon. No Leo. Idris had waited there until sundown. As the day wore on, his emotions had downshifted from elation, through apprehension and fear, to despair.

He had looked for Leo for two days, searched up and down the streets and back alleys of Bentiu, prowled through the bars, questioned anyone who would listen to him, used what little money he had to bribe people for information. But he could not find a single person who knew, or would admit they knew, a man named Leo with scars on his arms and a flattened nose.

He had finally given up. He had no food and no money to buy food. He wasn't sure how he had ended up on the steps of the mission church. He must have seen the cross. And his memory of the compassionate aide worker who listened to his story and offered him a ride was equally muddled. She was on her way to the Kakuma Refugee Camp in Kenya, and he'd traveled with her in the back of her truck until she'd let him out south of Bor. He had walked the rest of the way home.

His friends saw the heartbreak in his eyes, and it broke their hearts as well. He wasn't the only villager who was suffering, of course. Women had lost husbands; men had lost wives. Brothers, sisters and children had been killed in a bloody carnage that would forever mark the memories and souls of the survivors. But those people were gone—beyond the sun. Akin was still alive, and they did not realize how much hope they had pinned on Idris, that he would be able to do the impossible, that he would be able to save just one little girl.

Idris turned in silence and went to his tukul. Aleuth greeted him, and they shared grief, pain and heartache with just a look. Idris had had nothing to eat, so Aleuth gave him injera bread and fruit; he was exhausted, so Aleuth took his small pack and put a sleeping mat on the floor so he could lie down and rest. But he did not eat and he did not lie down. He merely sat beside the door of the tukul, too exhausted to do anything else, and stared with sightless eyes into the embers of the cooking fire. Shema did not even acknowledge his presence. He didn't know that his face and Shema's now wore the same blank, dead look.

Idris and Aleuth said little to each other. There would be time enough tomorrow, and all the other tomorrows out there, to talk about their loss and figure out what to do with no money and no cattle. For today, it took all their strength to live in the moment, struggling not to look at the smooth spot in the dirt where two sleeping mats once lay. They did not speak of Shema. Tomorrow. Tomorrow they would try to figure out what to do, try to help the child. But now, she merely looked with emotionless eyes that recognized her father, but held no joy in that recognition. It was like someone had blown out the light in her soul and now there was nothing left but darkness.

When Aleuth lay down beside her husband on their sleeping mat that night, he took her into his arms.

"We must pray," he whispered into her hair. "We must pray that the God who loves us will help us somehow. That he will make a way for us where we cannot make our own way."

So they held each other in the darkness and prayed. Neither had any sense of the presence of God, any hope that their prayers were heard. But what else were they to do?

* * * * *

When Ron sat up, he moved slowly. He was stiff and sore from another uncomfortable night sleeping—well, at least lying down—in the back of the jeep. The likelihood that he had actually slept more than an hour or two was pretty slim.

"Two days, Masapha, and still no game. You don't suppose we heard those fellows wrong, do you?"

The Arab did not get up. He lay flat on his back for a moment and rubbed his eyes with his fists, just like Ron's nephews did when they woke up.

"Perhaps our hearing of the words was not right." Masapha squinted into the sun as it cleared the horizon. "But still is this the most excellent spot for the slave traders to meet. They proved that by coming here two days ago. Even if we did not hear the words we thought we heard, it is still a good spending of time to wait here. The slave auction pictures we took are the first ever anybody has taken, and we took the pictures here."

Masapha rolled out his prayer rug, knelt and began to pray shurug, the sunrise prayer. He seldom managed all five daily prayers, but he did the best he could.

Ron climbed out of the jeep and put his shoes on after he shook out each one to make sure it contained no multi-legged stowaways. He folded his sleeping bag and tossed it into the back of the jeep. Then he leaned against the vehicle and waited quietly for Masapha to finish his prayer before he spoke.

"Well, if we don't see something soon, we're going to have to head back," he said as Masapha rolled up his prayer rug. "We've got enough water for three more days. Enough food for the same, though we can maybe grub up some stuff to stretch it."

Masapha nodded. "Three days it is."

They set up their equipment on the hilltop, then seated themselves a few feet behind and below its crest, constantly shifting to keep up with the small umbrella of shade provided by the handful of skinny, almost leaf-less acacia trees that grew there.

The two observers scanned the horizon, dispensed hourly rations of water and waited. For entertainment, they tossed the crumbs from the morning's roll into the air to be snatched by the circling sparrow larks.

A sand grouse that had a large chunk of bread clasped in its beak flew a few feet into the air and then dropped it on the sand at the top of the hill. Ron reached out to pick it up and froze. A moving column of dust was progressing slowly across the desert, headed straight at them.

The two men flattened themselves on the ground and hastily made one last check to ensure that everything was operating properly. There were no problems with the equipment, but there was a problem of a different sort. A floating advertising billboard of larks and sand grouse gyrated up and down a few feet above their heads announcing their presence to the world.

Ron couldn't very well stand up and shoo the annoying birds away. But he could remove the food supply so the birds would tire of hovering and go somewhere else for lunch. He picked up the bread, tucked it into his carry pouch and tossed the pouch onto the sand beside him. Then he turned to watch the swirling clouds of dust.

Five... six... seven... nine... eleven... twelve trucks! A dozen trucks! And maybe a couple more obscured by the dust. His heart raced. This was it, really it, this time. This was what he had been waiting for.

The undulating heat waves on the horizon warped and fractured the image, slicing the vehicles into shimmering, horizontal layers so the convoy emerged from the swirling whirlpool of dust in sections.

As they neared the area where the other trucks, jeeps and camels had parked several days earlier, the vehicles moved into position to form a large semicircle with an open area in the center. Because there were so many more vehicles, the line of them stretched all the way across the hollow, with the nearest one directly below Ron and Masapha's hilltop perch.

Each truck carried captives from a particular tribe, who spoke only their own dialect. When the trucks unloaded their wares in the open-air market, buyers could select a few slaves from each tribe. It was easier to train and dominate the slaves if they were isolated, unable to communicate with their fellow captives. Absent a common language, the slaves could not plot with each other, could not band together for revenge or escape.

Once the trucks rumbled into position on the desert floor and stopped, their trailing dust clouds overtook them and shrouded the area in an impenetrable haze. Though they could see nothing through the veil of dust, Ron and Masapha could hear the Arabs shout orders, truck doors bang and tailgates slam open. Gradually, the dust dissipated and the transports and their cargo materialized.

Ron swallowed hard. His fingers were sweaty as he focused his camera, and it had nothing to do with the heat.

"It's as bad as people have been telling us." He was awed at the immensity of the evil. "There must be 300 of them, maybe more."

The soldiers herded the captives out of the backs of the trucks as the dust cleared. Boys, girls and women were tied together by lengths of rope, and the soldiers tethered them to the trucks or to stakes driven into the ground, much like the villagers tethered their cattle outside their huts at night.

Masapha felt a small stir behind him. He turned and spotted two hungry grebes. Bolder than the others, the birds were only a few feet away, pecking at the remaining crumbs of bread left from lunch. He waved them off, much to the satisfaction of the crew of smaller larks waiting hopefully in the tree above him.

Ron concentrated on a group of captives in front of the last truck that had just pulled to a stop directly below them. As a guard pounded a stake into the ground, he pulled the focus in tight and captured the face of one little girl—frightened, bewildered, like a lost rabbit. She turned toward the morning sun, squinted and crinkled up her pixie face. When she did, Ron could see that she had dimples.

* * * * *

Akin looked up and squinted into the sun as the guard drove a wooden stake into the ground in front of the truck. Akin, Mbarka, Omina and Shontal had been batched as a package deal, tied together with a rope the guard looped around the stake. Once the rope was secure, the guard walked back to the puddle of shade beside the truck, leaving the girls to broil under the sun.

Better here than in the truck, where the girls had struggled to breathe in the cloud of dust that had swirled for hours around the last truck in the convoy. Still dizzy and disoriented, her wrists raw from the rough rope that tied her hands together, Akin was totally and utterly miserable. But in the noisy world that ebbed and flowed around her, nobody noticed one hungry, thirsty, frightened little girl, sitting despondent in the sand.

Except Ron. Click-click. Click-click. Click-click.

The auction unfolded faster than Ron or Masapha expected. They photographed, video taped and recorded the action, amazed at how quickly the buyers selected their wares, paid for them, loaded them up and left. There was a steady stream of arriving and departing vehicles, and the number of captives quickly dwindled.

When only about 50 or 60 remained, Ron slid down behind the crest of the hill to load a fresh roll of film into his camera. Masapha scooted down beside him to adjust a setting on the camcorder. They couldn't have been away from their observation posts more than a couple of minutes, but that was long enough for them to miss the departure of three soldiers.

The soldiers were guards for the captive villagers in the truck next to the one parked directly below the crest where Ron and Masapha were filming. When the last of their prisoners had been purchased and hauled away, they set their rifles aside to take a break, laughing and talking as they walked together toward the base of the hill. Then they separated, moved about 50 feet apart for privacy and began relieving themselves in the bushes.

Sudan

When the soldier nearest the hill finished and turned to head back to the truck, he noticed something odd nearby. At least a dozen larks and grouse circling in the air above the hill were diving at something on the ground there. He straightened his robe and headed around the side of the hill to see what so interested the birds.

Something in the squawking and chirping caught Ron's attention. He glanced over his shoulder and realized he had knocked his pouch of bread down the embankment when he'd loaded the last roll of film. The pouch had opened and spilled its contents onto the dirt.

He set his camera aside and scooted down until he could stand without being seen from the other side of the hill. He stepped to the sack and shooed the birds away. Then he reached down to pick it up.

They saw each other at the same instant. Ron as he leaned over to pick up the sack of crumbs, the Arab as he rounded the corner of the hill. Ron froze in mid-reach; the Arab froze in mid-stride.

Eyes wide, their gazes fastened on each other.

The frozen moment lasted only a heartbeat before the soldier started to back away. He took two steps, then turned and ran, shouting as he stumbled around the corner of the hill toward the trucks.

Ron leapt up the hillside, grabbed his equipment and hissed at Masapha, "Outta here, now!"

He slung the strap of the camera over one shoulder, the camera bag strap over the other, snatched up the camcorder and was running full out toward the jeep within seconds. Masapha grabbed the sound equipment. His short legs pumped frantically as he tore out for the jeep only a couple of steps behind Ron.

Ron and Masapha reached the stand of scraggly trees and bushes where they had hidden the jeep just as the Arabs started shooting. The guns sounded like cannons, and bullets sang through the air above their heads. The soldiers couldn't see them; they were shooting wildly. But they were shooting in the right direction!

The two men chucked their equipment into the back of the jeep, pushed away the branches of camouflage in one quick sweep and dove into the front seats. Ron turned the key in the ignition, and there was a second of silence during which both men aged 10 years before the engine caught and hummed to life. Ron jammed the gearshift into first, smashed the accelerator to the floor and popped the clutch all in one movement. The back tires kicked out a jet stream of small rocks as the jeep lurched forward, fishtailed slightly in the sand and then took off like a jackrabbit, bounding and bumping over the rutted trail.

In less than a minute, they were out of range of the soldiers' rifles. But the Arabs kept firing anyway. Ron and Masapha could hear the gunshots until they faded to distant popping sounds, like fireworks in the sky a long way off.

❋　❋　❋　❋　❋

Idris lay in the dark in the tukul, fighting the despair in his heart, struggling to banish the haunting memories so he could rest.

He didn't know that at that moment, he was the only man in all of Mondala who was trying to go to sleep. In fact, he was the only man in the village who was even lying down.

What had happened to Idris had been the lone topic of conversation in the village from the moment the men in the millet field spotted him trudging down the mountain path.

Shortly after the evening meal, Durak and several other men had gone from tukul to tukul throughout Mondala and announced that the village elders had called a special meeting—not just of elders, but of the heads of every remaining family in the village. The meeting would convene after sunset around a fire in the open space in front of the two large rocks that marked the entrance to the village.

The men began to arrive as the pink glow of sunset faded from the western sky, walking alone or by twos and threes out of the village into the flickering firelight. They squatted on the ground or leaned against the rocks and murmured quietly among themselves. Every family in the village was represented. Except one. Idris Apot, whose hut was on the back side of Mondala overlooking the river, had not been invited to the meeting and knew nothing about it.

Many of the men knew, or had figured out, why the meeting had been called. Others could not even have guessed. When everyone was present, Durak stood and addressed the group. There were no preliminaries; he got right to the point.

"We all know that our neighbor Idris is back and that he did not find his daughter," he said. "We know the story, that a man took his money and cheated him."

The crowd nodded in agreement. Yes, they all knew the story.

"Idris was deceived," Durak said. "He failed in his mission. But failure does not make him wrong. It does not make his mission wrong."

The crowd grew quiet.

"That is why we are here tonight. We have come together to talk, to decide if we..." he made a broad gesture to include the whole group, "...if we as a village should help Idris get his daughter back."

For those who didn't expect it, the statement was stunning. The shocked silence was followed by a rumble of sounds. Surprised reactions. Grumbles. Half sentences. Questions.

Finally, a man spoke in a voice that could be heard above the rest, and the rumble died down. He was a young man, early 20s, and not as sure of himself as the wise, old elder. But what he lacked in confidence he made up for in passion.

"I do not understand why we would even talk about this," he said, confused and exasperated at the same time. "What is the point? We could not fight off the raiders when they rode down on us. And many died because we could not."

He stopped and unconsciously looked around. They all were acutely aware of the empty spots, the blank spaces in the meeting and in their lives that were once occupied by good men now buried in the nearby field out there in the darkness. The young man who spoke had lost his father, his brother and sister-in-law in the raid.

"If we were helpless on our own land and in our own village, how could we hope to fight these monsters in their land?"

Heads bobbed up and down; the men muttered in agreement.

An older man, thin and wiry, without a single tooth, looked kindly at the young man and spoke with great patience. "No one is suggesting that we use sticks and clubs to fight a rogue lion, my son. To fight a rogue lion, you need a bigger lion!"

A third man's words tumbled out behind those of the toothless man. "At least Idris *tried*," he said. "He was not like a wounded dog that sits around and licks his sores. He had the courage to walk through the wilderness to the city, alone. He had the courage... " he glanced at the older man "...to go looking for a bigger lion."

A stocky man, short by Dinka standards, spoke then, trying to offer a voice of reason. He had an ugly, still-healing slash across his back, courtesy of a raider's machete. "But we don't know where she is," he said and turned to the last man who had spoken. "Our trackers lost their trail in the rocks. Even if we had, as you say, a bigger lion, what good would it do if we don't know where she is? She could be anywhere."

Another man shot back, "So we don't try? So we just sit here and do nothing?"

The man's name was Magok and he was notorious for his hot temper. His wife and only son had died in the attack. "We let them have her without putting up a fight? She is alive! Alive! We cannot help those who have gone beyond the sun... "

There was a moment's hesitation as his own pain took his words away. Then he went on more fiercely than ever.

"But she is not there," he pointed into the darkness in the direction of the burying field, "in the ground, cold under the dirt. She is still alive! She is one of us, a child of ours."

"She is not the only child of ours who needs our help," said the younger man who had spoken first. His 2-year-old had escaped with only minor burns when the raiders torched their tukul, and he'd taken in his dead brother's two orphaned children. "We need to do all we can do for the children right here in the village who have lost mothers or fathers, or both."

Magok weighed back in again, his voice rising: "If Akin had been cornered by jackals, would we say, 'We cannot go and help her because there are other children in the village to care for?' No! We would grab our weapons and fight them off and bring her home. We would not sit here and do nothing and let them tear her to pieces!"

For several minutes, the men hotly debated the opposing viewpoints. The mood of the group went first one way and then the other, swayed back and forth, persuaded by one speaker and then convinced of the opposite view by the next. Both sides presented reasonable arguments, but after almost an hour of furious debate, they were no closer to reaching a decision than when they started.

The big man had not said a word since the start of the meeting. He had only listened, leaned back against the tree in the shadows just outside the puddle of light from the fire, chewing a blade of grass.

In the silence that followed a particularly impassioned speech, he put down his straw, stepped into the light and walked purposefully the few steps to the fire where everyone could see him.

Akec Kwol stood quiet for a moment and thought about what he was about to say before he spoke.

"You all know I am the richest man in the village," he began.

Spitting on the ground in contempt, one of the men leaning up against the rock spoke with derision, "Akec, this is not the time to squawk like a parrot!"

Akec's demeanor didn't change. His next words were as carefully chosen as his first, "I am not here to squawk like a parrot. I am here to speak from my heart."

That got everyone's attention. His tone of voice was quiet, not belligerent. He seemed different somehow, though no one in the crowd could quite put his finger on how. They didn't know that they were responding to the non-verbal, to the big man's body language. He was not standing chest out and arrogant. His head was down, his hands palm-up.

"I have been a proud and boastful man," he said quietly. "I have," he looked at the man who had made the remark, "indeed, squawked like a parrot, making sure all who heard me knew that my herd of zebu was the largest herd in three villages, or that my millet crop was twice as large as the crops in the next fields."

He stopped, and let out a long breath. "I do not squawk now because none of that matters now."

As the tallest man in a village of tall men, the force of Akec's presence made an impression. He could look down on every other man in Mondala, and did. All his life, he'd used the force of his presence to press his advantage. Tonight, he knelt on one knee and fed sticks into the fire as he continued.

"I have lived in the tukul beside Idris for many years." He stared into the flickering blaze. "I know better than any of the rest of you the measure of him. He is a fine man."

As Akec watched red hot sparks float into the black night sky, he thought of the times Idris stopped and talked to him when other villagers avoided him. All the men gathered around the fire had known Idris all their lives; each plugged his own memory into the momentary silence.

The man whose daughter had been snatched by the raiders was not a splashy man, a man who stood out as a leader, a chief. He'd been a quiet, in-the-background neighbor so interwoven into the fabric of the community it was only when the men began to look at the individual threads that they realized how many ways Idris' presence had knit the village together, or kept it from unraveling. When he became a Christian, Idris had not changed dramatically. He had simply become more the man he already was.

"Idris is not just a good man, he is also a wise man," Akec continued. "Wiser than we realized. He is a hunter, the best shot among us. But it was not just his skill with a bow and a spear that made him a good hunter. He could track and kill gazelle and reedbucks because he knew their habits, knew where to look for them, knew where they were likely to hide. That is why he knew he must find a hunter who understood his prey."

His voice darkened. "A lion who knew their habits and their hiding places to track down the rogue lions that attacked us without warning and killed without cause or remorse."

Akec reached for a larger stick that was lying beside where Durak squatted in the dirt, listening intently. He placed it in the fire, then rose to his feet.

"Idris was deceived and lost all he had, but who among us has not been deceived at one time or another? Sometimes we even deceive ourselves." He spoke the next words softly. "I have deceived myself for most of my life."

There was a questioning murmur in the crowd.

"I told myself that my cattle, my crops and my wealth were all that mattered in life. I told myself that it wasn't important that none of you liked me."

Many of the men looked away, didn't want to make eye contact with Akec. But Akec didn't notice; he wasn't looking at them anyway.

"I deceived myself into believing that I was a happy, successful man."

He turned and gestured toward the village.

"My tukul was not burned; my cattle and goats were not lost. And yesterday, my daughter brought my new granddaughter here for me to see for the first time."

He smiled at the memory. The child had been born in a village downstream on the day Mondala was attacked.

"I held Aleul in my arms." He paused, emotion making his words thick. "If someone took my Aleul away, to beat her and abuse her and turn her into a slave, I would give every possession I have, every cow, every goat, every stalk of sorghum to get her back. It is the same with Idris."

He turned slowly and looked into the men's faces, lit by the dancing firelight.

"I saw many of you in the church when Pastor Maluong came to talk to us," he said. "Do you remember the last time the pastor spoke? Do you remember what he talked about?"

Some of the men nodded. Most just waited for Akec to continue.

"I remember. He told us that God gave richly, without holding anything back. He gave his son, everything He had, to set us free. Idris held nothing back. He sold his cattle, took all his money, gave everything he had to bring his daughter back out of the mouths of jackals and lions."

Akec looked back at the sleeping village and watched its few remaining fires send sparks into the velvet night.

"As the sun was setting, I held my Aleul in my arms. I would have given my life to keep her safe! But where was Akin at sunset? Where is she now? Who is taking care of her? What terrible thing might be happening right now, this minute, to little Akin?"

He stopped and turned back toward the other men and the steel of determination was in his voice.

"It will cost much to get her back, whether we hire someone to find her or pay a ransom ourselves. But let my words and this day be a witness that I will give as many cows and as many possessions as it takes to bring back Akin Apot, the daughter of Idris."

When he finished speaking, there were no dissenting voices. No arguments. There was only silence.

The next morning Akec appeared at Idris' door shortly after sunrise.

"You must come with me," he said simply. "Both of you."

With no further explanation, he turned and headed down the path that led along the outside of the village toward the road. Idris and Aleuth looked questioningly at each other and then followed, confused. When they looked around, they saw no one. The village was empty.

When they passed the tukul that sat a short distance back from the big rocks at the front of the village, Aleuth and Idris stopped in their tracks. They were too surprised to do anything but stand and stare at the wide, flat area where the preceding night a meeting had been held to determine the fate of their family.

Stretched out silently before them, several people deep, was every surviving member of their Dinka village, every man, woman and child. No one had stayed behind to tend a fire or make a meal. No one had gone to the field to work their millet crop or stake out their cattle.

At least 10 zebus were tethered to the tree Akec had leaned against the preceding night. Nearby, several goats were roped together, held by two small boys. Laid out in the dirt in front of them were woven reed baskets that contained everything imaginable, everything the other villagers considered valuable. Assortments of nuts and fruits, open baskets of threshed millet, knives, a pair of scissors, dried animal skins, all were neatly spread out like an elegant tablecloth on the ground.

Idris said nothing. His mind stumbled, fumbled for a frame of reference to figure out what it all meant.

Durak made his way through the grand display of gifts toward the stunned, speechless couple.

"Idris, you were right," the old man said. "To save your daughter, you went looking for a hunter who understood the prey you were seeking. You went looking for a bigger lion, and you failed to find one. But you were right to try. Take this," he spread his arms in an expansive gesture that took in all the valuables the villagers had gathered, "all of this, and try again."

Idris felt his knees go weak, and he struggled to remain standing. Beside him, Aleuth cried softly.

"We will help you search for Akin until everything of value in the village is gone," the old man said.

Chapter 10

After half an hour of frantic flight, Masapha turned around and sat down in the seat. He'd been peering through the dust the jeep's back tires shot into the air like a plume of water behind a racing boat.

"What?" Ron dared to take his eyes off the trail for a moment.

"We are not being chased by somebody," the Arab said matter-of-factly. "When we came up that last hill, my vision could look a couple of miles. No dust. Behind us, nobody is coming."

Gradually, Ron's heart rate returned to normal. The speed he was driving didn't. It was more than an hour after they had leapt into the jeep with bullets whizzing over their heads before Ron let off the accelerator.

The two rode along in silence as the afternoon sun dropped slowly toward the horizon. The landscape gradually changed. The desert sand dotted by scrub brush in varying shades of brown gave way to patches of farmland and clumps of stunted trees.

"Now what?" Masapha finally asked. "What is the next happening in your life after you present to your friend at the BBC the film and the words you will write?"

Ron gave Masapha a big grin. "Surely, you don't think we're finished with this story."

"Well, yes. We came to do a thing and we have done it, didn't we?"

Ron wagged his finger in Masapha's face. "Oh, no, no, no! As somebody important, whose name escapes me right now, once said, 'We have only just begun to fight.'"

"Fight what?"

Ron considered trying to explain that one but thought better of it. "You and I, we're going to get it all, the big Kahuna. I want interviews with slaves. And their masters. Shoot, I'd interview a slave trader, too, in fact, if I could get one to talk to me!"

The stunned look on Masapha's face was almost comical.

"You know that's not a bad idea at all, not at all! Maybe I could use a wire... "

Masapha didn't reply. He wasn't really listening anymore. He was looking at something in the distance, over a line of trees.

"Slow down," he said.

Ron let up slightly on the jeep's accelerator and followed Masapha's gaze. Vultures circled high above a stand of trees just ahead. Not odd, by any means. But that many vultures, that was odd.

Masapha touched Ron's hand on the stick shift. "Pull over. There is a thing that is not right about this. We should go on our feet to see."

Ron stopped the jeep, grabbed his camera bag and followed Masapha. As they drew near, they could hear the scavengers, the raucous cry of the coffee-colored vultures, their wings flapping as they settled down out of the sky.

The men moved cautiously forward, edged around a small bend in the road, and passed the brush that blocked their view of the trees. The sight and the stench slammed into their chests like twin wrecking balls.

Ron couldn't speak, couldn't breathe.

Before him was a sight that would forever define evil incarnate. Hanging in the trees all around them were corpses, rotting corpses obviously dead for days. There were probably two dozen of them.

If the dead could have told their story, they'd have described how the raiders had descended on their Nuba village with guns, swords and machetes, how they killed, maimed, raped and finally burned the village to the ground.

Because the villagers were Christians, the leader of the Mura-haleen had marched every man who had survived the raid to this stand of trees. And there, he had crucified them all.

Twenty-seven men had been nailed alive to the trees. The most hardy probably survived for as long as a day. Now all their heads hung down in death, hands and feet still impaled on tree trunks and limbs, with insects and buzzards picking to pieces their lifeless bodies.

Ron turned away, nauseous, shaking. Only a monster from hell walking the earth posing as human could have done such a thing. His head spun, and he was afraid he was about to be sick. The stench... he couldn't breathe. No one in the world would ever believe that atrocities like this really happened.

Oh, yes they would.

His fingers were clumsy as he flipped the catch on his camera bag, lifted the Nikon out and hung it around his neck. He steadied himself, then turned and resolutely began to fire. He snapped one ghastly, grotesque picture after another. Click-click. Click-click. A guarantee that the world would not be able to turn its back and pretend it hadn't happened. And a guarantee that each image would be seared into his soul, to haunt him for the rest of his life.

He had shot one entire roll and a few shots off a second before Masapha, who stood nearby visibly shaken, croaked, "Ron, look!"

Stretched out on the ground facing the crucifixion scene, a limp form lay in the dust, a boy, motionless.

Ron and Masapha ran and knelt in the dirt beside him. Masapha put his ear to the boy's chest, below the swollen, festering wound in his shoulder, and could barely detect a heartbeat. "He is alive, but it is a near thing. We must find a doctor."

* * * * *

It was late afternoon when the two camels and two horses rode into the camp. This camp had the feel of a village, not like the transitory-one-night camps the girls had lived in since their capture.

When the slave auction in the desert had exploded in pandemonium, two soldiers had grabbed Akin and her three friends and hoisted them up onto horses. Then the men leapt onto camels and took off across the plain with the horses in tow.

They traveled for days after that, until the girls' tender legs were raw from the saddles. Now, the Arabs quickly dismounted the camels, handed the reins to servants and left the captives tied to the horses. Akin and the others looked around in wonder.

The centerpiece of the camp, the hub around which all the rest revolved, was a large, white canvas tent. It dominated the camp the way the man inside it dominated the people in the camp. There were half a dozen smaller, colorfully striped tents encircling the big white one, each about 50 yards from the next. A handful of even smaller tents were scattered around the compound.

Beyond the tents to the north, a herd of camels grazed, each staked to the ground with a long tether rope. In the pastureland south of the encampment, a herd of horses was tethered to graze.

The camels, the horses, the camp—and now the four Sudanese girls—belonged to Sulleyman Al Hadallah, who lived in nomadic luxury in the center tent in the compound.

The men who had brought the girls to the camp untied the ropes that bound them to the horses, lifted them to the ground and shoved them across the compound, past the tents and up a small incline toward a palm tree set off by itself. Under it was a faded green army tarpaulin stretched across a center pole and tied to four shorter poles driven into the dirt. The space beneath the tarp was only about three feet high, and it was open on all four sides, but it provided shade from the blistering desert sun. What the shelter also provided was the down-wind stench of the camp's latrines, located only a short distance away.

When the men got to the shelter, they shoved the girls under the tarp. One of the men bound the girls' hands and then tied a length of rope to each girl's ankle. He pulled the knots so tight they winced in pain. The ends of the tether ropes were tied to the shelter's center pole. The lengths of rope were long enough for the girls to scoot as far as the edge of the tarp but no farther.

For the rest of the evening, the men celebrated loud, noisy dinners in the tents. The girls could hear shouts and raucous laughter. A small herd of black-robed women scurried back and forth carrying trays of food and urns of drink from what must have been the cook tent at the far end of the campground. Every time one of the women lifted the canvas flap of one of the tents, the clamor from the inside spilled out into the evening air.

The girls were ravenous and so thirsty their dry tongues stuck to the roofs of their mouths.

Finally, a small, bowed woman in a light-colored robe huffed and puffed up the path toward where they sat. She carried a bucket of water and a straw plate. When she reached the shelter, she sat the bucket down and flung the tin cup toward the nearest girl. Hesitating at first, but spurred on by the woman's gestures and unintelligible urging, Mbarka picked up the cup and quickly jabbed it into the bucket. She took a long, gulping drink, then handed the cup to Shontal, who drank and then passed the cup on down the line.

In a rare burst of generosity, the unknown woman had culled some scraps from the table where the men had been eating and brought the girls their only meal of the day—some pita bread, dates, couscous and feta cheese made from camel's milk. She watched the girls devour the food until a large woman came out of one of the tents and called to her, and she turned quickly and hurried back down the path.

The celebrations ended in the gathering dusk. Most of the men headed toward sleeping quarters in three of the striped tents. The girls could hear their voices as they talked to each other in their strange tongue. In fact, the girls could hear the sounds of the encampment surprisingly well. Even small sounds like cooking pans banging carried a long way in the cool, dry air.

The girls talked quietly and studied this new environment. If it was a village, it was an odd one. While there were easily 50 to 60 men, they had yet to see a single child and only a handful of women.

They had never met a Bedouin.

The Arab nomads had come south only temporarily to graze their herds in the lush green meadows and to trade livestock in Kosti. Once he'd sold off his stock, Sulleyman and his herders would return to Qadiq, the town in the north where the Hadallah clan lived. He made enough money to support a very comfortable lifestyle there by selling and trading camels and horses, and he supplemented his income by the sale of slaves he picked up on his trips south.

With his connections in Mauritania, Sulleyman could sell the slaves for twice what he had paid for them. And he had the use of them during his stay in Sudan. Occasionally, he kept slaves for his household, but his general policy was to use the women and girls for his personal pleasure and then sell them off when he returned home. It would take a rare slave to catch his fancy; he had bedded hundreds of them over the years. He was particularly fond of virgins, virgins who still looked like little girls. He liked their childlike bodies and how they fought and screamed when he took them. But a virgin was only a virgin once; as soon as she was de-flowered, she was interchangeable with any other slave.

The four slaves he had sent his men to buy at the slave auction would bring a good price, and if he decided to purchase any others, he would negotiate with his broker in Kosti, Faoud Al Bashara.

Akin's eyes were drawn to the big center tent in the gathering darkness. She saw a lamp flicker and then begin to brighten until the whole tent was bathed in a golden glow. When night fell and the stars appeared in the black sky, the white tent became a ball of light.

As she watched, the flap of the tent flew open and two men came out. In the puddle of light in front of the tent, she could see that both wore white headdresses, with fabric covering the lower portion of their faces. A man inside the tent barked at the two men, obviously gave an order, and they strode purposefully away.

Akin turned her attention from the men back to the tent, where she could see the man inside, the one who had issued the order, silhouetted by the golden glow of the lamplight in a perfect shadow on the tent wall. As she watched, the man began to take his clothes off, tossing his long flowing robe aside, and Akin's face flushed with embarrassment. She quickly averted her eyes and caught sight of the two men who had left the tent. They were striding up the path toward the shelter where she and the other girls lay in the darkness.

Instantly, her heart began to hammer, her mouth went dry and she began to pant, making little whimpering, hitching sounds as if she were crying. But she was way too scared to cry. She desperately wanted to run away, like she had run in terror from the men who attacked her village. But she couldn't run fast enough to escape them then. And tied to a stake, she couldn't run at all now.

When the men reached the open shelter, they ducked under the tarp. They reeked of wine, camels and body odor, and the girls shrank from them as far as they could. One of the men grabbed Mbarka's arm and yanked her out. She gasped, just a little squeak, before terror stole her voice and she could make no sound at all. She stood quaking as one man untied her hands and the other untied the rope attached to her ankle. Tossing the ropes aside, one of them seized her right arm, the other her left, and they turned with the terrified teenage girl between them and hustled her back along the path to the white canvas tent in the center of the encampment. When they got there, the men shoved her through the open tent flap, then turned and stood guard just outside.

The startled girl caught herself on a tent pole as she fell into the tent. Slowly, she lifted her head and her eyes widened when she saw

Sulleyman Al Hadallah. He was totally naked, lying back against a stack of pillows. Beneath his bearded face, his hairy, dark-skinned body glistened in the flickering lamplight; his fat belly trembled with his rapid breathing. Gold earrings sparkled behind his drooping jowls. His eyes were dark and menacing, his lips twisted in a predatory smile.

From her vantage point, Akin could see the scene played out in shadows on the glowing tent walls. She could see Mbarka's shape near the tent flap, but the man's shadow wasn't there. He must have left the tent, or he was lying down where she couldn't see him.

Mbarka had never seen a man like this. The sight of his naked, quaking body made her stomach heave. She instantly averted her eyes to the floor of the tent, just keeping him in the upper periphery of her vision. He had been lying back with his arms spread out expansively, and he sat up slightly, waved his hand slowly in a come-here motion and said something in Arabic. She clung to the tent pole, unable to move even if she'd wanted to.

He spoke again, his voice gravelly, his tone beckoning, and he motioned again for her to come closer. She did not move, and his face darkened. Ponderously, he got up off the pillows and plodded menacingly toward her. Suddenly, her terror exploded, she let go of the tent pole and bolted. She barely made it through the tent flap before one of the guards grabbed her and shoved her roughly back inside. She stumbled and fell, landing on her back, and when she looked up, the overweight man was standing above her, leering down at her.

Akin watched the scene play out in shadows. She saw the man get up and begin walking, his black silhouette approaching the thin one huddled at the front of the tent. She saw Mbarka lurch toward the tent flap, and watched the guard shove her back inside. And she saw the man reach down, grab her arm and drag her to the back of the tent. When the man's shadow vanished, she heard Mbarka's shriek, a cry of terror that split the darkness. She screamed and screamed, and suddenly her shrieking changed tone and became an anguished cry of pain that sounded like an animal captured in a snare.

Mbarka's initiation into womanhood was terrifying, painful, and humiliating. The two older girls quickly understood that she was being raped, and they bowed their heads and turned away. Little Akin, still not sexually mature, pondered what type of horrible thing must be happening to her friend in the white-canvass tent.

For half an hour that seemed like an eternity, the girls could hear Mbarka scream and cry. Then there was silence. Only silence. But Akin thought she could just make out the sound of someone sobbing softly, and she lay in the darkness listening to Mbarka's grief, feeling frightened, confused and totally alone. Her mind was shouting one question—what had happened to Mbarka?—and whispering another: What will happen to me?

* * * * *

With unmarked roads and an outdated map, finding medical help for the injured boy would not be easy.

"He is still hanging up," Masapha said. He had leaned over the seat to check on the boy as they rocked along the rutted path.

"Hanging *on*."

"Yes, but just barely."

It was clear on the map that about a dozen tributaries fed into the Bahr Al Arab River west of Bentiu. They had to find one of those tributaries—any one of them would do.

As he alternately peered at the map and then at the countryside, the pieces fell into place. Masapha grabbed Ron's sleeve and pointed at a line of low hills that marched across the horizon.

"I think the river that is here," he tapped a spot on the map with his finger, "is on the other side of those hills. If it is, the map is telling me a town is not far downriver."

Darkness had fallen like a thick, heavy blanket by the time Ron and Masapha roared into the small settlement of Lusong. And just as quickly roared back out again when villagers told them there was a medical facility run by a Swiss missionary doctor not far away.

A few minutes later, Ron drove up to a gate in a fence, and the jeep's high beams lit up a hand-lettered sign. *"Federation des Missions Evangeliques Francophones Medical Societe."*

For the next three hours, he and Masapha stood just outside the spill of light from a row of operating room lanterns while an elderly Swiss doctor performed surgery to remove a bullet from the boy's shoulder and repair the muscle it had torn away.

When the old man finally stepped away from the make-shift operating table and removed his mask, he sized up Ron and Masapha.

"Looks like you've had a long day," he said. "My people will watch over ze boy. My wife has made beds for you on ze floor in our home. You get zum rest, and we'll talk in the morning."

Ron did not unroll his sleeping bag, which smelled like the dirty sock hamper in the Indianapolis Colts' locker room. He just plopped down on top of the fresh blankets and fell into an exhausted sleep. Masapha collapsed in a heap beside him.

Chapter 11

The next morning, the doctor's wife prepared a hot breakfast. When Ron breathed in the aroma of freshly baked bread, he almost drowned.

"We have not been properly introduced," the doctor said as they sat down around the table. "I am Dr. Hans Greinschaft." He nodded his head toward his wife and smiled. "And this is my lovely wife, Helena. Ve are Christian missionaries and we work for the Sviss Medical Society."

The doctor and his wife were small, chubby, cheerful people with hair as white as strands of cloud. They reminded Ron of Mr. and Mrs. Santa Claus. The doctor had no beard, but he did sport a thick-as-a-broom white mustache and wire-rimmed spectacles.

When they went to check on the young tribal they'd brought into the clinic, Dr. Greinschaft's assistant said that the boy's fever had broken during the night.

"Ze boy will be fine," the doctor said. "Tank goodness for antibiotics. He will be unconscious, I tink, for the rest of the day." He gestured toward the door. "Come, let's go somewhere ve can have ourselves a talk."

The doctor eased himself down on the top step of the front porch on his small house. Ron and Masapha seated themselves on the steps as well.

Ron was the first to speak. "Doctor Grein...shaff?"

The old man smiled. "That's close enough."

"We appreciate all your help for the boy and your hospitality. It's been a rough couple of weeks. This is the first break we've had."

"It shows. You both look like you vent through a wringer washer backwards. What kind of verk do you do?"

"I'm a free-lance journalist. And a photographer, too, if taking pictures with a camera that won't focus itself still counts as photography."

"What are you doing in this," the doctor gestured at the world around them and searched for a word, "this nothing place in Sudan?"

Ron looked a question at Masapha. The doctor caught the look.

"You do not have to tell me vhat you do not want to tell me. I'm a nosey old man and... "

Ron didn't let him finish. "You need to understand that what we're doing in Sudan will very likely get our names crossed off Gen. Bashir's Christmas card list."

"That vould be a shame," the doctor said, dryly. "I understand he sends out bright shiny red ones."

Masapha was totally lost, but he smiled as if everything the two men said made perfect sense.

There was no good humor in Ron's voice when he continued. "You're probably better off not knowing anything about us but name, rank and serial number. But you asked. I'm working on a story about the slave trade in Sudan. When I'm done, the world won't be able to pretend it's not happening."

"Good!" the doctor said. "All the killing, all the... " His voice trailed off. "The Arabs will not stop unless the vorld makes them stop. I do not want to treat babies with limbs blown off. I want to go back to immunizations and nutrition."

Ron told the doctor about the slave auction.

"Everything we shot, and the equipment we used to shoot it, is in that canvas bag your sweet wife said we could store in the bottom of her pantry."

Masapha spoke for the first time.

"Can you tell us the way that is most safe and short to get to the capital? We have to send from this country our information." He smiled. "It will be like to Khartoum dropping a plane load of bombs on their heads."

"Vhat you have you must take very great care to disguise. Government soldiers go through everyting that is shipped into or out of Sudan—everyting."

Then the doctor told them about a "reasonably decent" road four or five days' by jeep from the clinic that would eventually dump them out in Ed Da'ein. From there, they could travel more bad roads to Khartoum.

"There is noting between here and that road except plenty more noting, so you will need supplies. After lunch, vhy don't you drive me into Lusong. I need to check on zum patients, and you can get what you need for your journey."

Ron and Masapha dropped the doctor on the outskirts of the village and continued down toward the dock on the river. They pulled up in front of the only store in town, a dilapidated structure in danger of immediate collapse, and purchased dried fish and beef jerky for Masapha, pork jerky for Ron, fresh fruit and two cans of petrol.

But they discovered they wouldn't need the gasoline after all. When they stepped out of the store with their supplies, their jeep was gone. It had been stolen.

* * * * *

Akec had arranged for six villagers to accompany Idris to tend the cattle and goods until they could be exchanged in Rumbek for money, the language of the westerners and Arabs. Then he, Magok and Durak would help Idris search for a bigger lion. Their route to Rumbek took them through the neighboring village of Tiresta the second night of their journey.

Though that village had not been attacked, they had suffered at the hands of the Murahaleen. A group of two dozen women and girls had been washing clothes at the riverbank when guerillas swooped down and hauled off nine of them. Their best hunters and trackers had searched for days, but could find no trace of the marauders. They just seemed to vanish.

The village elders had been debating what they should do, and Durak and Akec told them Mondala's plan. A man stood just outside the glow of the firelight and listened as they spoke. His name was Chewa Enosa. He was a Dinkan farmer who was visiting Tiresta from his home in a village several miles away. When the discussion around the campfire finally ended, he went to speak privately to Idris.

"My brother, Michael, was an SPLA soldier until he was wounded last year." Chewa told Idris quietly. "He has only one arm now. As a soldier, he traveled all over southern Sudan fighting government troops. He now lives in Kadriak on the Pibor River."

Idris had never heard of Kadriak and had no idea where the Pibor River might be located.

"It is a town where the SPLA has found many soldiers." Chewa's face darkened. "It is an ugly, dangerous place and there are many mercenaries there. I think my brother would be able to find in Kadriak the kind of man—the bigger lion—you are looking for."

Idris was instantly interested, but his experiences in the last few weeks had taught him caution.

"Why would he want to help us? He does not know me or my daughter."

Chewa said his brother would help because he had a personal ax to grind with the Murahaleen.

"Michael's wife was a beautiful woman, and one day when she was walking home from the marketplace, she ran into three drunk raiders," Chewa said. "They took her, all three of them, then beat her with their fists, sticks and clubs so you could not tell who she was when they were finished. And then they left her for dead on the side of the road."

Somehow, the woman had survived, but she had suffered brain damage.

"Her face is pushed in, she is blind, and something is wrong in her mind. Her speech is slow, and she is like a small child again. She lives with her parents in a village far south in the mountains, and when Michael goes to visit her, she does not know who he is."

The two men stood silent for a moment before Chewa continued.

"If you would like to talk to Michael, I will take you to him. He will help you if he can. I know he will." Chewa paused and looked into Idris' eyes. "I, too, have a little girl."

Idris told the other men from Mondala about Chewa's offer. Akec knew where the Pibor River was and said that it would be a long journey across the plains on the other side of the White Nile. But they agreed that going there was a better plan than wandering the streets of Bentiu talking to strangers.

They set out together early the next morning, but instead of making for Rumbek, they headed toward Bor, a city on the White Nile where they could sell their cattle and their other goods, and then catch a ferry to the other side of the river.

They bartered for two days in Bor to convert everything they'd brought with them into cash. Three of the six villagers, the ones who'd accompanied Idris to help with the livestock, left to go home to Mondala. Idris, Durak, Akec and Magok went with Chewa to find his brother, Michael.

Akec purchased tickets for the five of them on a bus that traveled the 150 miles between Bor and Pibor City twice a week. It was a dilapidated vehicle without a door, front or rear bumpers and so dented and scarred it was impossible to tell what its original color might have been. The bus left Bor shortly after sunup, bounded along the rutted gravel road, and did not arrive in Pibor City until well after dark. The bus driver allowed the villagers to spend the night in the bus, and the next morning they set out along the bank of the Pibor River for a town called Kadriak.

That evening they made camp on the outskirts of town and

Chewa went to find his brother and tell him Idris' story. Two days later, he returned.

"Michael has found someone he thinks you should talk to," Chewa said.

They met Michael in town, and he led them to a squatter settlement by the river, a collection of shacks, lean-tos and makeshift tents strung together by a labyrinth of interconnecting trails and passageways. It was a place defined by hopelessness and despair, a dark place even in the bright light of day.

Dirty, naked children darted in and out among the hovels like small animals. Other children stood unsmiling in doorways, watching the group pass, their eyes old and tired, their bellies swollen from malnutrition. Timid young women, their skin tones differing shades of darkness, listlessly shooed flies off the sickly babies in their laps.

Animal bones picked clean littered the ground, the hum of flies buzzed in the hot, stagnant air, and the choking stench of open sewers filled every breath. Even the uneducated Mondala villagers understood that this was not a normal living environment. Nowhere in their experience had they ever encountered anything that compared to the overwhelming filth and fetid squalor of the encampment; it disgusted and offended them.

When they came to an alley between two of the buildings, Michael turned down a narrow passageway. At the end of the passageway, he held up his hand, indicating for the men to wait. Then he opened the door of a small building literally vibrating with loud music. He and Chewa stepped inside and pulled the door shut behind them.

Idris and the others looked around, in wonder and disgust. Empty cans and beer bottles lay on the ground at their feet, along with piles of human excrement. What looked and smelled like vomit was splattered on a nearby wall.

Suddenly, the door opened, and Chewa indicated for the others to follow him. They stepped into the dimly lit room where an assortment of oil roughnecks, gamblers and other malcontents sat at makeshift tables or on crude stools that faced a bar made of planks stretched across oil drums. A battered boom box rested on the far end of the bar, blaring loud rock music in a language no one in the room understood.

Most of the bar/gambling hall's patrons cast curious glances at the tall Dinka tribesmen, Akec towering above them all, as Chewa threaded his way through the tables toward the far end of the building.

Michael stood near a group of three men sitting at a makeshift table of concrete blocks and wood slabs in a corner of the room that was shrouded in shadow. Idris could not quite make out their faces. Chewa stopped and his brother leaned over and spoke quietly to a tall figure seated in the middle.

Turning to Idris and the others, Chewa told them, "Michael will interpret for you."

The big man in the center of the group said something and his two companions rose and pushed briskly past the Dinkas without acknowledging their presence. Michael motioned for the villagers to come closer.

"I have already told Omar your story," Michael said to Idris. "He wanted to see you face to face and tell you his price and his conditions. If you can meet them, he will help you. For a price. He says everything is for a price."

Idris studied the seated man as he spoke to Michael, trying to make out his features in the dim light. He was a heavily muscled man, with massive shoulders and a wide, broad chest, where a thick mat of black hair curled out of the V of his shirt. Idris could see several tattoos beneath the dark hair on his arms; one of them was a snake wrapped around his right forearm, the head on the top of his hand, its forked tongue licking out toward his knuckles. The tattoo was so detailed and lifelike it seemed almost real, like the snake was an added weapon Omar could use against an adversary. And in an odd way, that was comforting. The mercenary spoke in a deep, raspy voice, and his smirk—he did not smile—revealed a gold cap on the left of his two front teeth. The brim of his hat cast an ominous shadow, but Idris could make out deep, unblinking dark eyes and a hawk nose that hooked over a thick, black mustache. The man had the face of a predator. The hat reminded Idris of Leo, but he resolutely pushed the memory out of his head.

"He says that you do not need to know his name," Michael said. "Omar will do for now. He wants to know if you have brought dinars or pounds."

Akec pulled out some Sudanese pounds for them to see and then shoved them back into his traveling pouch.

"Omar also says he works alone."

Idris responded immediately. "I am going with him. I am paying. Besides, he doesn't know my daughter."

A quick exchange followed, then Michael reiterated, "He says he works alone."

"Where our money goes, I go." For Idris, the point was non-negotiable. "The others will be turning back, but I am going on, with or without him. He can stab me in the back if he wants to, but he will have to kill me to take my money. I will never again give it freely to someone who disappears."

After hearing Michael's translation, Omar snorted a short, guttural laugh and then spoke in gruff Arabic.

Michael turned to Idris. "He says he will tell you one final time: do not come! But if you refuse to listen, you may accompany him. Just understand that if you cannot keep up, he will leave you behind. If you get hurt, he will leave you behind. He will use you as bait if he has to. You have been warned. Omar works alone."

Michael let that sink in for a moment and then continued.

"He says the price will be 500 Sudanese pounds plus expenses, whether he finds the girl or not. It will be another 500 if he brings the girl back alive."

Akec stepped forward and laid a handful of bills on the table.

Another exchange took place between Omar and Michael, this

one longer and more animated. When it was over, Michael translated for the group what Omar had said.

"Another thing is, he says there are to be no questions asked about his methods. He says very bad things sometimes happen along the way. He hates the Murahaleen and the Fedayeen, and it would be a privilege for him to kill any that he comes across—along with returning your daughter, of course."

Magok stepped up and spoke for the first time, his words, as always, blunt and to the point. "How do we know he will do what he says?"

Michael already had the answer. "You don't. But he's the best chance you have of getting the girl back."

Chapter 12

Akin and Omina were pack animals. They hauled wood for the cooking fires—armload after armload, from small sticks to logs it took both of them to lift. They carried water for cooking and for clean-up afterward, huge jugs of it, all the way from the river to the cooking tent at the far end of the encampment.

Their day began in the dark before sunrise, preparing for the morning meal; it ended in the dark after sundown, cleaning up after the evening meal. Every minute in between was filled with drudgery.

On stomachs so empty they were sometimes dizzy, they served food they could not eat. Their clothes filthy rags, their bodies dirty and tormented by bug, spider and scorpion bites, they scrubbed and cleaned the clothes of their Arab masters. They slept in the cold, were tied in their shelter during the heat of the day, were beaten, slapped, kicked, humiliated and intimidated.

The older girls were raped, too. Every night.

Mbarka and Shontal quickly discovered that being a slave meant they existed for the sexual pleasure of the men in the camp, and they were handed around from one man to another like what they were—property.

In southern Sudan just to fatten and trade his horses and camels,

Sulleyman Al Hadallah had brought only a few of his household servants and staff, and none of his five wives or 17 children. He and his herders accepted that as Bedouins they must spend time away from their families. But none of them expected or intended to give up sexual activity. Mbarka and Shontal, both virgins and both pledged to be married before the raids, had been deflowered by Sulleyman and then given to any man in the camp who wanted them. Every night, soldiers came for them and took them to the men's tents. Usually, there was more than one man waiting for them there. And every night or two, one or the other of them would be summoned to Sulleyman's tent. They always spent the whole night there, and both girls dreaded those nights the most.

A pretty girl with a well-shaped body, Mbarka had caught Sulleyman's fancy. He had decided the night he took her virginity that he would give her to one of his sons instead of selling her to a brothel as he had planned. Shontal was a different matter altogether. She was almost as pretty as Mbarka, but there was a deadness in her eyes that made Sulleyman uncomfortable.

And he was very aware of the other two slave girls as well. He particularly lusted after the little one, the child. He got his greatest pleasure from bedding the young slaves.

Mbarka held up remarkably well under the humiliation and degradation of unending sexual assaults. Her experiences with the men in the camp had toughened her, made her stronger. Though not defiant, neither was she broken. She was a fighter, a survivor.

Shontal had neither Mbarka's courage nor her strength of character. Every encounter with the debasement of rape left her more shattered inside. It grew harder and harder for her to disassociate from the brutality; the psychological shield that protected her soul from total destruction was wearing gradually away.

Akin and Omina watched in horror as Mbarka and Shontal were dragged away to the Arabs' tents. Every night when the men came up the hill to their shelter, the two younger girls cringed back into the darkness, terrified that this would be the night strong hands reached out and grabbed them, too.

Though only the older girls had to endure the brutality of the men in the camp, they all shared an equal dread of Pasha Drulois. In her black dress and turban, she was a daily angel of torment to the slave girls—vicious, brutal and merciless. Decades of cruelty, abuse and humiliation had warped her iron will, twisted her into a bitter, angry woman, as callous and ruthless as her master.

Pasha had a hair-trigger temper. Carrying a heavy bundle of wood too slowly or not fetching water quickly enough would occasion a tirade of unintelligible Arabic and a flurry of blows from her leather camel strap. Its tough surface bit into the girls' flesh, leaving angry, painful welts. If she hit hard enough, the whip would break the skin and draw blood.

Since the nightmare morning when the raiders attacked her village, life for Akin had become mere survival, a struggle simply to endure. Though she and the others were unaware of it, their psyches were being transformed, molded into a "slave mentality" that asked for nothing and expected nothing. At different levels, all four had come to accept that they were the property of someone else, and that they existed for no other purpose than to serve their master. They were slowly losing all concept of personal rights.

The only break from the torturous existence in the camp came during trips to the river to wash clothes. It was hard work. The clothes baskets were heavy, the camel fat used for soap was disgusting, bending over and washing the filthy garments in the river was back-breaking labor. But for Akin, clothes-washing days were the only ray of light in a dark existence totally devoid of hope.

She longed for river days so she could push her toes down into the sand and feel the water rush over her feet. Trips to the river brought back some of her humanity. The river was a connection, a tiny thread that kept her tied to a life filled with love, an emotion she had not seen a single Arab display toward anyone.

But like every other aspect of her life now, the river held danger, too. Crocodiles lurked in the reeds not far from the shore on the other side of the river. They watched, always alert, ready to strike.

The girls never ventured more than a few feet from the riverbank, never got more than ankle deep in the water.

Pasha always brought along one of the hired men with a rifle to the river. If a crocodile became too brazen—and it had happened a time or two—the soldier would fire a few shots at the creature to hold it and its cronies at bay. It would take more than a round or two to kill a crocodile, of course, but a few shots were enough to make the creatures think twice about the source of their evening meal.

* * * * *

At dawn, the Sudanese farmer and the mercenary set out from Kadriak in Omar's jeep, which was in much the same state of disrepair as the bus Idris had ridden from Bor. Without mechanics or spare parts, few vehicles in southern Sudan fared any better. As soon as he struck a deal with the Dinka, Omar had begun to put together a strategy. If anyone would know where to look for a slave girl, it would be Julian Barak, who owned a bar in Jonglei.

The issue, of course, was getting from Kadriak to Jonglei, which lay almost due west on the edge of the Sudd Swamp about 150 miles away. The dirt tracks stretching out in that direction from Pibor City petered out after about 40 miles. In the 322,000 square miles of southern Sudan, there were only four miles of paved road. There was no road of any kind across the vast southeastern plains, no towns, no villages, no people. Omar would just have to follow the setting sun overland until he came to the main north-south road between Jalle and Kangor that lay a few miles east of Jonglei. He was prepared; he'd packed plenty of supplies and gasoline for the trip.

The sun climbed into the sky, turned up the burner on the day's heat, and the two men bumped along in silence. Idris's companion never uttered a word nor returned a glance. Omar had warned the villager not to come along. He had said he worked alone. And as far as he was concerned, he was alone. Idris's physical presence didn't change that. Besides, they couldn't have talked even if Omar had been the kind of man who wanted to chat. Neither could speak the other's language.

Omar focused the intensity of his attention on the task at hand—finding the girl. If he could locate the girl, he could make more money than most Sudanese made in two years.

Born to a Lokuta slave and her Mauritanian master, Omar Akbar El Shammri was a portrait of toughness, a huge, powerful man—6-foot-7 and a heavily-muscled 275 pounds—who had grown up wild on the streets and wharves of Port Sudan. His deep-set eyes and heavy black eyebrows gave him a brooding appearance that matched the condition of his tormented soul. He feared nothing, certainly not death. He'd eluded it many times, in Angola, Liberia and other dark places where he'd plied his trade as a paid assassin. He'd seen death, inflicted it, and occasionally even reveled in it. He was immune to the pain left in its wake.

When Akbar was 6 years old, his mother had angered his father, and in a fit of rage, he had sold her to a farmer to work in the fields. She'd taken her son and escaped, eventually landing in Port Sudan where she'd sold her body in the back alleys and slums near the wharves to support herself and her little boy. The bi-racial child, neither black nor white, was rejected by the Arabs and the Sudanese alike. He learned early about survival of the fittest. He learned that he had to be tougher, meaner, quicker and smarter than everybody else in his world. That's how he stayed alive.

In the shadowy ecosystem of paid killers, Omar had a reputation as a trustworthy man. But his code of honor had nothing to do with any sense of morality. He'd learned over the years that men who kept their word and could be trusted made more money than those who didn't. He would not trick Idris or rob him. He would keep Idris' expense money in a leather bag in his pocket, separate from his own money, which he kept in a pouch attached to his leg—the 500 Sudanese pounds initial payment for finding the girl, along with another 100 that constituted all the money he had in the world. He would use the expense money in the bag wisely, spend it carefully. And he would apply every skill he possessed in an effort to earn the additional 500 pounds' ransom payment. But the idea of "rescuing" a kidnapped child and returning her to her family was totally meaningless to him. He would find the girl because he had been hired to find her, nothing more. It was a simple business transaction.

They made good time along the trails, but eventually the trails ran out. It was much slower after that. At the end of the last trail, they set out west through yellow grass so tall the grill of the jeep parted it like the prow of a ship. With bone-jarring jolts and bumps, the suspension-less jeep lurched up over red anthills and slammed down into animal burrows as they wove around the islands of trees and brush that dotted the flat landscape.

It was just before noon on their second day out from Kadriak that they encountered a herd of grazing antelope. As Omar drove slowly forward, the stocky creatures with white patches on their eyes, ears and throats and s-shaped horns, parted quickly to get out of the way. He was careful not to spook them. It appeared to be a large herd, and it probably wouldn't be a good idea to cause a stampede. Omar assumed they would pass through the herd in a few minutes, but the expanse of animals went on and on, eventually stretching for as far as they could see in every direction. They inched their way through the herd all afternoon. The Arab began to fear that the sun would set and they would be stuck in the middle of a herd of antelope all night, but shortly before sundown they came out the other side.

The engine on the jeep blew mid-morning of the third day. Though Omar saw it coming, he was helpless to do anything about it. Steam began to spew out from under the hood, but there was no water anywhere in sight. The vehicle lurched ahead for another quarter of a mile. Suddenly, there was a loud clattering sound deep in the bowels of the motor. Then there was silence and the jeep rolled slowly to a stop.

Omar was livid! He pounded the steering wheel with his fists and shouted Arabic invectives to the wind. Long before Omar calmed down enough to be rational, Idris understood and accepted the reality that from here on, they would have to walk.

Omar rummaged around in the back of the jeep until he found a large canvas bag and a back pack. He loaded into the bag the essential supplies, water and food, and put his equipment into the backpack along with all the ammunition for the .375 H&H Magnum safari rifle he carried. He pulled his hat down over his eyes and shoved the bag at Idris.

"Here," he barked, still furious. "Make yourself useful and carry this."

Those were the first words Omar had spoken to Idris since he met the tribal in the bar. They were the last, too. The Arab strapped on the backpack, picked up his rifle, squinted into the sun and stalked off, with Idris half a step behind him. They had only gone about 50 yards when Omar suddenly stopped. He turned and looked at the vehicle for a moment, then put his gun and backpack down on the ground and walked back to it. He reached into the jeep and pulled out a can of gasoline, opened the lid and splashed the liquid all over the sides and top of the vehicle. When the can was empty, he threw it aside, backed away, lit a match and tossed it.

There was an instant "whoomp!" sound as the gasoline caught, and within seconds, the jeep was an inferno. When Omar turned back toward Idris, he was smiling; his shiny, gold tooth sparkled in the noonday sun. They had walked about a 100 yards before the jeep's gas tank blew. When it did, Omar laughed out loud.

They set their faces toward the sun and moved across the plain all afternoon. Omar was a machine; he strode along on legs the size of tree trunks, mile after mile. Idris easily kept pace. He was 3 inches shorter than Omar and 125 pounds lighter. He had walked the 275 miles to Bentiu in nine days; another 75 miles across these plains didn't matter.

After their second day on foot, they stopped for the night under the broad limbs of a tall, emerald-green balanite tree, and Idris made the fire, as had become customary. Omar dug into the food bag, got out dried meat and water, and handed some to Idris without comment. Then the two men on opposite sides of the campfire ate the tough, mostly tasteless meat, stared into the flickering flames and thought their own thoughts.

When he finished eating, Omar took his boots off, set them next to his backpack, and stretched out on the grass with his rifle and knife beside him. Idris wore nothing but a loincloth and a bead necklace; he had no shoes to take off. He merely knelt briefly to pray, then curled up next to his spear, close to the pile of kindling so he could keep the fire stoked. Omar watched the tribal's prayer routine every night with a sneer twisting his mouth beneath his black mustache.

Up as dawn was turning the sky pink, Idris took the water bottles to refill them. He was still about 50 yards from camp when he heard Omar scream. It was a cry of surprise and pain, and Idris dropped the bottles and bolted toward the sound, even though he had left his spear and bow in the camp and had no way to defend himself. When he came around the trunk of the big balanite, he found Omar on the ground with one boot on, holding the other bare foot, rocking silently back and forth in agony. The foot was literally swelling before Idris' eyes. When he got closer, he saw a dead scorpion on the ground beside Omar's other boot—no, two dead scorpions!

Omar knew better than to put on a boot without shaking it out first. As soon as he felt the lightning bolt of pain in his right heel, he knew, but he couldn't shift his weight fast enough to keep from crushing the insect. A scorpion determines with each sting how much venom to inject into its victim and only rarely uses it all because it takes several days to replenish the supply. But step on the creature while it's stinging you, and you squirt in the whole load, like pushing in the plunger on a syringe. Omar fell backward on the ground, clawed his boot off and the smashed bodies of two small yellow scorpions tumbled out. Omar groaned. Death stalkers.

The scorpions that lay dead in the dirt were among the most

deadly scorpions on earth. To compensate for their smaller size and narrow, weak pincers, death stalkers were equipped with far more potent venom than larger species, an excruciatingly painful neuro-toxin that could cause fever, convulsions, respiratory paralysis—even coma and death. Omar looked at the crushed bodies lying in the sand as the screaming agony in his foot began to march relent-lessly up his leg, and fervently hoped they hadn't both bitten him. If they had, he was in big trouble.

* * * * *

When the girls woke up in their shelter under the tree, the sun was already up and the camp was quiet.

"I think the men have gone on a trip," Omina told the other girls.

Shontal's face twisted in a grimace of anger and revulsion. "I hope they all get killed, every last one of them. I hope jackals rip them apart and eat them alive!"

Two days after Mbarka was raped, the 14-year-old Shontal had been escorted by the two soldiers to Sulleyman's tent for her initia-tion of humiliation. Unlike Mbarka, she'd known what was coming and had retreated into herself, had hidden somewhere deep down inside where no pain or humiliation could touch her. She had been emotionless, as compliant as a rag doll. She had not cried out or begged him to stop. That was a mistake. Sulleyman enjoyed hu-miliating, liked to inflict pain. She'd come back to the shelter with a black eye and a split lip.

Omina lived in unrelenting terror of the day she would be snatched up and taken to Sulleyman's tent. She understood that the older girls had been raped. She was 12, and her mother had explained to her what happened between a man and a woman—to prepare her for the beginning of her monthly menses. Although Omina looked sexually mature, that had not happened yet, and she didn't know that she was safe from rape until it did. According to Muslim law, a man could not have sex with a child, and she was considered a child until she started her monthly flow.

Akin, on the other hand, had no idea what happened to Mbarka and Shontal in the Arabs' tents, and would never have dared to ask them. Oh, she understood that animals mated in order to have babies. She'd seen it happen many times and grasped that something similar happened among people. But Aleuth hadn't yet prepared her little girl for womanhood. The child neither understood human sexuality nor grasped the horror and brutality of its perversion.

Finally, the eerie silence was broken by a sound. But the sound was as eerie as the silence. It was the sound of chanting. The sound of castanets. A procession of half a dozen women came out of Pasha's tent and walked in single file toward the girls' shelter. They chanted a high-pitched mantra with the same foreign words and phrases repeated again and again. The chant was accompanied by the ceremonial click-click of the wooden castanets. It felt old, very old.

The chanting women stopped when they reached the shelter. Every woman in Sulleyman's service was there. Akin was struck by the looks on all their faces. They were blank, devoid of any expression.

Pasha barked an order, and two of the women stepped forward, untied the rope that bound Mbarka and pulled her to her feet. Then the women took hold of her arms like the guards had, one on each side, and made Mbarka a part of the procession.

They marched down to the riverbank and stopped by a collection of granite rocks. The two women holding Mbarka's arms shoved her toward two large, flat rocks, one about a foot taller than the other. They indicated she was to sit down on the shorter rock in front, facing where Pasha stood chanting, her steady voice repeating in Arabic, "You are being prepared for your master. No pleasure will you find in any other man." As soon as she was seated, the chanting stopped.

Mbarka looked up in wonder and dread at the women who stood above her. Something was about to happen, and she was the center of it. Though what it might be she could not possibly imagine.

Pasha turned and reverently placed a wooden box on top of a rock. Carefully, she began to remove her instruments.

Mbarka didn't notice the signal. Pasha gave a barely perceptible nod of her head, and the two women who stood on either side of Mbarka reached down and grabbed her arms, then clamped their knees tight around her shoulders. It happened so quickly Mbarka had no time to respond. She tried to struggle, but her whole upper body was completely immobilized, her shoulders in vice grips between the women's knees, her arms held rigid. Then the women began to lean the top of her body backward onto the taller rock behind her, leaving her buttocks on the rock in front. As they did, the two olive-skinned women clasped the sarong wrapped around Mbarka's body and yanked it away to expose naked hips and legs. They grabbed her legs and pulled them open as if she were about to give birth. Then each of the women took hold of one of Mbarka's legs and wrapped her arms around it to keep it still. Spread-eagled by the four women, Mbarka was completely powerless; she could move nothing but her head, her fingers and toes. Now Pasha could perform the ceremony of induction into Islamic womanhood.

For generations, the clitorectomy had been a culturally accepted rite of passage among the Arabs in Africa. Millions of young women had undergone the bloody procedure, performed to keep a woman from being unfaithful to her husband by removing her source of sexual pleasure. It was required of every woman before she could become the wife of a Muslim man. In fact, many Muslim men would refuse to have sex with any woman who had not had a clitorectormy, so prostitutes in brothels suffered the same fate as proper Muslim women.

Mbarka's eyes darted from one woman to the next in growing panic. They were going to do something to her, something so terrible they had to hold her down to do it. Little whimpering sounds of terror escaped as she struggled uselessly.

Mbwena, the Nuer cook, knelt between Mbarka's legs, and suddenly the girl felt hands touching her where no woman ever had.

She gasped and looked up at Pasha. When she saw what the woman held in her hand, she screamed, shrieked with such force the exploding air seared her vocal chords.

The three-inch blade sparkled in the morning sun, honed to razor sharp precision. Its handle of polished gray stone fit snugly in Pasha's palm. She had held it there many times before.

The world froze as Pasha held the knife out in front of her and leaned forward. Mbarka would forever remember that under the thin, black veil, Pasha was smiling.

Wailing, shrieking and crying all at one time, the girl struggled to shrink back from the knife that moved relentlessly toward her. She shook her head frantically no, she begged, pleaded—*Oh, don't, please don't!* before the world exploded in the most excruciating pain Mbarka had ever felt.

Mbarka was conscious for the first two of the four or five cuts it would take to remove forever the most sensitive organ of her body. Then she passed out.

She would have been far better off if she had remained unconscious. But she didn't. When she came back up to the surface out of the darkness, Mbarka kept her eyes squeezed tightly shut. She could taste salty tears and heard herself sobbing hysterically. The iron hands still pinned her to the stone. Searing pain beyond description radiated from between her legs. It ran along nerves she didn't know existed and sent her entire lower torso into writhing spasms of agony. A warm pool of blood was forming beneath her.

Slowly, she opened her eyes. Pasha had waited until she was awake. She smiled again, leaned over and sliced into Mbarka's body again. The pain hit her like a bolt of lightening, worse than the first time. She shrieked an agonizing wail and passed out again.

Akin, Shontal and Omina stopped breathing when they heard Mbarka shriek and scream. Their eyes were huge, their hearts hammered in their throats. What were they doing to Mbarka? Whatever it was, it was more heinous than what had happened to her the first night in Sulleyman's tent. Her screams that night had been horrible; her screams now were unbearable. Each girl thought the same two thoughts: What are they doing to Mbarka? Will they do the same thing to me?

Chapter 13

The morning after their jeep had been stolen, Ron was in a foul mood, but shortly before noon, Masapha crashed his pity party.

"The boy is awake and he is talking!" he said.

Inside the clinic, Dr. Greinschaft stood by the bed where the teenager lay. The boy didn't appear frightened, but it was evident he was confused. As Ron and Masapha came into the room, the boy was trying to communicate, but the doctor could not understand.

"I do not know this tribal language," the doctor said.

"It's Lokuta," said Masapha, as he crossed the concrete floor to the foot of the bed.

Greinschaft peered at the little man over his wire-rimmed spectacles. "You speak it?"

"I can understand it better than I can say its words. But from most of the words, I believe I can know what he is saying and at least tell him the place where he is."

With the aid of facial expressions and some creative hand gestures to boost his struggling Lokuta, Masapha gave the boy a brief description of finding him beside the road and bringing him to the medical facility.

The boy launched into an instant stream of questions, laced with bits and pieces of his own story, all spewed out as fast as bullets from an AK 47. The boy already had demonstrated that he was remarkably resilient; it was quickly becoming evident he was as bright as he was strong.

"Ask him to stop for a moment, Masapha," Dr. Greinschaft said. "And tell us what he said."

Masapha interjected three words and held up his hand. The boy stopped in mid-unintelligible-sentence and was quiet.

"His name is Koto Manut," Masapha said. "He is from Nokot, a very small village in a valley in the Imatong Mountains."

"Imatong Mountains?" The doctor sputtered. "That's on the Kenya border! How did he get *here*?"

"Soldiers attacked his village, and many were the people they killed and the captives they took away. He was marched with other captives for many days, to a place where there would come people to buy them."

Masapha suddenly stopped and looked at Ron. "I wonder... "

He turned and asked the boy a few more questions. When he finished, he looked back at Ron and smiled broadly.

"It is so I thought!" Masapha said. "The how Koto got shot was from the slave traders. It happened when he escaped to freedom from the slave sale and hid in thorn bushes where the soldiers would not go."

Ron suddenly realized what Masapha was suggesting.

"This can't be the kid who got shot and just kept going!" At the auction, Ron hadn't looked closely at the boy's face through his view finder; it had all happened so fast. "Those gunmen fired hundreds of rounds into the bushes that kid dived into. Nobody could have survived."

"On the other side of the bushes next to the wall of the rock outcrop, there was a long stone, leaning there. Koto crawled behind it, like into a cave, and no bullets came there to hit him."

The small Arab turned to the doctor. "When we were taking the photographs and video of the slave auction, this boy was making an escape from it. He ran, and we were taking his picture when the bullet hit him and knocked him flying, and he hit the ground and rolled over to be up running again."

Masapha looked at the boy in admiration. "This is a sturdy boy!"

"*Tough* boy," Ron corrected.

"He is indeed tough and sturdy," Greinschaft said, then gestured toward the door. "But he needs rest."

They left the clinic and Ron turned to the doctor with a resigned sigh. "Without a jeep, the only way for us to get to Khartoum is by steamer," he said. "Words cannot describe how thrilled I'll be to climb back aboard one of those floating dung heaps."

The doctor laughed. "The steamer's schedule is unpredictable. Sometimes it comes; sometimes it doesn't. But you are velcome to wait for it here. Helena and I vould be glad for the company."

"Many are the times you have wanted to talk to a run-away slave," Masapha pointed out. "Inside that room is a run-away slave to be telling you his life."

"Yeah, you're right. It might make a good little story."

* * * * *

For three days, the girls endured the heat of the desert sun under their tarpaulin, helping Mbarka swat away the flies attracted to the dried blood on her lower body. Every morning, one of the servants brought out a single bowl of dura for the whole group to share. With each trip, she also brought a small dish of foul-smelling black goo, the consistency of well-cooked oatmeal, for Mbarka to put on her incisions. When Mbarka refused to do it the first time, the woman returned with two other women and the three of them held her down and forcibly smeared it on her. After that, Mbarka complied, to avoid further humiliation. Thankfully, the mixture provided some measure of relief. The stench from the goo, potent and rank, was heightened by the heat under the tarp. At least it masked the smell of the latrines and helped keep the flies away.

Mbarka was still in excruciating pain. Every night, the girls suffered through the dark hours with her, awakened by her moans, groans and bouts of uncontrollable sobbing. They couldn't help her; she wouldn't let them touch her. So each passed the scorching days and cold nights imprisoned by her own fears.

At breakfast on the third day, Mbarka was able to move around a little. She sat by the bowl of dura with the others and dug her hand with them into the communal dish of tasteless gruel. They all looked at her, their eyes asking questions their lips dared not form and waited for whatever explanation she chose to give about what the Arabs had done to her.

Mbarka ate in silence, weighed what she would and wouldn't tell the other girls, and finally resigned herself to the reality that the same fate was likely awaiting all of them, too. They had a right to know what was coming.

"They took me to the riverbank, to the flat rocks where Pasha sits when we wash clothes in the river," she began.

And she told them everything. How the women had grabbed her and pinned her down so she couldn't move. How they had ripped her clothes off. How Pasha had come at her with the shiny knife—smiling, always smiling.

"She cut off...she took away my... " Mbarka couldn't continue.

She didn't know the word for that part of her anatomy. Finally, she simply pulled up her dress and showed them her wounds.

"Here," she said, deeply shamed and humiliated. "She cut me here. See! She cut out... took... "

Mbarka burst out sobbing, surprised that she still had tears left to cry. Barely able to speak, her words came out in strangled gasps. "I have dreamed about going home. About getting away from these evil people. About having a *life* again."

The full horror of reality sank in again with sickening finality and she stopped crying. Her voice was as hollow and dead as the look in her eyes. "But now I can't. I can never have a life. I can never marry any man. I'm not a woman anymore."

Mbarka turned away and lay down on her side with her back to the other girls, who sat frozen where they were in horror and terror and disbelief. Though there was dura left in the bowl, none of the starving girls wanted any more. Shontal was the first to move. She suddenly scrambled over to the outer edge of the tent and tried to vomit, but nothing came. Then she collapsed on the ground, panting. She didn't even rise when the gagging began again, just lay there heaving violently long after what little she had eaten was splattered on the ground in front of her.

Omina's face looked like somebody had slapped her. Her eyes were huge. She looked around frantically for a few seconds, as if she could find someplace to hide. Then she curled up in a fetal position beside Mbarka.

Akin looked at the other girls, from one to the other. They all had their backs turned to her, all imprisoned in their own torture chambers of horror and fear. She was so scared she thought for a moment that she, too, was going to be sick. But the nausea passed. She bowed her head and began to cry softly, making little mewing sounds like a baby animal separated from its mother.

For the rest of the day, each girl gravitated to a different corner of the shelter, each sought as much isolation as possible to nurse her grieved soul, to be alone with her thoughts.

Late in the afternoon, Omina broke the silence.

"Look." She pointed to a rising cloud of dust on the horizon. "They're coming back."

Soon, the girls could hear and feel the pounding of the galloping camels' hooves. The reprieve was over. The men had returned from their trip to Kosti, a city on the White Nile River an hour and a half by jeep, three by camel, from the camp. They had gone there to purchase supplies and for a few days' recreation. With their return would come the return of work. Carrying wood, water, cleaning, washing clothes. Jobs fit for slaves.

That night after the men had their dinner, two soldiers came to the shelter, untied Shontal, and led her away into the darkness.

Mbarka was off limits; Shontal was all they had. The other girls saw her ushered to a tent close to where the horses and camels were tethered. When the soldiers raised the tent flap, light spilled out, and the girls could hear boisterous laughter and the voices of the men inside. There were many voices. The soldiers shoved Shontal in front of them, and the tent gobbled her up, the flap closed and there was only darkness.

The next morning, Pasha took the four slave girls to a tent full of sweat-soaked garments. The accumulated dirty laundry and musty saddle pads from the men's trip lay in piles on the tent floor. Pasha pointed at the heap, barked instructions and gestured outside; the four knew the rest of their day would be spent washing clothes in the river.

Pasha began parceling out the filthy laundry, handing each girl a huge stack. She filled 12-year-old Omina's outstretched arms with a pile of saddle blankets too heavy for a grown woman to carry. Omina staggered away, and Akin glanced at Shontal, who was next in line. Her glance hung there on the older girl, who stood ramrod straight waiting for her load of laundry.

Something was different. Shontal looked odd. In fact, Shontal had behaved strangely all morning. The moon already had risen high in the sky before the soldiers brought her back from her evening in the men's tent and shoved her under the tarp. When they left, she didn't crawl to the outside edge of the shelter where there was a little grass to sleep on. She didn't move at all. She sat where she landed, staring out into the darkness.

And now that she thought about it, Shontal had been sitting in the same spot when the morning sun in her eyes woke Akin hours later. Had Shontal been sitting there all night?

There was a trance-like quality to the girl's slow, deliberate movements when she stepped up to receive her share of the load. Pasha was too busy piling clothes and blankets into her arms to notice. When a small black turban fell from Shontal's stack of clothes to the floor, Pasha pointed to it and kept stacking. The stare on

Shontal's face never changed; she didn't move. Pasha paused, gave a sharp command, and nodded her head at the fallen turban. Nothing. Pasha's temper flared. She drew back and slapped Shontal hard in the face, her fat hand striking the girl's cheek and glancing off her nose. Shontal's head snapped back, and life returned to her eyes. This time, when Pasha pointed to the turban, Shontal balanced the rest of the pile of laundry in one arm, leaned over and picked it up. Then she stood waiting for Pasha to load the other two girls like pack animals, too.

Once loaded, the overburdened caravan of slaves set out for the river behind Pasha. Akin stepped past the two older girls and hoped to partially shield them from Pasha's view. Mbarka grimaced with every step, barely able to keep up with the others. The weight of the mound of clothes in her arms put added strain on her tortured body; every movement tugged and pulled at her still-raw wounds.

But Akin could see in Shontal's countenance a different kind of pain than the one that kept Mbarka bent and moaning. Her facial features were totally immobile, frozen in a vacant stare. She moved like the walking dead, totally oblivious to her surroundings. Akin wanted to say something to her, but what was there to say?

Each girl dropped her pile of laundry on the rocks, then took turns at the bucket of camel fat that served as their soap, digging their fingers in deep and scooping out double handfuls. Akin stepped into the ankle-deep water and started on the first saddle blanket on her pile. She smeared on soap and scrubbed the two sides of the blanket together. Alternately scrubbing it and beating it on the rocks to loosen the dirt, she slowly cleaned away the grime, then rinsed the blanket in the water that flowed over her feet.

Pasha paced back and forth along the water's edge, leather crop positioned comfortably behind her back. She carefully inspected each girl's work as she passed.

Akin glanced over her right shoulder at Shontal, who had taken up the last position at the water's edge. She still moved slowly, like she was walking in her sleep.

When Pasha reached Shontal, the slave girl was scrubbing her wash with the feeblest possible range of motion. Pasha yelled at her and raised her crop. Akin returned to her work, certain Shontal would begin scrubbing furiously—and she had better do the same! Every girl knew the pain of Pasha's rage. The throbbing welts from her camel crop stayed raw for days.

But Shontal did not scrub any faster. She merely raised up and dropped the camel blanket in the water, didn't even lay it on a rock to dry. Then she slowly reached down for another blanket to clean, even though the first one wasn't done yet.

Pasha's face contorted in rage. The other girls heard her furious scream and then the sickening "Whap!" of the crop as it whacked down on Shontal's back. They cringed involuntarily at the cry of pain that would follow. But there was only silence.

Again, Pasha shrieked at her, and again she lashed the girl's back with the crop. The expected cry of anguish never came. Akin looked up from her own work, reluctant to witness her friend's beating. Shontal's blank expression remained unchanged, even after two brutal blows. Akin watched, sickened, as Pasha screamed at Shontal and raised the crop again. This time, she brought it down with the full force of her considerable strength. Whap! Akin winced; Shontal did not respond at all. Although the wounds on her back and shoulders were now streaming blood down her back, she remained bowed over the rock, mechanically scrubbing the blanket in a slow, circular pattern.

Pasha was flabbergasted. She was so enraged it took every ounce of self-control she possessed not to beat the girl to death right there on the spot! She yearned to flail away at the dumb slave, ached to hit her again and again and again until her back was a river of blood and mangled, torn flesh, until she was totally broken, begging for mercy, pleading for her life—and she would have, too... but the girl was her master's property. She could not damage her master's property.

Afraid if she stayed there she'd lose her temper and kill the stupid, lazy slave, she turned her back on Shontal and marched back toward Mbarka, at work on the other end of the line. She needed to calm down and think. She needed to consider a fit punishment for the girl's insolence. She would make her sorry. Oh yes, indeed, she would make that girl rue the day she dared to disobey Pasha Drulois. She would find a way to hurt her, to cause her pain she never dreamed existed—without decreasing her value, of course. She just needed some time to figure out how to do that.

Akin went back to work on the stack of clothes beside her. She scrubbed feverishly to avoid a confrontation with a headmistress already pushed all the way over the edge.

As she worked, she caught a glimpse now and then of the crocodiles that kept vigil 70 yards from shore. Akin studied the eyes of the two closest, floating motionless in the water and tried to determine which of the girls they were watching. The eyes, unblinking and glass-like, were impossible to read. But the stares made Akin's skin crawl.

Two other huge crocs swam behind the two motionless observers, back and forth, like pacing lions, each one more than 10 feet long. She hadn't needed Pasha's constant warnings. She had sense enough to go no farther than ankle deep in the water by the rocks—close enough to shore to scramble away before one of the beasts had a chance to strike.

Akin pulled her eyes away from the stalking predators and concentrated on the blanket she had to clean. As she usually did when she worked in the river, she began to lose herself in her thoughts. The coolness of the water around her ankles soothed the sand flea bites, and soon the harsh reality of Pasha Drulois and the camp began to fade away. She established a rhythm; the work flowed smoothly. She released her mind, set it free and allowed her thoughts to follow the path of the river to her village…

Suddenly, she caught a movement out of the corner of her eye. She straightened up and saw that it was Shontal. The blanket she had been cleaning lay on top of the washing rock, the water lapping at its edges. With the fresh wounds from Pasha's beating sending streams of blood down her back, Shontal stood knee deep in the water, motionless, gazing out into the river at the crocodiles.

Akin stole a quick look at Pasha, who was beside Mbarka, her back turned toward the other girls.

"Shontal!" she hissed, loud enough for her friend to hear, but not loud enough to alert the headmistress. "Look where you are! You're too far out. Get back here!"

The older girl did not respond, except to take another step deeper into the water. The crocodiles began to edge toward her.

Akin's heart leapt into her throat. She looked at the predators—it was clear which girl they were watching now—and half-screamed, half-pleaded with her friend, her voice still low. "Shontal! Come *back!*"

When the girl's response was to move further out into the river, Akin began to shriek. "Shontal! No, don't! Shontal!"

Her scream roused Pasha and the armed guard as well. Both whirled around immediately.

Pasha strode angrily toward the spot where Shontal had left the river's edge, and yelled commands at her.

Now waist deep in the water, Shontal moved slowly out, step by step.

The other two girls dropped their laundry and began to scream at her, too. "Shontal! Come back! Don't! Come back, come back!"

Shontal didn't hear them. Or if she did, it didn't matter. Nothing mattered anymore. The final mooring binding her fragile spirit to sanity had been torn loose yesterday by Mbarka's horror story of mutilation. And it had been ripped completely away last night when she was gang raped by so many men she couldn't count them. She had passed a point of no return, gone beyond redemption, her soul shattered beyond repair.

Now she yearned for peace, only peace, for a place where no one could hurt her anymore, where she was free from the brutality and debasement of stinking, drunk men who... A place where she was no longer hungry or cold. A place where it was dark and quiet and she could rest. She ached for oblivion. In her tormented mind, death in the jaws of crocodiles was better than life as a slave.

Akin frantically slapped the water with a blanket to distract the huge beasts that now swam purposefully toward Shontal. She was yelling at her friend and crying hysterically at the same time. Omina and Mbarka were screaming, too, sobbing. All of them watched helplessly as Shontal walked out into the water to meet her doom.

By the time the guard realized what was happening and grabbed his rifle, Shontal was up to her armpits in the slowly swirling river. The crocodiles had moved in so close to the girl that Shontal was between him and his targets. He couldn't shoot them without hitting her. He ran down the bank to get a different angle for a shot. But it was too late.

Shontal was almost neck deep in the water when the nearest crocodile sank slowly below the river's surface and a powerful surge of water moved toward her. Suddenly, the huge beast bit down on her legs with his massive jaws and yanked her down into the brackish water. But she quickly surfaced again with an awful gasp, shocked back into reality. That's when the second crocodile lunged at her, mouth open, and clamped his huge jaws on her torso. She let out a small cry as its teeth ripped into her chest, a scream cut off after only a moment, and then the 10-foot monster pulled her under.

Within seconds, the spot where Shontal had been became a mass of churning, bubbling water as the other crocodiles moved in for a piece of the kill. The boiling water turned crimson as the churning continued. It seemed to go on for a long, long time. Finally, the surface began to smooth out, the dissipating crimson grave marker washed away downstream, the river was quiet again.

Shontal was gone.

Even the battle-scarred guard was visibly shaken by the attack. He ignored the remaining girls and the headmistress, turned and stalked away.

Pasha stood for only a moment immobilized, staring at the spot where there was now no trace of the slave. Then she grabbed her skirt with one hand and waded over to Shontal's pile of blankets. She picked up the dripping laundry and plopped pieces from the pile down by each of the other girls.

Under her breath, she swore at the stupidity of these lazy, black animals. And she berated herself for her lack of attention. She knew she would pay dearly for it; the price of the slave would be taken out of her hide.

For a moment, Akin continued to stare at the dark water where Shontal had disappeared. Surprisingly, no tears came. Then Pasha screamed a command at her and she tore her gaze away. She reached down, picked up a filthy saddle blanket, smeared camel fat on it and began to scrub.

Chapter 14

Omar's foot swelled bigger with every heartbeat.

Idris stood frozen for a moment, then reached over the big man, yanked Omar's knife out of the scabbard beside his rifle and began to slash the balanite tree with the razor edge of the blade. He hacked deep gouges into the trunk—whap! whap! whap!—and pried off the loose pieces of bark with his fingers.

Omar sat quiet in the dirt, tenderly cradling his throbbing foot in both hands.

Once he had cleared a spot on the trunk of bark, Idris stabbed the knife point into the bare wood again and again, and had just managed to gouge a hole deep enough to draw out pulp and sap when Omar started to gasp for breath.

Idris shoved the bitter wood pulp into his mouth, chewing frantically, softening it as best he could without his front four bottom teeth. Water would have helped, but he didn't have time to run back to where he had dropped the containers. As he chewed, he scanned the ground beneath the tree, searching for a piece of fruit. He spotted one wedged between the tree and a large rock next to the trunk, dug it out and sliced it open. Inside the fleshy exterior lay a hard inner shell. He put the shell on the rock and hit it hard with the razor edge of the knife. When it split open, Idris scooped up the two halves before the oil inside could ooze out. He spit the wood pulp out of his mouth into his palm and mixed it with the oil from the piece of fruit. He didn't know if a balanite poultice would help, but he couldn't stand by and not try.

By the time Idris knelt beside Omar with a handful of sticky goo, the mercenary's calf had swollen so large Idris could barely fit the blade of the knife between the man's skin and the fabric to slit open his trousers so the leg could continue to expand. Omar didn't seem to be aware of Idris at all; he just sat in the dirt with his foot in his hands, each breath more ragged and labored than the next. Though he was awake, he didn't appear to be really conscious. His eyes moved as if he were looking at something Idris couldn't see.

What Omar saw that Idris didn't was the straw ceiling and mud wall of a hut. He was looking at the world through the eyes of someone very short because when the old black man came into the hut and stood in front of him, his eyes were level with the tribal's bony chest. The man reached out his gnarled hand and put it tenderly on Omar's shoulder.

"Come, tenyatta. Help me gather firewood in the forest," the old man said.

But the scene was oddly transparent. Omar could see it, but he also could see through it. He could see the morning sunshine and the tribal Idris kneeling beside him, and his own foot, huge and distorted.

Slowly, the village scene began to melt. Walking beside the old man under the trees, the birds singing—the images blurred together like a freshly painted picture splashed with water, until there was only a mass of random shapes and colors. Then the light in the scene began to dim, and as it did, the light in the world he could see through the transparency of the image slowly went out, too, until there was nothing in front of his eyes but darkness.

As Idris prepared to place the poultice on his foot, Omar suddenly went limp, fell backward in the dirt and lay there gasping. Idris grabbed him under the arms and dragged him to the base of the tree. The stone he had used when he cut open the balanite fruit was about three feet tall and flat on the top. Using the smaller stones around it as stair steps, Idris hauled the unconscious mercenary up onto the flat-topped stone in a sitting position. His back rested against the tree trunk and his legs hung over the edge of the rock.

Idris wanted Omar upright so he could breathe and so the scorpion bites would be lower than the rest of his body.

Once he had Omar propped in place, Idris knelt in front of him and applied the poultice to the bottom of his foot. The sole had turned completely black, with two lumps the size of plovers' eggs on the heel.

There were times throughout the rest of that sweltering day that Idris thought Omar would stop breathing altogether. Every breath was a gasping effort; he feared each one would be the big man's last. He applied the poultice to Omar's foot until noon, then made another one, this time using water to soften it—mostly because it made him feel like he was doing something other than just watching the man die.

Idris didn't know that the oil from the seed of a balanite tree, called the heglig tree by the Arabs, was rich in steroidal sapogenins—naturally occurring steroids. If Omar had been taken to a hospital emergency room, doctors there would have treated the scorpion bites with steroids.

Throughout the afternoon, Idris sat by Omar's side. He tore off a piece of cloth from Omar's pants leg and used it to hold the poultice on the bottom of the mercenary's foot, and replaced the poultice with a fresh one every couple of hours. It was desperately hot, and Idris considered trying to give Omar something to drink, but feared he couldn't swallow and would choke.

Toward evening, Omar's breathing improved some, so Idris left him alone for a little while to gather firewood. He sat up with the mercenary through the night, tended the fire and applied fresh balanite tree poultices. Shortly after noon the next day, Omar opened his eyes and looked around. Idris wasn't sure he was completely conscious, but he was responsive enough for Idris to give him a drink of water.

For the rest of the day, Omar drifted in and out of consciousness. By nightfall, an awareness came into his eyes. He was there, confused, but there. Idris tried to give him another drink, and the big man reached up weakly, snatched the water bottle out of the tribal's hands and drank it by himself. Omar was back.

They remained camped under the balanite tree for two more days, while Omar suffered the agony of putting weight on his right foot and regaining mobility. Idris went out with his spear every day and came back with small game—quail, partridge, guinea fowl and hares—that he cooked over the fire at night. He could have killed an antelope instead, but he didn't want to draw scavengers to the smell of blood.

As Omar watched Idris work, he was both angry and baffled. Any loss of control triggered rage, and Omar certainly hadn't been in charge of anything for the last few days. Idris had provided food, fire, water, even protection. And the vague, uncomfortable memories of the tribal taking care of him set his teeth on edge. But he was confused, too. If Idris had been stung, Omar would have left him there to die. Certainly, Idris needed Omar to find his daughter, but the tribal could have taken the money and hired somebody else to do the job. Why didn't he?

Omar was in turmoil on another front as well. After they broke camp and headed west again, the big man limped along, leaning on an acacia limb he had whittled into a crutch. They hadn't traveled more than a couple of miles before he began to have flashbacks. It was like he was looking at a series of still photos, but so vivid that the real world around him, the hot dirt under the tender sole of his bare foot, the sweat trickling down between his shoulder blades, the tall Dinka, striding along beside him—all of that was gone. The picture was reality. For a heartbeat or two, then the world came back into focus.

The venom-induced delirium was over, but the images from it

hadn't faded away like the smoke from a dying campfire. They had hung on a nail somewhere in his head. He knew where the hut was. He knew who the old man was who wanted the boy to go with him to gather firewood.

As he limped along, Omar remembered.

When his mother escaped from her Mauritanian master, she took her 6-year-old son and went home. She'd been kidnapped when she was 9 years old and had only the vaguest memories of any other world. But she had traveled the whole length of Sudan to the Imatong Mountains on the border of Kenya to find her family and her life. The hut in the snapshots was his mother's home; the old man was his grandfather. The hallucination had pulled the scab off his memories, and for the first time in more than 35 years, Omar recalled the day he'd found his mother sitting by herself on the riverbank, sobbing. He'd run and put his arms around her and tried to comfort her, but nothing he said or did made any difference. She cried until she was limp, too weak to cry anymore. When she spoke, her voice was a despairing whisper.

"You must gather all your things together," she'd said. "We are leaving in the morning."

"Leaving?" the boy had cried. "No, I want to stay here!"

Life in Mauritania had been a brutal, terrifying nightmare, and the village in the mountains was better than any little boy's fantasy. He loved the damp, tangled undergrowth in the forest, the cry of the birds and the monkeys in the trees. He loved fishing in the river, the smell of the campfire, and the feel of rough, gnarled fingers wrapped snug around his small hand. He was the old man's beloved "tenyatta"—grandson. He didn't want to leave!

But even as he cried out in protest, some part of Omar knew. He had seen how the other women in the village treated his mother; he had suffered the taunts of the village children, who called him names he didn't understand. Some part of him had expected this.

"I can't stay here," his mother said. "I don't belong."

"But this is your home, our home."

"No, it isn't my home. Not anymore. Once, when I was a little girl, before... " Her voice trailed off. Then she looked into her son's eyes and saw the pain there, and tried again to make him understand. "The little girl an Arab raider snatched out of her dying mother's arms is gone. She doesn't live in me. She's dead. *They...*" she spit the word out in disgust, and Omar knew who she meant, "They used her, fouled her and killed her! And the woman I am now... " she struggled for words again. "Who I am is a disgraceful thing."

She pulled her son into her arms and began to cry softly. "And you, even your grandfather cannot make the rest of the village accept you."

At the thought of her father, she burst into tears and rocked back and forth with Omar held tight to her chest. Though her crying garbled what she said to him then, the little boy understood every word.

"It would be better for my father, better for me and you—all of us," she cried, between hitching, halting sobs, "if I had died with my mother and sister in the raid on our village."

Omar and his mother had left the next morning and he never saw the village or his grandfather again. They finally settled in Port Sudan, where his mother spent a decade as a prostitute, using what she earned to feed her son and to feed her growing addiction to the narcotic quat. Eventually, the addiction cost more than the boy. Omar came home one day when he was 16 and found her dead.

The memory of how she had looked, sprawled in a pool of her own vomit on the floor of their filthy, one-room shack, vanished in a cry of pain when Omar's bare foot landed on a thorn that buried itself deep in his flesh. He fell to the ground in a heap and lay facedown in the dirt for a moment, wounded more by the memories than the thorn, grateful to be back in the real world, even if it hurt. Then he rolled over, sat up and began to dig the thorn out of the sole of his foot. He waved away Idris' efforts to help him, staggered to his feet, picked up his crutch and set out walking again.

It took the two men five days to cross the remainder of the plains, and as they walked, the ghost images in Omar's mind mercifully faded away. They came upon another herd of antelope but managed to make their way around rather than through it. They disturbed a family of warthogs in the bush, saw giraffe in the distance and heard the trumpeting of elephants. And for one long afternoon, they could hear the roar of lions. Idris led that day's trek, bearing west but circling downwind of the sound.

They came out on the north-south road at noon, only a few miles south of the track that led from it to Jonglei. At sunset, Omar hoisted a beer in a dark, smoky bar, and questioned an old friend about slave traders.

* * * * *

Koto's shoulder was still puffy and swollen, but it had started to heal. Antibiotics and a steady stream of intravenous nutrients had done a remarkable job, aided by Helena Greinschaft's African-flavored home-cooking. Dr. Greinschaft's surgical repair of the trapezoid muscle in the boy's shoulder had been successful. The arm had a limited range of motion now, and with time, it would get better. But the wound and the chipped clavicle beneath it created a deep indentation on the top of his shoulder that the boy would carry for life.

He sat propped up in the bed on pillows, a new, cushy experience Koto had decided he enjoyed. But it was obvious Koto's shoulder still hurt badly. It was equally obvious that he wanted nothing in the world more than to tell the people gathered around his bedside what had happened to him, to his family, his village and to the other captives kidnapped by the slave traders.

Ron and Dr. Greinschaft sat on the empty bed on the left side of the boy. Masapha sat on the edge of Koto's bed. The boy smiled at the little Arab not much bigger than himself. He had instantly bonded with the only person in the room he could talk to. The bond went both ways.

Masapha had set up the recording equipment to make an audio tape of the boy's story. The microphone lay on the pillow beside the boy's head; the recorder sat on the bed beside Ron.

"I'm going to ask the boy to begin at the start and from there go to the finish of the story," Masapha said. "Already, I have heard part of it."

The Arab had taken a couple of shifts sitting at the boy's bedside, and they had talked long into the night. It was plain to see that his affection for the boy had grown along with his command of the Lokuta language. It was nothing short of astonishing how quickly Masapha had become fluent in the dialect.

"But all of you need to hear the whole of it." He pointed to the recorder and told Ron. "What you must do is punch the button—here—where it says 'on.'"

"Tough job, but I think I can handle it."

Masapha turned his attention back to the boy, patted his arm and said to him in Lokuta, "Now it is time for you to tell us all of it, the whole story." He paused, then continued, "even the parts it is hard to say. Yes?"

The boy nodded and began to speak.

Even though none of them, other than Masapha, knew what the boy was saying, they were mesmerized by the tale and held spellbound by the boy's intensity as he told it. As he relived the horror, the others watched the drama play out on his face.

This time, the men allowed Masapha to proceed for long periods without interruption. Finally, the boy began to slow down. His words came haltingly and his voice began to choke with emotion.

Masapha stopped him, patted his leg and turned to the others.

He let out a sigh and cocked his head toward Koto.

"The boy needs to have some breath," Masapha said.

"Needs a *breather*?" Ron asked.

"Yes, that, too," Masapha said. "And, actually, I do as well. This is the story of the happenings in his life. Koto was up early to take the family's zebu to eat grass in the pasture. He was on his way back when he saw two silver *things* in the sky. He didn't know what they were, but they were flying faster than an arrow shot from a bow, right to his village. He said they made a sound like rumbling thunder." Masapha looked at Ron. "Gun-ships, you think?"

Ron nodded. "I'm thinking Antonov fighters, maybe. From what I understand, that's the government in Khartoum's weapon of choice to annihilate its own people."

Masapha took up the story again.

"He stood in the field, and the airplanes flew low over the village and suddenly there were explosions, making big holes in the ground, blowing zebu apart; huts turning to fire. In two minutes, the world of his life was gone."

"And he had a box seat," Ron shook his head in anger and disgust. "Got to watch his whole village go up in smoke."

"With his family in it," Masapha added.

"His family... " Ron groaned. "OK, tell me about them," he said, and scratched notes furiously on the pad in his lap.

"His mother's name was Dada." He turned to the boy. "Dada?"

The boy nodded and Masapha turned back to Ron. "Dada Manut and her husband, John. He had a baby sister named Reisha, and two little brothers, twins, 8 years old, Isak and Kuak, so much the same face it is hard to tell them from each other—except for the butterfly mark here," Masapha pointed to the top of his right hand, "on Isak's hand."

When Ron was sure he had the names down right, he nodded his head and Masapha continued.

"Also there was a grandfather, uncles, aunts and cousins, too."
Ron noted it.

"So he was standing in the pasture, with his village flaming into the sky, and he didn't know what to do. And then he remembered his father, his grandfather and his mother's brothers were working in the millet field, so he went in search for them." Masapha bowed his head. "And he found them."

He continued in a quiet voice.

"He got to the edge of the field and crouched in the tall grass where he couldn't be seen. All the men who had been working there—probably 40 or 50 of them—were running to the burning village. And Koto thought they had come to save his home. He saw his father in front—a big man, Koto said he was a very big man."

Masapha stopped and smiled just a little. "Of course, Koto is a runt, as am I a runt, so I don't know how big that would make his father."

The smile faded. "For just one moment, Koto was proud in his heart that his father was coming to fight the soldiers, and then he saw the real reason the men were running. Soldiers in jeeps were chasing them. And the soldiers had rifles, and they were shooting as they were driving behind the villagers, and the men with his father began to die."

Masapha paused, and each of the men became a 15-year-old boy, staring in disbelief at Arab soldiers and panicked farmers, listening to the crack of gunfire and the cries of the fallen.

"He watched his father be killed," Masapha said quietly. "He was one of the last ones to fall because he was big and strong and tall and could run fast—that's what Koto said. His father almost made it to the village."

Masapha described the convoy of trucks and jeeps full of soldiers in combat fatigues that roared into the village. Koto had frantically searched for his mother and his sister and brothers, but a soldier caught him, stuck his rifle barrel in Koto's face and gestured toward the trucks.

"He was pushed from behind to the center of the village where the soldiers were loading his people into trucks—the ones not dead, on the ground, bodies to step over. That is when he saw a soldier come from the road, dragging his little brothers. They cried and struggled hard to be away. Koto tried to go to them but a soldier hit him in the chest with his rifle butt and knocked him down. When he was back up to standing, his brothers were in the truck. The soldiers slammed shut the tailgate and drove away. He never saw them after that anymore again."

Masapha stopped and looked at the boy, who sat quietly listening to him talk.

"He was tied together with others of his village and marched down the road. That is the end of what he was saying. He was telling of that when he could not keep talking."

They had all seen the boy choke up, watched the tears spring into his eyes.

"Tell him he doesn't have to unpack the whole trunk right now," Ron said hurriedly. "There's no rush. If he wants to wait, we can come back later. "

"No," Masapha said. "I think he needs to take all the things out of the trunk at this one time. And then it is over."

Ron glanced questioningly at the doctor. The old man looked at the boy and reluctantly nodded. Masapha turned back to Koto and spoke a few words. The boy took a deep breath.

"We were tied up with thick ropes, each one to the next, in a line," he told Masapha. "And so I couldn't see far ahead. I was behind a large woman, and I couldn't see around her when they marched us down the road. That is why I didn't see them... until they were there, right there... "

His voice grew thick. He fought manfully to keep his lip from trembling as the image formed in his head. But he couldn't stop the tears. They streamed silently down his face.

"My mother was in the road. She had been shot... " He stopped. "Shot in the leg. I could see it as I walked to her. And then I saw they had shot her in the head, too."

He drew in a deep, shaky breath and continued. "Beside her on the ground, my baby sister, Reisha. I think. It had to be my baby sister, but I couldn't tell... "

And then the words came out in a rush of pain. "Because they had blown her apart!"

Masapha patted his leg and the boy stopped. His breathing hitched in his chest. But he wasn't crying. He had decided he was never going to cry again.

Koto watched the group's reaction as Masapha translated what he had said. He could see the shock, the revulsion and the sympathy on all the men's faces, even on the doctor's and the tall American's. No, *especially* on the doctor's and the American's. And he decided that he had been right, the white men were good men. Just being light-skinned like the raiders didn't make them evil. They had helped him, sure. But seeing on their faces that what had happened to him sickened and saddened them, told him they could be trusted. He needed to know that.

The boy continued to talk and Masapha continued to turn his words into pictures that all the men could see. The soldiers had loaded some of the captives into trucks, and others, like Koto, were herded along on foot for days. The forced march was brutal, he said—the captives were beaten and starved, babies were thrown into the bush, children who couldn't keep up were left to die.

He described his brief stay at the slave auction, how he untied a rope and got free, but he was understandably vague about exactly what happened after that. He and Masapha talked back and forth for a bit when he finished his story, but Masapha didn't translate the conversation for the others.

"Does he remember when we found him?" Ron wanted to know.

"I do not think so," Masapha said. "I am certain that if that was in his memory, he would have told me."

The doctor pointed out that often trauma victims had blank spots, amnesia about what had happened just before or right after they were injured.

"It is likely he remembers noting about what happened before he collapsed," Greinschaft said.

Ron exchanged a knowing glance with Masapha.

"Good," they said in unison.

The doctor got up off the bed slowly, painfully. He'd been in one spot for so long he was stiff. "So, we are done here, yes?"

"I think so," Ron said. "Looks like we're finished with Koto's story. "

"Actually, no, we are not," Masapha said.

The two men stopped and looked at the small man still seated on the side of the boy's bed. When he didn't say anything right away, Ron primed the pump.

"And that would be because... ?"

Masapha was uncharacteristically tongue-tied. "What the boy said is, Koto wants... ".

"Come on," Ron said. "Spit it out. What?"

"Koto wants to go with us," Masapha said bluntly.

Ron was taken totally off guard. "You want to run that by me again?"

"The boy said that when we leave to go to the north, he will accompany us. He wants to find his brothers."

Ron smiled. "I admire his courage, but you need to teach him about an American concept called 'looking for a needle in a haystack.'"

Masapha looked blank, then shook his head. "It will not be easy to talk him from this."

"Talk him *out of* this."

"Or that either," Masapha said, and Ron rolled his eyes. "You must understand, he has no one left but his brothers. There is no village for him to go back to. It has been burned on the ground."

Ron thought about telling him, burned *to* the ground, but decided to let it go.

"He understands what is a slave. He knows what waits for his brothers. He cannot leave them to that fate. Among the Lokuta, boys must hunt a lion before they are called a man. This will be Koto's lion."

"That's got a nice ring to it, but... " Ron stammered.

Masapha held up his hand. "He said that you are a white skin, but your heart is not full of worms and maggots like the raiders. He knows because he watched your face when he was telling his life. Your heart is pure. He says that your white skin will make them listen to you. They will not listen to him because his skin is black. They will just capture him again."

Before Ron had a chance to argue, the doctor ended the discussion. "You can talk about this another time. Right now ze boy needs rest. Visiting hours are over."

Ron hit the "off" button on the tape recorder, picked it up and they all filed out of the room.

● ● ● ● ●

Alonzo Washington walked slowly around Dan's office and studied the pictures on the walls. An oil portrait of the wife—curly red hair, good-looking woman. Individual studio pictures of the three kids. Even with no front teeth, the little strawberry-blonde girl was the image of her mother; the youngest had a mischievous gleam in his eye you could see even when he was posed in a coat and tie. Then blown-up snapshots—those were better. All three of the kids burying Dan in sand at the beach. The oldest at the free-throw line, concentrating hard. One of them, probably the youngest, as a toddler, his hands buried up to the wrists in a chocolate birthday cake.

Washington moved farther down the wall to a picture in an ornate silver frame—an older couple, distinguished man and a wispy-haired wife. The parents, probably, he could see the resemblance. And there were scenic shots, too, arresting, breathtaking black-and-white photos of shadows on sand dunes and a fireball sun on the horizon of some vast plain. The last picture, a portrait of a smiling, sun-tanned man who bore an uncanny likeness to Dan, only younger, thinner and blond. That must be the brother—the one stirring up so much trouble in Sudan.

"Alonzo!"

The congressman turned and extended his hand as the big man from Indiana strode into the room.

"Sorry to keep you waiting." Dan made a have-a-seat gesture toward a yellow-and-orange plaid couch. "Make yourself at home."

The couch and a matching chair had been Sherry's idea. She'd said his office needed brightening up. So she'd added a couple of touches of her own—lamps, two end tables and the furniture. Dan had hated it at first, but after he'd watched one visitor after another relax in the homey feel of the office, he'd concluded—yet again—that he had, indeed, married the right woman.

Washington sat down on the couch and let out a small sigh. Sherry had scored again.

Dan sat in the chair. "I hate watching you in the gym," he said.

Washington smiled.

"No, I'm serious. I hate it. You're out there running laps like a cheetah, and I'm on the basketball court with the old guys, huffing and puffing my way through a game of three-on-three."

"A cheetah? Maybe once. Now the only cat I look like when I run is Garfield. I'm getting old, man, slowing down."

Actually, the light-skinned African American was only 34. He appeared even younger than that, with chiseled good looks that had done him no damage as a television news anchor in Detroit, and yelled "charisma" on a campaign button.

"If you're slowing down, I'm a Chinese airplane pilot." Dan leaned back in the chair and stretched his long legs out in front of him. "Surely, you ran track at... ?"

"Michigan State."

"Oh," Dan groaned. "A Spartan, huh? I liked you a whole lot better before I knew that."

"And you would be?" As if he didn't know.

"A Boilermaker!"

"I'll try not to hold the sins of your youth against you."

"Big of you, Alonzo. I forgive you, too, and I won't tell a soul. Your secret's safe with me."

The two men talked Big Ten sports, past, present and future. Which team they liked for the NCAA Final Four, and how the upcoming match-up between MSU and Purdue was likely to turn out.

"I've got season tickets," Dan said. "And the next game's in West Lafayette. You want to go with me?"

Washington laughed. "A Spartan fan sitting smack in the middle of a herd of Boilermakers? I'd be about as popular as... " He stopped, then decided this was as good a time as any. "... as you are among my black colleagues right now."

Dan had figured that was why Washington had come to see him and was glad to have it out in the open.

"You got that right! What's up with that? I can't get anywhere near those guys. Do I smell bad?"

"I've never been downwind of you in the gym so I couldn't speak to the issue of your personal hygiene," Washington said. "But I can tell you that my friends of the African American persuasion are very uncomfortable with your Sudan crusade."

"How about you? Do you think I stink?"

Washington reached over to the end table and picked up a hand-carved wooden statue of a lizard with a bright orange head and tail. Ron had given it to Dan for Christmas, said lizards like that were to Africa what chipmunks were to Indiana. Sherry had liked it because the orange matched the couch.

"It's not about whether or not I think you stink. It's about whether or not I can afford to let your stink rub off on me."

"You still haven't answered my question." Dan looked the young lawmaker in the eye. "Do *you* think I stink?"

"I'm sure it's safe for me to assume that what's said in this room stays in this room."

Dan nodded.

Washington put the statue down, leaned forward with his elbows on his knees, his hands clasped between them. "OK, Readers Digest Condensed Version of my position: I think you're right, but if I say so right now I could get tarred and feathered."

"Who's heating up the tar and plucking the chicken?"

Washington sighed, stood up and walked to the window. Outside, the trees were swaying in the gentle morning breeze, casting dappled light through the leaves into the room.

"What you need is a birdfeeder right here." He pointed to the window ledge. "My wife put one outside my office window. Other people stare into fish tanks, I look at birds when I'm trying to get my thoughts straight."

Dan smiled. "When I want to relax and think, I play my guitar."

"Oh, I've heard about your guitar! Everybody on the Hill has heard the story of the fundraiser where you played *Johnny B. Goode*, holding your guitar behind your head!"

"Evidence of a misspent youth."

Both men were silent for a beat.

"I think what's going on in Sudan is abominable," Washington said quietly. "I started hearing about it years ago from my mother."

"Your mother." It was a statement, not a question.

"She belongs to a couple of Christian mission organizations, and she's been sending me copies of their mailings for going on three years now. Studies from Human Rights Watch and some other organization whose name escapes me right now."

Dan nodded. He knew all about Human Rights Watch and he could probably have named the Christian mission organizations, too.

"And I know what happened to the delegation of clergyman and NAACP members who went over there a few months ago," Washington continued. "I know they were wined and dined and given the scenic tour."

"I hear the feeding centers, the refugee camps and the slave auctions aren't very popular tour bus destinations," Dan said.

"But I don't know how much of that kind of information has made it into the hands of my fellow black legislators."

Dan started to protest, and Washington waved him off.

"Ok, I know the information has made it into their hands; I just don't know how much of it has made it into their heads or their hearts."

Washington paused for effect. "And I do know that the gum arabic and soft drink lobbies have turned up the heat hot enough to fry pork rinds."

Dan picked up the orange-headed lizard and turned it slowly around in his hand. "It would be hard to miss them galloping up and down these hallways. They make more noise than a herd of caribou." He dropped the bantering tone. "They've put a lot of money into a lot of political war chests, and they carry a big club with jobs in a lot of districts." He paused and set the statue back on the table. "And this is an election year."

"Look, I'm just a junior congressman from the tundra in the great frozen northland, and I still have trouble finding the executive washrooms around here." Washington was being humble. In fact, he was a rising star, acknowledged as a man with a bright future in Congress. "But I do bring one thing to the party. I'm your best connection to the Black Caucus."

Dan sat up in his seat. Backing by the Black Caucus on any issue, but particularly on one involving black slavery, would be huge.

"You're proposing?"

"I'm in good with Walters and a couple of the others, but that inner circle, whew, that's a tough nut to crack. There are a handful of men, you know who they are, who call all the shots. Most of the others are hesitant to vote against them for fear of looking like a traitor to the race."

Dan slapped his hand down on the arm rest, "Alonzo! We're talking about *helping* blacks!"

"I know that. Just hear me out." Washington crossed the room and sat down again on the couch across from Dan. "My big ace in the hole is that Avery Thompson is one of the big three and he's been sort of my mentor ever since I got here."

Dan was impressed. Washington's star must, indeed, be rising if he'd caught the eye of one of the most powerful men—black or white—in the House.

Washington leaned toward Dan and spoke slowly and deliberately. "I've thought about this long and hard, and there is only one way I can do you any good right now. And that's to arrange a meeting for you with Thompson and the others."

Dan felt like he had just been handed the pole position at the Indianapolis 500.

"You come in and do your dog-and-pony show, answer questions, that kind of thing... "

"That's all I've ever asked, Alonzo, a chance to give people the facts. Simple reality here is so compelling it doesn't need ribbons or wrapping paper."

"But I want to be straight with you about one thing up front." Washington's tone held none of Dan's exuberance.

"I always like to know what to expect."

"I can't afford to go down with you if this ship sinks, Dan. I'm telling you right now that whichever way the wind blows, I go. I'll introduce you, set you up. You'd better have all your ducks beak to tail feathers before you get there because once we're in that paneled room, you're on your own. If they support you, I'll support you. If they don't, I don't."

There was a long pause before Washington asked, "You in?"

Dan put out his hand and gave Alonzo's a firm shake. "I'm in."

⁕ ⁕ ⁕ ⁕ ⁕

Ron had wrapped the last roll of film in a pair of socks and was about to hide it deep in his knapsack when Dr. Greinschaft walked into the room.

"The radio message I sent out on the high frequency the other day got to Chumwe OK," he said.

Greinschaft's mission organization operated a feeding center in Chumwe, and he had offered to get in touch with associates there and ask them to help Ron and Masapha.

"I told them who you are and hinted at vhat you are doing in Sudan. They vill figure it out; they are smart people. I know they will serve you in any way they can. For sure, they will send zumbody to meet you at the dock in Kosti. And they will pass a message on to your BBC contact in Cairo, too."

"Now you're talking, Doc!" Ron was delighted.

"But ve've got a problem."

Ron stuffed the film into the bottom of his sack. "How so?"

"Come with me and see for yourself."

Masapha and Koto were sitting on the steps outside the clinic when Ron and Greinschaft approached.

"What's up, Masapha?" Ron asked.

Masapha pointed to the boy. "He says he is going with us."

When he saw Ron's response, he hurried on. "I have told him we go to the north to do another thing that is not about him, but he is certain anyway that we are going to help him."

"You need to tell him that wishin' don't make it so. That boat's actually going to be here today, and you and I have a lot of lost ground to cover!"

Ron was approaching an urgency-anxiety meltdown. The decision to wait at the clinic for the steamer had cost them almost a month. The first steamer had been 10 days late, then blew a boiler the morning they were set to depart. The second steamer never showed up at all. Dr. Greinschaft had confirmed by radio that the third would be at the dock in Lusong within the hour.

"We've been sitting on our thumbs here for way too long, and I'm not wasting any more time." Ron knew as soon as he said it that "thumbs" was not going to compute. "Look, just tell him no. Plain and simple. No."

Ron had taken only a couple of steps toward his stack of equipment when Masapha spoke. "Ron... "

Ron's shoulders slumped.

"Masapha, we can't go on a hunting expedition for this kid's brothers." He turned back to face the two small people—one Arab, one black—sitting on the porch. "I know you want to help him, and we did. Shoot, we saved his life! But we have a job to do now, and we've got to keep the main thing the main thing."

"You know what he will do if we do not take him with us," Masapha said. "He will do what you or I would do. He will go alone to find his brothers."

Ron could feel himself getting sucked into an argument that wasn't going anywhere. Why were they even talking about this? They couldn't possibly help this kid find two slaves among hundreds of thousands.

"How in the world do you expect us to... ?"

Masapha interrupted him; he had it all figured out.

"I would like to proposition you." Ron let it pass. "Your plan is that you are to go to Khartoum while I stay behind and ask more information, right?"

Ron nodded.

"We can help the boy only this much—we can take him with us to Kosti. I will stay there with Koto while you make the journey to Khartoum. When you return, you and I will take the boy to the place of the doctor's friend in Chumwe. He can stay there safe with the workers at the feeding center and we can be away to do our job!"

Masapha's plan had more holes in it than a wino's raincoat! That boy would not stay "safe" in Chumwe. If he was determined to find his brothers, nobody could stop him from looking. Besides, what the boy did or did not do was none of their business; he wasn't their problem anymore.

Ron was about to point all that out to Masapha when it suddenly hit him what was really going on. None of this made any sense because it didn't have to make any sense, at least not to Masapha. The truth still in the husk was simple: Masapha wasn't ready to give this kid up. Maybe he never would be—which opened up another huge can of worms!—but he certainly wasn't ready now. All the rest of it was smoke and mirrors.

Ron threw in the towel. "OK," he said.

"OK he can come with us?"

"Yes, OK he can come with us." Before Masapha had a chance to respond, Ron continued firmly. "But we need to have an understanding here. When I get back from Khartoum, you and I go bye bye and the boy stays in Chumwe. Are we on the same page about that?"

"Our pages are the same." Masapha beamed.

He turned to translate the verdict for Koto, but the boy had read their faces and said something to Masapha in Lokuta.

"Koto said to tell you that on your outside you are a white man, but," he tapped his chest, "on your inside, you are a Lokuta warrior."

"Swell. That'll be a real conversation-stopper around the operating table if I ever have my appendix out."

Masapha didn't understand and Ron didn't expect him to.

The steamer actually pulled in at the Lusong dock only three hours late. Ron picked up his assorted gear and the sack of food— including home-made bread!—that Helena Greinschaft had prepared for their trip.

"Doc, I don't know how to thank... "

"You tell your story, that will be tanks enough." The old man took Ron's hand and shook it firmly. "Helena and I vill pray every day that God keeps you safe."

"You do that!" Ron said.

And he meant it.

Chapter 15

The meeting room door was open. Inside, an assortment of House members and Senators milled around, talked and enjoyed their after-lunch coffee, served on a table by the window.

When Alonzo Washington spotted Dan, he smiled and crossed the room to greet him.

"Glad you could make it." He reached out and shook Dan's hand, then held on a beat after the handshake. "I look forward to what you have to say."

Dan's arrival served as a signal and the legislators began to take their seats around the long conference table in the center of the room. Dan's assistant, Chad Mattingly, went to the window and closed the heavy drapes, then quietly hooked his laptop to cables that came out of the wall.

At Rep. Washington's cue, Dan set down his briefcase and joined him behind a small lectern at the head of the conference table.

"I want to thank all of you for coming to this special meeting," Alonzo began. "I know we're all busy, so we'll get started."

He turned and nodded toward Dan. "We've all read Congressman Wolfson's statements in the congressional newsletter and the newspapers, so we don't need to talk about why we're here. Our colleague is the sponsor of PL. 99-057, the Freedom from Religious Persecution Act. You all have copies of it. In brief, the act is an effort to force the government of Sudan to stop human rights violations or face steadily stiffer sanctions from the United States. The representative from Indiana has requested a private, confidential meeting with the leaders of the Black Caucus. And that's what you have agreed to—nothing beyond that. We're here to listen to what he has to say."

Alonzo glanced at Dan and smiled. "I would like to remind each of you that in the past, Dan has strongly supported initiatives dear to our hearts."

Two light claps of applause sounded at the end of the table and Washington relaxed a little at the show of support.

"He has been a friend to the state of Michigan, and I am honored to present him to you... even if he is a Boilermaker."

A few chuckles around the table lightened the atmosphere. Alonzo moved over to give Dan the space behind the lectern.

As Washington made his way to his seat, Dan surveyed the room. He had worked with some of the men and women seated there on key legislation; others he had strongly opposed on issues. They all sat expressionless; there was no way to read them. The only thing clear right now was that they wouldn't give an inch. If he wanted two points, he would have to dribble the ball all the way down the court and dunk it by himself.

"Thank you for allowing me to speak to you today," Dan said, his normally booming orator's voice subdued for the smaller room. He nodded to Chad, who pushed a button, and a screen slowly descended from the ceiling on the wall to Dan's right while he spoke.

"I care deeply about Sudan and I passionately believe that we will have to answer to our consciences, to history and to God, if we sit idly by and allow the carnage there to continue unchallenged."

He nodded again and Chad started the Power Point presentation. A brightly colored map of Sudan flashed on the screen. The young man stepped to the wall switch, and the paneled room was plunged into semi-darkness, except for the glow from the screen that lit up Dan's face.

"This is simplistic, but in general terms, the northern part of Sudan is populated by Muslim Arabs, and the southern part is a conglomeration of more than 500 different tribal groups who are predominantly Christian, though there are a good many animists there, too."

Dan gave a succinct history of the origin of the turmoil in the region, as Chad deftly coordinated his words with bullet points on the screen.

"After Sudan split off from Egypt in 1953, Khartoum allowed a separate regional government to administer the affairs of the south. But when Lt. Gen. Omar Hassan Al Bashir and the Sudanese People's Armed Forces took power in 1989, the south's democratically elected government was dissolved."

A picture of Al Bashir, in full dress uniform, flashed on the screen. Dan looked up at the picture as he spoke.

"Al Bashir's government is controlled by a fundamentalist group called the National Islamic Front, and they instituted a program to force everyone in the whole country to convert to Islam."

Dan stood in shadow with the light from the projector behind him, but even in the dim light, the legislators seated at the table could see the intensity on his face.

"And when the 6 million southern tribals didn't play ball, the north began to systematically wipe them out—massacred them by the thousands."

Chad flashed a more detailed map of Sudan on the screen. Dan walked over to it and pointed to southern Sudan.

"This is where the atrocities have been reported. In the last 14 years, more than 2 million Sudanese, most of them black Africans, have been killed there—*by their own government*. More people have died in Sudan than in Rwanda, Uganda and Kosovo put together."

Dan turned and walked back to the conference table. He placed his hands on it and leaned toward his listeners.

"And more than 150,000 Sudanese have been sold as slaves to the highest bidder."

He let that point sink in for a beat or two before he continued.

"The pictures I'm about to show you were sent to me by a BBC correspondent in Cairo. They're hard to look at, but they're reality. The photos were shot by an undercover reporter inside Sudan."

A woman's voice came from the darkness. "Your brother?"

"Yes," Dan said, and he was surprised at the swell of pride he felt. "My brother Ron is risking his life to document the bloodbath in Sudan."

Then the black legislators looked through the view finder of Ron's camera at a nightmare world; one awful image after another filled the screen.

In one, a blank-faced child cradled the body of a dead little girl in her arms.

"See these marks." Dan stepped to the screen and pointed to red welts on both girls' shoulders. "Slave traders don't brand captives. These children had already been purchased when they escaped. The little one died when she angered her master and he put insects in her ears, stuffed wax in behind them and let the bugs eat out her brain."

Dan heard a muffled groan from somewhere in the darkness.

Another picture: bullet-riddled bodies lying in pools of blood, with huts in flames behind them.

"The government's usual game plan is to send in fighter planes to strafe and bomb the villages, then the troops come in behind... "

An image appeared on the screen of a pile of dead bodies slashed and hacked apart, many of them missing body parts.

"...and attack the defenseless villagers with guns and swords. But their weapon of choice is the machete."

The images flashed one after another. Dead children. Bombed villages. Burned crops and dead livestock. After awhile, Dan stopped his narration and moved out of the glow of light from the screen. These people didn't need him to tell them this was genocide.

After the last image, Chad turned the lights back on and Ron returned to the lectern.

"General Al Bashir has already massacred hundreds of thousands of his own people. I have drafted legislation to force him to stop the bloodbath or face serious consequences." He paused. "And right now, ladies and gentlemen, that legislation doesn't have a snowball's chance in hell of passing."

There was a murmur in the group; Dan's candidness surprised them.

"I need your help, plain and simple. Without it, the scenes you saw on the screen will be replayed again and again and again until there are no southern tribals left to slaughter."

Dan could have said more. But it was time to hear from his listeners. "Questions?"

The most senior member of the group was a congressman from Louisiana. "We have already made a commitment to help the U.N. raise another $50 million in aid support." Rep. Charles Dubois had left the bayou but not the accent behind. "That's not enough?"

Dan shook his head. "It would be a good start to relieve the suffering in the south, if it actually got to the people who needed it. But it doesn't."

Dan explained that the United Nations notified Khartoum where and when an aid drop would be made, which ensured the slaughter of anybody foolish—or hungry—enough to show up to claim it.

"And humanitarian aid doesn't address the basic issue here," he said. "We have to do more than provide the survivors a hot meal and a blanket after their government has bombed their villages and soldiers have hauled off their women and children to sell to the slave traders."

His final two words drew a response from a well-groomed New York Congressman. When Lamont Walters leaned forward in his chair to speak, Dan had time to think: OK, here it comes.

"As you may or may not know, I am a Muslim," Rep. Walters said in a resonant baritone. "Like many other people, you condemn what you do not understand. And it is obvious to me you don't understand Islam."

He picked up the pen beside the notepad in front of him and pecked it on the table to emphasize his next words.

"Islamic law forbids slavery; Christianity does not. For 200 years, American slave owners used the Bible to justify kidnapping the ancestors of every man and woman in this room."

There were murmurs in the group, but Dan couldn't tell if they were agreeing or disagreeing with Walters.

"Actually, I know enough about Islam to know that the Koran does not allow a Muslim to enslave *another Muslim*," Dan fired back, a little stronger than he meant to. "But if you're not a Muslim, all bets are off! And the people hauled away in trucks to the north to spend their lives in bondage are Christians or animists. Sharia law allows Muslims to enslave them—they're fair game."

The Congressman from New York responded with fire of his own. "Rev. Chavis and Benjamin Grover traveled to Sudan to see for themselves what was really going on, and there were no signs of slavery. If that many people had been hauled off in bondage, surely somebody would have noticed."

"Those men were wined and dined and shown only what Al Bashir wanted them to see," Dan retorted. Then he grabbed hold of his emotions—nothing to be gained by a shouting match—and continued in a more measured tone.

"You saw pictures right there," Dan pointed to the screen on the wall, "of things they never saw. I didn't invent the pictures. That's reality, not the five-star hotel tour the government gave Chavis and Glover."

Dan turned and asked Chad Mattingly for the bound folder the young man had carried in with his laptop.

"Rep. Burns and Johnson didn't get a guided tour." The two congressmen had traveled to Sudan unannounced and had gone unaccompanied to inspect the southern provinces. Dan had included their report in the information he'd dispersed in recent months to members of both the House and the Senate, so its contents shouldn't have been news to anyone in the room.

"Right here is what they found." He held up the dossier. "It's all documented—everything I just showed you."

Then Dan paused and returned to a previous point.

"If that many people had been hauled away, surely somebody would have noticed." Dan quoted what Walters had said earlier. He paused again, and then quietly launched a single word out into the air and let it hang there.

"Who?"

A beat or two later, he continued. "Who would have noticed? Who is there to see, to come and tell the tale? If it weren't for men like Burns and Johnson—and my brother—nobody would ever know. The victims are nobody's favorite religion and nobody's favorite color, and they can vanish without a trace, are vanishing without a trace, and nobody will ever notice or care unless we do."

The Congressman from New York was undaunted. "It will take more than some pictures—horrible pictures, I grant you—to convince me. Those are photos of what happens in a civil war. The two halves of Sudan are fighting each other, and people get killed in wars. It's deplorable, but it is reality. None of that proves genocide. And it certainly doesn't prove slavery."

Margaret Bryan, a Congresswoman from Missouri who was one of the most respected members of the delegation, took a verbal step in between Dan and the fiery New York representative.

"Excuse me," she blatantly interrupted. "I want to talk about the elephant in the middle of the room."

She put down her pen and aligned it carefully on the top of her legal pad, just for a moment or two, to let the dust settle. She was a veteran of many heated debates and she wanted to turn the burner down on this one. Then she leaned forward and looked all around the table.

"Can anybody say Tri Cola and American Gum?"

There it was, out in the open. Dan knew they'd get to it eventually.

"Those guys—and some others—are heavy hitters," she said. "They have huge investments in Sudan. Sanctions will not make them happy, and they can bury everybody in this room with their pocket change."

Rep. Dubois spoke again in his soft Cajun voice. "Tri-Cola and American Gum both have branch offices in my district. They're good corporate citizens, models in minority hiring. Now, if I turn against them and vote for economic sanctions in Sudan, that chicken is going to come home to roost in my front yard when they start laying people off."

There was a momentary silence while each person at the table did a mental tally of the hit he or she personally would take if they crossed giant corporations whose sales exceeded the gross national product of two-thirds of the countries in the world.

Dan walked to the window, pulled back the drapes and spilled afternoon sunlight into the room. "I know what you're saying." There was no boom in his voice now. "I'm up for re-election myself."

He turned and faced the table. "And the soft drink and gum companies have put more than $400,000 into my opponent's campaign chest already."

Rep. Dorothy Warden from Ohio spoke for the first time.

"Why you, Dan?" Her voice that was almost too deep and husky for a woman.

Dan looked puzzled.

"You've grabbed hold of this Sudan thing and held on like a pit bull."

Dan was a neighbor of sorts. Warden hailed from Cincinnati, a couple of hours upstream from Dan's hometown on the Ohio River in Indiana. Middle America. Fly-over country. There was a bond there.

"And hanging on could very well cost you your career. I'm just curious. Why?"

"That's a legitimate question, Dottie, and I wish I had a smooth, sound-bite answer for you. Truth is, I'm not sure."

He stepped to the side table under the window where the coffeepot and empty cups sat. He picked up a crystal water pitcher and poured himself a glass, then slowly drank half of it. He was stalling. When he turned back around, he had made his decision.

"My family owned slaves." He watched the surprise spread over their faces. Even Chad Mattingly looked a little shaken. "So did my wife's family. Our ancestors in Virginia and North Carolina. We looked it up."

The representative from Maryland, the powerful Avery Thompson, leaned forward in his seat. Dan had expected to be grilled by the politically savvy Thompson, Alonzo Washington's mentor. But the man had not said a word, made a comment or asked a question. He had merely listened, as he listened now.

"And that would tie it up nice and tidy, wouldn't it? Wolfson wants to absolve his guilt, cleanse the family name of shame. Case closed. And I'm ashamed to admit that's probably at least part of it."

Dan's tone changed as he grew speculative. "It's interesting... even though we're a couple of hundred years removed from slavery in this country, we still don't want to talk about it. I don't want to talk about it. You don't want to talk about it. It makes us uncomfortable."

He spoke his thoughts as they formed in his mind. "Maybe acknowledging that slavery is alive and well somewhere else in the world forces us, as a nation and as individuals, to revisit our own trauma. And we just flat out don't want to go there. That could be why we try so hard to pretend it's not happening."

He turned and set the glass down. When he turned back around, his face was hard.

"But it *is* happening. Right now. This minute. As we sit here safe in this comfortable room, on the other side of the planet Arab raiders are kidnapping women and little kids, tying them with ropes and hauling them off to an auction where they'll be sold, branded, beaten, raped, mutilated and forced to work against their will." He walked back to the lectern. "I don't need some other deep psychological explanation for why I'm so passionate. That's reason enough. It's wrong."

His voice got quiet. "It's just *wrong.*"

He looked down the long table; the faces that looked back at him were unreadable.

"Sure, this is a religion issue. Absolutely! Militant Muslims in the north are forcing Islam on Christians and animists in the south. But it's a race issue, too. Arabs are enslaving tribals."

He put the palms of both hands on the table, leaned over and said quietly, "I appeal to you today as survivors of the Middle Passage. The question isn't: 'Why haven't African Americans responded to this crisis?' What I want to know is why African Americans *who are descendents of slaves* won't fight to stop the enslavement of others."

Dan straightened up. The orator was back in his voice, not in volume but in intensity. "Rarely does history grant an opportunity to confront a tormentor lost to time and place. You, we, I, have that opportunity right now."

No one moved. Dan reached down and picked his briefcase up off the floor.

"Thank you for hearing me out. If you need to hear any other arguments on this issue, just listen to your conscience."

* * * * *

Akin was sick. A pain deep in her belly had awakened her and it still gnawed at her. It wasn't like anything she'd ever felt. She knew she'd incur Pasha's wrath if she didn't grind the grain in her bowl, but the pain took all her strength away.

She hadn't felt this bad since a millipede sting when she was 5 years old kept her on her sleeping mat for days. A sense of terrible loneliness suddenly washed over her. She felt so hopeless and abandoned she feared she might burst into tears.

Pasha came out of the tent with a larger pestle for Omina. As she approached the girls, she stopped a couple of paces away from Akin and just stood there without saying a word.

Akin finally looked up to see what she wanted.

Pasha spoke, but Akin didn't understand. She repeated the phrase again and pointed at Akin's legs. The little girl didn't take her eyes off Pasha's face, just lowered her hand below the wrap-around skirt that reached halfway down her thigh. She felt something warm and sticky. When she looked at her hand, her eyes widened. Her fingers were red, covered with blood, and she saw a trickle of blood working its way down from between her legs on a slow journey toward her knee.

She stepped back in horror and looked up terrified into Pasha's face. She had seen Mbarka and Shontal going through menses, but the sight of her own blood drove all those thoughts from her mind. Pasha turned abruptly, walked back into the supply tent and emerged a few moments later with a brown rag.

In the closest thing to kindness she'd ever shown to any of the girls, she walked to the still speechless Akin and handed her the rag. Akin began to daub frantically at the small streaks of blood. In a moment, she felt Mbarka's arm around her shoulder

"Don't be afraid. We all go through it."

For the next few minutes, Mbarka helped the shaken little girl clean herself, and showed her how to attach the rag to her wrap-around, so it could catch the flow of blood. When Mbarka had finished her explanation, a thought popped into Akin's mind. She couldn't remember the last time Mbarka had been off limits to the men, which she was during her monthly flow.

"Does it happen always? I haven't seen you with blood like this in a long time."

Mbarka looked into the distance and said quietly. "I am pregnant." She turned her gaze back to Akin. "When a woman is pregnant, with child, she stops her monthly flow of blood until after the baby is born."

Pasha couldn't wait to tell her master the little slave girl had become a woman. She had seen how he lusted after her.

When he heard the news, a wide smile spread across Sulleyman's face and he instructed his stewardess to have the girl prepared for her master's bed after the celebration meal on their last night in camp.

"In the morning after I have taken her, I want you to circumcise her before we break camp," he said. "She will be healed enough by the time we arrive home that I can use her until my youngest son returns from Senegal."

He had planned to give Mbarka to his son, but she had turned up pregnant. After her baby was born and he disposed of it, she'd be sent to a brothel. Akin would be a good substitute.

"But my son cannot have her until after she has developed." He was not talking to Pasha, he was thinking aloud. "As long as she looks like a child, she is mine."

● ● ● ● ●

Omar's mercenary friend, Julian, had squinted over the top of a glass of aragi in his smoke-filled bar in Jonglei and roared with laughter when Omar described his mission. Find one slave girl? Impossible.

But if he was determined to try, Omar should start his search in Kosti. Slaves passed through the river city 230 miles south of Khartoum like dark ghosts. Julian gave Omar the names of people to contact, and two days later, Idris and the mercenary were on a barge floating slowly north on the White Nile River through the largest swamp in the world, 12,000 square miles of black water. The Sudd was roughly the size of Belgium.

Idris sat on the side of the barge, watched the pattern of ripples spread back from the bow, and prayed. Prayer was all that brought him peace. The silent Omar leaned against a mango crate nearby. He watched the tall grass glide by, and saw flocks of birds rise and settle in the swamp beyond the riverbank in a choreographed ballet of color. But he was not at peace. He never was. He mulled over the names Julian had given him, made a mental list of the people he would approach first, which ones he would pay and how much. And which ones he would threaten and with what.

When he turned from the sun's glare on the water, Omar's gaze fell on Idris. Even in repose, the African's face had a determined set to the jaw. Omar had learned in the past weeks that there was absolutely no quit in the man.

"You would have been far better off to stay in your country village," he said. Idris looked up. Omar knew he couldn't understand. "I doubt that you will ever see your daughter again, and even if Allah smiles on us and we find her, " he paused, and there was something akin to pity on his face, "I don't know that you will be able to stand what you see."

Chapter 16

Leo Danheir had developed many skills over the years and plied many trades. All his endeavors had one thing in common: The only rule was there were no rules. Leo did whatever Leo wanted to do. His behavior was bound by no moral code of any kind; self-gratification was his only aim in life.

He and his black sidekick, Joak, had traveled from Bentiu to Kosti to lose themselves in the mosaic of the city, to blend into the layer of society there that had no soul. The pair had money. They had conned or stolen enough in the past few weeks to set themselves up for awhile, so they could afford to be a little selective about their next business enterprise.

Such was the joy of life in a country torn apart by civil war. With government-sanctioned, no *encouraged,* murder, rape and pillaging unleashed on half the population, who would notice, or care, about the petty larceny of a sewer rat like Leo? Anarchy was, indeed, a fertile ground for the common criminal.

Leo and Joak were an effective team. Leo's skin and language granted them access and unhindered travel through the Muslim portion of the country. And Joak, though he dressed garishly in brightly colored floral shirts and miss-matched western-cut pants, was a clever chameleon. He could use his skin color to find out what he wanted to know from the SPLA or to gain the trust of an unsuspecting tribal, like that stupid villager in Bentiu looking for someone to find his kidnapped daughter. Seldom in his checkered career had Leo met an easier mark. Fleecing that naive farmer had been a joy and a privilege.

In the past few years, the pair had gravitated more and more toward slave trading. You could make good money with little effort working as middlemen. If you were clever, you could find slaves to purchase at a bargain price from the Murahaleen, the guerillas, soldiers, anybody who had flesh to market, and then sell the captives to a larger, established slave trader who had customers in northern Sudan and other neighboring countries.

The standard operating procedure for Leo and Joak was to set up shop in a seedy bar or gambling house. There, they would simply wait, watch and listen. Criminals for hire could always find sources of income if they were willing to be patient and see what flotsam and jetsam the river of life washed their way.

The bar they selected in Kosti had been a thriving, fashionable business establishment, with a polished wood floor and shutters on the windows, in the early 1950s when Sudan was under British-Egyptian sovereignty. It had once had a name, too, but nobody remembered what it was anymore. Nothing was left of the sign that proclaimed its identity but two rusty hooks stuck in the ceiling of the roof that stretched out over the big double doors.

To its patrons, it was merely "the bar." Like most everything else in the country, it had rotted like the carcass of a dead tree, and was infested with the kind of slithering creatures that only come out at night. Roaches as big as a man's thumb lived on the accumulated grime, spilled food and liquor on the uneven wooden floor. Pieces of wall had crumbled away, exposing holes and tunnels where rats came and went like paying customers. In the back of the dilapidated building was a room divided into three small sections by hastily erected cypress poles and scrap pieces of lumber. In those sweltering cubicles, smaller than most American closets, desperate

Sudanese and Ethiopian women plied their trade and spread disease throughout the quarter.

Leo and Joak ordered a bottle of rice wine and found a table. The fermented liquid smelled so strong and tasted so bitter most westerners couldn't swallow it. Leo and Joak drank it like water. They made their best plans a little drunk.

As the brew began to warm their insides like the relentless heat warmed their outsides, Joak turned to Leo. "Are you sure it is such a good idea to do business with Faoud?" He didn't often question Leo's leadership, but he was far more frightened of the slave trader than he was of Leo.

"Oh, it is never safe to crawl into bed with a snake. But Faoud's got the connections and the reputation to sell anything he can lay his hands on. If we hook up with him, we could buy cheap from freelancing soldiers who don't know the value of their captives and sell them to Faoud at a good price."

Joak nodded agreement, though he was far from convinced it was a good strategy. But Leo was a dangerous man to cross too.

"Maybe we can get on his good side by showing up for our meeting this afternoon with a few 'presents' to sell to him cheap," Leo thought out loud.

"In Bagwe, I heard that the Murahaleens made a good haul in the south," Joak said. "They could go up for sale any day now."

"Go into the market and nose around. See if there's any word yet on the Murahaleen raids. Maybe we could get to them early and buy something to take as a present to Faoud. I do not want to meet that man empty-handed."

●　●　●　●　●

Ron, Masapha and Koto browsed the fruit stands in the Kosti marketplace and loaded up their packs with raisin cakes, bread and fresh fruit. They were scheduled to hook up with Dr. Greinschaft's contact from the Swiss feeding center in Chumwe, several hours' drive from Kosti, mid-morning at the dock next to the market.

As Koto wandered around nearby, drinking in the sights of the first city he had ever seen, Ron and Masapha sat down to rest in the shade provided by a pile of boxes leaning against the last fruit stand on the street. Only a few passers-by took notice of the light-skinned foreigner; Ron certainly took no notice of a particular African, dressed in a brightly flowered shirt and smelling of rice wine, who had edged up to the other side of the boxes of fruit in an effort to eavesdrop on their conversation.

Joak did not often see white men who were not Arabs, and the big blonde man obviously was not. That made him out of place here, and the out-of-the-ordinary was always worth investigating. Joak took a position behind the stretched muslin awning the vendor had erected over the ripest fruit. Cocking his head, he concentrated hard to block out the ambient noise around him.

"You have not written *any* of the stories yet?" Masapha asked incredulously. "Not a word? All that time at the doctor's compound, and you did not write?"

"How was I supposed to do that—in longhand on the doc's unlined typing paper? I've never met a reporter anywhere who could write a story in longhand. Olford's got a laptop I can use."

Ron was so dedicatedly non-techie that it had grieved him mightily to purchase a laptop several years ago, which was loaded with a word-processing program and absolutely nothing else. He had left it with his darkroom equipment at the Canadian refugee center, hundreds of miles away.

"I can type just about as fast as I can think, which says something about the speed of one or the other of those processes. If I tried to write with a pen and a piece of paper, the words would back up in my brain like a clogged sewer." Ron reached down and wiped pineapple juice off his hands onto his pants. "Can't be done, my friend. Can't be done."

Joak's command of the English language was not perfect, but he understood enough to know that the white man on the other side of the fruit stand must be a journalist working on a story. He leaned closer, as if examining the fruit, and strained to hear more.

"Then do not let a bus to run you over!" Masapha told Ron earnestly. "Without your words, the pictures and the video and the sound recordings have not any value anymore."

"Aw, come on, Masapha. If something happened to me, you could write this series," Ron teased. He nudged the little man and grinned. "You know as much about the slave trade in Sudan as I do."

Joak slowly lowered the mango in his hand, replaced it on the fruit stack and backed away from the little alcove. When he was sure he had gone unnoticed, he disappeared into the crowd.

Ron squinted at the sun's position in the sky. "I think it's late enough. Let's head over to the dock and find our friend from Chumwe. I should be easy for him to spot. I probably have the only white face in Kosti."

Masapha gestured for Koto to gather up the food, and the three of them dove back into the sea of humanity and swam toward the river.

●　●　●　●　●

Leo spotted Joak as the garishly-dressed man wormed and weaved his way through the crowd and limped toward him. His gimpy right leg was not the result of some battle injury. He'd had some disease as a kid that withered the limb.

Excitement animated Joak's ugly face, and he grinned a wide, toothless smile. "I found something!"

Leo held out a piece of blackened fish. Joak took it, but was too wired to eat.

"I think it's something important. Very important."

Leo crunched down on his own piece of fish. His gaze told Joak to give him the rest of the information and not leave him hanging.

"You said you did not want to go empty-handed to Faoud, that you wanted to have some little present to put him in a good mood toward us."

Leo nodded and kept eating.

"I saw a white man, an American."

So? Leo had seen plenty of Caucasians from time to time, petroleum company representatives, cotton buyers, gum brokers, U.N. envoys.

"He's with an Arab from the north. The American is a journalist. He has information and is going to write a story about... " Joak couldn't resist a pause for effect. "About the slave trade in Sudan!"

Then Joak played his ace. "And he has pictures and video and sound recordings to go with the story!" His grin broadened to reveal upper and lower dark pink gums. "Would this not be a thing Faoud would want to know?"

Leo's face did not return the smile, but Joak could tell he was interested. "Take me to them. I want to see for myself."

"This way." Joak pointed toward the north end of the market by the dock. Leo dropped his half-eaten fish into the dirt and followed.

*   *   *   *   *

Near an old block building ringed with empty oil drums by the river sat a jeep, a slightly newer model than the one stolen from Ron in Lusong. The man in the driver's seat wore rounded glasses and had shaggy blond hair so sun-bleached it was almost white. He looked like a California surfer. A tall African dressed conventionally in pants and a shirt sat beside him.

Both men quickly climbed out of the vehicle as soon as they saw Ron emerge from the crowd.

The Swiss driver, about Ron's age, reached out his hand with a smile as bright as polished crystal. "You must be Mr. Wolfson! Lars Bergstrom."

"Agot Maruta," the African said and shook hands all around too.

"Glad to meet you both," Ron introduced Masapha and Koto.

"No, Mr. Wolfson, it is we who are glad to meet *you*. Dr. Greinschaft has told us all about you. If there is anything we can do to help—anything at all—you have only to ask."

Ron was surprised and touched by Bergstrom's earnest welcome. No, not really surprised. These people were Christian missionaries with the same organization as Dr. Greinschaft, and the good doctor had been the real deal.

"Actually, I *could* use your help on something." Ron looked around and spotted a pile of rubble, probably the remains of a collapsed building, just down the road from the last market stall. There was one wall still standing, and it cast a shadow over the rest of the rocks. "Let's have a seat over there out of the sun and talk."

The group crossed the dirt road and settled themselves as comfortably as possible on the rocks.

"Anybody want a guava?" Ron asked.

Bergstrom nodded, and Ron pulled out a piece of fruit, pitched it to him and tossed a raisin cake to Maruta. Then he extracted a banana for himself and held it up as if it were a wine glass to clink with the other "glasses" in a toast.

"Here's to... what are we celebrating? I don't even know what day it is."

"It is Wednesday, May 21," Bergstrom told him.

"Well, then, here's to... " Ron thought for a moment, did some mental arithmetic, and his face broke into a huge grin. "Here's to Memorial Day!"

Blank stares all around.

"Memorial Day is next Monday, and it's an important holiday in my country. It's a day to remember the people who gave their lives for America—and it's the official first day of summer vacation."

But it was more than either of those things to Ron. It was Family Day. The holiday never fell on Sunday when his father was busy from morning services to evening worship. And since 75 percent of his father's congregation left town on Memorial Day, it had become a tradition that the whole Wolfson family spent the day together— with *no* interruptions, that was the rule. Ron and Dan both liked it better than Christmas.

Bergstrom held up his guava.

"Here's to Memorial Day!" He clinked his fruit with whatever the others held up.

Then he lowered his voice and spoke softly. "We know why you're here in Sudan and what you're doing. I think we can help you in several ways, but first you must tell us your needs."

Ron peeled back the yellow skin, took a bite of the banana and began to tell Bergstrom his plan. He explained that Masapha and Koto would remain in Kosti nosing around while he traveled to Khartoum to hook up with a friend from the BBC. He would give his friend the film, video and sound recordings he'd already made—write the stories to go with them—and then return to Kosti for the final part of his investigation.

"I don't know where Masapha and I may go from here." Ron said nothing about leaving Koto at their feeding center when he and Masapha struck out on their own. He figured he'd sort of ease into that information later. "I'm not sure where we'll have to go to find what we're looking for."

"And that is?" Bergstrom asked.

"A slave owner," Ron replied. "I want to talk to somebody who owns slaves, somebody who holds another human being hostage. I want to hear their side of the story."

Both men from the feeding center looked surprised.

"And exactly how to you intend to pull that off?" Maruta asked.

"I don't have any idea," Ron answered honestly. "I'll cross that bridge when I get to it."

Bergstrom shook his head. "You Americans! Is there anything you won't try?"

The glasses that magnified his pale blue eyes repeatedly slid down the sheen of sweat on his nose. He pushed them back up, over and over again, so he could see.

"Well, if you're looking for a slave owner, you do not have to travel all over Sudan to find one," he said. "You don't have to go any farther than right here in Kosti. Plenty of people in Kosti own slaves. In fact, I wouldn't be surprised if some of the slave traders didn't live here, too."

Ron and Masapha exchanged a grateful look. It would be nice to find what they were looking for right under their noses instead of having to arrange transportation—on a boat, a bus, a donkey cart, or yet another jeep—and traipse all over the country peering under rocks.

"Then while I'm in Khartoum, Masapha can shake some trees right here in Kosti and see what falls out."

"About your trip to Khartoum," Bergstrom began. "I have some thoughts about that, if you'd like to hear them."

Ron reached into the sack and pulled out a rice cake. "Shoot, I'm listening," he said.

"We've been in touch with your contact, Mr. Olford, at the BBC."

Ron stopped in mid-bite. They'd reached Olford? Without the Crocodile Dundee code? That was impressive. The meticulous Brit was way into codes and passwords and secret handshakes.

"We discussed with him the danger of trying to get any information out of Sudan through Khartoum. Three weeks ago, a bomb was discovered in the Khartoum airport—or so officials said. I don't know if the story was true or if the government just wanted to make the SPLA look bad. But either way, the incident gave them an excuse to crack down on airport security. Now, they search everything—all your belongings—and every person, head to toe."

Bergstrom leaned closer for emphasis. "One wrong step, Mr. Wolfson, and all you've worked so hard to gather up will be confiscated—and your friend, Mr. Olford, will be presented a one-way ticket to a Sudanese prison cell. He won't need round-trip because most people who go in never come back out again."

Ron had often considered the possibility that it might be difficult to get his series safely out of Sudan, but in Scarlet O'Hara fashion, he had determined to "think about that tomorrow." He had begun to put serious worry time into it, however, as soon as he got pictures of the auction. They were so incriminating, so one-of-a-kind, so important. The chips that Masapha described as "not so big as the nail on your thumb" from the audio and video recorders might slip through, but his rolls of film? He resolutely forced out of his mind the opening stanzas of Olford's digital photography song.

Masapha reached out and took the sack of food from Ron's hand and rummaged through it in search of something that suited his fancy. He had said nothing in the conversation, only listened. But he hadn't missed a word of what was said.

Koto, on the other hand, hadn't understood anything anybody had said all day. He wandered away from the group and amused himself by tossing rocks at a tin can on the other side of the road.

"And you have a better idea than Olford taking the tapes out with him when he flies back to Cairo?" Ron asked.

"Yes, I do," Bergstrom said. He paused for a beat. "You could give the tapes to me." He saw the knee-jerk alarm on Ron's face, and hurried on. "We have supply planes that fly a regular route from an airstrip near the feeding center to food depots in Eritrea. We could send the material out on a plane this afternoon, and Mr. Olford could pick it up in Asmara this evening. No one in Eritrea would confiscate the tapes of a BBC reporter bound for Cairo."

Ron said nothing when Bergstrom finished. He glanced at Masapha, who shrugged. Then he looked back at the bespectacled Swiss aid worker.

"Two things," he said. "First off, you guys must have some clout with somebody somewhere to get my contact at the BBC to talk to you without using an Australian accent." That blew right by them. "And secondly, you must think I'm either a fool or have a lot of faith in your organization to hand this footage over to you."

Bergstrom laughed, and the sound boomed like an echo inside a grain elevator. "Faith is what makes us tick, Mr. Wolfson."

He tossed the skin of his guava onto the rocks, then looked around in vain for somewhere to wipe his sticky hands, finally settling for the seat of his pants.

"Listen, this is a generous offer," Ron said, feeling his way along. "But I gotta tell you, I have more reservations than the Washington Hilton." A blank look. Another swing and a miss. "OK, let's say I'm reticent to... "

He finally gave up his effort to put it well and just spit it out. "I have pictures here," he reached into his bag and pulled out a sock, extracted one of the 10 film cartridges inside and held it up for Bergstrom to see, "of an actual slave auction—in progress!—of human beings on sale to the highest bidder."

Ron dug around until he found his worn navy blue passport with the golden eagle on the front. He opened it to the center, carefully lifted the video chip nestled with the audio chip between the pages, held it up and continued. "I've got video that documents the whole thing, including footage of that young man," he cocked his head toward Koto, who was on the other side of the road positioning his tin-can target, "getting shot as he escapes from the slave traders."

Bergstrom glanced at Koto and noticed the bandage on the boy's shoulder.

"I have all of it recorded as well." He pointed to the audio chip in the passport. "And, as an extra added attraction, I have still shots of two dozen Nuba tribals who were crucified, nailed alive to trees!— likely for committing the heinous crime of being Christians."

Bergstrom was stunned. Dr. Greinschaft had hinted that what Ron had was explosive, but the aide worker hadn't been prepared for an atomic bomb. His mouth didn't drop open, but Ron definitely had his attention.

He also had the attention of two men leaning against the wall of a nearby building. When Ron held up the film canister, the one in the flowered shirt broke out in a wide, toothless smile.

"So tell me," Ron continued, "why I ought to trust you with information that will expose the greatest evil of this century?"

Bergstrom swallowed hard. "You are not the only person fighting against slavery, Mr. Wolfson. There are *many* other people, people you have never heard of." He pushed his glasses back up on his nose and looked intently at Ron. "With only a handful of relief agencies allowed to work in Sudan, we've been asked before, by others like you, to be a conduit of information in and out of the country. We have always said no. The work we do is too important to endanger it. If we are thrown out of Sudan, thousands of people will starve."

Bergstrom glanced at Maruta, and their silent communication spoke volumes. His glasses started to march down his nose again and he reached up, took them off and dropped them into his shirt pocket.

"But you have a chance to make a real difference, Mr. Wolfson. With your political connections in the U.S. and your access to the world press, we believe you are a... good horse to put the bet on. So to speak."

This time Ron was the one who chuckled.

"I've never been called a horse before. A horse's ass, yes. A horse, no."

"You would be less than a horse's buttocks if the Sudanese soldiers catch you with that film. You would be dead." Bergstrom paused, then continued softly but with intensity. "And so would we."

He stared unblinking into Ron's eyes. "It is a risk you have been willing to take, and now it is a risk we are willing to take also."

Ron studied Bergstrom's earnest face. There was no guile in the man. He was an associate of Dr. Greinschaft's—a Christian too, like the missionary doctor—and Ron had never met anybody more trustworthy than the old man who looked like Santa Claus.

If Bergstrom was prepared to risk his life to get Ron's information safely to Cairo, then Ron would take a chance on him. There was no story yet, but that was probably best too. It made sense to wait to write the piece until he was safely outside Sudan so he didn't have to try to sneak it out of the country. And there was the final piece of the puzzle, the slave owner piece. When he had that, he could write the whole thing at once.

Ron nodded. "OK, you've got a deal."

He and Masapha stood and the men shook hands all around. Then Ron unloaded the precious rolls of film he'd hidden in the bags, along with his notes for the stories. He gave it all to Bergstrom, then handed him the audio and video chips. The Swiss aide worker slid them carefully into his shirt pocket and buttoned the pocket closed.

"When you are finished with your investigation, come to our feeding center in Chumwe. We will send out the rest of your information, too. Then you can fly out of Khartoum and not worry about what a security guard might find in your luggage."

Ron thought about mentioning, oh by the way, that he'd be leaving a certain Lokuta tribal boy at the center when he left the country. But there was plenty of time later to drop that little bombshell. Instead, he just reached out his hand to his new Swiss friend. "Thank you," he said.

"God be with you," Bergstrom said.

Ron laughed. "God, the United Nations, the House, the Senate, and the New York *Times*."

● ● ● ● ●

Leo and Joak watched the relief workers get back into their jeep and drive away, then they turned and quickly blended into the crowd flowing down the street. Masapha called out to Koto, who dropped his rock ammunition and joined the Arab and the American. Leo and his limping friend were half a block away before the Oreo-cookie trio, Ron in the middle, the dark Arab and African on the outsides—strolled off toward the marketplace.

"You said the American had not written this story of his about slave trading—is that right?" Leo asked Joak as the crippled man struggled to keep pace with Leo as they walked together down the dirt street.

"The Arab asked him, and he said he had not written even one word yet."

Leo smiled. "So maybe Faoud would like to meet this journalist. He might be able to talk the American out of ever writing anything at all."

Chapter 17

As the sun sank below the horizon, leaving the world briefly gray before darkness stretched out to claim it, Ron began to look for somewhere for the three of them to spend the night. Cities in Sudan were not safe places after dark.

There were only a handful of overnight accommodations in all of Kosti. One of them was the Al Jubari Lodge. The lodge sat beneath a red sign with white Arabic lettering that stood high up on tall posts. It was actually freshly painted and a lion glared down from beneath the letters, its mouth open in a silent roar.

Unfortunately, the excellence of the establishment ended with the sign. The lodge itself was a pit.

All the single and double rooms were full. That left only the 24 beds in the travel room—a shoe-box shaped dormitory for one-night travelers that jutted off the side of the building. The wooden slat bunk beds there were lined up 12 to a side down the walls of the narrow room. Three feet of center aisle space separated the rows of beds; lumpy, canvas-covered straw mattresses lay bare on each bunk.

In the "lobby" of the inn, a tired old man sat at a desk and collected room fees and the one-pound-each charge per bed for one-night travelers.

Ron paid the three pounds for their beds, opened the creaking door into the travel room, then stopped and began to gag. "What the... ?"

Masapha walked in past him.

"Unwashed bodies and sweat make a large odor," he said casually. "I don't imagine the mattresses have been cleaned for all the years they have been here. Maybe your senses can't handle?"

"Oh, I can handle, I can handle." Ron waved him off, but continued to gag at the thick, musky smell. "I just hope my death certificate doesn't read: 'Cause of death: BO.'"

Masapha's gleaming, gap-toothed smile reflected the light generated by the candles that flickered on the wall. Americans were so pampered.

⁕ ⁕ ⁕ ⁕ ⁕

The canvas-covered truck that Faoud Al Bashara and his men normally used to transport slaves now transported them. Faoud sat in the front seat beside the driver. He was quiet, brooding. Seething. He replayed in his mind what the witless mercenary had told him.

Leo Danheir could not be trusted; he would slit his own mother's throat if the price was right. But what the man had said tonight had the ring of truth to it. For one thing, the mercenary was not creative enough to make up such a tale. And to what end? He might be stupid, but he was certainly smart enough to know that Faoud would kill him if his story did not pan out.

And a vague memory had surfaced as the fat man bounced along in the truck. There had been an incident at a slave auction in the oil fields. One of his hired raiders had stumbled upon a white man—a blond—behind a hill overlooking the site. The soldier had said the man was feeding birds, which made absolutely no sense at all! The soldiers fired on the man, but he got away. Could it have been the American? Perhaps he had a camera the soldier didn't see. How many blond white men could there be in that part of Sudan?

It was dark when the truck rolled into Kosti.

"What are the places in Kosti where a white man and an Arab could stay for the night?" Faoud asked the driver of the truck.

"There are only a few," the man replied.

"We will search them all!"

Faoud's face darkened with growing rage. How dare some imperialist pig from the Great Satan set foot in his world. If he found such a man, Faoud would make him very, very sorry he'd interfered in the affairs of Faoud Al Bashara.

Clouds of dust followed the truck up and down the dark, sandy streets as it traveled from one lodging place to the next. They had searched for almost two hours when they turned down a narrow, hard-packed dirt road and the headlights of the truck lit up a lion on a red sign. The whitewashed walls of the Al Jubari Lodge glowed as the lights swept across them when Faoud and his men pulled up out front.

* * * * *

Ron had slept only fitfully. It was not so much the smell. He'd almost grown accustomed to that. But as soon as he began to drift off, advance scouts for the regiment of chiggers inside the straw mattress performed a search-and-destroy mission on his neck. Once they'd planted their flag, they sounded the chigger claxon and the rest of the teeming hordes charged out of the mattress and mounted a full frontal assault on his back and arms. He decided that if he didn't win the battle with them in another five minutes, he would head outside and take his chances with the mosquitoes. On the edge of sleep, he heard a loud motor, probably a truck. It sputtered for a few seconds and then shut down.

He didn't hear the front door of the lodge open when two men with guns went inside to talk to the proprietor. But he did hear the door of the sleeping room squeak open and then bang shut a few minutes later and had time to think, *Hey pal, don't you know people are trying to sleep in...* before hands grabbed his arms, picked him up off the bed and set him on his feet on the floor beside it. Men on both sides of him dragged him down the narrow center aisle between the rows of beds and out the front door into the night.

Masapha heard scuffling sounds beside Ron's bed. When he rolled over and opened his eyes, the barrel of an automatic rifle was inches from his nose. A gruff voice ordered him in Arabic, "Get up!" Masapha got up.

Koto was asleep in the bed next to Masapha. Awakened by the commotion, he opened his eyes and instantly identified the dress and guns of the raiders. He froze in terror.

One of the gunmen ordered Masapha to gather his possessions and Ron's, and Masapha stooped and pulled the packs out from under the bed. The other gunman grabbed them out of his hands and shoved him down the center aisle between the beds to the door.

Masapha followed the gunman's instructions and never looked back, never cast so much as a glance in Koto's direction. None of the patrons in the other beds made a sound or stirred. They were awake, but had no desire to get involved with men carrying automatic weapons.

The elderly Muslim lodge keeper moved out of the way as Masapha and his captors stepped through the door into the night. He tucked the Sudanese pounds he'd been given into his shirt, went back into his cubicle office and closed the door behind him.

Koto wanted to get up and look out the door to see what was happening but he was too scared. He just lay in the bed trembling.

Faoud leaned against the front grille of the truck between the headlights on high beam. The two men who'd been shoved in front of him squinted into the bright lights.

He let the pair stand there for a few moments, struggling to see, before he posed a question to Ron in Arabic.

The answer came back from Masapha who understood it. "He is Ron Wolfson, an American; my name is Masapha Kamal Mbake. I am from Khartoum."

The slave trader fired out another question.

Masapha's answer was steady and sure. "We are compiling pictures for a travel magazine in the U.S."

Another question came from the still faceless man who stood between the bright lights.

"We wanted to get an accurate picture of Sudan and Egypt, so we had to go around Sudan shooting scenes in different places all over the country... even here, in Kosti."

"You speak Arabic and English? How do you know both?"

"I taught at the university. I speak several tribal languages as well."

The soldiers rummaged through Ron's back pack and equipment bag while Masapha answered questions. Any other time, Ron would have been angered by their disrespect for his property; but at that moment he was so scared he didn't care if they stole everything he owned. When they came upon Ron's Nikon, they gave it to Faoud. The slave trader took the camera and began to roll the film forward until it was completely fed into its housing. He opened the back of the camera, removed the film canister and placed it into a pocket in the folds of his robe.

Then he turned toward the truck cab and obliterated one of the lights for a moment as he passed in front of it. That was Ron and Masapha's first glimpse of Faoud, the slave trader. When the big man gave an order to his men, Masapha understood it. They were on their way to Faoud's for questioning.

The goons prodded the two men toward the canvas-covered back of the truck and gestured for them to get in and sit on the benches that stretched across both sides, where other armed men had been stationed to keep them company. Ron and Masapha did as they were instructed, the most recent in a huge list of captives who had sat on those same benches on their way to bondage.

Ron looked back for his pack and saw a soldier give it to Faoud; Masapha looked back in the direction of the lodge where Koto lay in the darkness. The boy had managed to survive on courage and determination before; Masapha hoped he could do it again.

Koto heard doors slam, a diesel engine start and the rattle of a truck as it pulled out and drove away. The silence that followed throbbed in his ears and kept time with his heart as it hammered in his chest. Gradually, his heart and breathing returned to normal, but the emptiness inside him grew.

Ron and Masapha were gone. He was alone.

* * * * *

Rupert Olford pushed his glasses up on his head, leaned back in his leather chair and looked out the window at the lights of Cairo. The BBC reporter closed his eyes and rubbed them with his thumb and middle finger, then opened them and blinked. It would be dawn soon, and he'd been up all night.

The image of Ron Wolfson's face came suddenly into his mind, and Olford broke into a wide, toothy smile. Well done, Yank, he thought. Well done, indeed!

He'd watched the raw video footage all the way through three times already. Once the film editors worked their magic, it would be spellbinding. The slave-traders shooting that boy—amazing! And his story!

Olford stood up, arched his back, stretched his tall, skinny body and sat down again. He'd heard Koto's taped interview on one of the audio tracks and had decided to send the interview to Ron's brother, Dan, in Washington. It was a compelling story; maybe the congressman could use it, with the vote on his bill set for the first part of next week.

It was a shame Ron didn't know when the vote in the U.S. House of Representatives was scheduled, so this slavery series could run before the vote. But there was no way to get in touch with him. Ron was out there somewhere in the wilds of Sudan; he'd bagged the story of his life.

* * * * *

The converted army transport stopped in front of a stone building. One of the gunmen banged on a door on the side of it and shouted, "Ahkmad!"

The door creaked open on heavy hinges. Inside stood a rangy man in worn army fatigues, with a wide, thick scar on his face that extended from above his right eyebrow all the way down his cheek to his chin. He nodded, and the guards shoved Ron and Masapha out of the truck, into the building, and down a cool, dark hallway.

Ron was in front. He held his arms out as he stumbled along, hardly able to see. Behind him, the footsteps of the man who'd opened the door sounded like tympani drums exploding on the cold, stone floor. The man had a flashlight but could obviously negotiate the corridor without it. He turned it on, the splash of light chased the shadows into the corners for a few seconds, then he turned it off again. The first time he turned it on, all Ron saw was the floor in front of him and a large gray rat that quickly skittered off into the darkness. The second time, Ron could see a couple of unlit lamps on the walls and barred doors on both sides of the hallway. The cells were dark and silent.

A burst of the scarred man's flashlight lit up the wall at the end of the hallway. There was a stone bench there and a cell door on the right. Ahkmad, the jailer, produced a large key and stuck it into the cast-iron lock, and like an ancient dungeon gateway, the door creaked open. Ron stumbled along the path of the jailers' flashlight beam into the room and felt, rather than saw, Masapha come in after him.

Then the cell door clanged shut with a resounding bang and the key scraped in the lock to seal it. Ron and Masapha heard the sound of footsteps as they retreated down the hallway. Then there was silence. They were probably no more than three feet apart; in the total blackness, they couldn't see each other. But they each could hear the other's ragged breathing, and though neither of them could see it, there was obviously a window or an opening of some kind in the room because they also could hear Faoud outside shouting orders.

"What's he saying?" Ron whispered.

"Just giving scar-man charge over us until he comes back tomorrow to ask information from us."

Masapha's reply was equally hushed, though neither of the men could have said who it was they were afraid would overhear them.

Then Masapha fired out the question that had clawed at his mind since their brief interrogation in front of the truck's lights. "What are the pictures on the roll of film the man took from your camera?"

"There aren't any pictures on it," Ron told him. "It's blank."

"Blank?" The Arab let out a breath he didn't even realize he'd been holding.

"As soon as I finish a roll of film, it's out of the camera and right into the zipper pocket of the camera case. I emptied that pocket into my sock at the doctor's place, and I'm sure I gave all the rolls in it to Bergstrom."

Ron felt his way around in the dark, his hands reaching out for something solid.

"I always load a fresh roll in the camera as soon as I take the spent roll out—that's what our charming, fat friend has confiscated."

Masapha put is hands up in front of him and stepped forward to locate a wall.

"So he cannot know you are not taking traveling photos..." Masapha thought out loud.

"...unless we tell him," Ron finished for him.

He didn't have to draw Masapha a picture. Both men had figured out that the fat man was probably a slave trader who had gotten wind somehow of a photographer on his turf and had come to check him out.

If the slave trader found out that Ron had captured a slave auction on film, he'd kill them both in a heartbeat. Their lives depended upon telling a convincing story when the man came back to "ask information" from them in the morning. They'd just keep it simple—Ron was taking pictures for a travel magazine. That's all. It was a plausible story, and it was the only one they had.

Ron's hand touched cold stone and he felt his way down it to the floor and sat down in what felt like straw.

"Hey... maybe the beds here don't have chiggers." He tried to sound cheerful, and he might have pulled it off if he could have kept the shakiness out of his voice. But as the reality of their situation sank in, fear had clutched his belly and squeezed so tight he couldn't stop the tremor.

The inky blackness began to give way slightly as his eyes adjusted to the lack of light, and he imagined he could almost make out the classic lines of Masapha's movie-star face. It was no use looking for his friend's shiny white teeth, though; Masapha didn't have any more to smile about than he did.

Chapter 18

The squawk-squawk of a testy secretary bird awoke Masapha. He looked up and saw a barred window far above his head that directed shafts of dusty sunlight into the cell. Ron sat with his back propped against the jail wall, his forearms on his knees.

"Good morning," Ron said when he saw that Masapha was awake.

"Is it?"

"I'm sure it's a good morning somewhere on the planet."

Masapha no longer had a prayer rug; it had been taken the previous night, along with everything else he owned. So he merely knelt on the dirty cell floor and prayed. When he finished, he moved to the wall opposite Ron and leaned against the stone. The rock was cool, and he figured it was probably several feet thick. The jail was like a cave; at least it wouldn't turn into an oven during the midday heat.

The two sat in silence for a time.

"So, what do you think?" Ron finally asked.

"I think we are in big trouble." Masapha hoped his voice didn't sound as shaky as he felt. "I would not think in all our lives up to this point, either of us ever has been in so much trouble as we are now in." Masapha paused. "It's bad."

"How bad?"

"All the bad."

＊　＊　＊　＊　＊

When Idris and Omar stepped off the barge onto the dock in Kosti, the same smell of rotted fish carcasses met the mercenary and the tall tribal that had met Ron, Masapha and Koto when they walked down the same dock the day before.

Their barge trip downstream had taken them through swamp and wetlands, and past savannah that slowly became dry plains like the one they had crossed on foot. But in the last few days, Omar and Idris had moved into the Sahel, the hot, arid next-door-neighbor to the Sahara, where brush and stunted acacia trees dotted a desolate, sandy landscape.

Kosti was an Arab city. Men wore long white or black robes, with Arabian shora scarves or kuftis on their heads. Women wore flowing kaftans and shayla wraps that revealed nothing but their faces. A few women were dressed in burkhas. Idris had never seen a world like this one, and he gawked unashamedly at everything around him.

Omar signaled for Idris to follow him up a set of steps that led to the market. He found a rock wall where no one was sitting, put down his backpack and rifle and motioned for Idris to stay there to watch them.

A few minutes later, he returned with two wrapped packages of blackened perch and some peaches. He laid Idris' portion on the ground beside him, then sat down on the rock wall and began to eat his.

But Idris did not eat. He knelt in front of the mercenary and made motions with his hands in an effort to communicate. Omar looked at him blankly, so Idris began to draw in the sand with his finger, crude stick figures. He pointed from the drawings to the crowd in the marketplace and then back to the drawings. Suddenly, Omar understood.

He looked out into the market and could see them everywhere—

Arabs accompanied by two or three dark-skinned Africans who carried their bundles, held their purchases and moved along slowly behind them. Omar looked at Idris and nodded his head; yes, Idris was looking at slaves.

The tribal was stunned at first, then horrified and outraged. Omar watched the emotions play across Idris' face. Then he followed his companion's gaze to a young black girl on the other side of the street behind a fat Arab woman. The girl carried a large bundle and walked with her head down. When she looked up briefly so the men could see her face, the expected look of despair wasn't there. What was there was worse: resignation.

Omar turned and studied Idris as the tribal watched the child. Even though his own mother had been a Haratine, he had never before considered slavery from a tribal's point of view. He felt a momentary sadness for the thin black man beside him, then brushed the emotion aside and turned his attention back to his fish.

After they'd eaten lunch, Omar left Idris with his gear and went in search of information. Julian had given him the names of people in Kosti involved in all sorts of enterprises, both legal and illegal. He'd find out what they knew about recent slave auctions. He'd bribe or threaten whoever he had to bribe or threaten. He'd find out something. Tomorrow, he and Idris would head inland to follow up the leads. And to do that, he would need a jeep.

❋   ❋   ❋   ❋   ❋

Leo sat on a warped fruit crate and studied the crowds that passed the bar as he sharpened his knife, running the whetstone over it in smooth, fluid strokes. Joak sat on a crate next to him.

"When will Faoud pay us for telling him about the American journalist?" Joak asked. "He will pay us, yes? He is a man of his word?"

"Oh yes, a real gentleman." Leo was tired, and the little man got on his nerves. "Faoud will pay us whenever Faoud gets ready to pay us—and not before."

With that, Leo stood, slipped his knife into its scabbard and the whetstone into his pocket. "I want a drink. And I want to see one of the girls in the back."

Joak thought about their sleeping accommodations. "Give me some money then, and I will go and reserve our rooms for the night." Without paid-in-advance rooms at the inn where they were staying they'd have to spend the night like cattle in the traveling room.

Leo turned back and glared at the little man irritably.

"I will pay for us when we get there," he snapped, then stepped up on the porch, marched through the big double doors and was lost in the dim interior.

Joak sighed. Leo would be drunk within the hour—drunk and mean. The girl he picks will earn her money today, he thought. Then Joak got up and went to find something to eat.

* * * * *

About mid-morning, Ron heard the sound of boots in the hallway. He and Masapha exchanged a glance; both men swallowed hard.

The key scraped in the lock and the heavy door swung open with a clang. Two of Faoud's men entered, followed by the jailer. And then Faoud himself.

It was Ron and Masapha's first daylight look at the slave trader, and he was even scarier than the shadowy specter in the dark had been. Uglier, too. Way uglier. Ron thought that if he were casting somebody to play a slave trader in a movie, he probably wouldn't have picked this guy. He was so sinister and evil looking it was overkill.

Faoud Al Bashara was a big man, well over six feet tall, who had probably in his youth been heavily muscled. Now, in middle age, it had all gone to fat. He weighed at least 270 pounds, probably closer to 300. For comfort around his huge, pendulous belly, he wore a white African dishadasha, a shapeless, one-size-fits-all robe, with an equally shapeless blue outer garment called a jubbah. His thinning black hair was slicked back in a short, greasy ponytail. The skin on his round, fat face and neck was pockmarked with deep craters from what must once have been a horrific case of acne. His nose was flat, his nostrils wide—like a pig's snout. His eyes were black and unusually small. They glowered from beneath a lone, heavy black eyebrow that stretched across the length of his forehead. Gold earrings hung in each of his large, drooping earlobes behind the jowls that sagged from his jaw.

The slave trader stared down with equal parts outrage and loathing at the blond man on the floor at his feet. How dare this infidel interfere in his world!

"What are you doing in my country, you American *khawaja?*" Faoud spit out the Arabic word for "foreigner" with disgust. "How dare you even set foot in Sudan."

Faoud turned to Masapha and growled, "You are Sudanese. Tell me what this infidel is doing here! It will go easier for you if you tell me the truth now. If you do not, you will suffer the same fate as the imperialist pig."

"I can only tell you the same thing he has said," Masapha replied, with what he hoped was a good imitation of calm and confidence. "He hired me to show him around Sudan so he could take pictures for a travel magazine."

Masapha had it all worked out in his head what he would say, how he would describe the pictures they had already taken and explain the shots they sought now. When he wasn't in prayer, he'd spent the better part of a wide-awake night fleshing out the details of his story. But it was a tale Masapha never had a chance to tell.

"Liar!" Faoud roared. "Both of you are liars! I want the truth! I want to know what you are doing here and I will find out."

He turned toward the jailer, who unfurled a thick black whip he held coiled behind his back.

"They only want to lie to me. Drive the truth out of them, Ahkmad. One of them will talk. Whip them until they do."

Masapha choked. *Whip?* Ron didn't understand what the ugly

Arab said, but he understood the whip in the jailer's hand and the look of fear on Masapha's face. He knew something very bad was about to happen.

The two soldiers put their guns on the floor, grabbed Ron and Masapha and pulled them to their feet. They shoved their bodies face first up against the wall, pulled their arms up over their heads and fastened their wrists in the sets of shackles that dangled from iron spikes driven into the stone at five-foot intervals all around the room. Masapha was so short, he had to stand on his tiptoes.

Faoud watched for a moment. A cruel smile twisted his ugly face, then he spat on the floor at Ron's feet and stormed out.

Ron's cheek was pressed against the rough, clammy wall. He could smell the musty odor of the fungus that grew in the stone cracks where water occasionally seeped in. The smell made him gag. Even as he hung from shackles next to Masapha, he wrapped his denial snug around himself for a few final moments of protection from reality. They couldn't... they wouldn't...

One of the soldiers stayed behind with the jailer. He grabbed Ron's shirt collar from the rear, inserted a cold blade of steel beneath it and with one quick move, the knife separated Ron's shirt from his back. The soldier stepped over to Masapha and repeated the procedure. Then he moved back into the corner of the cell to give Ahkmad plenty of room.

Ron's heart hammered in his chest, fear a cold knot in his belly. His back felt bare and vulnerable. No, they weren't *really...*

From the blindsiding jolt an unspotted safety had given him in a football game his senior year in high school, to the time he had cut his leg with Uncle Thomas' chainsaw, Ron had never known such pain. As the whip sliced a groove down the right side of his back, every nerve anywhere near the blow exploded in agony, and his body recoiled, arched into the wall against the cold stone. The entire middle of his back felt like someone held a torch to it. He gasped a huge lungful of air with such force his throat throbbed, and held onto the scream that threatened to tear out of his mouth.

All of his senses were so heightened by the pain that when the jailer stepped over to take his turn with Masapha, it sounded like an elephant had stomped across the dirty hay.

The crack of the whip as it whistled through the air sounded more ominous than the rebel rockets fired at his hotel in Liberia. The lash landed on Masapha's back with a sickening thud, and Masapha's moaning gasp was a stifled cry of agony.

The footsteps turned Ron's way again. He heard them halt. Like the tide recedes before a great wave, Ron sensed the whip draw back. His skin crawled and he instinctively shrank away, tensed...

Whap!

The second blow was slightly lower than the first, harder. It cut a deep canyon of lacerated flesh as it sliced downward. Ron's body arched and jerked in an involuntary spasm; a gasped moan escaped his lips. Like broken underground water lines, the shattered capillaries sent a surge of warm blood down his back. He heard the jailer's steps shift to repeat the blow on Masapha's back.

Whap!

This can't be happening! Ron thought, it can't be hap... !

Whap!

Whap!

The men screamed now. Both of them. Every time the whip sliced into their backs, they screamed.

Whap!

By the fifth blow, Ron and Masapha were limp, their weight supported by their wrists in the shackles.

Whap!

After the eighth blow ripped into Ron's swollen, bloody back, he slipped mercifully into unconsciousness.

The unconsciousness is a color. Blue. Blue and gray. The sky at the gravesite after his father's funeral. He and Dan are standing by the casket at Hillcrest Gardens while Uncle Thomas escorts Aunt Edna down the cemetery path to the waiting limousine. Most of the crowd has left. Dan stands tall and straight, his hands in his pockets, gaz-

ing at the shiny silver casket with fresh roses strewn on top. Only 18, he already has the air of a young man who's going somewhere; Ron, long-haired and sullen, looks like he has nowhere to go.

Gusts of frigid wind cut across patches of snow on the ground and whistle among the grave markers. Dan and Ron are quiet, each in his own world. Then a deep, rumbling voice makes ripples in the silence.

"Pastor Wolfson was the bedrock of this community," Mr. Albertson, the chairman of the local chapter of the NAACP has come up behind them and stands next to Dan. "I never knew a finer man than your father, ever! Black or white."

He reaches out and pats Dan on the arm.

"You should be very, very proud of him, son," He pauses and looks each of the boys in the eye in turn. "You just make sure you make him proud of you, hear?"

The old man turns and crunches across the frozen ground to his car.

Before either of them has a chance to respond, Ellen Birkeman comes gushing at them, her dyed platinum hair football-helmet perfect, her dress under the fake fur coat a little too tight and a little too low-cut for the occasion.

"Boys, I am so, so sorry," she says in her shrill, nasal voice.

She pauses and looks at the casket. "You know where I'd be today if it weren't for Rev. Wolfson."

Actually, they didn't, specifically. But judging from her appearance, they could make a pretty good guess.

"You boys had the best father in the world!" She squeezes Dan's hand, pats Ron on the shoulder, turns and walks away.

A door slams shut, and the car bearing their father's sister pulls away from the curb. When it does, the dam holding back Ron's emotions bursts.

"He never should have been on that road in an ice storm," he says quietly, but with so much emotional intensity he sounds like he's shouting. "And he wouldn't have been out there if he had said no—

just one time, no, I'm going to stay home with my family, you'll just have to solve your own problem! But he couldn't do that; he couldn't put us first just once! And now he's gone."

Dan tries to put his arm around Ron's shoulder, but Ron pulls away. "He did the best he could, Ron."

"That was the best he could do?" Ron shouts back in a rage. "The best he could do was never showing up at a single one of your games, not one? The best he could do was never taking us fishing or building a snow fort with us or showing me how to shoot the .22 rifle he got me for Christmas, or teaching me to drive?"

"He wasn't perfect, but... "

"Oh, yes he was! Just ask all those people out there he helped and they'll tell you he was perfect. They'll tell you all about how he fed the poor, built shelters for the homeless, stood up to the legislature, took on the river boat casinos and the pornographers, child abusers and drunk drivers."

Ron is sputtering, his words coming out in a great rush, "All those people will tell you he was a great guy.... a wonderful guy!"

Some of the air whooshes out in a tired sigh. "Wish I'd known him."

Dan stares at the casket for a few moments before he speaks.

"He screwed up, Ron. He was a good man who made a lot of mistakes. But I think he would have figured that out someday. I think he'd have changed if... "

"If he wasn't dead?" Ron retorts viciously. "Yeah, being dead more or less limits your ability to interact with people, doesn't it. Dead is... gone."

Suddenly, Ron turns on Dan and spews it all out on him like the time when they were kids he had vomited all over Dan's shoes.

"And for what? Can you tell me that? For what? Look around you, Dan. The same prejudices, the same problems and battles to fight. Nothing changes. The only difference is we don't have a father anymore."

Dan is struggling, too. As the oldest, he has a special treasure— a few memories of his father playing catch or reading him stories when Ron was too little to remember. Back when the legendary Dr. Paul Wolfson was just beginning his ministry. Those memories slice into his heart now like a rusty can lid, and he wants to cry, to sit in the dirt beside his father's grave and cry.

But he knows his father would want him to be strong for his younger brother, who is hurting in a way Dan can't quite fathom. So he swallows hard and does what he knows his father would want him to do. It is the first time his father's character has served as his guide; it won't be the last.

"Sometimes change takes a long, long time." Dan speaks slowly, chooses his words carefully. "And sometimes it doesn't happen at all—never will happen. But that doesn't mean you don't try, that you just throw up your hands and walk away. Dad fought for a lot of important things, and I don't think his story's over yet. "

"Oh, his story's over all right!" Ron reaches down and picks up a handful of dirt and holds it out to Dan. "It's over! This is the dirt those guys over there in the blue shirts are going to shovel in on top of him as soon as we leave."

Dan can't think what else to say. He finally just blurts out, "He loved you, Ron. And he loved me. But he was struggling, too. He adored Mom—I saw how they were together!—and he missed her every day of his life. Did you ever think about that, about the burdens he carried, how hard it was for him? He was a single parent and he did the very best he could to balance it—to be a pastor, to stand up for what he believed in, to be a mother and a father, too—all at the same time. He tried! He just didn't get everything right. Can't you forgive him for that?"

Dan reaches out, but his younger brother pushes his hand away.

"Leave me alone." Ron turns his back but after a few moments speaks softly. "Maybe someday I'll think what he did was as wonderful as everybody else does. But not right now. It hurts too bad right now. I just want my father back."

His shoulders begin to shake and he turns to Dan with tears streaming down his cheeks.

"I miss my dad!" The last word comes out in a strangled sob and Dan wraps his arms around Ron and holds him while he cries.

Whap!

When another searing lash sent a shock wave through him, his body jerked and he heard a wailing scream. He realized it was his own before he slipped quietly away again.

This time, the scene playing on the screen of his mind is set almost a decade after the death of his father. It is the New Albany Newlin Hall ballroom in the Floyd County, Ind. district that has just elected Dan the youngest state senator in the history of the Indiana General Assembly. The party is in full swing. Confetti is flying, champagne is flowing, a band is playing rock 'n' roll songs from the '80s, and a large group of well-wishers encircles Dan.

Ron smiles and begins to shoulder his way in to see his brother. He finally gets close enough that Dan sees him. The new state senator parts the crowd like Moses parting the Red Sea and folds his younger brother to his chest in a mammoth bear hug.

"Congratulations, big guy!" Ron shouts above the noise of the crowd and the music. "I'm proud of you! And Dad would be, too!"

Dan looks into his brother's eyes and they connect. They have a moment, the two of them, alone in the middle of the crowd. Dan nods his head and says softly, "Yeah, I think he would. Thanks." There's too much noise for Ron to hear the words, but he reads Dan's lips and the look on his face.

Someone shouts Dan's name and he looks up and smiles, but keeps his arm draped across his brother's shoulders.

He might even be proud of me, too," Ron continues to shout. "I got my letter from the Peace Corps today. I'm in."

Dan can't understand because of the crowd noise. He leans down to put his ear closer. "What did . . . ?" Then he suddenly sees the Indiana lieutenant governor, one of his biggest political supporters. He straightens up and waves, then turns back to Ron and shouts, "I'm sorry, what? I didn't get that."

Ron responds with a big smile and shouts really loud, "I'll tell you later!" Dan nods his head vigorously and smiles back, and Ron turns and vanishes into the celebrating crowd.

Whap!

Ron's body convulsed and smashed his nose into the rock wall. He groaned, the agony in his back so excruciating he had no air to scream.

Through the jackhammer of his heart in his ears, he heard Masapha scream. But the sound came from a long, long way away. Then Ahkmad stepped back behind him. He wanted to cry, but he had no air for that either. He tensed, didn't breathe, cringed...

The jailer said something in Arabic, and Ron heard the big door open and slam shut. The key clanked in the lock and two sets of boots stomped down the hallway. Then there was silence.

● ● ● ● ●

Omar's quest had been successful on two fronts. He'd found both information and transportation.

Julian's sources had given him the names of two men they believed worked for slave traders. He'd talked to the sister of a Murahaleen guerilla who captured tribals and sold them and made lots of money. It was a place to start.

A local entrepreneur had a jeep that he normally leased to government officials or businessmen on their way to the oil fields. Even though Omar drove a hard bargain, it was still a lot of money, and the supply Idris had given him was steadily dwindling. Omar kept meticulous track of every pound. He would stretch the tribal's funds as far as possible, but when the money was gone, the game was over. Without a vehicle, there was no chance at all of finding the girl; with a vehicle, there was very little.

Omar motioned for Idris to follow him and led the way to the inn where they would spend the night before they picked up the jeep to start their search by daylight. They turned the corner and headed down a dusty side street toward a building with a sign high above it. It was a big, red sign with a roaring lion on the bottom: the Al Jubari Lodge.

* * * * *

Masapha's voice was breathy; it was hard to talk when your entire back from the neck to the waist was an agonizing, throbbing wound.

"That day we found Koto, remember?"

Why in the world was Masapha worried about Koto now?

"The kid will be fine," Ron gasped. He tried to remain perfectly still. It hurt less if he didn't move. Much of his body now was turning a hideous mixture of blue, black and red from the merciless flogging. The fiery agony throbbed with the rhythm of his heartbeat, and the pain traveled around his rib cage, where the whip had several times wrapped itself around his torso. A sticky pool of gel had formed in the crack of his buttocks with the blood that flowed down from shattered capillaries. His right eyelid was fluttering—the result of the eighth lash, when the tip of the whip came over his shoulder and caught his eye. For the last hour, he had slipped in and out of consciousness, and he had to focus his foggy mind to speak.

"Koto will make it; he's a survivor."

What he didn't say was, I hope the two of us are, too.

"No, I do not mean that... the crucified men... "

Before Masapha could continue, they heard the footsteps of the jailer and the soldier in the hallway. The man with the scarred cheek opened the heavy door and stepped into the cell. Omar's henchman followed, and the rusty hinges again creaked as the heavy door thudded shut.

Ahkmad understood the psychology of torture. He had learned to inflict serious injury and then withdraw and allow the victim time to suffer, to experience his agony. It was when you returned for the second round that the prisoners always broke. Already in torment, they were willing to bargain away everything they had, do or say whatever you wanted—anything to avoid more pain.

Ron looked at Masapha. His limp body, already lean, looked

emaciated from water and blood loss. Now covered with bloody, bruised stripes, the man hanging from the shackles resembled an antelope carcass that had just been field dressed. Ron imagined he probably looked just as bad.

There was a heartbeat of silence before they heard the whip unfurl and make a rustling sound as it uncoiled on the straw-covered floor. The soldier said something to the jailer in Arabic, and the scar-faced man moved from behind Masapha to behind Ron. The heavy whip dragged through the straw, as ominous as a viper snaking its way across the ground.

There was a pause, and Ron was afraid he was going to be sick. He tensed for the blow he knew would come and cringed away from it, tried to melt into the cold, stone wall. Though he tried to stifle it, a whimper escaped his lips.

Suddenly, Masapha cried out in frantic Arabic. Ahkmad stepped up to him and fired questions. Masapha answered each one, a desperate urgency in his voice. They spoke for several minutes. When he was finished, the jailer said something to the soldier. They both laughed. Then the jailer crossed the room to the door, and from a peg on the wall beside the door frame, removed a key. He used it to unlock Masapha's manacles and then Ron's. Both men immediately collapsed and curled up beside the wall.

The jailer left, came back with a small bucket of water and placed it in the center of the cell. Neither of the men on the floor had the strength even to crawl to it. He motioned to the soldier and the two of them walked out and locked the door behind them. Ron and Masapha could hear the men's footsteps retreat down the stone hallway.

As soon as they were out of earshot, Ron spoke. "What did you tell them?" He was sure he knew already. What else could Masapha have said that would have satisfied their tormentors?

"Everything."

In short, pain-filled sentences, Masapha explained that he had told the men what he and Ron had really done in Sudan, what they had photographed, what had happened to the film, and why they had remained in Kosti.

Well, that's the ballgame, Ron thought, and the realization sliced pain into him as real as the blows from the whip.

"You do not ask me why I spoke," Masapha said. "But I will tell you. You could not understand the words of the soldier to the whipping man. He said to forget about the Arab and concentrate on the American. He said Faoud had given instructions to make you talk or kill you."

Masapha let that sink in for a heartbeat before he said softly. "There are easier ways to die, my friend, than to be beaten to death. And we are going to die."

Ron looked at Masapha, who lay bleeding in the straw beside him. His mind reeled, stumbled, tried to track what the Arab was saying. But he backed up from the reality of it like a calf from a branding iron.

"I was in such pain, I dreamed about the crucified men," Masapha continued. "And that is when I remembered. When we were there, you took pictures, a whole roll, then you loaded in another roll in your camera, yes? But only you had shot a few frames, and then we saw Koto and... "

The memory dropped into Ron's mind with the force of a refrigerator dropping on his head. Those were the last pictures he'd shot! But he didn't finish the roll so he didn't unload it! That roll was still in the camera!

"The slave man has that film, and when he sees the pictures, he will know crucified men are not for a magazine of traveling," Masapha said. "He knows who only would take pictures like that. He is aware who we are or can figure it out."

Masapha grimaced in pain when he tried to sit up, so he gave up and remained where he was. "Why would this slave man let us live? He will say, 'Oh, you have tried to destroy me, so now you can go free?'"

Ron said nothing.

"Who will come to rescue us from this death? Even who knows we are here?"

Masapha's words were like ice picks that jabbed again and again into a smooth, hard, frozen surface, and sent little cracks in all directions.

"We are going to die, my friend. You Americans think the guy always wins who wears the white hat. You do not really yet understand Sudan. It is death here all around. Only you can avoid it for a while, and then it catches you. For that death, it is time now to prepare. I will make peace with Allah; you should make peace with your God."

Masapha turned on his side to face the wall, in what he hoped was the direction of Mecca. He began to gasp out familiar words, long-ago-memorized phrases. Allah might listen to his prayers; he might not. It was impossible to know. He could only hope that he had done a sufficient number of good things in his life to earn Allah's favor.

Ron lay where he had fallen, wondering what in the world he ought to do to prepare to die.

* * * * *

Koto had never felt so lost. Not even when he'd escaped from the slave traders and wandered wounded through the bush. He'd been alone then, but he'd been in his own element. He knew how to survive in the wild.

Nothing was familiar here; everything was foreign. As long as Masapha and Ron had been there with him, it had been exciting—the sights and smells of the marketplace, the strange people in odd clothing who spoke languages he didn't understand. With Masapha to translate, to talk to, to—yes, take care of him!—it was an adventure.

Now, he was alone with no one to understand. He had spent the day in the marketplace. He had listened, searched for his own sound, his language. But he found no one who spoke Lokuta. He was hungry. He'd had nothing to eat since the meal he, Ron and Masapha had had the preceding night. And he was frightened, not just for himself, but for the two men who had so quickly become family to him. Out of nowhere, armed men had snatched them up and carried them away. Where? What was happening to them? What would happen to him?

Koto returned to the Al Jubari Lodge because it would be night soon and he had nowhere else to go. He squatted in the dirt under the big red sign, put his head in his hands—and even though he'd said he never would again—he began to cry.

* * * * *

Omar had decided to spend the night at the lodge because he had no desire to tangle with the gangs that wandered the streets of Kosti at night. Tomorrow, he and Idris would pick up the jeep he'd leased and begin following the leads his sources had provided.

Three or four men were talking with the lodge owner. Omar had to wait until they finished before he could make arrangements for the night; Idris stood behind him, looking around. That was when he spotted a boy with a bandage on his shoulder. The teenager sat beneath the lodge sign crying.

Omar paid the proprietor and motioned for Idris to accompany him into the building. Idris didn't follow. Instead, he walked over to where the boy sat with his head in his hands. Omar made it all the way to the door before he noticed Idris wasn't with him. He turned, called Idris' name, and motioned "come on" with his hand. Idris shook his head no and pointed to the boy.

Then Idris motioned for Omar to come to him and again pointed to the boy. Idris said something in Dinkan and pointed to the boy a third time. Omar couldn't speak Idris' language, but you couldn't miss the intensity of his tone. And he had come to know the farmer well enough in the weeks they'd spent together to know that the thin black man would not budge from that spot until Omar came.

He stepped out of the doorway with a sigh and wondered why

he'd ever allowed himself to be talked into bringing the soft-hearted father with him.

The boy looked up when he sensed Idris in front of him. He saw only kindness in the man's face; but there was no kindness in the face of the Arab who stalked toward them. Koto began to inch away and glanced quickly from side to side for an escape route.

Idris spoke several phrases to the boy in Dinkan. The boy caught a word or two and replied in Lokuta. Idris was about to try again, when over his shoulder, he heard the gruff voice of the mixed-race mercenary, son of a Lokuta woman.

As soon as Omar spoke, a wave of relief washed over Koto's face. Omar barked only two words, a callous, "What's wrong?" That launched Koto into a 10-minute, blow-by-blow description of the raid on his village, his capture, escape, meeting Ron and Masapha, the hospital and arriving in Kosti.

Without any understanding of how damning the information could be in the wrong hands, the boy told Omar in detail what Ron and Masapha had done in Sudan and what they were looking for in Kosti.

Then he described what had happened the preceding night, how the men had come in the dark with guns and hauled Ron and Masapha away.

Omar listened intently to the boy's story. He asked a question or two now and then. His mind raced. An American and an Arab who snooped around the slave trade are kidnapped and hauled away in the middle of the night? You didn't have to do mental cartwheels to figure out that someone must have gotten wind of what they were doing, someone who didn't want the light of international scrutiny focused on the slave business. And who might that be?

Omar didn't care what happened to Koto's friends, but their abduction provided a great opportunity for the mercenary. The most logical jumping-off point in a search for a slave was a slave trader. Obviously, there was one around here close by and Omar intended to track him down. The proprietor had likely been bribed when the

American and his friend were taken—by whom? Somebody in the lodge or the neighborhood saw the pair hauled away, probably a lot of somebodys. Somebody noticed what kind of vehicle the thugs were driving. Omar was confident that if he waved a few pounds under "somebody's" nose, he'd get the answers he needed.

Yes, indeed, this chance meeting could provide a wealth of information. Omar intended to be up early in the morning to track it down. He motioned for Idris and the boy to go in ahead of him while he paid the proprietor for Koto's lodging, too.

Chapter 19

Joak had almost fallen asleep when the door at the front of the room grated open—again. For the third time that evening, the lodge keeper had admitted more people. Well, he couldn't let many more in; there were only a few beds left.

Leo had passed out in the bed beside Joak's even before the sun began to set. He'd been drinking all day, and the high alcohol content of the home-distilled liquor finally hit him. He'd been so drunk when Joak guided him to the inn that he hadn't even tried to get the two of them private rooms, just staggered into the dormitory and collapsed on one of the bunks.

Joak was furious. If Leo had let him come earlier, they would be asleep upstairs in real beds, not down here on canvas cots crawling with chiggers. Every bite made him more irritable; he hoped when Leo woke up his body was one gigantic itch from head to toe. And he also hoped these were the final travelers the innkeeper let in for the night. Joak wanted quiet, so he could toss and turn in peace.

He squeezed his eyes shut, willed himself to relax again, as someone padded down the aisle and lay down on a bed on the other side of the room. Suddenly, a particularly vicious chigger chomped into his calf, and he rolled over to scratch the spot. That's when he saw a tall, thin tribal enter the room. Although four candles burned in the wall brackets, Joak couldn't see his face well. But there was something about him that looked familiar. Joak half sat up on one elbow and peered at the bare-chested black man in the dim light. The thin face with tribal marking scars on his forehead, the bead necklace, the ebony spear. He could swear he had seen this particular tribal somewhere.

Omar came in and made his way down the aisle past Idris and the bed on the other side of the aisle where Koto already had stretched out. The big man located the next available bunk near the end of the row, slid his rifle carefully under it, sat down and pulled off his boots. He took the small leather pouch of Idris' money out of his backpack and placed it on the mattress beside him, then shoved the pack under the bed beside the rifle.

Joak took no notice of Omar at all; his attention was focused Idris.

The tall tribal leaned his ebony spear against the stucco wall by his assigned bed. He placed the small roll that was his pack under the bed, knelt on his knees beside it for a moment and then stretched out on the canvas mattress.

Joak lay back down, his mind whirring. Where had he seen...? That face? That bead necklace? Where? Oh, forget it! Joak was annoyed that he couldn't remember, so he resolutely dismissed the tribal from his thoughts and concentrated on going back to sleep. That's when it clicked. *The southern tribal they had scammed up-river.* Leo had promised to help him find his daughter, and had conned him out of a lot of money!

Joak's heart began to pound. No use trying to awaken Leo; he was out cold. Joak lay still, didn't move for half an hour. He gave the African plenty of time to settle into his bed. Then the toothless man in a flowered shirt sat up, got to his feet quietly and limped slowly toward the door. As he did, he swerved by the African's bed to get a closer look at the now motionless form. It was the same villager they'd scammed weeks ago and 350 miles south of here! Joak eased the door open, signaled to the manager that he needed to relieve himself, and escaped into the night.

* * * * *

Prepare to die.

For some reason, those words made Ron think of the movie *The Princess Bride*, when the Spaniard had announced time and again in his heavily accented English: "My name ees Inigo Montoya. You keeled my father. Prepare to die!"

But that fleeting connection was the best Ron could do to be flip about his situation, and that didn't last long. Then he was back in a stone jail cell as evening dissolved into night, his back a screaming agony, his mind running madly around in all directions in an effort to come to terms with what Masapha had said.

Masapha's logic was too sound to argue.

Unless they could escape, the ugly slave trader would kill them. And they couldn't escape.

Unless someone came to rescue them, the fat man with the little rat eyes would kill them. And there was no one to rescue them.

Unless...

Ron quickly ran out of unlesses. Exactly how the man would kill them, Ron couldn't imagine, and it turned his stomach to think about it. But he couldn't pretend that it wouldn't happen. Ronald Joseph Wolfson, 385 Barrington Ridge Blvd., Fairfax, VA, the proud owner of a 4-year-old Honda Civic, a little condo full of mismatched furniture, a cat named Scrubs that lived at Dan's, and a storage shed loaded with scuba gear and rock climbing equipment, was going to die.

The full impact of that realization hit him like a left hook to the chin. It staggered him.

The sun was about to set outside. Very little light filtered in from the lone window high above his head. Masapha lay on his side facing the wall—either asleep, unconscious or on his own private journey. And as the light dimmed, Ron became more and more terrified. Not afraid of dying; afraid of the dark! He knew the room would soon be blind-man black, and that thought sent his heart on a thudding rampage that threatened to explode out of his chest.

While he still could see, he forced his pain-wracked body to move, and crawled/scooted across the room to where Masapha lay. When all the light was gone, he had to be able to reach out in the darkness and touch another human being. He couldn't be alone; not now. After the torture he'd endured, he couldn't be here in the blackness by himself.

And he remembered the nights he'd crawled into bed with Dan because he was afraid to sleep by himself. Ron would never have confessed such a weakness to his father, but as soon as the lights were out, and his father had gone to bed, Ron scrambled out of his top bunk and crawled in beside his big brother in the bottom.

Dan had never complained, had never told Ron, "Go sleep in your own bed." He'd just scooted over to give Ron room. And better than that, Dan had never said a word about it. Not to their father, not even to Ron.

Whenever their father was home at bedtime, the big man always came in and said prayers with the boys. They'd all three kneel beside Dan's lower bunk, his father in the middle, and pray. Though Ron struggled now to remember what they'd said in those prayers, he couldn't recall a word.

But he could remember vividly the first time he had refused to pray. He'd been home from college; Dan, from law school. Aunt Edna had asked him to say grace before supper and he said no. It just popped out. He didn't mean for it to. Dan had swooped in to save the day, as he always did, so the moment wasn't awkward. That night, though, they had it out on the front porch, Dan yelling at him that he had been rude; Ron countering that he was only being honest.

"Why bother to pray?" Ron shouted at his older brother. "You think God listens? You think he cares?"

Dan stopped shouting then and just looked at him. Ron wasn't expecting what he said next.

"You think God's just like Dad, don't you."

Suddenly, it all made sense to Dan. He understood. "You think God created us and then bailed, left us out here to fend for ourselves, to sink or swim."

Dan stood for a moment, shaking his head. When he spoke, he sounded sad. "Ron, just because you think Dad was a lousy father doesn't make God one."

He opened the screen door and went back into the house, leaving Ron outside staring up at the stars in the Indiana sky. Ron couldn't see the stars here. The cell was almost completely black now and Ron's heart pounded in his chest like a fist on a door.

There are no atheists in foxholes, he thought.

OK, God, I'm here, and I'm scared, and there you have it, my life in a nutshell, he said inside his head. *The scared part... I really am scared. It's so dark!* And he thought miserably, *Oh please, God, help—don't let me cry!*

He drew in a deep, shaky breath. Then another. And another. Gradually, his heart stopped its tap dance and began to beat normally again. And he didn't feel alone anymore. Maybe it was his friend's presence nearby, but somehow he didn't think so. It was something more than that.

God, I need to do this like a man. With dignity. I need to die like—he could hear his father say, "Now son, you remember, you're the child of a King. Act like it!"

OK, G... He stopped himself. *OK, Father, help me die like a man.*

Then he remembered an old Bible story and added in a rush: *But you got the Apostle Paul out of jail. Please, please—get us out of here!*

* * * * *

Pasha suddenly appeared beside Akin as she scrubbed a pot blackened in the fire when the cooks prepared breakfast. The woman took her by the arm into the dining tent and gave her a loaf of warm bread to eat! Akin was stunned, but quickly gobbled it down before

Pasha could change her mind. Then the head mistress returned with two female servants who carried towels and soap, and indicated that Akin was to go with them down the path to the river.

At the water's edge, the women pulled off Akin's ratty T-shirt, so filthy and faded the smiley face was almost completely gone. They took her into the water and gave her a thorough soapy bath, then dried her with towels and dressed her in a small white wrap. Akin had not felt so clean and so comfortable since the day she'd been stolen from her village, and she was totally mystified by what was happening.

The women took the child back to her shelter. One of them had a small blanket, and she placed it on the ground for Akin to sit on. The other woman produced a swatter made of horse hair to drive away the flies from her clean body. Then the women left Akin alone under the tarp.

Why? Why the special treatment?

The little girl had seen too many horrible things to be naive enough to believe that what was happening to her was a good thing. Nothing here was ever a good thing. But whatever bad thing was about to happen, it was not happening right now. If captivity had taught her anything, it was to live in the moment, and she seized it, savored the small measure of humanity shown to her. She picked up the fly swatter and made up a game. How many of the huge, green latrine flies could she swat? The pile of them would be something to talk about when the others returned to the shelter that night.

* * * * *

The sun had risen above the riverbank trees and the streets were already filled with people who'd brought their goods to the Kosti market when Idris stepped out the door of the lodge. Though normally an early riser, he'd slept a little later than usual this morning. When he awoke, he'd found many of the room's occupants already gone, including Omar and Koto. He saw their beds empty, and his heart had risen into his throat, but then he saw Koto's small roll still on the bed where he had been sleeping, and he knew they would return.

Omar and Koto had left the lodge that morning before anyone else was awake. Omar had taken the boy with him to the market to buy food so he could question him more about what had happened to the American and his Arab friend.

Among a group of men across the street from the spot where Idris waited for Omar were two men who knew exactly what had happened to the American.

Joak had returned to the lodge before first light and awakened Leo, whispered in his ear, "Get out of here, now!"

Leo knew enough about fast exits not to ask questions. He simply stood up and left the room as silently as a cat. Once outside, Joak told him about the villager. Now, they waited across the street for the tribal to emerge from the dormitory room so Leo could confirm for himself that it was the same man they'd swindled.

Leo's mind had been spinning ever since Joak awakened him. How had that Dinka tribal—villager, farmer!—made it all the way to Kosti by himself? The only possible answer was: he hadn't. Somebody had helped him. But who? That was a good question, one Leo considered as he waited. Finally, the tall, slender villager with his familiar ebony spear came through the doorway.

Leo rubbed his coarse beard and stared across the street. That was him, all right, the father so desperate to get his daughter back.

"We're going to kill him, right?" Joak asked impatiently. He'd thought about it, too, and had it all figured out.

"No, we don't kill him." Leo said flatly. He hadn't taken his eyes off Idris and a plan began to form in his head. "If I listened to you, we'd have been broke, in jail or hanged a long time ago."

Leo continued to stare at the tribal and what passed for a smile twisted his face under his crooked nose.

"What?" Joak's eyes shifted from Leo to Idris and back.

"You look at him, you see a dead man," Leo said. He turned to face Joak. "I look at him, I see a present."

Joak was lost. "A present?"

"A present for Faoud," Leo said and returned to his inspection of the tribal. "Faoud paid us well for the American, didn't he? Why was that?" He didn't bother to wait for Joak to respond; the fool probably didn't know the answer. "Because the American was interfering with Faoud's business, and Faoud never allows anybody to do that."

Leo pointed at Idris, "Now this man, he's trying to find a slave and take her back from the master who bought her! Faoud can't very well let people get away with that, now can he? That wouldn't be good for business."

A toothless smile broke out on Joak's face. No, that wouldn't be good for business at all.

"And there's more going on here than this stupid villager." Leo muttered to himself as he thought out loud. "How did he get here, all the way to Kosti—a tribal, who only speaks Dinka?"

He turned to Joak, and his ugly face grew sinister. "That's a question I am sure our friend, our *partner* Faoud will want to ask him."

* * * * *

Koto totted a burlap bag full of food as he and Omar approached the lodge. Just ahead of them, a cloud of dust made its way down the street and rose over the tops of the small concrete dwellings. The transport bus had come to pick up the lodgers and take them to the work camps. As the vehicle neared, Omar spotted Idris standing behind the waiting group of workers in front of the lodge, and he smiled. The tall African held his familiar ebony spear and stood faithfully beside Koto's bedroll.

The bus rounded the corner and pulled up to the waiting crowd; diesel fumes and dust clouds swirled in its wake. The group surged forward to board the bus, but as Omar watched, a figure suddenly pulled out of the crowd of men and grabbed Idris.

Surprised by the hand that encircled his wrist, Idris' eyes followed the scarred arm up to the menacing face of Leo Danheir. He would not have been more shocked if he'd been attacked by a lion in the middle of the street. As soon as Idris identified Leo's vengeful face, he also identified the point of steel that applied pressure to the middle of his back. He remembered Leo's knife. It had been very sharp.

"Come on, my determined little farmer friend," Leo said pleasantly. "I have someone I think you should meet."

Leo shoved Idris around the group of men boarding the bus and through the cloud of dust behind it. He held Idris' left arm, walked about half a step behind him, and poked the point of the knife into Idris' back often enough to remind him it was there. Joak yanked Idris' spear out of his hand and tossed it on the ground. He grasped the tribal's right arm and held on as if Idris were supporting him as he limped along. The threesome moved along the street, turned a corner and headed down an alleyway between two tall warehouses.

Omar had watched the whole drama; so had Koto, his eyes wide with horror. The mercenary turned to the boy and told him quickly in Lokuta to take the food, go back to the lodge with their belongings and wait for him. Then he set out behind Idris and his captors.

For the next half hour, Omar followed Leo, Joak and Idris through the streets and alleyways of Kosti. Well before they got to it, Omar saw the top of a two-story stucco house behind a rock wall on the edge of town.

After he watched the three men disappear through the gate under a stone archway in the wall, Omar began to make a wide circle around the dwelling through the trees and brush. When he got directly behind the house, he saw a gray stone building with high barred windows outside the rock wall. There was a tall gate in the wall opposite a wooden door in the side of the building. He continued his orbit and discovered a trail on the other side of the rock building that wound out to the road on the other side of the house, presumably for the use of vehicles that transported captives to and from the jail, for that was surely what the stone building was.

Satisfied that he knew the lay of the land around the house, Omar made his way back to the stone building. Hidden in the brush nearby, he leaned back against the trunk of a tree, made himself comfortable and prepared to wait.

* * * * *

Faoud sat on the patio, where a servant had just brought him a second pot of mariamia tea to go with his breakfast of mammoui, date-filled cookies. He smiled, chuckled under his breath, in fact. Today was going to be an enjoyable day, he thought—yes, indeed, a most enjoyable day. Then the servant returned and announced that Leo Danheir wanted to see him.

"Most noble Faoud, I know you are a busy man," Leo fawned. "I have come to you with more information, *new* information to sell."

Faoud's eyes narrowed. He liked small, quick facts, not the long story he suspected he was about to hear from Leo. "Explain."

"I rented a bed last night in the Al Jubari Lodge." The name clicked instantly with Faoud. That was where he'd found the American and his Arab friend.

"And while I was there, I saw a man from the south who weeks ago had tried to hire me to find his daughter. She'd been carried off from some village by... " Leo paused for effect, "a black-robed man named Hamir riding a white horse. You have a captain who fits that description, do you not?"

Faoud nodded, and Leo plunged breathlessly ahead. "And this farmer was willing to pay me a lot of money to find this girl, take her from her owner and bring her back to him."

Leo cast a glance at Joak and grinned. "Of course, I took the fool's money and left. I did not think I would ever see him again."

"So what are you saying?"

"I am saying that this," Leo pointed to Idris with contempt, "farmer could not have found his way from Bentiu to Kosti all by himself."

Faoud looked at Idris, and the tribal returned his look with an icy stare. All of these men, including the fat one—no, *especially* the fat one—were as evil as puff adders, and Idris refused to be cowed by evil.

Leo was right, Faoud thought. This was a simple tribal. Somebody must have brought him to Kosti. And who might that be? Who might be helping this farmer find a slave, one Faoud's men had taken and Faoud had sold?

Leo continued to prattle on. When he said something about the American, Faoud held up his hand for the mercenary to be silent. He wanted to process this information. Leo was suggesting that this tribal was in some way connected to the American. How could that be? Why would the American help him? He had come to Sudan to take pictures of slaves, not to help some farmer find his daughter. But *somebody* brought the tribal to Kosti, and he was staying in the same lodge the American had stayed in.

"I am tired of guessing who is helping this farmer look for his daughter. We will get him to tell us, and then we will not have to guess anymore."

He clapped his hands and two guards with automatic weapons appeared like ghosts out of the shadows.

"Take him," he indicated Idris, "to Ahkmad. Tell the jailer to find out... " He stopped and turned back to Leo. "What tribe is he?"

"Dinka."

"Do you speak Dinka?"

"No, but my man here does." Leo pointed to Joak.

"Then your man will be the interpreter." Faoud turned back to continue his instructions to the guards. "I want to know who brought this villager to Kosti. I want to know everybody who is involved in any way. Everybody."

He addressed Leo, "I am going to kill the American and the Arab tomorrow morning. I will kill this man, too, and anybody else who dares to interfere in my business. And when these men die, I want all my problems to die with them."

The guards grabbed Idris and headed down a stone walkway that led from the patio to the rock wall; Leo and Joak trailed after them.

From his vantage point in the woods, Omar watched fatigue-clad guards put Idris in the jail, just as he thought they would. Two of them, along with the two men who had kidnapped Idris, came out the gate in the wall and knocked on the door. Someone let them in and the guards came right back out. The others remained—the two troublesome strangers and the tribal who'd insisted on coming along on this quest. Well, Omar had warned him not to sign up for this adventure.

The mercenary shook his head and whispered softly under his breath, "I told you, father, that I might have to use you as bait."

Chapter 20

When footsteps sounded in the stone passageway outside their cell, Ron and Masapha froze, instantly terrified. But the men who came through the ancient dungeon door had no interest in them.

There was scar-face, the jailer who moonlighted as an enforcer for the Arab Gestapo; a crippled, toothless, black man in a flowered shirt; an Arab whose nose looked like it had been hit with a baseball bat—more than once; and two guards escorting a tall, thin tribal between them.

The guards dragged the tribal across the cell to the far wall where the manacles hung, clamped his hands in the shackles and left.

Ahkmad turned to Ron and Masapha and said something in Arabic.

"He says we are to get from the way so he can work," Masapha told Ron.

The two of them exchanged a look and moved their injured bodies carefully into a far corner of the cell.

The two other men got out of his way as well when the jailer unfurled his whip and swished it around in the straw on the floor before he reared back and slashed the tribal's bare back with it. The man jerked forward into the wall, grimaced in pain, but made no sound.

"Joak, tell him he can save himself a whole lot of grief and pain if he just tells us what we want to know right now," the smashed-nose man said, and the weird-looking man translated what he had said into Dinka.

Masapha leaned over and translated it quietly for Ron.

"Tell him he will answer our questions eventually anyway," the man continued. "Why not do it now before we have to hurt him, why wait until we break him? And we will break him."

Joak spoke to the man who hung on the wall, and the man said nothing.

Whap!

The whip ripped a new canyon of agony down the tribal's back. Again, he jerked forward soundlessly.

"Tell us how you got to Kosti," Leo said. "Who helped you?"

Joak translated the question, and the man who hung on the wall replied in pain-filled Dinka.

"No one helped me. I came on my own. I got information from farmers who had seen the raiding bands on the move, and I followed after them. I worked in the fields to support myself. I came with no one."

"Liar!" Leo roared, and Ahkmad went to work again.

Over the course of the next hour, Ron and Masapha pieced together what the men named Leo and Joak wanted to find out from the tribal. But the tribal stuck to his story. And he never cried out. Not once. Ahkmad hit him again and again, and he never made a sound.

Idris believed with all his heart that his daughter's life depended on his silence. Over the course of the past weeks, he'd become convinced that against all odds, defying all logic, Omar could find Akin, *would* find Akin. But the mercenary would not have the chance if these men found out about him. They would kill him.

As the lash ripped his thin back, the Dinkan farmer focused on his little girl.

Whap!

Her dimpled smile.

Whap!

The sound of her voice.

Whap! Whap!

The pain was so excruciating that Idris began to pray desperately to die. He begged God to take him away from the agony. He would go and be with Abuong and trust that the man named Omar would find Akin and take her home.

After 16 lashes, Idris slipped into unconsciousness. Leo was disgusted. He stalked out of the cell and Joak limped along behind him. The jailer unlocked the shackles and let the tribal's limp body fall to the floor. As soon as the cell door slammed shut, Ron and Masapha did what little they could for the injured African. They washed the wounds on his back with the remaining water from the bucket the jailer had given them the preceding day to wash their own shredded flesh.

"This is one tough tribal!" Ron said, as he picked pieces of straw off the man's slashed back. "He's a better man than I am."

Ron knew that if he'd suffered the beating Idris had taken, he'd have told the jailer anything he wanted to know.

"He is protecting someone," Masapha said. "And that someone means more to him than does his own life."

Leo and Joak stood outside the jail as the late morning sun began to fry the day.

"I don't think he knows anything," Joak said. "The jailer said most men buckle and talk after half as many lashes. He didn't say a word."

Leo said nothing. He was thinking.

"I don't know of a man alive who wouldn't talk after a beating like that," Joak prattled on. "If that won't make him talk, what will?"

"His daughter," Leo said quietly.

"What?" Joak had no idea what Leo meant.

The big man sighed. Joak was so stupid you always had to draw him a picture. And even then, sometimes he still didn't get it.

"He's a father, right?" Leo said. Joak nodded. "He sold everything he had to find his little girl, came all this way. Do you follow me?"

Joak nodded his head again. "He hired somebody to help him find his daughter just like he tried to hire us. You could beat this man to death, and he'll never tell you who it is. If he'd die to protect his daughter, he'd die to protect whoever is looking for her."

"So what do we do?"

"What if we found his daughter?" Leo said. He spoke the idea as it popped into his mind and he liked the sound of it when he heard it. "Don't you think he'd spill his guts all over the floor to keep us from hurting her?"

"But how can we find his daughter?" Joak was mystified again.

"We know this dung-toting farmer's name is Idris Apot, and his daughter's name is Apin, or Aleen or Akin... something like that. That's what he told us, isn't it?" Leo asked.

Joak nodded and smiled in agreement; in truth, he had forgotten the farmer's name as soon as he heard it.

"And Faoud's man Hamir raided this guy's village. It's a long shot, but maybe Faoud knows who bought the slaves from that raid."

Leo was proud of his own deductive prowess, eager to impress Faoud with how smart he was.

"Let's go find out," he said, turned on his heel and headed toward the gate in the rock wall.

Omar saw their conversation from his hiding place in the woods. He was close enough to the jail that he could hear the kidnappers' voices, but not close enough to make out what they said. He suspected it likely had something to do with Idris, so he continued to watch and wait.

* * * * *

"You're in luck!" exclaimed Faoud. "Instead of five hundred haystacks to look through, you only have two."

Leo eyed Faoud warily. The big man was far too accommodating. It made Leo nervous. It was possible he had been smoking the narcotic drug, quat. Leo couldn't tell for sure. But he knew the slave trader's moods could change faster than a cobra could grab a mouse.

"I remember the raid on Mondala because my captain, Hamir, remembers it. The villagers killed five of his men and injured seven others in that raid. I do not know how many captives he took—but all the captives from that area were sold at sales in the oil fields. And most were purchased by customers who are here in Kosti or nearby."

Faoud looked up and gave Leo a crooked smile.

"The boys—50 or 60 of them—I sold to a brick-maker who needed workers. I sold two different groups of girls to camel herders who do a lot of business here. Hadim Raja Shad bought a large group; Sulleyman Al Hadallah bought only a few."

Faoud paused to finish the remainder of his tea. Then he picked up a set of keys off the woven reed stand beside his chair and tossed them to Leo.

"Take my jeep," he said. "My man Sadiq downstairs will give you directions to the camel camps."

Leo grinned happily; even Joak could tell this was good fortune.

"I don't know if you'll be able to find the camel herders," Faoud said. "They may be gone already. Some of them have already broken camp and moved back to the north."

* * * * *

The call had come right after Dan confirmed his family's tickets on the noon flight home to Indiana. He and Chad Mattingly had been listening for the third time to the gripping interview Rupert Olford had sent, when Dan's secretary buzzed in that Alonzo Washington wanted to speak to him.

Could Dan come right now to the conference room at the end of the hall on the second floor of the Senate Office Building? The Black Caucus had convened a private session to talk about his bill, and the group hadn't been that divided since Justice Clarence Thomas' appointment to the Supreme Court.

"I'll be there in 10 minutes." Dan hung up the phone and sat very still, thinking. Then he looked at Chad.

"Son, you know a whole lot more about this kind of thing than I do. Is there any way to get this interview, what this kid is saying, out of there," he pointed to Chad's laptop, "and to this meeting in a form I can use, that people can hear?"

"I can do that for you, sir. I'll edit out most of the tribal language, too."

Dan looked dubious. "Can you do it in 10 minutes?"

Chad responded with the two words Dan wanted to hear: "Yes, sir!"

Rep. Washington met Dan at the conference room door and whispered as he led him into the room. "Remember, this meeting never happened. We've already been here for over an hour, and it's been brutal! As soon as somebody stops shouting long enough to take a breath, I'll throw you to the wolves."

"Thanks a bunch, Alonzo."

Dan glanced at his railway-flag watch, the birthday gift from Ron to commemorate the electric train the two of them had as boys—the one that ran on tracks spread from one end of the manse to the other. He smiled when he thought of his brother, then did the time zone math—six hours difference, 9 a.m. here, 3 p.m. there. He wondered what Ron was doing in the middle of this Friday afternoon in Sudan.

* * * * *

Ron couldn't stifle a groan when the soldiers threw him down on the hard clay tiles at Faoud's feet. The slave trader had waited patiently on his patio while the guards half dragged, half carried the bruised, bloody American down the stone pathway from the jail.

Faoud was seated in a rattan chair with wide arms, a high back and bright orange cushions. It rested in the shadow of a canvas awning that stretched over the patio to protect it from the flaming mid-afternoon sun.

"Welcome," Faoud said. In English.

He caught the look of surprise on Ron's face and smiled broadly.

"You do not know that I speak English, Mr. Wolfson?" he asked in feigned surprise. "Ah, but you will find that there is much you do not know about me. With languages, as with everything else in life, it is always wise to pretend to know less than you do. You find out many things that way."

Faoud turned and gestured through the patio doors into his house.

"I am sorry that I could not invite you inside, but you are not," he paused and wrinkled his nose at Ron's condition, his raw, bruised back with bits of straw and dirt stuck to the caked, dried blood, "fit to go into my home as you are."

His voice darkened. "An infidel is never fit to go into the home of a follower of Mohammed, may his name be praised."

Then the expansive hospitality returned to his tone. "So I will make you as presentable as possible and entertain you here."

He clapped his hands once and an African in a white robe appeared out of nowhere. "Clean him up," he told the African.

The African disappeared into the house and returned shortly with a large basin of water, a pitcher and towels. With a gesture of his head, he summoned the guards who stood beside the patio door. They grabbed Ron by the arms, picked him up off the floor and shoved him into a kneeling position. The African stepped behind him and began to pour water over his bruised and lacerated back. It felt cool and soothing on his enflamed skin. But it was not soothing when the African scrubbed away the straw and dried blood with the dry towel. The pain was excruciating; it felt like acid had been applied to his back from his neck to his hips. Ron sucked in great gulps of air and gritted his teeth not to cry out. The servant repeated the procedure twice.

Then the guards picked Ron up and deposited him roughly in a chair opposite Faoud. Ron instantly leaned forward so his lacerated back would not touch the chair back, and for the first time, was on an eyeball-to-eyeball level with Faoud. He made a quick assessment. The man, undoubtedly the ugliest human being he had ever seen, was either drunk or high on something.

The slave trader nodded his head unconsciously up and down, as if he were very slowly saying yes, yes, yes. His small eyes were open too wide, and they were coal black, the pupils fully dilated. It seemed to take an effort for the fat man to focus on Ron, to pull his attention from some fixed point over Ron's left shoulder. When Faoud spoke, his speech was slow—not slurred, but carefully articulated, the way a drunk cautiously puts one foot in front of the other during a sobriety test.

"I would offer you a smoke," the fat man said, and for the first time Ron noticed a bong on the floor beside Faoud's chair, and the thin pipe from it in the man's hand, "but I know that you will want your wits about you because I am about to give you your heart's desire."

Ron figured it probably wasn't tickets on the first flight out of Sudan, or even the Big Mac he'd dreamed about last night. In fact, it was a pretty safe bet that whatever the man had to offer, he wouldn't like it.

The slave trader smiled a vacant smile and continued, "As a gift, from me to you, I will grant the last wish of a man about to die."

That hit Ron in the belly. He understood clearly that his life lay in the palm of this man's hand. The Arab with the squinty eyes, the pig nose and the pock-marked face would determine how many moments his life would have and when they would run out.

"I have been considering what your small friend told my man in the jail cell about your purpose here in Sudan," Faoud said. "You have apparently gotten all of the story you wanted, except one part. It was your desire to talk to a slave trader, was it not?"

Ron was surprised that Masapha even remembered the remark

he'd made in the jeep after they'd escaped from the slave sale in the oil fields.

"I have decided to fulfill that desire, " Faoud said.

He leaned toward Ron and even from across the table, Ron could smell the rancid odor of his breath, mixed with the stench of whatever he smoked.

"You will interview me, Faoud Abdul Al Bashara, the greatest of all the slave traders in Sudan! You will have a story like no other journalist has ever had."

He paused and the hard, angry edge replaced the fake joviality in his voice. "You will not live to tell the story, of course, but you will hear it because I want you to hear it. You wanted to see my world? Then I will show it to you."

Faoud clapped his hands again, and the mystery servant appeared out of nowhere again. He said something to the man in Arabic, and he returned a few moments later with a glass of liquid that he set in front of Ron.

"Drink it," Faoud said.

Ron looked at it fearfully, and when Faoud saw his expression, he burst into a real, full, belly laugh.

"There is no poison in it, you stupid American!" he sputtered, genuinely amused. "If I wanted to kill you right now, I could do it in any one of a dozen different ways. I certainly would not have to trick you into drinking poison. It is water, you fool. If your throat is dry, you cannot speak, and I want you to speak. Drink it."

Ron picked up the glass, turned it up and let the cool liquid course like a fresh stream down his throat. Faoud had not lied; it was just water.

Ron drained the glass and set it back down on the table in front of him.

"Thanks," he said.

Faoud's smile widened, and there was merriment in his glassy eyes. "You are welcome, my American friend. Anything else I can do to make you comfortable?"

Ron could think of about 50 different things.

"No" he said. "I'm good."

"Splendid! So we will begin, yes?"

Then he sat with an expectant look on his face. Ron was a little confused.

"You want me to... ?"

"Interview me! You are a reporter. That's what reporters do, isn't it? You may ask me any question you like."

Ron was nonplussed, but he understood that he couldn't refuse to do what the slave trader wanted; that wasn't an option. He shook his head and tried to focus. He didn't bother to point out that if this were a real interview, he would have a notepad or a tape recorder. He concentrated, tried to pretend it was just like any other interview.

"OK. Tell me how you got into the business."

Faoud smiled and leaned back in his chair. For five minutes, he described his work as a paid assassin, that he'd learned how to kill silently, quickly, or slowly and painfully, whatever he was assigned to do. It was easy, really; he was smarter than the men he killed. But it was obvious that he was smarter than the men who hired him, too. And the ones with the pockets full of money and the big houses all were slave traders.

Over time, he'd figured out how to buy slaves cheaper than the other slave traders and where to sell them for more than his competition, and his business flourished.

Buy low, sell high. The guy could have been an American stockbroker, Ron thought.

Occasionally, Ron stopped Faoud to ask a question or clarify a point, and the fat man positively beamed at the attention. He continued to take drags off the pipe attached to the bong and grew just a little less focused as time went on.

Ron asked how many slaves he had bought and sold over the years, where they came from and where they went. Faoud told him whatever he wanted to know. The man had a keen mind for numbers; he either had amazing recall or was running a good bluff. Ron asked how much money he'd made and what he had done with it, did he have dealings with other slave traders or the government in Khartoum, what did he think his business would be like in a year? In five years? When the Arab responded, Ron paused for a moment, trying to get his mental arms around such mind-boggling numbers.

Faoud was impatient.

"What is your next question? What else to you wish to know from this slave trader?"

The reporter in Ron leapt out before he could grab it.

"I want to know how you can do it, how you can steal children away from their parents and sell them like cattle..."

Faoud didn't let him finish.

"Oh, but they *are* cattle. They are animals." He sneered, "You Americans act like they are people, human beings. They are live-stock."

* * * * *

"...they are livestock," Dan said. His eyes searched the faces of the legislators seated around him. "The tribals of southern Sudan are nothing more than animals sold to the highest bidder."

He'd spoken to the members of the Black Caucus for 15 minutes, answered the same questions, got the same response. It was time to play the only card he had left.

"I can sit here for the rest of the morning and give you facts and figures, and still not convey the horror of life for hundreds of thousands of people," he said. "So I won't tell you all the stories, I'll just tell you one. It's the story of a 15-year-old boy named Koto Manut, and it's in his own words."

Dan explained where the interview they were about to hear had come from and that Chad had cut much of the Lokuta dialect so they didn't have to listen to long stretches of it. Then he nodded to Chad and leaned back in his chair to listen.

Koto's voice filled the conference room—the mouse that roared. Though the members of Congress couldn't understand his words, they could not mistake the intensity behind them. Soon, Masapha spoke, translating the boy's story—the raid by uniformed government troops, bombs blowing up his village, watching his father die, his own capture and the sight of his 8-year-old twin brothers, Isak and Kuak, being tied up and hauled away.

And they heard his voice crack before Masapha translated the last part of the story.

"He said his mother was in the road lying there, and they had shot her leg and her head," Masapha said. "And he said his baby sister, Reisha, was there on the road beside her... at least he thought it was his baby sister. The little body of the baby had been blown apart."

There was a communal groan around the room.

Masapha told the rest of the boy's story—the forced march, the slave auction, his escape, the bullet that ripped through his shoulder and how he was determined to go north and rescue his brothers.

"He understands what is a slave," Masapha said. "He knows what waits for his brothers. He cannot leave them to that fate. Among the Lokuta, boys must hunt a lion before they are called a man. Finding his brothers will be Koto's lion."

When Chad hit the stop button on the recording, the room was deadly quiet.

Into that silence, Dan spoke softly. "Isak and Kuak are out there somewhere. They're 8 years old and they're somebody's property. Think about that. Think what could be happening to those little boys right now."

* * * * *

Faoud clapped his hands together twice and twin servant boys appeared out of the shadows, dressed in identical white knee-length robes. They ran to Faoud's chair and stopped behind it, their eyes downcast.

"Come here," he said, and the children stepped up beside him.

"The blacks exist to serve the Arabs. That is why Allah put them on the earth."

He continued to talk but Ron wasn't listening anymore. One of the boys had put his hand on the arm of the chair as his master spoke and Ron saw a mark, the shape of a butterfly, like a tattoo just behind the boy's knuckles.

Masapha's voice spoke into Ron's mind. "Two little brothers, twins, 8 years old, Isak and Kuak, so much the same face it is hard to tell them from each other—except for the butterfly mark on the top of Isak's right hand."

Could these be Koto's little brothers, the ones he wanted to come north to rescue? Ron's mind backed up from the thought in horror and revulsion. No! Not here, not captives of this tarantula spider in a human being suit. But even as he cried out internally that it couldn't possibly be so, he searched the faces of the children and saw more there than an uncanny resemblance to each other. He saw Koto.

Faoud's voice suddenly penetrated Ron's thoughts. "...and of course I castrated them as soon as I got them," he said as matter-of-factly as "pass the salt."

Ron took in the boys' faces; they were as blank and lifeless as dolls. He measured the distance, wondered if he could leap across the table and strangle the fat man before the guards shot him.

Faoud saw the look of revulsion on Ron's face and smiled.

"You Americans." He shook his head. "You do not approve of what I do with my property. But as a good reporter, it is your job to capture reality, right?"

The slave trader clapped his hands and summoned a servant. He said something in Arabic and the man returned a few moments later with Ron's camera bag and set it on the table in front of him.

"Take my picture!" Faoud commanded.

Ron hesitated.

"Did you not hear me? I said, 'Take my picture.'"

He would not say it a third time.

Ron fumbled with the clasp, pulled the Nikon out and slipped the camera strap around his neck. He picked up one of the two remaining fresh rolls of film in the case, opened the back of the camera, fit the tag of the film onto the sprockets on the advance wheel and pulled it tight. He flipped the case shut, fired a couple of shots to advance the film, and then turned back to the slave trader seated across from him.

Faoud smiled the phony, plastic smile people paste on their faces when they look into a camera. Ron put the view finder to his eye and began to shoot. He caught the whole scene, the ugly slave trader and his twin slaves—click-click. Then close-ups. Faoud's evil, grinning face—click-click. The boys' faces, blank and desolate, their eyes dead—click-click. A half dozen frames and he was done.

And then he thought of something.

Why not, what have I got to lose?

Still peering through the view-finder, Ron moved his elbow slightly to the left on the table and sent the camera case sliding over the edge. It fell to the tile floor, scattering empty film canisters, two lenses and a lens cap under the table.

"Oops, sorry," Ron said, and leaned down to pick up what had fallen; the camera still dangled from the strap around his neck. The table blocked Faoud's view, and the man was more than a little distracted by whatever he was smoking.

Could Ron do it?

Ron had been the undisputed champion. He could change the film in his camera faster than any foreign correspondent in the Middle East, Southeast Asia or the Pacific Rim. Combat soldiers could assemble their rifles in seconds; photographers had to be able to load film just as fast. You could miss a Pulitzer Prize-winning photo while you fumbled around in your camera case for a fresh roll. Back before digital cameras and memory chips turned Ron's manual Nikon into a dinosaur, correspondents even staged competitions. Ron always won. Every time.

Faoud took a long, slow drag on the pipe connected to the bong on the floor. Ron's fingers worked their magic. The spent roll out; a fresh roll in, badda boom, badda bing. Ron sat back up and placed the camera bag on the table, bent down and picked up the lens and the cassette case, took the camera from around his neck and placed all of it inside the bag. The film he had just shot was in his pants pocket; the roll of film in the camera was blank.

"Now, you have all of your story, complete with pictures." He nodded his head at the boys and they ran back into the house. "Pictures to stir up sympathy for the southerners so you interfering infidels can tell us how to live our lives, imperialist Americans... "

He leaned forward slightly and dropped the next words one at a time, individual stones plunked into a pond. "Like your brother, Dan Wolfson."

* * * * *

"Dan Wolfson," Alonzo Washington said and nodded to the place where the big man sat at the end of the table, "has spoken eloquently and passionately about his Freedom from Religious Persecution Bill."

Washington turned to Dan. "I want to tell you how grateful I am that you were willing to come before us today on such short notice. Do you have anything further you'd like to say?"

Alonzo had passed him the ball. This was his last chance, his last shot. He felt like he was about to attempt a three-pointer from mid-court, and recalled what his coach always told him about the nobility of trying: "Dan, 100 percent of the shots you don't take, don't go in."

He smiled his warmest smile and began a quick summation.

* * * * *

Faoud watched Ron's face carefully and when he saw the look of shocked surprise, almost laughed out loud.

"Ahhh, so he *is* your brother The last names are the same—it was a guess. Excellent. *Excellent!*"

Ron was so stunned his mind reeled. Faoud saw his look of confusion.

"Do you think I am a stupid man?" he asked contemptuously. "Do you think I stay here and never go to Khartoum or Cairo, or Addis Ababa, or Nairobi? Do you think I do not know what is going on in the world and how it affects my business?"

Faoud smirked. "You Americans always underestimate your enemies. Your brother does not yet know the hive of bees he has shaken, but he will soon."

Faoud leaned back and took a long drag from the tube that led into the bong. He let his breath out slowly.

"You will not get to tell your story, Mr. Wolfson," he said quietly. "But I will get to tell mine."

The slave trader liked to play with his mouse, to watch the American squirm. He looked forward to further torture, not just mental but in every way that makes a man scream.

"Have you not wondered why you are still alive? Why I did not kill you as soon as I found out who you were and what you were doing here?"

He paused, and Ron realized this was not a rhetorical question.

"The thought did cross my mind." He hoped his voice didn't shake.

"I have sent for someone whose services I need, and you have been allowed to remain alive until he gets here—tomorrow."

The big man got up ponderously. His movements were slow, either because he was high or because his body size made movement difficult. He walked to a cabinet, turned and faced Ron.

"He is a man who understands electronic equipment, a man who knows how to operate... " he paused, reached down and opened the cabinet, "the video and sound equipment we found in your belongings."

There lay all the recording equipment Ron and Masapha had used, the not-on-the-market-yet equipment the Putz had sent to them. Whoever planned to use it had better be able to figure out how to operate it on his own, Ron thought; that stuff didn't come with an operator's manual.

Faoud watched Ron try to piece it all together in his head.

"The equipment you used for your story, I will use for mine." Faoud answered Ron's unasked question. "And you will be the star of your own movie, for a little while at least."

Faoud waddled back, sat in his chair and looked at Ron. He was coming down a little off his high and was growing weary of his cat-and-mouse game with the American.

"I am told that there is to be some vote in your government next Tuesday," Faoud said contemptuously. He got louder as he grew more outraged. "That your brother wants to punish Sudan for doing whatever we choose to the black tribals in our own country..."

* * * * *

"...to punish Sudan for doing whatever they choose to the black tribals in their own country, their own citizens—massacred in the largest full-scale genocide the world has seen since Hitler's reign of terror in Nazi Germany." Dan looked from one legislator to the next. "This bill is an effort to stop the carnage."

Dan leaned forward in his chair so he could see every face around the table. He held a pen in two fingers and unconsciously tapped it on his thumb. "It is a profound experience when an adversary stops running and turns to meet you in battle. When a plunderer points to his spoil and hurls a challenge—'Yes, I did it! What are you going to do about it?' What are we going to do about the rape, plunder and enslavement of Sudan? A window in time has re-opened. It has given us the opportunity to confront a specter lost to us in another age."

He slid his chair back and stood. "When the House reconvenes next Tuesday morning after the Memorial Day holiday, this bill will come up for a vote. Without your help, the United States will not intervene in Sudan, and hundreds of thousands of black people whose faces we will never see and whose names we will never know will suffer and die and be sold into bondage."

He paused and looked around the table before he continued, in a quiet, measured voice.

"Next week, I will stand up against an evil I thought our forefathers had dispatched to the bowels of hell over a hundred years ago. I only ask: 'Who will stand with me?'"

* * * * *

"Who will stand with him, your brother?" Faoud sneered. "Perhaps no one, when they see how much it costs. I will send your brother a message. Actually, you will send your brother a message."

Faoud took a final drag off the tube but the bong was empty.

"You see, I am going to make a video of you and your Arab friend. And I will get those who know how to do such things to put it on the Internet for the world to see. For your brother to see. I would like very much to appear with you, but I must remain anonymous. The SPLA cannot know who I am, or I am a dead man."

He stopped, and crooned in mock sympathy. "So, I do apologize, Mr. Wolfson, but I am afraid you will have to tell this story all by yourself."

The feigned sympathy vanished from his voice.

"The video will show your brother, your government and the world the price to be paid when Americans interfere where they do not belong."

He smiled. He had waited a long time for this, to watch the American's face.

"In the video, you will speak a few words to your brother, whatever you want to say, I do not care... Goodbye, perhaps."

He leaned forward and spoke the next words softly, like the hiss of a viper. "And then Mr. Wolfson, I will chop your head off."

He smiled broadly when Ron's face went totally white.

"That's right, my American friend. For the first time ever, the whole world will witness the execution prescribed by the Qur'an for infidels. You will be beheaded!"

Chapter 21

It was the hottest part of the afternoon by the time Leo and Joak drove into the camp of Sulleyman Al Hadallah. The campsite of Hadim Raja Shad had been deserted; he had already left for his home in the north. If the girl was not here, the search would come up snake-eyes and they would have an hour and a half drive back to Kosti with nothing to report to Faoud but failure.

Pasha spotted the two men in the jeep before the dust had settled from their arrival. Sulleyman and the other men were out of the camp; she was in charge.

The headmistress in her black turban strode out to meet the visitors. What was their business here, she demanded to know, and make it quick. She had better things to do than stand in the sun and talk to strangers.

Leo put on his best imitation of a submissive smile and explained that they had been dispatched on behalf of Faoud Al Bashara, who did business from time to time with her master.

"Faoud sold a group slaves to your master not too long ago," Leo said. "And we would like to ask those slaves some questions."

"What kind of questions?"

The mercenary had killed men who spoke to him in that tone of voice, but he swallowed his anger and replied as pleasantly as possible.

"Actually, I need to know their names first," Leo said. "We're looking for a particular slave, so if you could just tell us... "

"My master's slaves have names if he gives them names," Pasha retorted. "I do not know the names they had when they got here."

The stone maiden in a black turban didn't give an inch. He realized too late that he'd allowed himself to get sucked into an argument, when there didn't need to be any discussion at all. So Leo took the gloves off.

"If you will not allow us to talk to the slaves, we will wait until your master gets back and speak to him personally," Leo told her coldly. "And I will tell him you refused to cooperate with the representatives of his business associate."

Pasha flinched; Leo had her!

She left the two of them out in the sun, stalked off to the cook tent and returned a few minutes later with Mbarka and Omina in tow. Joak spoke to them in Dinka and their faces lit up. They had not heard their own language in months.

Akin sat in the shelter with her fly swatter and added victims to her ever-growing pile. She had seen the two men arrive in a jeep and had watched them speak to Pasha. She paid closer attention after Mbarka and Omina were summoned from the cooking tent. When Mbarka pointed in her direction, Pasha and the men turned and looked her way. Then they headed up the hill to the spot where she sat, squeezed into the tiny slice of shade left in her shelter. Leo wrinkled his nose at the overpowering stench of the nearby latrines as they approached.

"Good day," Joak said to Akin in Dinka, his tone friendly. Like Mbarka and Omina, Akin was surprised and delighted to hear her own language. Her smile planted twin dimples in her cheeks.

"Hello," she said tentatively, afraid to say more.

Life as a slave had changed her bubbly, outgoing personality. She was cautious with people now, wary, careful. Punishment for a mistake, even if you didn't know it was a mistake, was swift and painful.

"I wonder if you can help me," Joak said. "I'm looking for some-one."

"Who?" Akin looked at the odd, toothless man, confused.

"A little girl named Akin Apot."

Akin's jaw dropped. "I am Akin Apot!" she gasped in stunned surprise. "Do you know my family? My father is Idris. My mother is Aleuth. Have you seen them?"

Leo and Joak exchanged huge smiles. The excited little girl con-tinued to pepper them with questions but they ignored her. They had found out what they wanted to know; she didn't matter any-more.

Pasha did not understand Dinka, so she had no idea what the men or the slave said. And she really didn't care. She just wanted the men to leave so she could return to her work. There was much to be done before their departure in the morning.

Leo turned to Pasha, "My master would like to borrow this slave for a little... "

Pasha didn't let him finish. Her master's property would stay right where it was, she informed him sternly. She would not lend him any slave—and certainly not this one, not today.

"This slave is a virgin and has just become a woman," she told them. "She has been made ready and tonight my master will take her."

Leo and Joak exchanged a glance. It was clear they wouldn't be able to persuade this woman or her master to give up the little girl. But in truth, they didn't actually need to take the slave back with them. Now that they'd seen her and could identify her, they could make Idris think they had her. He would tell them anything they wanted to know to keep his sweet, dimpled child from harm.

"We understand completely," Leo told Pasha. "Thank you. You have been very helpful. Very helpful indeed."

With that, he and Joak went back to their jeep and drove away. Pasha shielded her eyes with her hand to make sure they actually left and then returned to work.

Akin sat in her shelter alone, totally baffled by what had happened to her since she woke up. The bread, the bath, the clean clothes and now this man who knew her name. None of it made sense. The only certainty in all the confusion was that for some reason today was a special day. *Something important is going to happen to me today.* She was realistic enough to concede that it wouldn't likely be a good thing, and that scared her down to her core. Still, she couldn't shake the certain conviction that this would be a day she'd never forget.

* * * * *

Ron had returned to the jail cell from his interview with Faoud a different man, quiet and withdrawn. Beyond a brief summary of the events, Masapha couldn't get him to talk about what had happened. The only time there was any spark at all in Ron's eyes was when he reached into his pants pocket and pulled out a film cassette, then described how he'd managed to swipe it out of the camera.

Masapha was glad to see a genuine smile cross Ron's face, but he didn't really get it.

"It a good thing any time you can put over one on the ugly, rat-eyed man," Masapha said. "But I do not understand the point. Why did you do it?"

"Because I *could!*"

Faoud called all the shots in his world, got whatever he wanted. No one crossed him. What Ron had done wasn't much, but he had reclaimed his dignity in some small way by his act of defiance.

"He won't be hanging *my* pictures on his wall to commemorate his depravity."

Then Ron lowered his head and told Masapha that he'd found Koto's little brothers. In a cold, dead voice, he said that Faoud had them, they were his personal slaves and he'd castrated them both. The information made Masapha nauseous.

The rescue of his little brothers was to be Koto's lion; but the young tribal was not prepared to fight a dragon. The hopelessness of the situation suddenly settled over Masapha like a choking fog. Those little boys were lost—*lost!* They'd been gobbled up by an evil of such monumental proportions it defied understanding, just like his blood brother's son had been gobbled up all those years ago.

It was a long time before Masapha noticed that Ron had fallen uncharacteristically silent. When he asked the American what was wrong, Ron had a plausible explanation.

"Faoud said the vote on Dan's bill will be Tuesday, in four days. The pictures we took, the video and the stories would have made a difference in that vote. I really believe that. Now, it's too late. Not a thing we did matters; it was all for nothing."

It wasn't like Ron to be so negative, and after that, Masapha couldn't get another word out of him. Something had happened to Ron during his encounter with the slave trader, but what it might have been, Masapha couldn't guess.

When Idris came to after his beating, he told Masapha—who translated his Dinka for Ron—his story. He described the raid on his village, the death of his son and how his precious little girl was kidnapped.

"I buried my son and then went to find my daughter and bring her home," he said simply.

Ron and Masapha exchanged a look; this man was certainly not your average Dinka tribal!

Idris told them about being swindled by Leo, and how his village had financed his second try. He wouldn't tell them anything beyond that, but it seemed clear that he'd hired somebody else to look for his daughter, and that "somebody else" had brought him to Kosti. It was equally self-evident that the tribal would give his life to protect the identify of the "somebody else" he believed still could save his little girl.

When they heard the sound of a jeep outside late that afternoon, and the voices of Leo and Joak, Ron and Masapha knew what was coming. The duo had returned to ask the tribal more questions, and the tribal would die rather than answer them.

There was a wide grin on Leo's face when the jailer let him and his partner into the jail cell. It was an evil grin.

"Tell him we have just come from a long conversation with a pretty little girl," Leo told Joak.

When the words were translated into Dinka, Idris lifted his head off the floor where he lay in pain, a look of surprise and wonder on his face.

"Tell him the child had great big eyes—and *dimples*."

When the word "dimples" was spoken in his language, a look of joy spread across Idris' face that erased every hint of pain and suffering, and he whispered a single word, "Akin!"

"Yes, Akin," Leo said. Idris ignored the agony in his back, sat up and looked at the two men who stood in front of him with shock, then joy, then fear.

"Ask him if he would like to see his daughter," Leo told Joak.

A knot formed in the pit of Ron's stomach. This was about to get ugly.

Idris, of course, responded, "Yes, yes! Please, take me to Akin."

"You have something we want and we have something you want," Leo said. "We propose a trade. You tell us who brought you to Kosti and we will take you to your daughter."

Masapha started to say something to Idris, to warn him, but Ron shook his head no.

Idris was confused and stunned. This man had actually seen Akin! And he'd take Idris to her if... then reality settled in. He had known Leo was a bad man the first time he saw him. He had had no such intuitive response to Omar. Omar was dangerous; Leo was evil. There was no honor, there could be no truth, in this evil man.

Leo and Joak watched the emotions wash over the tribal's face, watched his jaw set firmly and his gaze turn to steel. He said nothing.

The short fuse on Leo's pent-up rage burned all the way down in an instant.

"Then tell him we will bring his daughter to him!" he roared. "Tell him we will bring her here, strip her naked, and whip her as he was whipped."

His voice grew cold and menacing. "Tell him Ahkmad will hit her again and again and again, he will beat her to death unless he tells us what we want to know. Who brought him to Kosti?"

Idris heard the words translated and terror leapt into his eyes. He had not been afraid when he was taken to the slave trader. He had not been afraid when they whipped him. But he was afraid now. Whip Akin? *No!* But if he told, she would remain in bondage, would remain a slave...

"Idris, if you won't tell him, I will!" Ron blurted out. He knew the tribal couldn't understand what he said. He turned to Leo and spit out two words: "We did."

"What?"

"You heard me. I said we did," Ron lied as smooth as a satin pillow. "We brought him to Kosti, Masapha and I. He was trying to go north by himself, and we found him collapsed on the side of the road. We took him to a missionary doctor outside Lusong. He was half dead, hadn't had anything to eat or drink ..."

Ron glanced at Masapha and his friend took the lateral pass from the American like an expert rugby player, and headed toward the goal line with it.

"The doctor wanted him not yet to leave there because his body was not healed," Masapha continued the story. "But he would go north if it meant to crawl, and we were headed this way."

"And we felt sorry for him so we said he could come with us," Ron said. "Soon as we got to the dock in Kosti, he vanished and we didn't see him again 'til you guys brought him in here this morning."

There it was, the line in the water. Would Leo bite?

"If that's true, why didn't he just say so?" Leo asked warily.

"You got me, pal. Why don't you ask him." Ron cocked his thumb at Idris, then winced in pain from the movement. "Come on, he's just a dumb tribal. He's probably so stupid he actually thinks we could get out of here alive, and he didn't want to get us in trouble. Blacks may not be real smart, but they're loyal as hound dogs."

The American certainly got that right, Leo thought. Joak was a prime example. The mercenary's face suddenly lit up in a wide smile. He had known all along the American was tied up in this somehow! And he, Leo Danheir, had solved the mystery! Faoud would be delighted with the information, thrilled that he had all the rats in one trap and could snap it shut on them once and for all in the morning. They would die, and Faoud's problems would die with them.

Idris had watched the exchange in perplexity. He guessed they were talking about him, and had no idea what they'd said. But none of that mattered to him. All he cared about was Akin, all he wanted was to protect her from harm.

"My little girl... " He looked at Joak "Please do not... "

Leo didn't even wait for Joak to translate what the tribal said. He knew. His smile took on a cruel edge. He enjoyed suffering, felt powerful when he inflicted it. And he was about to cut this man's heart right out of his chest.

"Tell him what we found out at Sulleyman's camp," he told Joak. "Tell him his precious little girl won't be a little girl anymore after tonight."

Masapha groaned and translated for Ron. The two of them watched Idris, saw the shock, the revulsion, the horror. They saw more pain in his eyes than the jailer had been able to inflict with 16 lashes from his vicious whip.

"Tell him Master Sulleyman is notorious for his taste for young girls," Leo said. "And when he's finished with her, he'll give her to his men, and they will... "

"That's enough!" Ron told the smashed-nose mercenary. "Leave him alone." But it was obvious his body could not deliver on the promise of menace in his voice.

Leo took two steps toward him and buried his boot in Ron's

belly. The blow knocked all the air out of him in a whoosh and he instantly doubled over. "Don't tell me what to do, you American swine!" Leo roared. "I'll be there in the morning when Faoud chops your head off, and I'll spit in your face then just like I'm spitting in it now."

He spewed a gob of saliva at Ron, who lay a ball at his feet, then turned and stomped toward the door with Joak on his heels. He stopped before he left the cell and turned to his partner. "Tell that tribal if his precious Akin is still alive when Sulleyman and his men get through with her, she won't be when I'm finished."

Joak spoke in Dinka, then slammed the door shut and left the three men locked in their pain.

Ron suspected Leo's boot had cracked a rib.

Masapha scrambled to wrap his mind around "chop your head off."

And Idris' heart cried out in agony, "My little Akin... *No!*"

Leo and Joak chuckled as they left the jail cell.

"Let's go tell Faoud his troubles are over," Leo said, and the two men headed toward the gate in the rock wall.

* * * * *

Omar watched them go. He had spent the day observing the jail— who came, who went, what time. He'd seen the American taken to the house and dragged back out. He watched Idris' kidnappers leave and then return. He had seen all there was to see here and understood it as well as he could. Now, it was time to go back into Kosti. He needed to find out who owned the big stucco house on the edge of town. He needed to rent a jeep. And he needed the boy. Omar got up silently and melted into the woods as the sun left its last tracks in the evening sky.

* * * * *

The sun set. The jail cell grew steadily darker. Idris' mind, heart and soul were consumed with the fate of his daughter; he didn't give a moment's thought to himself.

But as the room sank into the deepest ditch of the night, Ron and Masapha grasped that they were not alone with Idris in the featureless gloom. Like a bloated, hairy-legged spider, its fangs dripping, Death had crawled into the dungeon to keep them company. They recognized his face, looked him in the eye, sat in the sightless oblivion and waited for him to come for them.

A portion of Ron's agony in the dark of the jail cell was ragged grief for Dan. Watch somebody cut your little brother's head off—what do you do with a thing like that? Where do you put it? How do you cope? And Dan's would be a very public grief. The broadcast death by beheading of the brother of a U.S. congressman—a well-known congressman who had launched a personal crusade against the atrocities in Sudan—would grab international attention, center stage in the world arena, front page news from Bangor to Bangladesh.

Ron marveled that the stupid slave trader had no idea how such an act would backfire, explode in his face. If there was any way to galvanize grass-roots America, to launch them into a holy war of their own against Sudan, chopping the head off the brother of an Indiana congressman in front of the whole world was a good place to start.

And in that way, Ron made his peace with dying. He would give his life to show the world the horror of slavery in Sudan. Ron's death would be the best story he ever wrote.

❋　❋　❋　❋　❋

Faoud stood on the porch that encircled the front side of his house. He was deep in conversation with one of his soldiers when he spotted Leo and Joak coming toward him across the lawn.

Most of Faoud's men lived in a compound on the other side of the road about half a mile from his house. The stables where Faoud kept his prize horses were located there, and the pasturelands around the cluster of buildings provided grazing for Faoud's Arabians, as well as for his men's horses and camels. Four of his most trusted guards lived downstairs in his rambling two-story home.

On this particular evening, about 15 of Faoud's soldiers from the compound had been invited to join him and his guards for the evening meal, served on a large veranda on the side of the house.

Faoud dismissed the soldier as the mercenary and his monkey approached. "Good evening. You have good news for me, I trust." The slave trader's smile never quite reached his eyes.

Leo began to babble, gave Faoud far more information than he needed or wanted. But the fat man waited patiently for the mercenary to finish, satisfied with the report.

"The American, huh," he mused. "Makes sense. Those fools operate their lives on sympathy."

He shifted gears. "Excellent. When they all die tomorrow, my problems die with them, and their deaths will send out a message to the meddling American imperialists. You have done well, Leo Danheir."

He gestured toward the veranda where the soldiers were lined up for dinner.

"You may eat with us," he said, then turned and walked away.

"We're in," Leo whispered to Joak. "We're *in!*"

● ● ● ● ●

Seated at a table in the small room with a cot that served as his bedroom just inside the front door of the jail, Ahkmad was playing Solitaire in the glow of a lantern when someone knocked on the door and called out his name.

He did not recognize the voice.

He picked up his semi-automatic rifle, went to the window slit in the door and shoved it open. Outside stood a huge Arab and a tribal boy. The boy's hands were bound tightly, and the Arab held the end of the rope.

"What do you want?" Ahkmad asked.

"I picked up this run-away." Omar gestured to Koto. "Faoud said to put him in jail for the night until he can decide whether to kill him or keep him."

Ahkmad was wary.

"Faoud didn't send me word anybody else was supposed to be locked up tonight."

"Of course he didn't, you desert jackass!" Omar sneered. "I just got here with the slave a few minutes ago. Faoud didn't expect me to track him down so fast." Ahkmad could hear the cockiness in his voice. "But no one is a better tracker than Omar Hassan!"

The jailer still wasn't convinced. "I don't know you. I've never seen you before."

"Are you deaf as well as stupid?" Omar's voice had a hard edge now. "I said I just showed up five minutes ago. Faoud hired me to chase runaways and this is my first catch, which I am tired of looking after. Open up so I can dump him in there and go get something to eat!"

"I'm not supposed to..."

"I said, open the door!" Omar exploded. Then he grabbed hold of his temper with great effort and continued, intense and menacing. "You don't want to make me angry. And you definitely don't want me to go back, get Faoud and make him angry. I'm a dangerous man when I'm angry. Faoud is deadly."

Without another word, Ahkmad reached up and took the key from the peg on the wall. He opened the door to the Arab and the tribal, picked up the lantern off the table and led them down the hallway. It was not totally dark; two small lamps cast dancing yellow puddles of light separated by stretches of darkness.

"He can sleep in here with the others," Ahkmad said as he got to the last cell.

He set the lantern and his rifle down on the stone bench beside the door and fit the key on his key ring into the lock.

"They'll all be gone tomor... "

A thin wire pulled tight around his neck. Before he could make a sound, the wire sliced through two layers of muscle and his carotid artery. With only a slight gurgle, his life spewed out on the front of his shirt.

* * * * *

Leo pushed his chair back from the table, stood and let out a loud burp. Joak had just sat down to eat, with his plate on his lap on the veranda steps. Tribals didn't eat at the table with Arabs. They had to wait until all the Arabs had eaten their fill, and then they were given the leftovers. Leo wondered if it had ever occurred to Joak that he could just as easily be a slave as any of the unfortunates they had sold over the years. No, probably not; the toothless cripple was too stupid to make the connection.

Leo picked chicken out of his teeth as he wandered over to where Joak was seated.

"I'm going to get the jeep we left parked by the jail and take it back to Faoud's garage," he said.

Faoud kept several personal vehicles parked in a building next to his house. All his other vehicles—trucks and the jeep—were housed in a garage at the soldiers' compound down the road. "I'll be back in a little while."

He turned and headed around the side of the house toward the stone pathway leading to the gate in the back wall. When he passed a table where the soldiers had been eating, he spotted a half empty bottle of rice wine. He picked it up and took it with him.

* * * * *

The prisoners had heard the sound of footsteps in the hallway and Ahkmad's voice. It was totally dark in the cell and they could see the glow of a lantern through the window in the cell door.

Ron was nauseous with a fear that had grabbed hold of his guts when Faoud said the word, "beheaded," and had gripped tighter and tighter as the minutes of his life ticked away in the darkness of the cell. Now, terror clenched so hard he couldn't breathe. Had the slave trader's techie friend arrived early? Was it Showtime already?

Lantern light spilled into the cell as the door opened and into the light stepped Koto.

Ron would not have been more surprised if Elvis had hip-twisted his way into the dungeon singing *Blue Suede Shoes.* Masapha could only whisper, almost reverently, "Koto!"

The hulking form of Omar appeared one step behind the boy. Idris' face, expressionless from the moment Leo and Joak had left hours ago, came back to life. Ron and Masapha instantly made the connection; this muscular man was "somebody else"—a really *big* somebody else!

Omar set the lantern on the floor and began to untie Koto's hands. He looked at Idris and motioned toward the door. "Let's go. We don't have much time. We're getting out of here."

He knew Idris couldn't understand the words, but was certain the tribal could figure out what he meant.

Ron's voice came from just outside the lantern's light. "Is this party invitation-only, or can anybody come?"

"The door's open," Omar said off-handedly. "All I've got's a two-man jeep, and there's only room for... "

He stopped. As Idris struggled to his feet, he moved into the glow of the lantern, and Omar saw his shredded back for the first time. An unexpected wave of pure rage drilled through Omar's body like a comet slicing open the night sky.

"Who...?" he began.

Omar had watched the guards take Ron to Faoud and then return him to the jail; he could see the American had been savagely beaten. But Idris? He'd sat right outside the jail, so close he could hear the kidnappers' voices when they stopped to talk. He would have heard the screams of a man being whipped.

 "The jailer whipped him this morning when they brought him in," Masapha answered Omar's half-asked question. "He hit him again and again to make Idris tell him about you, where to find you so the rat-eyed man could hunt you down and kill you. But Idris made no answer. He made no sound at all."

Idris had refused to identify Omar; had taken the beating in silence. Omar was shocked, sickened. But why was he surprised?

They could have beaten Idris to death and he'd have remained silent! Nothing could have forced the Dinka farmer to betray his daughter's only hope. Omar reached out and took Idris' arm to steady him, a surprisingly gentle gesture for such a big man.

"Speaking of scar-face, where is he?" Ron asked.

"Dead," Omar said. Oh, how he wished he'd let the man live so he could have killed him slowly! He stepped to the door, bent down and began to drag Ahkmad's body into the cell. "We'll lock the place up... "

Suddenly, there was a knock on the front door of the jail. Everyone froze.

"Get over there!" Omar hissed at the three injured men and pointed to the far corner of the cell. "Cover the lantern!"

He pulled the jailer's body back out of the cell and hefted it into a sitting position on the stone bench outside the cell door. He yanked the door closed, whispered something to Koto in Lokuta and shoved the boy into the open door of the next empty cell. Then he vanished in the shadows of the dark cell across the hall.

The rapping continued, followed by Leo's voice. "Ahkmad, come on, open up. I've got wine, have a drink with me."

He knocked again. No response. *Well, fine,* Leo thought irritably, *I'll drink it all myself.* He dealt the jail door one final frustrated blow and the door moved slightly. It wasn't locked.

Leo knew the condition of Ahkmad's only prisoners, so he had no concern that they'd overpowered the big man and staged a jail break. But he was curious. Why wasn't the door locked?

He pushed the door open and called out, "Ahkmad?"

There was no response. But there was somebody... He could just make out a figure seated on the bench outside the last cell. He took a few steps down the hallway and saw that it was the jailer.

"You idiot," he muttered under his breath and marched toward the slumped figure at the end of the hall. "Do you have any idea what Faoud will do to you if he catches you asleep or drunk on guard duty?"

As he passed the last set of empty cells, Koto stepped out of the darkness into the hallway in front of him.

"Where did you come from?" Leo sputtered. Koto began to back slowly toward the body of the jailer and Leo took the bait. When he lurched to grab the boy, Omar came up behind him from the other side of the hallway. He shoved the barrel of Ahkmad's automatic into Leo's back, and the "click!" when Omar cocked it echoed in the stone hallway like a gunshot.

"Breathe, and you're dead," Omar whispered.

Leo froze.

Koto went ahead of the two men and opened the cell door, and Omar shoved Leo toward it. He planned to kill the man when he got him into the cell and could use his knife or garrote; a gunshot in here would boom like a cannon.

As soon as Ron uncovered the lantern and Idris saw Leo, he started to babble at Omar frantically in Dinka. When Masapha realized Omar didn't understand, he translated. "This man knows where Idris' daughter is," he told Omar. "He was with her only ago a few hours."

Omar looked at Leo and a genuine smile lit his face under his black mustache. His gold tooth sparkled. "Well, well, well. Aren't we lucky our friend here decided to drop by!"

He spoke his next words to Leo. "Let's take a little jeep ride in the moonlight together—what do you say? I'm sure you're eager to show us where to find this little girl."

"And what makes you think... ?" Leo began brashly.

With the speed of a cobra, the huge mercenary clamped his arm around Leo's neck and shoved the barrel of the gun under his chin.

"You know where the girl is, so I will not kill you. But I can make you wish you were dead."

All the defiance drained out of Leo like water through a hole in a bucket. "I'll tell you, OK. I'll take you there. Whatever you want. Just don't hurt me."

Omar wasn't surprised at the man's reaction. He had yet to meet a bully who wasn't a coward.

"I thought you'd see things our way," Omar said. He turned to Ron, who had moved to the door, handed him the jailer's gun and told him, "If this guy blinks, shoot him in the crotch."

He quickly frisked Leo, took the quaking mercenary's knife and revolver and tossed them into the far corner of the cell. He picked up the garrote he had dropped on the floor after killing the jailer and wiped the gore onto his pants.

Then he looked at Ron and Masapha. "I've only got a two-man jeep..."

"He's got a jeep," Ron said, and nodded at Leo. "It's parked outside."

Omar felt Leo's pockets and found the keys. He turned back to Ron, who had dropped the jailer's gun in the straw and now leaned against the wall for support. "Can you drive?"

"My choices are drive or stay here? Yeah, I can drive!"

"Our friend will drive his jeep, and I will sit behind him with a knife at his back," Omar said. "You will drive my jeep. It's parked down the road. Let's go!"

* * * * *

Without any teeth, eating was a challenge, but Joak ate just about anything he wanted anyway. It took him a little longer to gum his food enough to swallow it, that's all.

He had finished his dinner at Faoud's and waited by the veranda steps for Leo to return from the garage where he'd taken Faoud's jeep. The servants had already cleaned up after dinner, and Joak was the only person still there. What was taking Leo so long? Had he forgotten that they still had to walk all the way back into town to spend the night in that chigger-ridden flop house?

Finally, the little man got tired of waiting and decided to go down the road to the garage and see if Leo had stayed there to have a drink with the soldiers after he turned in the jeep. If he couldn't find him there, Joak would go back to the jail. Maybe Leo and Ahkmad had gotten into a card game.

* * * * *

When the servant knocked on Faoud's bedroom door, the slave trader was furious. He did not want to be disturbed.

"What do you want?" he roared, and thought that if it was not important, he would have the African servant's hands chopped off.

The servant's voice called through the thick door. "The black who was with the mercenary today is downstairs. He says Ahkmad's throat has been cut and the prisoners are gone!"

"*What!*"

Faoud bolted out of bed and knocked one of the little boys—the one with the mark of a butterfly on his right hand—onto the floor. He opened the door and shouted orders as he dressed.

"Get them up—everybody! I want everybody up!" Servants came running and then dashed away to obey his commands. "Load the men into trucks."

He put his shoes on and started to waddle down the stairs.

"Split them into two groups," he shouted at his personal guards who stood at the foot of the stairs. "One is to search Kosti and the other will go with me."

"Go with you where?" the guard asked.

"To the camp of a camel herder named Sulleyman Al Hadallah!"

Chapter 22

The full moon cast a silver sheen over the desert and left pools of darkness in the shadows beneath trees and behind rocks and bushes. Five figures were hidden in one of those shadows. Behind a decaying sycamore log next to a hedge of bushes, Idris, Ron, Masapha, Koto and Leo waited for Omar. The big man stood at the end of the row of bushes and peered out at the moonlit landscape.

About 200 yards beyond them lay the camp of Sulleyman Al Hadallah—his horses, his camels, his tents, his men and his slaves.

Omar turned and strode past Idris and Ron, together in the darkness close to the bushes, and Masapha and Koto, side by side on the ground. He marched straight to Leo, pulled an eight-inch blade from its sheath and knelt on one knee beside the bound and gagged mercenary, who sat in the sand and glared at his captors.

"Your life depends on that little girl being in that camp," Omar said quietly, with an intensity that shouted. "If she is, I will set you free. But if I ever see you again, anywhere, under any circumstances, I will slit your throat. Do I make myself clear?"

Leo's eyes were wide with fear. Even in the cool night air, sweat glistened on his face and painted dark circles on his shirt under his arms. "But if she is not in this camp," Omar stopped and lifted the blade of the knife to within inches of Leo's nose, "I will castrate you, like their masters castrate the little boys you sell. That is where I will start. Before I am finished, you will beg me for death."

He leaned closer. "Now, tell me. Do you still say that the little girl, Akin Apot, the daughter of Idris, is in this camp?" Leo wagged his head up and down furiously.

Omar stood and turned to Masapha.

"Tell him," he nodded toward Idris, "that I'm going in after his daughter now. I will bring her back if I can."

Masapha rendered his words into Dinka and Omar watched for a moment as hope lit Idris' face. Then he turned and stared into the distance once more. Ron stepped up beside him.

"Did I miss something here?" he asked. "All we've got is your rifle, knife and garrote, and there's no telling what kind of firepower that chieftain has." Ron gestured toward the camp and had to stifle a groan when the movement reverberated in the open wounds on his back. He swayed slightly. The hour-and-a-half, jolting drive across the desert in the dark had been a nightmare. There were times he was afraid he would pass out from the pain.

Koto had ridden in the jeep with Ron and never took his eyes off the American the whole 90 minutes. The boy patted Ron's arm when the blond man looked woozy, and spoke what obviously was reassurance. It was in Lokuta, but Ron almost thought he could understand the words.

Though in truth, he was actually glad he couldn't understand, couldn't speak Lokuta. He was glad he couldn't tell Koto the horrible secret he knew about the fate of the brothers the boy had come north to rescue. Koto was such an unquenchable Rambo, he would go after them anyway, all by himself. And get himself killed.

Ron tried to stand straight and tall beside Omar as he continued. "You saved my life, our lives. I was set to go on the chopping block—literally—in just a few hours. I'd be dead if it weren't for you, and I'll help you do this any way I can."

He tried to grin, but couldn't quite pull it off. The effort became a grimace instead.

"I'm not sure how you intend to stand up against this guy's cannons with a popgun, a frog-sticker and a piece of piano wire, but I'll stand with you. I'm not worth much right now, but I'll stand with you."

Omar looked at the American, who could barely stand at all, with new respect.

"No one stands with me," he said. "I go alone.

"You will try to sneak from the camp this child?" Masapha asked, not at all convinced the hulking man was cut out for stealth. And the full moon would make hiding a little tricky.

"No," Omar said. "I will bargain for her. If the chieftain is in a negotiating mood, we have a chance."

He turned the handle of the large knife toward Masapha.

"If I do not return, kill this man," he said, and cocked his head toward the sweating Leo. "But remember the pain you suffered because of him and make him pay for it before he dies."

Masapha took the knife.

"He will have pain in his body worse than ever the whip gave to me." The menace in his voice promised a brutality Ron couldn't believe came from his friend. "I would have much honor to kill him."

Omar turned back to Ron. "If I don't make it back, take the jeep and the father and head south. That's your best shot. When Faoud discovers you're gone, he'll look under every rock in Sudan until he finds you."

Omar handed Ron the rifle and flashed a brief smile. "Now, we will see if I still know how to cut a deal."

Then he turned, walked around the end of the row of bushes and was gone.

The quiet of the desert night was so absolute the silence roared in their ears, and the men hidden in the darkness could hear every movement Omar made.

The big man's footsteps crunched heavily in the sand that led to the encampment.

* * * * *

The big man's footsteps crunched heavily in the gravel that led to the cemetery.

Huge purple, pink and white azalea bushes, aflame with spring color, lined the nearby fence, and a breeze stirred the multicolored carpet of fallen blossoms, changed and shifted the hues like a kaleidoscope.

It was a peaceful place, and right now, Dan wanted peace.

Sherry's father had picked up the family at the airport, and they'd visited for a while in the living room of the old farmhouse by the river where Sherry had grown up. Then David headed out to shoot baskets in the hoop attached to the front of the garage, Jonathan plopped down in front of a video game, and three generations of red-headed females chattered their way into the kitchen to whip up some gooey dessert for dinner that would add yet another inch to Dan's ever-expanding waistline.

Dan had come here, to the cemetery, to visit the grave of his father. He wanted to talk to his dad. And maybe to God.

* * * * *

Idris wanted to talk to God. When Ron turned back to the group after Omar disappeared into the night, the tribal with a shredded back dropped to his knees in the sand, raised his face to the sky and began to plead with God for the life of his daughter.

Ron didn't know what he was saying, but he understood the tone and the posture. He'd seen it before. Aunt Edna. Uncle Thomas. Dan. His father. As a boy, he'd seen all of them on their knees at one time or another, their eyes turned heavenward, their voices imploring.

He'd been there, too. Oh, not as often, but he'd been there. He'd begged for God's help.

On the slat seat of a rowboat, while he waited for his dog to come back up out of the murky water.

On the cold bench of an emergency room, while he waited for a doctor to tell him about his father.

On the filthy floor of a jail cell, while he waited for a slave trader to chop off his head.

There was a desperation in the tribal's voice that Ron knew well.

Idris's prayer was murmured, little more than a whisper of the wind. The tears that streamed down his face and dripped off his chin sparkled in the moonlight. Only Masapha could understand the farmer's words, but the others needed no more translation than Ron did.

* * * * *

One of Sulleyman's guards sat by the campfire in the middle of the camp, and he spotted Omar when he appeared out of the darkness. The man grabbed his rifle, shouted, "Halt!" and fired a shot into the air. The shout and the shot brought the whole camp to its feet, including Sulleyman Al Hadallah.

The final-night celebration had been long, loud and boisterous. The men were proud of the fine herds they would take back to the north. They were anxious to leave and looked forward to reunions with their families. They laughed a lot, ate and drank too much. The party had lasted late. But it had been over for half an hour now, and Sulleyman wanted the child, the little girl who had become a woman.

He had disrobed and was resting against the satin pillows, ready for his guards to bring the girl to him. He had looked forward to this for days.

Suddenly, he heard one of his guards shout, then a rifle shot. He grabbed his robe, flung it around himself and stepped to the doorway of his tent. He could just make out the form of the man who strode toward the campfire out of the darkness. Sulleyman straightened his robe, slipped his feet into sandals and marched out to meet him, to see who was stupid enough to disturb his evening.

By the time Omar arrived at the campfire, more than a dozen of Sulleyman's men held the unannounced visitor at gunpoint. One of the men had thrown several small logs and branches onto the smoldering fire, and it began to cast a bright glow of flickering light to give them a better look at the intruder.

It wasn't hard for Omar to determine who was in charge when Sulleyman strutted into the firelight.

He raised his hands as if in surrender and spoke calmly, "I come in peace. I am unarmed, as you can clearly see. I have come for one reason only—to do business."

Sulleyman stepped closer and looked carefully at the tall, heavily muscled stranger. He was an Arab and he carried himself like a guerrilla but had a relaxed, confident air about him. It was obvious the big man was not even mildly intimidated by Sulleyman's presence, or by the guns trained on him.

"What possible business could you have to conduct in my camp this late at night?" Sulleyman demanded harshly. "You must have a death wish! It is a miracle you made it this far before one of my men shot you."

"I'm sure your men could see that I pose no threat. I am unarmed. Who comes unarmed to do battle?"

"Tell me what business you think you can do in my camp alone at night. You are alone, aren't you?"

Omar nodded. "I am alone, as I am unarmed. You can see for yourself. I have nothing to hide. I came here from Atbara to buy slaves for my employer, Sadiq al Mahdi."

Sulleyman scoffed. "And he sent only one man?"

Omar smiled a confident smile that showed his shiny gold tooth. "I've bought for him for many years. He knows that I can do a better job than any six of his soldiers. I have his trust." He paused for effect. "And his money."

Omar patted the pocket where he kept the leather pouch with the remains of the money from Idris' village.

That got Sulleyman's attention. "So you've brought money. How much?"

Omar's grin was disarming. "Enough."

The level of Sulleyman's suspicion still rose slightly higher than the level of his greed.

"You have yet to tell me what I want to know! Why this late at night? No one but a fool goes out to do business in Sudan after dark."

Omar opened his hands, palms up. "Surely you don't think I intended to come to you at this hour! I didn't plan to arrive so late. I decided to travel through Dimari to get from Atbara to Kosti. And I misjudged the length of the journey."

He shrugged a little sheepishly.

"I will not travel that way again. It is a short route, but without roads, it takes much longer."

"I am well aware of the traveling conditions around Kosti," Sulleyman said condescendingly. "What does that have to do with your business with me?"

Sulleyman was irritable. He had been ready, eager for the little slave girl. The interruption had taken his desire away, distracted him.

"I went to Kosti to do business with Faoud," Omar replied easily. "When I got there and told him what I was looking for, he told me he had sold his best batch of slave girls to you."

Sulleyman stood silent; his look asked, "And?"

"Faoud said you are a shrewd businessman and always interested," Omar bowed respectfully, "in a good return on your investments."

Sulleyman grunted. "I am a businessman. Of course, I make a profit. If I did not make a profit I would be out of business."

"Exactly," Omar replied. "And I have a deal... "

"Sometimes I have more important things to do than business, however." Sulleyman cut him off. "The slave girls—they are for you, or your master?"

Omar smiled a hungry smile.

"Both," he said. His voice lowered an octave. "I get them... *ready* for my master. That is part of my payment."

Sulleyman recognized the longing in the intruder's voice and unconsciously connected to it. He identified with that kind of sexual need, that kind of raw, naked lust. Here was a man with a passion like his own, he thought, and his suspicions about the stranger began to melt away. The man obviously was who he said he was, so Sulleyman reluctantly shifted gears. He had lost his focus and had been interrupted at a very delicate time. But it was done, and there was no going back now. There would be ample time later to rekindle his desire. Perhaps he could make the man pay enough to make the intrusion palatable.

"You have interrupted my camp and my plans for the night, but I will still do business with you." He was fully engaged in negotiating mode. "Tomorrow we break camp and return to the pasture lands and our homes in the north. I had decided to sell one, maybe two of my slaves along the way, but if I can make the profit tonight it will save me the trouble of transporting and feeding them. You can go on your way, and we are both happy."

He clapped his hands and summoned Pasha Drulois.

She disappeared into the darkness and returned a short time later with Mbarka.

"Two hundred and fifty pounds, and you can take the girl and go," said Sulleyman with a wave of his hand. Pregnant, Mbarka would be more trouble than she was worth for awhile.

"She is suitable for a Muslim," he added as an extra selling point. "The procedure has already been performed. And as you can see, she has many fine... attributes." The teenager was naked from the waist up. Her pregnancy was visible now only in her swollen, engorged breasts.

The girl was too old and well developed to be the 11-year-old child Idris and Leo had described.

"Two hundred and fifty pounds!" Omar laughed. "Is she made of gold? For that bag of gazelle bones I wouldn't give you 100 pounds."

Mbarka bowed her head in humiliation as the two men bartered for her like an animal in the marketplace. Her dark cheeks flushed with shame.

"I seek very young girls. Girls who have not yet been used as this one has."

Sulleyman stopped. Apparently, he would not make money tonight after all.

"I am afraid I cannot help you. I have only one girl who fits your description." Sulleyman's voice grew suddenly ragged and hungry. "And tonight I will take this girl who has never known a man and initiate her into womanhood."

The thought of it instantly put him into a good mood. "You are welcome to sleep in my camp tonight by the fire and not venture back out into the bush." It was indeed a magnanimous offer to a stranger. "But it is not possible for us to transact any business."

Omar refused to back down. He stepped closer to Sulleyman. "I have traveled a long way. I seek very young girls and I will pay a premium price to get one. I am prepared to give you 400 pounds if you have such a girl in camp."

The soldiers who stood in the firelight murmured among themselves in surprise. Four hundred Sudanese pounds—for a slave?

"The going rate is 100 pounds per slave, yes?" He didn't wait for Sulleyman's reply. "You will get back four times the investment you have made. Pay 100, get back 400—you can only do that at the camel races."

Sulleyman certainly wanted to sell a slave tonight to this man who obviously had more money than good judgment. Just not the slave the man wanted. Since Mbarka's pregnancy did not yet show, perhaps Sulleyman could palm her off on the stranger. Then it would be his problem to put up with an undesirable slave and get rid of her useless offspring.

"I might be willing to make you a special deal on this one." He pointed to Mbarka. "Only because you have traveled so far and it is late, I will let you have her for 225."

Omar wouldn't budge.

"This one has known many men, probably every man in this camp." He gestured at the darkened tents just outside the glow of the campfire. "I seek young, less experienced girls. Faoud told me it would be weeks before he gets in another shipment and I need slaves for my boss now."

He lowered his voice and his tone was urgent. "And I need a virgin for myself...tonight!"

Sulleyman laughed.

"Faoud is sharper than an adder's fangs. Don't believe anything he tells you. He peddles more flesh than anyone in the country. He can find you what you want, and you won't have to wait two weeks to get it. He's just trying to jack up the price."

Sulleyman stopped, did some mental arithmetic and made a decision. "I tell you what," he said slowly. He hated to do it, but business was business. "This virgin girl I have, you can have her tomorrow for the 400 pounds you offered. You get a young girl, and I make a good profit."

Omar reached into his pocket and produced the leather money pouch. He emptied it, took from it every remaining pound Idris' village had given him.

"Everything Faoud said about you is true," he said respectfully. "He told me you were a shrewd businessman who drives a hard bargain. You are a better negotiator than I am. I will give you 500 pounds for the girl, the *virgin* girl. It is, as you can see, all I have."

The soldiers were stunned. Nobody paid that kind of money for a mere slave. Virgin or not, a girl's a girl. After their employer took the man's money, he would tell the tale forever afterward about the fool who came in the night and paid a king's ransom for a skinny little slave.

Sulleyman surprised them. With a wave of his hand, the Arab chieftain dismissed the pile of money and Omar.

"Again, my friend, you are welcome to spend the night by the fire." Omar could see twin flames of fiery lust burn in the man's eyes. "But the little slave girl is mine."

Sulleyman turned and strode back toward his tent. The soldiers shook their heads in disbelief and began to disperse to their sleeping tents. Omar stood very still for a few seconds, the look on his face unreadable.

"Master Sulleyman," he said, quietly, "I have one final offer."

Sulleyman didn't even turn around. "I don't care if it's another 200 pounds. I told you, I'm not interested."

Omar set his left foot up on a large stone beside the fire, leaned over and pulled up his pants leg. His personal money pouch was firmly attached to his calf. He reached into the pouch and pulled out a pile of bills, all the money he had in the world. "You might change your mind when you know what the offer is," he said.

* * * * *

Time was measured in breaths. In, out. In, out. The world shifted on its axis, but the men who waited for Omar's return in the moonlit desert night were suspended over infinity in a crystal Christmas ornament that swayed endlessly back and forth. There was no time, no past, no future. Life was a forever now.

In the profound desert silence, they would hear anything that approached long before they could see it. They froze at the tiniest sound, their hearing so focused they could have detected the slither of a snake across the sand.

The silence was a prison that held each man locked tight inside, a captive of his own thoughts, hopes and fears. Ron and Masapha still reeled from the pendulum swing of their circumstances. They'd been rescued from the razor's edge between life and eternity, returned from the world of the dying to the world of the living. Gratefully, their emotional response to the reversal hadn't hit yet; they didn't have time for that right now.

Masapha scooted away from Leo and whispered to Ron, who crouched in the darkness and strained with the others to detect any hint of Omar's return.

"Do you think maybe they have made of Omar a prisoner?"

Ron turned to respond and noticed that Leo had tucked his chin down close to his chest.

"Keep an eye on that snake," he told Masapha. "Looks like he's trying to loosen his gag."

Masapha pulled Leo's gag so tight it cut into the corners of his mouth. Then he sat back down and all was still and quiet again. The only sound that broke the stillness was almost no sound at all, less than the whisper of a breeze. It was the sound of prayer.

The tribal was no longer on his knees. He lay prostrate, face down. His whispered words gently moved the grains of sand in front of his mouth.

Ron, Masapha and Koto watched him as he petitioned the God of the universe to intervene in the fortunes of his child. Each of them had come to care for the Dinkan farmer. Koto remembered the kindness the tribal had shown to a frightened boy he didn't know, whose language he didn't speak. Ron and Masapha thought about the brutal beating the man had suffered in silence, how the whip slashed again and again into his back. All of them had been indelibly touched by the sacrificial love of the tall, thin African father.

* * * * *

His father's grave was next to his mother's, but each had an individual stone. Hers had been there for almost 20 years longer than his. The stones were under an oak tree with a fresh spring umbrella of bright green leaves. Dan had always liked that oak tree. He'd wanted so badly to climb it when he, his father and Ron had come to the cemetery to visit his mother's grave. If ever there was a good climbing tree, that oak was it.

A simple stone. Date of birth. Date of death. None of that "beloved father/brother/son/husband" stuff.

"Paul Daniel Wolfson," Dan read out loud. Then he leaned back against the big concrete crypt near his parents' graves, the final resting place of the dentist who'd filled his teeth when he was a kid. A breeze nudged the bushes, and purple, pink and white blossoms rained down onto the grass. Dan breathed in a lungful of air that smelled so clean it must have been freshly washed and hung out on the line to dry.

It seemed foolish to speak out loud to a headstone, but Dan did it anyway. "I wonder what it would have been like to know you—not as my father, but as a man. I think I would have liked you, that you and I would have been friends. I think we would have had some good times together. I know we would have laughed—you liked to laugh, I remember that. I remember the sound of it. It was booming, like your voice when you preached."

He smiled and shook his head. "Yeah, we'd have gone on some crusade together, too, I bet. We'd have climbed on our horses and gone out to attack some windmill somewhere. We're a lot alike, you and I."

He paused, surprised at the wave of emotion, at how very desperately he missed his father and wanted to talk to him, just once, right now.

"Dad, I don't know how to do this!" he cried out.

He looked away then, leaned his head back and blinked, so tears wouldn't run down his face.

A flock of birds fluttered overhead in the bright blue sky. They reminded him of the geese he used to watch from the porch swing when he was a kid, big, gray birds that honked their achingly lonely melody as they flew south for the winter.

"I know how to succeed," he whispered thickly, "but I'm about to fail. I don't have the votes, Dad. Plain and simple. I've counted and recounted; they're just not there."

He turned his face into the breeze and felt the chill of tears on his cheeks.

"The Freedom from Religious Persecution Bill isn't going to pass. And when it's voted down, the big corporations will heave a gigantic sigh of relief, they'll cut their political contribution checks right on schedule, the American people will keep pretending it's not happening." His voice began to break. "And men in Sudan with guns and swords and machetes will continue to ride down into villages and kidnap little kids. Make them slaves. *Slaves!*"

Dan let go then and put his head in his hands. For the first time since his father died, he cried. And some part of him he hadn't heard from in a long time spoke.

God, don't let this happen, Dan said in his head. *Please.*

* * * * *

God, don't let this happen, Ron said in his head. *Please.*

He looked down in pity at the Dinka tribal. *Don't let this guy lose his daughter after all he's been through.*

On his face in the sand, pleading with God to give him back his little girl, Idris suddenly heard the snap of a branch. They all did and froze, held their breath. Another crackle. Footsteps. Someone was coming. Idris rose to his knees and listened.

The others instinctively dropped to the sand and hunkered down behind the log. If it was a guard on sentry duty, maybe he would walk past them in the darkness. Or maybe he would change direction.

It's only one person, Ron thought, and if we had to, we could handle one person. We've got Omar's knife.

With everyone's attention diverted, Leo began to squirm in the darkness. Masapha had tightened the gag in his mouth but not the ropes that tied his hands.

As the steps neared, Ron whispered to Masapha, "It sounds like the same footsteps that left. I think it's Omar!"

The hearing of the two tribals, Idris and Koto, was much more refined and acute than the American's or the Arab's. Both figured out quickly that the footsteps that now approached had the same stride, rhythm and cadence as the footsteps that had left an hour earlier. But what struck Idris was not what he could hear; it was what he couldn't hear. The steps were solitary; they were not accompanied by the lighter, leaf-rustling steps of a child. Ron saw Idris's expression and suddenly understood what Idris already knew. Omar was on his way back, all right. Alone.

Ron couldn't bear to look at Idris's face. He had watched the man's heart break in the jail cell when Leo taunted him with what was in store for his little girl tonight.

The lone set of footsteps crunched closer and closer.

On his knees in the sand, Idris began to cry silently. He felt the same bottomless hole open in his gut that he had felt the day he knelt in the sand and cradled the butchered body of his little boy in his arms.

But Akin was not dead! Barbed thoughts ripped open his heart with jagged, nightmare images. A man held his little girl down. Akin struggled to get away, screamed, cried, pleaded with him to stop. The man came down on top of her, forced her, raped his baby girl!

He wanted to cry out, to shriek, to wail, to jump up and run into that devil's encampment and snatch his little girl into his arms and carry her away. But he could do none of those things. He had not the air to wail nor the strength to run. It was over. It was finished. He had given everything he had to save his child. And he had failed. At the moment his child needed him the most, he had let her down.

He knelt, staring with unseeing eyes into the darkness where Omar had disappeared, and sobbed, cried as he had suffered the lashes on his back—in silence. The footsteps crunched around the stand of bushes.

Suddenly, Idris froze. He sucked in a ragged gasp.

The footsteps stopped.

Ron lifted his eyes to Idris's face. He couldn't read the expression. He shifted his gaze to Omar.

Lying in Omar's arms, cradled against his massive chest, was a frightened, terribly thin, scarred and beaten 11-year-old girl.

Akin saw her father at the same moment he saw her. Her face exploded in joy.

"Papa!" she gasped.

Idris continued to sob. A smile filled his face with such profound joy it was sacred. He couldn't speak; he merely held out his arms. Omar set the child's feet on the ground. She flung herself into her father's embrace with such force she almost knocked him backward off his knees.

Idris held her tight to his chest. Tears streamed down his cheeks. He rocked her back and forth crooning, "Akin... Akin... Akin," with broken, sobbing breaths.

The child cried, too, the relief and release so overwhelming—the terror gone, her Papa here. Here! It was over, over! She cried harder and harder, let it all out in heaving sobs, her arms wrapped so tight around her father's neck he could hardly breathe.

The others rejoiced with Idris, their faces lit by the glow of his achingly tender reunion. Some of them had never felt the kind of joy that warmed their hearts. It was so pure and sweet it was almost holy.

Masapha handed Omar back his knife just seconds before Leo seized the warm, poignant moment to escape. Leo had freed his hands, and he suddenly leapt up, yanked down his gag and yelled as he sprinted toward Sulleyman's encampment.

Omar sprang like a cat. Within three steps, the big man caught up with Leo, grabbed him by the hair and jerked him backward off his feet—all in one fluid motion. Then the snake on Omar's hand struck, sliced the knife across the front of Leo's throat, and the flat-nosed mercenary settled to the sand in death.

"Out of here, now!" Omar whispered urgently.

They all jumped to their feet and raced for the jeeps, which they'd left parked on the other side of a small rise about 50 yards from where they'd hidden behind the bushes. As they ran, they heard the sound of voices in Sulleyman's camp, but they piled into the jeeps and were speeding across the desert before the guards could determine who had shouted in the darkness.

The jeeps had bounced less than half a mile down the dirt path that served as a road before they saw headlights coming from the other direction. Four sets of headlights, coming fast. Omar was in the front jeep and he slammed on the brakes. He hadn't turned on his headlights yet for fear they could be seen from Sulleyman's camp. Ron's jeep was dark, too, as he screeched to a halt beside Omar.

Nobody had to tell them who would be traveling in the middle of the night to Sulleyman's camp.

"They haven't seen us," Omar said. "But we have to get out of here and find somewhere to hide."

"Chumwe!" Ron said.

"What?" Omar asked.

"Chumwe. Can you get us to Chumwe? There's a place there we can hide, people there who will help us."

Omar nodded, turned around, angled past Sulleyman's camp and headed southwest across the desert.

* * * * *

Pasha Drulois was not about to allow her master to be disturbed again. Not now! When Faoud and his men roared into Sulleyman's camp, she marched out to meet Faoud before he even had a chance to get out of his truck.

"Where is Sulleyman Al Hadallah?" Faoud demanded to know. "I must talk to… "

Pasha didn't allow him to finish. "He has retired for the night and he… "

Just then there was a scream from the big, striped tent in the center of the camp. Everyone turned to look. They all heard the sounds of a scuffle and then a loud *smack* and the screams dissolved into hysterical sobs.

"My master is initiating a virgin slave girl into his clan tonight," Pasha said as she turned back to Faoud. "It is not the time now to disturb him."

Faoud grinned broadly. The virgin girl. The daughter of the tribal. *Excellent!*

Pasha had continued to talk and he suddenly tuned in to what the woman was saying.

" …man came and purchased the other slave girl, the little one I had prepared for my master… "

"Someone bought a slave girl here tonight?" Faoud roared.

Sulleyman's guards stood behind Pasha, ready to protect their master. When they heard Faoud's angry tone, they stepped forward, guns drawn.

The raiders Faoud had brought with him in the truck could make short work of this Bedouin's toy soldiers. But what was the point of such a fight? Faoud held onto his temper and asked coldly, "Who? Who purchased the girl?"

"I do not know his name, but he was a mercenary."

Pasha wanted to be rid of the strangers.

"He came out of the darkness and offered to pay my master a lot of money for the virgin slave girl and then he carried her away into the night."

She didn't tell the man in the truck about the shout the guards had heard, or about the dead man they had found just outside camp, his throat slit. She just wanted the stranger to leave. What was happening here in the camp tonight was private. Her master was doing what was *haram*—forbidden. He was taking the virginity of a child, a girl not yet a woman. After the mercenary left with the little slave girl she'd made ready for her master, Sulleyman sent her to bring to him the other virgin, Omina.

"How much?" Faoud demanded to know. "How much did the man pay for the slave girl?"

"A thousand pounds," Pasha said.

Then she turned on her heel and marched back into the camp, Omina's cries echoing in her ears.

❋ ❋ ❋ ❋ ❋

It was almost noon before Faoud pulled under the stone archway and drove up the driveway to his house. Even though he was exhausted, his head still spun. Where did a Dinka farmer get that kind of money? And Faoud still marveled that the lying jackal Leo had been smart enough to come up with such a complicated, convoluted ruse to trick him into producing the slave girl Leo had been hired to find.

Well, Mr. Danheir wouldn't get to spend whatever fortune he'd been paid by the Dinka to bring his little girl back. Or whatever the American had promised to get Leo to set him and the little Arab free, too. Faoud's men would track Leo down. They would look under every rock in the desert until they found him! And he would pay—oh, my yes, the mercenary would pay dearly for his deceit! Faoud would catch the American and the Arab, too. They all would pay when he caught them.

He looked up as he climbed wearily out of the truck. There on the porch steps sat Joak, Leo's loyal monkey, awaiting his master's return—too stupid to figure out that he'd been left holding the bag. A remnant of anger boiled up in Faoud's throat like acid.

He turned to his guard, "Kill him!" he said.

The guard had taken two steps toward Joak when Faoud commanded, "No, wait."

He had thought of a more fitting punishment.

"Take him to Hamid at the carpet factory," he said. "Tell Hamid the cripple is a gift, a free slave. Not a dime will I charge him. All I ask in return is that he chain this monkey to a loom and work him day and night, work him to death."

The toothless man was stunned and terrified. Where was Leo? He had waited for his partner to come back with Faoud, waited for his share of what Faoud owed them. What had gone wrong?

Faoud lumbered into the house, and mumbled under his breath as his guards grabbed Joak and threw him into the back of the truck: "He sold slaves; let's see how he likes being one."

● ● ● ● ●

Lars Bergstrom slipped quietly into the office where Ron sat hunkered over the desk, and set a cup of steaming tea down beside him.

Ron mumbled, "Thanks," but continued to write.

Bergstrom looked at Ron's back and winced. Many of the cuts already were infected. They needed medical attention. But Ron also needed to eat something and lie down and get some rest, and that wasn't going to happen either. He wouldn't do anything until he finished his stories—the American had made that patently, abundantly clear.

When the jeeps had roared into the feeding center in the middle of the night, it had taken Bergstrom less than ten minutes to hide the vehicles and provide shelter for the occupants in the back three rooms of his house. He and several helpers quickly treated the wounds of the tribal and the Arab, and prepared hot food for all of them, particularly the starving little girl. But the American wanted only one thing. He wanted paper and a pen—no, lots of paper and more than one pen. He said he had stories to write. And he'd sat down at the desk in Bergstrom's office six hours ago to do just that.

He wrote frantically, non-stop, scribbled as fast as he could. He scratched out, wrote over, marked through—and kept writing, so concentrated he was not aware of his injuries, his surroundings or anything else.

The only time he'd stopped writing was when he spoke to Masapha. The Arab had ridden to Chumwe in the jeep with Omar, Idris and Akin. The father had cradled his little girl in his lap while she sobbed out her story. The forced march. Tied under a tarp next to the latrines. Bug bites, scorpion bites, spider bites. Days of labor with nothing to eat but scraps. Beaten by the headmistress. And Shontal's gruesome suicide. She cried the hardest when she talked about Mbarka. That first night in camp when the teenager had been raped by her master, Sulleyman, and how she had been dragged away every night after that to the soldiers' tents. She described the clitorectomy and told her father Mbarka was pregnant. She sobbed bitterly as she spoke, her heart broken. Mbarka had been her friend, her protector—and tomorrow her master would take her and all his other property north to his home, where Mbarka would vanish forever into a lifetime of human bondage.

Ron had listened intently to the story, took a few notes and then went back to work. Bergstrom had never seen anybody so totally focused.

Ron was in his own world. He had gone there as he raced through the night across the desert toward Chumwe—as the cold wind kissed his face and cooled the raging fire on his back, the white orb of the moon in the charcoal sky lit his way, and fear, gut-gnawing fear, raced along behind.

Faoud was back there somewhere, Faoud with his little rat eyes and pock-marked face. The slave trader who planned to behead him, who raped women and children and massacred innocent villagers. Faoud was back there, and Ron was running from him like a man in a nightmare.

Somehow he had to communicate that terror. Somehow he had to make the world see what it was like to live in a country where monsters in white robes swooped down on you with machetes and guns, burned your home, raped your wife, kidnapped your children and hacked your friends and neighbors apart.

Somehow he had to tack words onto the kind of closed-throat terror he had felt when he stood at gunpoint in the blinding glare of headlights, when the scar-faced jailer swished the whip around in the straw before he pulled it back, when Faoud smiled his evil smile and said he would chop off his head, when he lay in the dark in a stone dungeon and tried to figure out how to die like a man. Nobody should have to live with that kind of fear! But for a tribal in southern Sudan, fear was the canvas on which every day of his life was painted.

Ron had to find the right words to describe that reality. He had to make the world understand. He had to drag his fellow Americans into the nightmare and rub their noses in the horror.

Unless his mind was completely fried, today was Saturday. Dan's bill would come up for a vote on Tuesday—that's what the slave trader had said. Perhaps there was still time for his story to make a difference.

Shortly after noon, Ron put the pen down, leaned back in the desk chair—and jerked instantly upright again as soon as his mangled back came in contact with the slat back of the chair. He'd returned to the real world, and the pain he had ignored slammed into him like a freight train made of broken glass. He picked a cup of tea up off the desk, cold now, and sipped it, as energy wheezed out of him like air out of a bald tire.

"Ron?" Bergstrom stood in the doorway.

Ron rubbed his eyes. He tried to turn around. "Lars, listen, I... "

But the pain of turning was so intense he moaned, and Bergstrom was instantly at his side. He looked with compassion down at the American and asked, "Will you let us help you now?"

Ron managed a smile. "Not yet. Not until you tell me you can have this," he nodded to the pile of scribbled papers, "and this," he leaned his weight over on one side, dug his hand deep into his pants pocket and fished out a film cassette, "on a plane to Asmara in... "

"How's 10 minutes?" Bergstrom beamed. "The pilot has been waiting for hours."

"Lars, thanks!"

Ron would have wrapped the surfer-dude aid worker in a bear hug if he could have. But it was all he could do to sit upright without swaying.

"I'm so zonked I'm probably not making any sense at all. I just hope what I wrote does."

"I have no doubt it will," Bergstrom said. "Neither does Rupert."

"Olford? You and Olford are on a first-name basis?"

"Our communication system here at the center is never reliable— you don't know from one minute to the next if it will work. We haven't been able to send or receive anything at all for more than a week—until last night when you arrived. It worked perfectly then, and I could tell Rupert what was coming."

Bergstrom smiled. "I told you—faith is what makes us tick, remember?"

Ron remembered.

"Rupert will be waiting for these papers when our plane lands in Asmara. He'll get back to Cairo on the first flight out. He said to tell you he'll try very hard to get the story put together before the vote on your brother's bill."

Ron's face shone like a 400-watt bulb.

"But he said to warn you that he could not promise anything."

That was Olford, all right.

"He said it is all about timing. Can he get the space he needs, the air time, on such short notice? He talked about things I know nothing about, but he said he would try."

Ron nodded.

"And when I described to him what had happened to you..." Bergstrom's voice trailed off as he looked at the raw wound that was Ron's back. "He got quiet and said he would try very, very hard."

"Can't ask for more than that." Ron thought of one more thing. "Oh, and get him to check the details in these stories against my notes, the ones I sent with the video and audio chips. I had to write most of this from memory." He smiled a little, even though it hurt. "In longhand, on unlined typing paper!"

Then he wobbled in the chair. Bergstrom steadied him and called over his shoulder for help. The American had finally gotten to the end of his strength. Now, he would have to let them help him. He couldn't stop them.

Chapter 23

Dan rolled over, opened one eye and looked at the clock. When he suddenly sat bolt upright in the bed, he almost knocked Sherry out on the floor.

"Dan, what in the world... ?"

Her husband looked around a little sheepish. "Oops, sorry. I thought I'd overslept. I saw the clock and... "

"Go back to sleep. It's Memorial Day, remember?"

Dan smiled. Memorial Day. His favorite holiday. And he had it all planned. The Wolfson family would spend this Family Day "in Vermont."

That was their code.

During Dan's last year of law school, the couple was so poor they could barely pay the electric bill. But they yearned for a break, a get-away. They dreamed of a vacation—didn't matter where as long as it was romantic. Say, in a ski lodge in Vermont!

So they had gone to Vermont—without leaving their tiny, one-bedroom apartment. They had closed all the drapes on the windows, locked the door, took the phone off the hook and for three glorious days pretended to be in Vermont.

After the kids came along, the little ones joined in the fantasy.

When Dan informed them that this year they would spend Memorial Day in Vermont, even their teenager, who was way too cool for silly games, dashed around the house with his brother and sister, closed the drapes and locked the doors. Then David patiently showed his father how to unplug/unhook/turn off all things electronic—computers, televisions, radios, telephones and cell phones.

The family retreated to the basement, had a picnic lunch on the floor and played Monopoly, Pictionary, Scrabble and charades all afternoon. Dan got out his Telly, a Fender Telecaster electric guitar, plugged in his booming amplifier, and Sherry and the kids sang old rock 'n' roll songs. The Beatles, the Rolling Stones, Simon and Garfunkle. He played country, too, folk songs, bluegrass—even disco. They scooted the furniture back to the walls and David did a John Travolta imitation as his father belted out *Stayin' Alive*. That night, they cuddled together on the couch in the dark and watched old black-and-white westerns and World War II movies.

They tuned out springtime in Virginia and for 24 hours, they ignored the world.

And for the same 24 hours, a good portion of that world was trying frantically to get in touch with U.S. Rep. Daniel Wolfson.

On Tuesday, Dan didn't even bother to check his voice mail when he got up. It would all hit the fan as soon as he got to the office anyway; why jump into the water with the piranha until it was absolutely necessary?

He drove into the congressional parking lot so early he thought it would be empty. Instead, he saw a huge phalanx of news media and wondered who they were ready to pounce on.

When they swarmed around his car as he pulled into a space, he honestly thought they must have mistaken him for somebody else. But as soon as he opened the car door, he figured out they'd found exactly who they were gunning for.

"Tell us what you think about your brother's stories, Rep. Wolfson!" That was the guy from the *Washington Post*.

The crowd of reporters gave him no time to answer, just shouted more questions, shoved microphones in his face and snapped pictures.

Is there a collective noun for reporters? Dan wondered, as he smiled his way through them and crossed the parking lot—*like covey or bevy or school or pride? Gang was for kangaroos, but it would work for reporters, too. Gang it is.*

The gang of reporters pushed and shoved and fired questions as they group-walked beside, behind and in front of Dan while he struggled to get by them and into the building.

"How did you manage to get the stories to run right before the vote on your Freedom from Religious Persecution Bill?"

"Have you talked to your brother?"

"What affect do you think these stories will have on the vote?"

News anchors, the big guns, lobbed questions at him like hand grenades.

Bam, Bam, Bam.

"Did you... ?"

"Are you... ?"

"Will you... ?"

He did a bob-and-weave around the questions and the reporters who asked them. He finally closed his office door almost literally in their faces and had time for one huge, heaving sigh of relief before his secretary and all his aides weighed in on him in a feeding frenzy of their own.

"Tried to call you... "

"Left you nine messages... "

"Associated Press wants to talk... "

"Sent you e-mails..."

"Rupert Olford tried to warn..."

"Hold it!" Dan's grand orator's voice could have drowned out a smoke alarm.

The room went instantly silent.

"I have been away and obviously I missed a major news event that involves my brother."

"I'll say it was a major news event!" Chad Mattingly gushed. "Why it..."

"And I don't have a clue what's going on!" Dan rumbled. "I go to the House floor for the vote on my bill in less than two hours. The press is barred from this office, no calls either—understood?"

Seven voices replied with the perfect unison of a Greek chorus: "Yes, sir!"

"Chad, I want video of everything that has run on any station, all the networks."

"Done." Chad scurried away.

"Shelly, get me copies of all the big daily newspapers, for today and yesterday."

"They're on your desk right now, sir."

Dan turned toward his private office. "Hold all calls. *All* calls for the next half hour."

Then he went into the office and shut the door firmly behind him.

* * * * *

Ron watched the never-ending line of starving villagers file into the largest of five buildings at the Chumwe Feeding Center. Faoud's jeep was hidden in a shed behind it.

Omar had returned the rental to Kosti. He'd nosed around while he was there and returned with a smile that highlighted his shiny gold tooth. He said the slave trader had pulled out all the stops to find the American, *and the mercenary, Leo,* who had helped the infidel and his friends escape.

"Faoud thinks Leo orchestrated the escape, and I am happy to let him keep right on thinking it," Omar said.

Masapha came out and sat down on the porch beside Ron and the two watched the flowing crowd. They sat in silence for a time. Five days after their beating, the bruises on their backs had gradually changed color, from angry red and purple to green and yellow. Only a few lacerations were still open wounds. The others had left puffy, red ridges that would one day shrink to white scars, permanent tattoos, a lifetime souvenir from Faoud the slave trader.

"You are thinking about your brother, yes?"

Ron knew that on the other side of the planet, it was the morning of the House vote on Dan's Freedom from Religious Persecution Bill.

"Just wondering if our stories will do any good, that's all."

"Your BBC friend said they splashed large."

Ron turned to his Arab friend with a smile. "Yeah, they splashed large. I just hope the water got the right people wet."

* * * * *

Dan stared at the picture of the little girl, big eyes, dimples, her ankle tied to a stake in the ground. He couldn't wrench his eyes away from the image. He had to force himself to put the newspaper down on his desk. Then he turned in his swivel chair and looked out the window.

Chad Mattingly knocked gently on the oak door, opened it a crack and stuck his head into Dan's office.

"Sir," he said tentatively, "I think you really need to see this."

Dan turned back from the window.

"What is it, son?" he asked absently. He couldn't get the story—a teenage girl walked into a river and let crocodiles rip her apart!—out of his mind.

"This, sir," Chad said.

He crossed to Dan, set his laptop down on an acre of cherry desktop, opened it so his boss could see the screen and clicked "play."

While the intro credits for the CBS Evening News rolled across the screen, Chad told Dan, "This story ran all day yesterday. It was on in the morning, the noon news, 6 and 11 p.m."

Dan stared at the screen, at trucks in a semi-circle on the desert floor. Groups of people, mostly women and children, were tied to each other and to the trucks or to stakes in the ground.

Dan watched in fascinated horror as a teenage boy raced away from the trucks, watched a bullet slam into him, watched him hit the ground, roll over, get up and continue to run. Koto. At the meeting that never happened, the members of the Black Caucus had heard that boy tell his story. Yesterday, they saw his words come to life.

Dan's secretary peeked in, saw Dan and Chad at the computer screen and seized the moment to speak.

"Sir, a man named Rupert Olford with the BBC wants to talk to you before you leave for the vote," she said breathlessly, in a rush to get it all out before Dan cut her off. "I know you said no media, but he said that your brother... "

"I'll take the call."

He nodded a thanks to Chad and lifted the receiver off the phone on his desk as the aide picked up his laptop, left the office and closed the door softly behind him.

When Dan replaced the receiver in the cradle a few minutes later, he dug through the newspapers on his desk until he came to one with the picture of a man on the front—the ugliest man Dan had ever seen. It was a tight shot of the man's face, and the caption warned that the pictures on the jump page inside were not suitable for children to see.

Dan read the story all the way through twice. In the past decade, just one slave trader had sold more than 20,000 people into slavery, and pocketed millions of dollars. He looked at the picture of the vacant-eyed twin boys. He thought about what this man with the beady eyes and the pock-marked face had done to his brother and what he had threatened to do.

Dan felt a sudden blind fury rise in his chest, a rage so raw and fierce it stunned him. Dan knew in that moment, with absolute certainty, that he could kill another human being. If that slave trader had been within his grasp, Dan would have fastened his huge hands around the fat man's neck and choked him until there was no breath left in his body.

Chad stepped into Dan's office again and pointed to his watch. "You have 15 minutes, sir."

Dan put the newspaper down and swiveled back toward the window. He stared out into nothingness for perhaps a minute, then stood and crossed to the coat rack beside Chad.

"My little brother is... " His voice was too full of emotion to continue. He picked up his suit jacket, slipped his arms into the sleeves, then patted his pockets and looked around. Chad went to the desk.

"Looking for this, sir?" He handed Dan his Palm Pilot.

"I sure hope it doesn't take me as long to get the job done in America as it did Wilberforce in England." Dan looked in the mirror and straightened his tie.

"Excuse me, sir?"

"Wilberforce. William Wilberforce. He worked his whole political career to get Parliament to ban the slave trade in the British colonies."

Dan picked up a folder from his desk and headed to the door. "That was almost 200 years ago, and it's still not over."

A gang of reporters pounced on him as soon as he stepped out of the elevator.

"How do you think the vote will go today?"

"Will it be close?"

"How did your brother manage to get the networks to run his slavery series right before the vote on your bill?"

Dan took that question.

"My brother didn't have anything to say about the timing of the series, and neither did I!" There was a hard edge to his voice the reporters couldn't miss. "Ron has been a little too busy lately to micro-manage the release of his series. This time five days ago, my brother had been whipped until he was unconscious and was lying in a slave trader's dungeon waiting to have his head chopped off."

Dan's words exploded like a howitzer and sparked a mighty roar of excited follow-up questions. Dan ignored them and used his size to snow-plow through the journalists and into the House Chamber. As he walked to his desk, he noticed that the chamber was as full as he had ever seen it, and the normal bank of radio and television microphones, cameras and monitors, was more crowded, too.

Good! The legislators would have to answer to more than their consciences for how they voted. There was nowhere to hide.

Dan noticed something else a little unusual, too. Several black congressmen looked up when he walked onto the floor. A couple acknowledged him with a slight nod as he took a seat at his desk.

What happened between the time he sat down at his desk and when the vote was called on the Freedom from Religious Persecution Bill blew by Dan in a blur. Pinned in the center of the bulletin board of his mind was a newspaper clipping with a picture of Faoud the slave trader. Dan tried very hard not to think about Olford's description of what had happened to Ron. Not now. There would be time for that later. Even so, words popped like firecrackers into his consciousness.

Dungeon. Shackles. Whipped. *Beheaded.*

The speaker's voice suddenly penetrated his consciousness in mid-sentence, and Dan's pulse kicked into a gallop.

" . . .all those in favor of PL. 99-057 please say "aye."

He had time to think, "This is it!" before he joined his grand orator's voice to a mighty rumble of other voices.

"Aye!"

"Those opposed, please say "no."

An equally loud roar filled the chambers.

"No!"

The volume of ayes and nays had been so similar Dan couldn't tell which had been louder. And volume was how the Speaker would determine which way the vote had gone. Unless . . .

Dan pushed his chair back and rose to his feet.

"Mr. Speaker, I respectfully request a standing vote."

A wave of murmurs washed across the chamber like ripples from a stone skipped across a still pond.

Dan didn't sit back down. He wanted to be the first to stand up against the evil of slavery in Sudan.

"As many as are in favor of PL. 99-057 will rise and remain standing until counted," the Speaker said.

He'd asked the members of the Black Caucus at the meeting that never happened who among them would stand with him. Now, he was about to find out.

All over the chamber, his colleagues began to get to their feet. Dan knew each of them, knew their stories, understood what this was costing them.

He watched the television cameras pan the room, stopping to focus on first one face and then another:

Alonzo Washington from Michigan. Alonzo fairly leapt to his feet. He had obviously decided Dan didn't stink, or he didn't care anymore if Dan's stink rubbed off on him.

Margaret Bryan from Missouri. Margaret had pointed out the American Gum/TriCola elephant in the room when Dan first met with the Black Caucus. She knew which side her political bread was buttered on but she was as tough as boot leather when she needed to be.

Charles Dubois from Louisiana. Dan recalled the elderly black Congressmen's concern that when the big companies started to lay off workers in his district, that bird would come home to roost in his front yard. The old fellow must have decided to make fried chicken.

Dorothy Warden from Ohio. Dottie was Dan's "neighbor" from Cincinnati who had questioned why Dan had gone on this crusade in the first place.

Raleigh Sutherland from South Carolina! Dan was floored. He tried to make eye contact with the old man who had opposed him on every bill he'd ever proposed, but Sutherland resolutely stared straight ahead.

Avery Thompson from Virginia. The oldest and the most influential member of the Black Caucus was the only one of the group who had asked no questions of Dan at either meeting. His stony silence had been deafening.

Lamont Walters from New York. The Muslim. Walters turned toward Dan, looked him in the eye, and gave a small nod, in clear view of the other delegates on the floor.

A simple glance around the room displayed the obvious: the Black Caucus had united around this issue, had stood together to make a decisive, powerful statement.

After the ayes had been counted, the Speaker called for the nay votes. Only one of those was any real surprise to Dan. Greg Alexander from Idaho stood beside his desk and refused to look at him.

When the Speaker stepped to the microphone to announce the results, the chamber grew instantly quiet and still.

"By a vote of 219 to 203, PL. 99-057, which calls for economic, and if necessary, military sanctions against the government of Sudan, shall be enacted, and shall remain in force until proof is supplied by U.S.-approved U.N. inspectors that all forms of human slavery there have been abolished."

Alonzo Washington rose to his feet and slowly clapped his hands. Dorothy Warden followed suit. Others joined them. And then others. The wave of applause spread to the gallery, where it became a thunderous roar. CNN and all the major network cameras pulled in tight shots of Dan. They captured the smile on his face and the tears in his eyes.

Colleagues seated nearby reached out to him, shook his hand or patted him on the back. Washington actually hugged him. But much of that response was a blur. Overwhelmed, Dan's mind was still in replay mode: the little girl with dimples, the teenage boy slammed to the ground with a rifle shot, and the ugly face of the evil slave trader, Faoud.

When Dan filed out of the chamber with other members of the House, reporters and photographers swarmed over him, pushed microphones at him, snapped pictures, babbled a cacophony of questions. He was about to make a statement when he noticed a group of his black colleagues just beyond the journalists.

"Excuse me, please," Dan's booming voice was loud enough to get everybody's attention. "I'll answer any question you have, tell you anything you want to know, give you as much time as you'd like, if you'll give me just a moment first. Deal?"

The reporters backed off and Dan approached the group of lawmakers. For a moment, no one spoke. Then the Muslim reached out his hand to Dan. Walters' grip was strong and firm.

"For the Middle Passage," he said.

With great emotion, Dan echoed, "For the Middle Passage."

● ● ● ● ●

Ron had returned to the front step of the building after dinner. It was cool there, and he'd watched the sunset, watched the stars begin to sprinkle the sky like freckles on a kid's nose. His mind was not a million miles away, but it was at least 11,000 when Bergstrom charged through the door and let the screen bang shut behind him.

"I just heard on zee radio." Excitement brought out his Swiss accent. "The bill passed. Your brother's bill passed!"

It took a beat or two for it to sink in. It *passed!*

Then a dam burst somewhere and a river of relief flowed over Ron along with a wave of salty tears in a delicious, warming flood. All the steam valves popped open, spewing out months of pent-up pressure in a glorious, liberating whoosh. Ron would have leapt to his feet and cheered, but his back wasn't up to so boisterous a celebration. Bergstrom would have slapped him on the back to congratulate him, but had the presence of mind to merely grab his hand and shake it furiously.

Somebody had finally noticed! Somebody had finally stood up to the bully. The U.S. House of Representatives had spoken with clear, moral authority. "No. This is wrong. It has to stop."

Finally!

The bill still needed approval in the Senate and the President's signature, of course. But it was on its way. And the whole world was watching.

Dan had made it happen. Oh, how Ron wanted to grab the big dude in a bear hug and tell him, "Way to go!"

But he would settle for finding a little dude, his partner, a man who had taken the same beatings he had for the same cause.

"Where's Masapha?" Ron stood up too fast and pain shot through his back. He didn't care. "I want to be the one to tell him. I want to watch his face."

Chapter 24

A villager at work in the millet field spotted them, leaned on his grubbing hoe for a moment and stared. A man was making his way down the hill-side trail with a little girl behind him.

Suddenly, recognition dawned. The villager turned, shouted at the other farmers in the field and pointed at the two approaching figures.

"Idris! Look, it's Idris! *And Akin!*

Word spread across the field and through the village faster than a sprinting cheetah. Every person in Mondala dropped whatever they were doing and ran past the pastureland and the fields to the base of the mountain trail. Then they stood in awe and wonder as the father and daughter came down the trail toward them.

Omar had driven Idris and Akin in Faoud's jeep as far as Malakai to catch the Nile Steamer to Bor. He'd brought Idris north; he would take him back and put him where he found him. Equipped with plenty of supplies from the feeding center, they traveled only at night, took no main roads and skirted around every village in their path.

The father and daughter babbled for hours as they bumped along in the back of the jeep. Sometimes they laughed, often they cried.

Omar didn't understand anything they said, just drove in silence and listened to their chatter.

Idris knew that when they got to the dock in Malakai, he had to communicate somehow with Omar. He had to arrange to pay Omar the rest of what he owed him—the additional 500 Sudanese pounds the mercenary was to receive if he actually found Akin and brought her back safely.

And Idris wanted to thank him, to somehow express the profound depth of his gratitude.

When they arrived in Malakai, Idris searched for hours to find somebody, anybody, who spoke both Dinka and Arabic. The tall tribal with the bead necklace and the ebony spear went from one person to the next, up and down the dock. The mercenary watched his efforts in amused silence. Idris could find no one.

Omar paid the fare for Akin and Idris to travel upriver to Bor with the last few dollars he had in the pouch attached to his leg. He had told no one the price he'd paid to return the little girl to her father. He pushed a protesting Idris toward the steamer and gestured that he and Akin were to get aboard.

Then he spoke, as he had spoken at times during the journey north—in Arabic. He knew the Dinkan farmer couldn't understand.

"You found her, father." His gold tooth sparkled in the midday sun. "You got a bigger lion and went north and found your daughter—before you did not get a little girl back at all."

Omar shook his head, an odd half-smile on his face. "A miracle. Take her home and guard her well, my black friend."

Then he turned and walked away.

Idris stood on the dock with an empty feeling in his chest. He watched the big Arab until he was lost in the crowd and knew he would never see Omar again. And he had wanted so desperately to communicate with him!

Then a slow smile began to spread across Idris' face. He *had* communicated with Omar, said everything he needed to say. He just hadn't used words. He reached down and took Akin's hand and they boarded the steamer together.

They rode the boat to Bor and walked the rest of the way home. Idris made sure they arrived in daylight. He wanted the whole village to see them coming.

Aleuth, with Shema at her side, raced up behind the crowd of villagers. She had been gathering firewood when a neighbor ran to find her.

"Idris is back!" the woman told her breathlessly.

Before her neighbor could say another word, Aleuth dropped the armload of sticks and dashed through the village, her heart in her throat.

She didn't dare hope. *Please God, oh please, please, dear God, please.* And then she swept around the last tukul and could see the trail. There was Idris.

There was Akin!

Aleuth was not aware that her knees collapsed and dumped her on the ground, where she laughed and cried in an unintelligible tangle of joyous sound.

She had prayed, the whole time Idris was gone, she had prayed, begged God for the life of her child. But she didn't really believe her prayers would be answered. Deep in her heart, she knew that Idris' quest was futile. She knew there was no way to find one lost child in all the north.

Her daughter was gone for good. She knew that, but she understood that Idris had to look for her, that he would not rest, would never come to terms with reality until he had done everything he could to find her. All she dared hope was that Idris would survive the quest and come home to her and Shema. They needed him, too.

Akin! Dear God, it was Akin!

Aleuth staggered to the base of the trail and gazed up at her husband and her daughter. When Akin saw her, she squealed, "Mama!" and scrambled down the remainder of the trail.

Aleuth snatched the child into her arms. She was so light! So thin. Aleuth could feel ridges on the little girl's back and shoulders through her dress. She hugged Akin to her breast, sobbed in joy and relief, and crooned the age-old mother melody, "Shhhhh, mamashere, mamasgotcha now, shhhhhh."

Tears streamed down Akin's face, too. Abuong was not here to greet her. Idris had told her about her brother's death. He was gone. So much was gone.

Over Akin's shoulder, Aleuth saw Idris. Their eyes met, their souls connected. He was thin, too, and he walked like an old man. But he was alive and home! She cried out his name, and he came and wrapped his arms around the two of them.

The other villagers stood in the glow of the Apot family's joy. Akin had been found; she was home! Her life was as real as the deaths of those buried near the road, where grass now grew over their graves.

Idris spotted Akec, tall above the other cheering villagers. He released his wife and went to greet him.

"So, you have brought your daughter home!" Akec beamed.

Idris looked deep into his friend's eyes. "The whole village brought her home. She belongs to them all."

In the raucous celebration of Akin's homecoming, everyone had forgotten about Shema. Except Akin. She felt the child next to her, holding onto her dress, and she pulled out of her mother's embrace and knelt in front of the 5-year-old.

Shema didn't look right. She didn't smile or laugh or even cry. She just stood there, her vacant eyes focused somewhere in the distance, her little face expressionless. Akin had seen that blank stare, those vacant eyes before. That was how Shontal had looked when she waded into the river to let the crocodiles tear her apart.

No!

"Shema!" Akin said sharply, and she shook the child. "Shema, look at me! *Look at me!*"

The little girl rocked back and forth, limp in Akin's grip. Then her eyes moved to Akin's face. And they focused. She actually looked at Akin, recognized her older sister.

"Akin."

It was just a whisper; so soft only Akin heard. It was the first word the 5-year-old had spoken since she led her father to the unconscious body of her mother, lying in the reeds where the robed man on the black horse had left her for dead.

Akin grasped the tiny child and held her close. Shema was still stiff in her arms, rigid. Akin just hugged her tighter. She understood. Akin knew that her little sister had gone away. She knew where Shema had gone because she had gone there herself in the months since the soldier snatched her out of the river. When reality had been too hard, too painful, Akin had checked out of reality, dropped out of life.

Shontal had checked out, too. But she had gone too deep into the darkness, too far beyond hope and she had never come back. Well, Akin would bring Shema back! She would go to the place where the little girl had gone, take her sister by the hand and lead her back out of the darkness into the light.

There was a church service two days after Akin's return. By the time it began, everyone in the village had heard the story, but they wanted to hear Idris tell it anyway. It would become part of the oral history of Mondala, handed down from generation to generation.

So the shy man stood before his friends and neighbors and told them what had happened to him. He told them what had happened to Akin, too, so she wouldn't have to talk about it. But he didn't tell her whole story. There were many things Akin told her father that he would never tell another living soul.

"I do not know the words to say such important things," he said humbly. "But I want to thank all of you for bringing home Akin, the daughter of Mondala."

*   *   *   *   *

The only sound he heard was a thump. It was an odd enough sound that it caught his attention briefly, but he was only momentarily distracted.

His bedroom door suddenly banged open, kicked from the outside by the largest of the half-dozen armed black men who swarmed in. They all held automatic weapons and all the weapons were trained on Faoud. It took him a few moments to process, to focus. How dare these...soldiers? They were SPLA soldiers!

The leader, a man named Jalal, stood silent as he took it all in. His shock turned instantly into a disgust and rage so violent he was only barely able to control it.

"You stinking swine!" he bellowed. "How I would love to blow your foul brains all over that back wall!"

When he saw instant terror register on two identical little faces, he lowered his voice and spoke quietly to the children. The boys didn't understand. He tried another dialect. Still, they didn't understand. One of the other soldiers tried. Nothing.

"Get them out of here," Jalal said. "Cover them up."

Two soldiers began to unbutton their shirts while the leader spoke to Faoud.

"You're even uglier than your picture in the newspaper."

Faoud sat up, grasped the sheet and pulled it around himself, then scooted back in the bed toward the pillows. His eyes darted frantically from one man to another. He began to pant.

The soldiers who had taken off their shirts wrapped them gently around the twins, picked them up and carried them out of the room.

The four remaining SPLA soldiers focused their full attention on Faoud.

"Get up, you stinking fat hog!" Jalal ordered.

Faoud slid over to the edge of the bed and tried to stand. But his knees were so weak they wouldn't hold his weight.

"If you don't get up, I'll kill you right here. I'd rather not, but I'm not going to carry a fat pig down those stairs."

When he finally found his voice, he began to babble hysterically. "Please, I can pay you... you don't understand, I can give you more money than you ever dreamed, make you rich... "

"Shut up and move." Jalal gestured toward the door with the barrel of his rifle. "Now!"

Faoud reached for his robe.

"Leave it!" the big black man sneered. "Let's see how *you* like being naked. Out now, I won't say it again."

Faoud waddled toward the door. He whimpered little squeaking sounds and trembled so violently his whole body quaked. The soldiers prodded him along with their rifle barrels and he finally made it to the bottom of the stairs. The bodies of his guards lay there in pools of blood.

Faoud began to sob. The soldiers shoved him out the front door of his house; it took two of them to heft him up into the back of a truck, where four other soldiers waited with automatic weapons drawn. A jeep and driver sat beside the truck. Each of the two soldiers who got into the back of it cradled in his arms a frightened little boy wrapped snug in a shirt.

Before he climbed into the back of the truck with the slave trader, Jalal told the driver, "Just drive out into the desert far enough that nobody can hear his screams."

The truck backed up, pulled out under the stone archway onto the road and drove slowly past the compound that housed Faoud's soldiers. The buildings were dark. They were either asleep or dead.

"Enjoy your last few minutes as a whole human being," Jalal said pleasantly. Then he leaned closer. "I wish I could make you suffer for years, just like those you have sold into bondage; but I will do the very best I can to make you suffer enough in one night to pay for them all."

Faoud's eyes were huge, sweat dripped off his pockmarked face and he breathed in hitching gasps.

"Your fat body will make quite a feast for the jackals. And they won't have any trouble tearing it apart. I will make it easy for them to chew."

Faoud's terror made Jalal laugh out loud.

"You do not need to be afraid, my friend," he said soothingly.

"I will not kill you. In fact, I will do everything I can to keep you alive."

He reached down and picked up a sledge hammer off the floor of the truck.

"I will destroy you slowly with this, pulverize every bone in your body, one at a time. I will place your hand on a rock and crush each finger, one after the other."

He smacked the head of the hammer into his palm as he spoke. "But I will make sure you can still scream, that you feel their fangs tear into your flesh when the jackals come to eat you alive."

Faoud's bladder released and he wet himself.

* * * * *

Ron and Masapha were still at the feeding center when they heard about Faoud's disappearance. One of Bergstrom's men from Kosti brought them the news as they sat down to breakfast.

"He was taken from his home in the middle of the night by SPLA soldiers who saw his picture in the newspaper," the man said. "No one knows what happened to him. But whatever it was, I am sure it was not pleasant."

Ron and Masapha exchanged a glance.

"Guess I got the last laugh after all, Pig Face," Ron muttered in soft triumph. "Hope you enjoy Hell."

But Ron cherished no illusions about Faoud's slave-trading operation. He was certain that some other savage already sat in the fat man's chair in the fat man's house and had already unleashed his army of ghouls to kidnap women and children and carry them off into the night.

After breakfast, Ron made arrangements for Bergstrom to take him to Kosti the next morning, where he could catch a launch downriver to Khartoum. Much as he dreaded it, after dinner he would have to say goodbye to Masapha. Ron hated goodbyes.

Masapha must have come up with the same timetable because as soon as dinner was over, he told Ron, "It would make me glad to speak to you on the porch steps."

Ron smiled. "It would make me glad to speak to you, too, Masapha."

As soon as the big American and the small Arab closed the screen door behind them, Masapha launched into his prepared speech. He'd obviously practiced it all afternoon; it sounded carefully rehearsed.

"You have come to my country from far away and done a great service, for which I am happy and grateful." He spewed the words out in a rush so he would say it right and not forget anything. "The evil of the militant Muslims in Khartoum makes sick all the rest of us who are Arabs, and brings shame and disgrace to all Muslims everywhere."

He took a breath.

"But their evil was in a secret place where no one looked until you came and dragged it out into the sun of morning for the whole world to see. I am grateful from my heart's bottom..."

"The bottom of my heart."

"That, too." Masapha plowed doggedly ahead. "And I have much pride and honor that I helped you do this great act. If ever a thing needs doing in all your life that I can do, you must promise to ask me first to do it before anyone else."

Masapha suddenly stopped and looked horrified. He had obviously forgotten the rest of what he'd planned to say.

Ron didn't let him struggle. "You're the best!" he said, his voice suddenly husky. He didn't care whether it was culturally sensitive or not, he grabbed the smaller man in a bear hug—a gentle one that didn't hurt the still-healing wounds on either of their backs.

"You and I have bled together," he whispered. "Just like you and Sharmad, we are blood brothers."

Then he stepped back. That was it. That was all he could do; he hated goodbyes.

"Where do you go from here?" Ron took the reins of the conversation and rode purposefully off in a different direction.

"The boy and I, we go in search for Koto's lion."

Ron felt a hole open up in the pit of his stomach.

"I have spoken to Koto about the little boys you saw at the slave trader's. When the SPLA took Faoud, they would not leave two little boys, do you think? Only 8 years old, in that place alone? I do not think. The boys are somewhere rescued, I believe. Koto and I will go in search for them."

"You know that Faoud... " Ron couldn't bring himself to say the word "castrated." "You know what happened to them. And I saw their faces. When you find them...I just don't know what you'll find. They won't be the little boys Koto remembers."

Masapha nodded and looked away. He'd already thought of that.

"Slowly, as time is passing, I will make Koto to understand what was done to them and the damage he will see. And if Allah is merciful and we find them, then we will try to make it right for them, the wounded ones."

He stopped, turned back to Ron, and added softly. "It is all that can be done."

"Yeah," Ron said. "It is all that can be done."

● ● ● ● ●

When Dan's secretary told him who was on line one for him, the congressman grabbed the receiver and fairly shouted, "Ron! It's you, right? I mean, it is you, isn't it? Talk to me, brother — say something!"

"Whoa!" Ron sputtered. "Do you want me to hang up and call back in five minutes when you're finished having a conversation with yourself?"

Dan began to chuckle softly. "Nobody likes a smart mouth. You know that, don't you? Fool with me, and I'll rub your face in a cow patty again."

That caught Ron by surprise and he laughed a full belly laugh. "As I recall, you got a category five backside tanning for that particular act of brotherly love. Apparently, it didn't teach you much. You're still bull-headed."

"Isn't that the pot calling the kettle black?"

"OK, we're both bull-headed. Runs in the family."

Silence hummed across the 11,000-mile phone connection. Dan reloaded first.

"You did it, Ron. Your slavery series, it was the most amazing piece of journalism I've ever seen. The bill wouldn't have passed... "

"Oh, no you don't! That bill was *your* baby, and you brought it kicking and squalling into the world, making a racket nobody could miss. Woke up the whole House." He paused. "It'll make a difference, Dan. I really believe it'll make a difference here."

"Are you all right, Ron? Truth, I'm serious. Are you all right?"

"I'm good."

"That's not what I heard."

Olford. It figured. Ron should have expected it. Now what? Did he blow it off and be cute, charming and evasive? Or real?

"It was a nightmare on steroids." Ron tried to keep his voice steady and level. "The only thing that could have been worse was dying. And I came closer than I ever want to come again to doing just that."

"Come home, Ron!" Dan struggled to keep his own voice under control. "I'll take some time off and we'll go... " He sputtered, tried to think of something. "...fishing together."

"Fishing?"

"Whatever. Look, the kids are dying to see their Indiana Jones Uncle Ron. They miss you." There was a beat of silence. *"I miss you."*

"Can't."

"What do you mean, 'can't'?"

"How many things can 'can't' mean?"

"Ron, you almost got yourself killed! I know what happened to you. I know what that slave trader did to you!"

The last words came out ragged and Dan took a few moments to regain his composure before he continued. "That's enough, Ron.

You've done enough. Come home. I'll get you booked on the first flight out—you name the city: Khartoum, Asmara, Nairobi, anywhere."

"Actually, what I really need is cash." Ron sounded like he hadn't heard a word Dan said. "I don't have a nickel to my name. And by the way, I don't say my name, our name, very loud around here anymore. Neither one of us is exactly poster boy for Hug an American Week."

"Then come ho..."

"I'm sitting in the lobby of the Baja Hotel in scenic downtown Khartoum and unless you wire me some money, I'll have to climb down the fire escape in the middle of the night and skip out on the bill."

Dan could hear a grin in his brother's voice. "I'm registered under the name C. Dundee, and if I do say so myself, I fake a pretty decent Australian accent. For a Hoosier."

"Don't be cute. This is serious. I want you to..."

"Yes, it *is* serious. And it's still happening. The world forgets quick. Compassion and concern have very short shelf lives. If what's happening here falls back off the world's radar screen... "

"Ron... "

"Dan... don't. OK? Just send me some money." There was a pause. "And I've got to get in touch with the Putz..."

"The Putz?"

"He's an old friend from college who's a soft touch for electronic equipment. Hey, I don't suppose you know where I could lay hands on an old metal Nikon. I... lost mine. And no way am I going to use one of those digital things."

"You're really staying, aren't you." It was a statement, not a question.

"Yeah, I'm staying."

Silence. Dan thought of a dozen things he wanted to say, things that had come to him in the night when he woke up in a cold sweat with dreams of Ron's screams fading to rags and tatters in his head.

He wanted to tell Ron how proud he was of him, how proud their father would have been. He wanted to tell his brother he loved him.

"You be careful now... hear?"

"I hear."

Ron drew in a deep breath. "I'm heading out. I hear the government in Khartoum is shifting attention to the western provinces."

"Where?"

"A place called Darfur."

● ● ● ● ●

Idris and Aleuth sat beside the dying embers of the cooking fire as it shot little red sparks into the night sky. Akin was asleep on her sleeping mat. Aleuth rose and stepped to the door of the tukul to look in on her. Just to check. The girl was sound asleep with Shema wrapped in her arms.

When Aleuth returned, Idris looked at her with a knowing half smile. He, too, constantly checked to see that Akin was there, that she was safe, that she really was home.

Aleuth sat down on a log in the flickering firelight, picked up a stick and pushed aimlessly at the coals. Finally, she forced herself to give voice to the thought that had been hiding just out of sight, like a puff adder in her mind.

"They could come back."

Idris looked at his wife. He wasn't surprised by her words, and he slowly nodded. "Yes, they could come back."

Now that the thought had been free, words spilled out after it in a torrent.

"They could come back anytime... tonight, tomorrow... and take her away again, steal her—steal *both* of them." Aleuth's voice had the beginning sharp edge of hysteria. "Idris, they could make Akin a slave again! They could take her and Shema away and beat them and starve them and..." Her husband didn't tell her the fate Akin had so narrowly escaped; he didn't have to.

"Idris!" This last was a frantic, desperate plea: "How can we protect our children?"

Idris stared into the glowing embers for a time before he lifted his head and looked into his wife's eyes. When he spoke, his voice was quiet.

"We can't."

———————